*As slavery divided a nation,
they were swept into the flames of desire
. . . into a war fought both
on the battlefield and in their hearts*

AUDRA—The wildly beautiful and pampered heiress to Brennan Manor, she believed in a way of life that couldn't last, even though loyalty meant breaking her own heart.

LEE—Committed to the Union cause and his own principles, he struggled to reconcile his passion for a Southern belle, his duty to his country, and the promise he had made to protect her no matter what happened. . . .

JOEY—To win his father's approval, he would don Confederate gray and risk his life on the killing fields of Shiloh, aching with the knowledge that his closest friend must now be his bitter enemy.

TOOSIE—Audra's exquisite golden-skinned slave, she kept the intimate confidences of her young mistress . . . and a shattering secret that threatened Audra's secure, charmed life.

RICHARD—A powerful and brutal Louisiana plantation owner, he convinced Audra that wedding him was her duty, never revealing his dark side until the night she became his wife.

Tender Betrayal

ROSANNE BITTNER

BANTAM BOOKS
New York · Toronto · London · Sydney · Auckland

TENDER BETRAYAL

A Bantam Book / October 1993

ISBN 0-553-29808-9

Published simultaneously in the United States and Canada

Bantam Books are published by Bantam Books, a division of Bantam Doubleday Dell
Publishing Group, Inc. Its trademark, consisting of the words "Bantam Books" and the
portrayal of a rooster, is Registered in U.S. Patent and Trademark Office and in other
countries. Marca Registrada. Bantam Books, 1540 Broadway, New York, New York
10036.

PRINTED IN THE UNITED STATES OF AMERICA

RAD   0 9 8 7 6 5 4 3 2

To two of my favorite people,
Laura and Harold Swope,
of Greentown, Indiana. To think
of them brings warmth to
my heart, and sweet memories
of visits to "Aunt Laura and
Uncle Harold's" house
when I was young.

FROM THE AUTHOR...

Historical events in this novel set during the Civil War are true, and certain officers placed in particular battles are real; however, the primary characters and their personal stories are fiction. It is my hope that readers will understand that many of the opinions expressed in this novel about slavery and racial prejudice are not my own. I have strived to show the beauty, intelligence, and strength of black Americans, while at the same time realistically portraying the situation as it was in our country just before, during, and after the Civil War.

Tendor Betrayal is a story of abiding love; it is also a story of hope, and of people, both black and white, determined to survive and to rise above disaster through faith, not only in God, but in the human spirit.

May 12, 1859 . . .

CIVIL WAR: APPROACH—The annual Southern Commercial Convention, an organization designed to promote economic development, meets in Vicksburg, Mississippi. After many years of considering the issue of reopening the African slave trade, the convention votes to approve the following:

> *"In the opinion of the Convention, all laws, State of Federal, prohibiting the African Slave Trade, ought to be repealed."*

The Southerners feel the Federal Government should play a role of positively protecting slavery.

—Arthur M. Schlesinger, Jr.,
The Almanac of American History

PROLOGUE

1867

Lee, my love,
Just as the sun shines
And the ocean wind blows wet and wild,
I love you as a woman loves,
But you see me as a child.

Audra read the words to the first verse of the song she had written for Lee Jeffreys so long ago, when her heart was full of innocence and dreams. The young see such hope in the impossible, she thought. If she had known what would come to pass after she met the handsome lawyer from New York, perhaps she would never have written the song.

But the past could not be changed, and now she must

decide if the song she had composed with such passion years before still meant anything to her. She was so tired of having to make decisions that tore at her very soul, so weary from the pain of all she had lost. The war had finally ended; but just as the South would take a long time to mend, so would her heart.

It was still easy to remember their first meeting in Connecticut. She could almost smell the seawater, hear the cry of the gulls and the soft splash of waves upon the beach. It seemed a lifetime ago, a time when she had lived in a world that no longer existed. She laid the tattered papers in her lap, buttoned the top button of her woolen jacket against the cold November air, and leaned back in the rocker to watch the wide Kansas horizon and think of Lee. . . .

PART 1

A house divided against itself cannot stand. I believe this government cannot endure, permanently half slave and half free. . . . It will become all one thing, or all the other.

—ABRAHAM LINCOLN, 1858

JUNE 1859

Lee guided his carriage beneath the row of huge maple trees for which his family's estate was named. Maple Shadows held sweet boyhood memories for him. He remembered watching men chop down some of the stately trees when he was a child, clearing the way for the curved, bricked drive that led to the ornate octagon-shaped home his father had built here in Connecticut. The estate was to be a summer retreat from the filth and noise of New York City; but in the last few years his father and brothers had made little use of it, finding their lives just too busy to take advantage of the family "paradise" on Long Island Sound.

Lee figured he and his mother were the only ones in the family who truly appreciated this place. There was a time when they all would spend their summers here on

Mulberry Point; but now that he and Carl and David were grown, and his brothers had wives and families, it just seemed as though getting everyone together at the same time for more than a few days was impossible. His mother still came every summer, staying from May until September.

Anna Harcourt Jeffreys loved it here, and Lee supposed she liked to pretend that her "boys" were still young, and at any moment they would appear at her door ready to take walks in the sand and climb the maple trees as they did a lifetime ago. He could hear the cry of the sea gulls on the beach beyond the house, remembered feeding them, chasing them as a child. He used to have a huge collection of seashells and snails, but somewhere in his growing-up years he had lost all of that.

He halted in front of a hitching post, then climbed out of the carriage and tied the handsome black gelding that had brought him here from New Haven. He studied the house he loved so much, remembering how he used to run all around it, counting all eight sides of the octagon-shaped structure. His mother had insisted on the addition of a porch that ran the full circumference of the house, its roof serving as a balcony for the second floor. The estate was so beautiful, she wanted to be able to sit on a veranda or walk out of her upstairs bedroom and see in any direction, the Atlantic to the east, Long Island Sound to the south, nothing but heavily wooded hills to the north and west.

A lacy-design black wrought-iron railing edged both the lower veranda and the upper balcony, and the white wood siding of the house was set off by the dark gray trim of the molded cornices and the decorative brackets that supported the eaves and ran around the groupings of double windows and French doors.

Everything was as pretty as ever, and he wished he could have come earlier; but at least the warmth of an early summer had already brought trees and grass and flowers back to life. He was the only family member who spent a good month here every summer, deciding he worked too damn hard the rest of the year not to take this time away. Before opening his own law firm, there had been the years of schooling, both at West Point and Yale. For four of those summers he had not been able to come here at all.

A dull ache returned to his heart when he remembered that one of those summers he had stayed away because of Mary Ellen Eastman. That was supposed to have been the best summer of his life. He was to have brought Mary Ellen here to marry her the summer after he graduated from Yale, but pneumonia had claimed her life before they could wed. He hadn't been able to bring himself to come that summer without her. He still visited her grave back in New Haven, but not as often as he once had. She'd died six years ago. The past was just that now . . . the past.

He paused, listening then to piano playing so splendid that it gave him a chill at its glorious beauty. That would be his mother, doing what she loved best, her slender fingers flowing over the keys of the grand piano in the parlor. No one could play and sing like Anna Jeffreys, but in the next moment someone's magnificent soprano voice joined the piano accompaniment. He knew his mother's voice, and she was not singing now. Whoever it was, she ran a close race with his own mother's magnificent singing abilities. The music flowed from the house, filling the air and the flowers and the trees beyond it, carried by a gentle breeze that drifted over the manicured lawn and brought with it the smell of the sea.

Music. It was his mother's life. The sound of her playing and perhaps some student of hers singing only added to the comfort he always felt when he came here. They were familiar sounds, and they told him nothing had changed. He approached the front door, putting a finger to his lips to warn Katherine, the housekeeper, to be still. She had just come through the door to prune some potted plants on the wide veranda when she saw him approaching.

"I want to surprise her," he said quietly.

Katherine nodded, her face lighting up with delight at his presence. "She'll be so happy to see you here," she answered.

Lee gave her a wink. He breathed deeply of the sweet scent of lilacs blooming at each side of the veranda steps.

His mother loved lilacs, and hundreds of bushes bloomed throughout the thirty-acre estate.

"Have old Tom take good care of that horse and buggy for me, will you? I rented them at the docks back at New Haven—took a merchant ship from New York. It was the only thing available at the time. Tell him to take the buggy back tomorrow for me. He can take an extra horse along to ride back home."

"I'll tell him." Katherine left and Lee entered the house, closing the screen door softly. The singing continued, floating through the many rooms of the house, filling every corner and stairway. All the windows and doors were open to the warm afternoon, and the music mingled with the soft spilling sound of waves as they rolled onto the beach at the back side of the house. A sea gull flew very near the front doorway, giving out a piercing cry before flying off again.

Lee removed his hat to hang it on the same cherrywood rack that had stood in the entranceway for years. The family's summer home was not nearly as big and ornate as his parents' home just north of New York City, but it was splendid in its own right. Nearby, on a beautifully carved pedestal, a Chinese vase full of fresh-cut flowers had been placed. Lee did not remember the vase or the pedestal. Perhaps his mother had bought them on her trip to Europe this past winter. She certainly did love flowers, but not as much as she loved her music. She had given up a career as a concert pianist and opera singer when she'd had her first son, his oldest brother, Carl. Then had come David, and then himself. There had been a fourth child, but he had died at birth.

Anna Jeffreys had missed being a part of the world of music, but wanted to be home with her sons, so she had found happiness in teaching voice and advanced piano to young people who had the potential to become the very best. At least he hoped she was happy. He remembered the day he'd caught her crying when he was younger, when she admitted that she had given up her career in part because his father had insisted on it. Maybe that was when he decided his father would never tell him what to do, that he'd rule his own life. He had, much to Edmund Jeffreys's chagrin.

He pushed the old hurts aside. He was here, and he was going to enjoy himself and forget family problems. When it came to his mother, there were no problems at all. She was generous and loving, accepting of her children's wishes. In her eyes he could do no wrong.

He headed toward the parlor, anxious to surprise her. She expected him tomorrow, not today. Her student's voice was superb. Lee's own ear for music had become trained over the years, but he had not inherited a talent at the piano, nor any particular desire to learn to sing or play. Still, being raised by Anna Jeffreys, he could not help but appreciate talent in others.

The last student that he could remember his mother having here was a young man who went on to play piano with a New York symphonic orchestra. Now his mother was apparently giving voice lessons to a young woman who dreamed of the kind of career his mother had had. Anna Jeffreys's own voice was still surprisingly strong for a woman of sixty years, but not as strong or as lovely as the voice he heard now.

He walked lightly over Oriental rugs that led past the home's wide central stairway, down an oak-lined hallway to the parlor. A teenage boy sat just inside the double French doors leading into the room. The boy peeked around a potted palm and smiled at Lee. *Two* students this year? Lee figured the boy was waiting for his turn at a lesson, either voice or piano.

He turned his attention to his mother's cherished grand piano, a full nine-foot, concert-sized instrument his father had purchased for her when she quit her career. Anna sat on the padded bench playing rich chords while her new student stood nearby singing her heart out, and Lee found himself staring. The student was a young woman of elegant beauty, her skin white as pearls, her auburn hair falling in a cascade of curls down her back. That hair glinted pure red when the sun hit it, and it was drawn up at the sides, revealing a slender neck, high cheekbones, and an exquisite nose and jawline.

Lee walked farther inside the room, and his mother, a graceful beauty in her own right, glanced in his direction. Her blue eyes brightened, and her aging but still lovely face broke into a smile as she rose. "Lee, what a nice surprise!" She came toward him, and Lee felt proud of how she had kept her figure over the years. Her once dark, but now graying, hair was twisted into a mass of curls on top of her head. She wore a soft yellow day dress, her skirts rustling as she came closer to embrace him.

Lee gave her a hug in return, wondering if he had grown taller in the year since he had seen her. The top of her head came well below his chin, and he thought now neither he nor either of his brothers seemed to resemble their mother, except for their dark hair. In his own case, he had also inherited his mother's very blue eyes. Carl and David both had their father's dark brown eyes. His mother would sometimes brag that his blue eyes made him the handsomest of her three sons, and he grinned at the thought of how she was always boasting about him and his brothers.

He looked past her then to glance at the younger woman, who remained standing beside the piano, watching him with exotic green eyes. She quickly looked down and blushed, apparently embarrassed he had caught her studying him a little too intently. Pictures of the family were scattered across the top of the piano, Lee's right in the center. He supposed she recognized him from that, and knowing his mother, the young woman had probably already gotten an earful about Anna Jeffreys's "boys."

"How are you, Mother?" He leaned back to get a better look at her.

"I've been fine, except for still having so many headaches these past few weeks."

He frowned. "Well, that's part of the reason I'm here. I'm concerned about you."

The woman patted his arm. "I'm sure it's nothing serious. Dr. Kelsey isn't sure what's causing them, thinks it's just from worrying about your father and the rest of you too much. Your father and brothers work too hard, you know, but at least *you* find time to get away from the summer heat and filth of New York City. I wish I could get all of you here at once. I'm having a devil of a time getting your father to come at all this year."

"You know Dad. He's supposed to be letting Carl and David take over the factories, but he just can't quite let go." He wondered if she knew deep inside that for the last few years he had made a point of *not* being here at the same time as his father and brothers. There would only be arguments, and he did not come here for that. His mother hated discord in the family, and he hated upsetting her.

"Lee, this is Audra Brennan," Anna told him, turning from him and introducing the young woman at the piano. "Her father brought her all the way from Louisiana by ship. She's to spend the summer here for voice training."

Lee nodded to Audra. "Well, I expect a summer in Connecticut must be much more comfortable than spending one in the unbearable heat of Louisiana," he told her with a smile. He watched her chin rise slightly, as though he had somehow insulted her.

"When you're born to a place, Mr. Jeffreys, you get accustomed to the weather there," she answered in a heavy but charming southern accent. "Only someone from the *North* would think the heat of Louisiana is unbearable."

Lee was intrigued by the way she stretched out her words in a rich drawl. North was "Naawth," and she had put a strong emphasis on the word, with a tiny hint of distaste. *So*, he thought, *she's one of those stubborn southerners whose father has probably been preaching that anyone who lives north of Kentucky is some kind of enemy.* "My apologies," he answered aloud. "I didn't mean to offend your lovely state. I haven't even been there, but I *have* been in Florida in the summer, and it *was* unbearable." He grinned. "To this *northerner*, at least. Maybe after spending a summer here in Connecticut, you'll understand what I mean. Either way, I'm sure my mother will make your stay here comfortable and momorable. Is your father here with you?"

"My father is very busy with the plantation this time of year, so he could not stay. He has gone back to Louisiana and will come for me in September." She paused, then added, "Father owns one of the biggest plantations in Louisiana, and he dares not be gone for too long at a time.

Brennan Manor takes a great deal of supervision, you know, especially with hundreds of Negroes running about."

Lee frowned. *Pompous little brat,* he thought. She spoke the words as though her father were the most important man ever born. And they owned slaves! God, he hated the concept of slavery. This girl apparently thought nothing of it. He'd like to have a damn good talk with her *and* her father about that.

"I met Audra's father at the opera in New York City the winter before last," Lee's mother spoke up quickly. She gave Lee a chastising look, as though to warn him not to start arguing with the girl. "Mr. Brennan was there on business. He is not only a farmer, but a cotton broker. He had brought Audra with him that year as an adventure for her, to let her see a bit of the world beyond their plantation, and because he misses her so when he travels."

Audra forced a smile as Anna Jeffreys spoke. Did the woman realize how she still suffered from a terrible homesickness? She had hated New York. It was cold and dirty and ugly. It made Brennan Manor seem like a piece of heaven.

Anna moved around the bench to stand near Audra. She put an arm around her. "Mr. Brennan wanted his daughter to see a real opera, because of her own lovely voice and love for singing," Anna Jeffreys continued. "When he discovered I had trained the lead female singer, he asked if it would be possible for Audra to spend a summer with me. He thought it might be a nice experience for her. Her voice has great possibilities."

"I heard," Lee answered. "Very beautiful."

"Thank you, Mr. Jeffreys," Audra answered.

"Audra was only fifteen then," his mother was saying. "Mr. Brennan wanted to wait until she was a little older to send her so far from home. He refused to send her north again in winter, as she hates our cold weather. Sending her in summer meant he could not stay with her, as that is his busiest time on the plantation, so he allowed her brother to come with her, as well as her personal ... servant."

Lee noticed her hesitation at the word "servant." Did the girl have a Negro *slave* along? He saw the look in his mother's eyes and knew it must be so. The woman knew how adamant he and his brothers and father were that slavery must be ended in this country. What a disgrace America was to the rest of the world, preaching freedom but owning slaves! He had himself helped the governor of New York, who was a personal friend of the family, work on creating new legislation designed to eradicate the practice.

"I am afraid our poor Audra has been quite homesick," his mother said. Anna Jeffreys had a way of loving and accepting all people, no matter what their way of life, especially if they were interested in music. *Music rises above all prejudice and hatred,* she had told him once. *It is a common ground shared by everyone and can bring people of all walks of life together in joy.*

"Maple Shadows is almost as pretty as Brennan Manor," Audra spoke up.

Almost? Was she trying to be nice, Lee wondered, or did she intend the remark as an insult? Probably an insult. He had worked a few times with southern businessmen and aristocrats and found them a proud, pompous bunch who seemed to think their South was the most beautiful place in the world.

"I did not at all like the bit of winter I experienced two years ago in New York," Audra continued. "I am not accustomed to such harsh weather. My father feared I might take ill, and being so far from home ..." Her eyes teared, and Anna Jeffreys gave her a squeeze.

Lee felt a glimmer of sympathy for the girl at the look in her eyes, but her attitude still irritated him, as though she were doing them a favor by her mere presence. He bowed slightly. "Well, welcome to Connecticut, and what I am sure will be a *very* pleasant summer for you," he said as he straightened.

Audra was convinced both the bow and the remark were in jest and not out of respect. Lee Jeffreys was indeed Anna's handsomest son, with the bluest eyes she had ever seen; but the way he looked at her right now did not make him terribly likable. He was laughing at her behind those eyes, she was sure.

"I think I'll go to my room and change," he told his mother. "I'd like to go for a swim before supper."

"Oh, Lee, the water is still very cold!"

"That's the way I like it." Lee turned and walked over to the young man who sat near the door. He put out his hand. "Lee Jeffreys. You must be Audra's brother. What's your name, son?"

The boy rose and grasped Lee's hand. He nodded, his face growing a little red as he glanced then at his sister, who was rushing to his side. "This is Joey," she answered for him.

Lee smiled and squeezed the young man's hand slightly. "Well, nice to meet you, Joey."

Joey smiled in return, but he still did not speak. The three of them stood there rather awkwardly for a moment, and Lee let go of the boy's hand, mystified by the embarrassing moment.

"You go right up and change," Anna told her son. "I'll tell Helen to begin preparing supper for you, Lee. How long will you be staying?"

Lee was grateful for her intervention. He turned to her and put an arm around her, sweeping her into the hallway. "A whole month," he announced. "How do you like that?"

"Oh, Lee, that's wonderful!"

"Well, it's my own law firm, so I guess if I want to take off for a month and leave everyone else in charge, it's my right."

"I just wish your father would look at things that way sometimes. He's not coming until late August this time, and I have a feeling he'll stay only a week or so. Carl and David aren't coming until then, either. I do so wish I could get you all together at once. Do you see each other very often in New York?"

Lee reached down to pick up his bags. "You know how it is, Mother. New York is a big city, and I'm not anywhere close to the factories. All of us are so damn busy, we have to come here to Connecticut to see each other, only this year it looks like we won't even accomplish that." He kissed her cheek. "It doesn't matter. What's important is being able to spend some time with you. What's this about gallivanting off to Florida and then to Europe? Usually you stay in the city with Father in the winter. My God, it's been a whole year since I saw you last night here at Maple Shadows."

Anna put a hand to her forehead. "Yes, well, you know how I have always hated the city. This is the place where I always feel the best, but I've gotten so I can't bear the cold winters, either in New York *or* Connecticut. I can't get your father to leave, so I spent part of the winter in Florida with your Aunt Grace. The two of us sailed on to England for a holiday. I truly enjoyed it, and I had only two of the really bad headaches. Mostly they're quite bearable."

She turned and headed for the stairway, and Lee suspected she didn't want to talk about her health, which worried him even more. "Come on up," she told him. "I'll show you which room to take. I've given Audra your room because it has such a wonderful view. I thought it would be nice for her."

The stairway curved past the parlor door, and Lee turned to glance down at Audra. She and her brother were both staring at him, but Audra quickly looked away again. Lee could not get over how beautiful she was, in spite of her haughty air. She wore a ruffled pale-pink muslin dress with tiers of white linen cascading in a V shape down the front and back. It fit her tiny waist invitingly, and he had already noticed earlier that it also fit her bosom perfectly, a bosom that looked very generous for a young woman so small otherwise. Too bad such a brat had to be so pretty.

A young Negro woman came down the stairway then, hesitating when she saw Lee. Lee felt instant irritation, realizing she must be the "personal servant" his mother had mentioned. She nodded to him, and he saw gentleness and intelligence in her dark eyes. *What a waste of human life*, he thought. She was a beautiful woman, her creamy brown skin clean and smooth. She moved past him then, looking over the railing at Audra. "Shall I prepare your change of clothes for supper now, Miss Audra?" she asked.

"Yes, Toosie, but we are not finished here. Mrs. Jeffreys is just taking her son to his room first. We have another half hour of lessons yet."

Lee could not help staring. The woman surely carried

white blood, for her skin was much paler than any Negro he had ever seen. He had heard stories about some white men in the South having literal harems of Negro women, with dozens of mulatto babies running about. Were the stories true, or just exaggerated by people who didn't know what they were talking about? "Hello," he spoke up. "I'm Lee Jeffreys. I take it you came here with Audra."

The woman glanced down, appearing suddenly nervous. "Yes, sir."

"How do you like it here in Connecticut?"

"Just fine, sir. I—"

"Toosie, don't be rattling on to the owner of this house," Audra called out sternly to the woman. "It's not your place."

The woman twisted her apron in her hands, still not having met Lee's eyes. "Yes, ma'am," she answered quietly. "I will go help the kitchen maid until you are ready to change, Miss Audra." She hurried past Lee and on down the stairs. When she walked past Audra, she kept her eyes averted, and Audra gave her a scowl. Lee noticed Audra's arrogant posture, and it annoyed him. He had never spoken to a servant the way she had just spoken to hers.

Audra looked up at him then, seeing his anger. "Toosie has been my personal servant since I was six years old," she explained. "She was thirteen when father gave her to me. You have to understand, Mr. Jeffreys, that slaves cannot be treated the way you people treat your help here in the North. If you are too easy with them, my father says they become cocky and belligerent. Please do not try to make idle conversation with her. I have already explained to your mother."

Lee felt his temper rising. "Look here, young lady, this is my house, and I'll speak with *whom*ever I want, *when*ever I want, be it idle conversation or discussing important issues, one of which is *slavery*, I might add." He frowned in disgust. "And I *don't* like the idea of having a Negro slave in my house!" How dare this young female tell him what to do and say! She had spoken to him as though he were some ignorant idiot who didn't know how to conduct himself. He was, by God, a grown man, a successful attorney in New

York City, and his family was probably ten times wealthier than this little snob's slave-owning, arrogant, southern bastard of a father! What the hell was wrong with these people from the South, still dealing in the abhorrent practice of slavery, talking about separating from the Union?

He glanced at her brother again, who just stood watching him. The young man still had not spoken a word. He turned his attention back to Audra. "I'll see you at supper, Miss Brennan," he said, a strong note of authority in the words.

He glanced at his mother then, who looked distraught, then stormed past her and on up the stairs. He was anxious now to change and let the ocean water cool his anger. It irritated him to no end to think that Miss Audra Brennan would be here the whole length of his own visit. He would rather have found just his mother here. If the girl had not brought her own damn personal slave along, it wouldn't be so bad. He'd by God talk to that poor Negro woman if he felt like it. Slavery was wrong, and he didn't like the idea of someone who believed in such things staying in his house. He gave his mother an angry glare as she hurried to catch up with him.

"I'll not go treating that slave woman like she's something to be squashed under a man's heel!" he told her, his blue eyes flashing with indignation.

"Calm down, Lee. You always did have the worst temper of you three boys. Please remember that Audra and her brother are our guests, and try to be more open-minded." Anna led him to the room he was to use and urged him inside, closing the door. "Owning slaves is all Audra has ever known," she continued. "If you want to talk to her about the right and wrong of it, you've got to approach the whole thing gently, calmly. She's only _seventeen_, son! She was brought up in that culture. It's as natural to her as breathing is to you."

She patted his arm and walked to a window to draw the curtains aside. "Audra is actually a very sweet young lady, and immensely talented. This is her first time so far from home by herself, and I think she is a little bit intimidated about being in the North, surrounded by people who think it's horrible that she has a slave with her. She's actually scared and very lonely, so be kind to her."

"Well, she's *not* by herself! She's got her brother with her, for whatever *he's* worth. What's the problem with him? He hasn't said a word since I got here!" Lee dropped his bags and walked over to help her open a window that was stuck. His irritation was enhanced by the fact that he had to give up his room with a view of the ocean. This room looked out on the front lawn, away from the sea.

"The boy stutters, Lee. I'm sure being in the presence of a successful lawyer like you, he feels very embarrassed for you to hear him talk. I think part of his trouble is his father. The boy seems to be very close to his sister, but his father did not treat him very nicely when he first brought them here. I noticed the man gives Audra all his attention and almost none to the boy."

Lee sighed, feeling like a bit of a heel. He shook his head in resignation. "Ever patient and understanding, aren't you? What would this family do without you, Mother?" He gave her a faint smile. "I'm sorry. I just don't like a woman I don't even know giving me orders in my own house, especially when she's more *girl* than woman!"

"I'll talk to her. Just remember she was raised by a very wealthy, slave-owning plantation owner. That's the only life she's known, and on top of that her mother died ten years ago. She's had no mother since she was seven years old, so she has grown up being trained to give her own orders and run the household."

"Yes, yes, don't worry. I won't cause a scene at supper." He picked up a bag and threw it on the bed. "Go on back downstairs and finish the lessons." The poor girl had no mother. He felt like an ass, and he had probably embarrassed her brother, who could not readily speak up in his sister's defense. "I guess I'm just tired from the long trip here. It takes a while to wind down from life in Manhattan."

"I know, son. It's the same way for your father and brothers when they first get here." Anna stepped back and looked him over. "Lee, every time I see you, you're handsomer than before."

He laughed lightly, feeling some of the steam going out

of him. He removed his gray waistcoat. "Your sons could be the ugliest things that walked the face of the earth, and you'd still say they were handsome. Go on with you. I want to change."

Anna breathed deeply, looking him over lovingly. "I'm glad you came, Lee." She wished she could tell him how frightened she was by her headaches. She carried a deep fear she could not name, fought the suspicion that the cause was something more than any doctor had been able to detect. She turned away so that he could not see the tears that suddenly filled her eyes. "I'll see you at supper."

Anna left the room, and Lee removed his clothes, putting on a cotton robe. He had always swum naked, and he damn well would today, guests or no guests. He went to the doorway and again heard his mother's lovely piano playing, joined by the incredible singing of Audra Brennan. He went down the back stairs and through a rear entrance, out to the beach. Soon the sound of the waves nearly drowned out the music. He threw off the robe and jumped into the cold water.

He swam out far enough that he could no longer hear the piano or the singing, but the icy wetness did little to cool his continued irritation at having an unexpected guest at the house when he had planned on being alone.

He came out of the water shivering. He quickly picked up the towel he had brought along and briskly rubbed his hair with it, then put on his robe. He stood watching the house for a moment, began to catch bits and pieces of Audra's singing again. He was surprised at how easily the girl had riled him. It was true he had a temper, but his years as a lawyer had taught him to control it, especially in the courtroom. He was a grown man who normally did not get upset so easily, especially at pretty young women.

He rubbed the towel at his hair some more as he headed toward the house. He told himself that Audra Brennan simply did not understand the folly of her own ways. She didn't know any better than to be rude to the help and give orders to others. She had been brought up that way, by a domineering father, and with no mother to teach her the gentler side of life.

He hated to admit it, but he knew his anger did not come so much from her bringing her personal slave here with her, but more from the fact that she was so damned beautiful, and he had no right thinking of her that way. She was just a kid, and a mighty spoiled one at that.

"The hell with her," he muttered. He had come here for a badly needed vacation, and he would enjoy it as much as possible, in spite of the unwanted company. As long as Audra Brennan stayed out of his way and didn't try to tell him again what to do in his own house, everything would be fine.

2

Audra opened the French doors that led to the balcony outside her room. She breathed deeply of the sea air and walked past an array of lawn furniture and plants to the wrought-iron railing. She gazed at the water, glittering from the light of a full moon. She liked it here at Maple Shadows well enough, but it was not Brennan Manor. At home she was the one in charge, adored by her own father, and by Richard Potter, the fine southern gentleman who, it was more or less understood, she would marry in another year.

She was not at all sure she wanted to marry Richard, but she hated disappointing her father, who was eagerly in favor of the match. Right now, the way people here were treating her, and the way Lee Jeffreys had deliberately tried to upset her this evening at the supper table, Richard seemed like the most wonderful man who ever walked. He was twenty-five years her senior, more like a father than a suitor and her future husband; but at least he respected her, understood her way of life. After all, Richard was the son of Alfred Potter, whose plantation was nearly as big as Brennan Manor. After their marriage, the two plantations would be melded into one huge enterprise that would dwarf all other plantations in Louisiana, perhaps the whole South. She would be the mistress of it all. Mr. Lee Jeffreys simply did not understand her father's importance and political standing, nor did he have any conception of life on a plantation, or why the Negroes were necessary to the survival of their way of life.

It was obvious Lee did not like her at all, and now she would have to put up with his arrogant attitude for a whole month. If not for Anna Jeffreys's uncompromising kindness, she would have asked to be sent right back to Louisiana. She missed Brennan Manor so much that she felt sick. At night, when she was alone like this, tears of loneliness came easily. The only reason she refused to give in and ask to be sent home was that her father thought the trip, and studying under Mrs. Jeffreys, would serve as a kind of finishing school for her. Through some of the opera music Anna Jeffreys was teaching her, she was even learning some Italian, French, and Spanish. Friends and family back home would be very impressed, especially Aunt Janine and Uncle John McAllister in Baton Rouge. Aunt Janine was her mother's sister, and she was always fussing that Audra did not have a well-rounded education, that she lacked refinement because she had grown up without a mother.

Aunt Janine's daughter, her cousin Eleanor, had been sent to Europe last summer. Audra didn't doubt that the reason her aunt was always flaunting her daughter as a well-traveled, worldly debutante was because she was trying to make up for the fact that Eleanor was so unattractive. Eleanor, who was four years older than Audra, had a heavy body with no curves, and a round face that was usually peppered with blemishes. Her dull brown hair was straight and difficult to manage, and even though Aunt Janine dressed her in the finest, most expensive European designs, the clothing did little to help her appearance.

She was sure her aunt was upset that Eleanor was

twenty-one years old and still had no prospects of a husband. She did have plenty of suitors, but none of them offered marriage. Audra suspected that was not just because of Eleanor's looks, but because the men who courted her did not respect her. Eleanor had whispered shocking stories to her about young men and the things she let them do to her that Audra knew would make Aunt Janine faint with shame.

Audra did not understand much about secret things men and women did behind closed doors, and she didn't care to know. No man, not even Richard Potter, was going to humiliate *her* that way, or court her just because she behaved like a harlot, whatever it was that harlots did. She only knew it was a label that carried shame with it. She had heard two young men at a party once talking about Eleanor. They had called her a slut and a harlot in the most disrespectful, insulting tone she had ever heard. She had never told her cousin about it.

Right now she actually missed Eleanor, missed *everything* about home. Brennan Manor might as well be a *hundred* thousand miles away as a thousand, but for her father's sake, she vowed to be strong and proud and stay the full summer. Ever since she could remember, she had been doing what she could to please Joseph Brennan, hoping she could make up for his disappointment in Joey. She felt a need to protect and defend her brother. Why couldn't their father see what a loving son he had? The man expected so much of Joey. That was another reason she felt she must marry Richard. Joey would never be capable of running the plantation himself. She had to marry someone who could take over when their father was gone, someone who would let Joey live there forever but who understood he would never be able to take full responsibility as master of Brennan Manor. Richard was the perfect answer.

She loved Joey so, had always felt responsible to care for him since their mother died. That was when he had begun stuttering. The problem had grown worse over the years instead of better, and she was sure it was because their father had made such a fuss about it and had made Joey more self-conscious about his speech.

Poor Joey had been embarrassed earlier when Lee introduced himself, and that made her even angrier with Lee. He had arrogantly ignored both of them during supper, had even talked to his mother about the next elections, accenting the fact that when it came time to vote for a new President, he would want someone who would support the total abolition of slavery. *I think Abraham Lincoln is our man,* he had said, glancing at Audra as though just waiting for her to argue his remark.

She had deliberately held her tongue, not wanting to express opposing views at the dinner table. According to her father, Abraham Lincoln would be the worst thing that could happen to the South. If that man became President, a lot of states *would* secede, but she was not about to go into all that with Lee Jeffreys. These northerners were so ready to preach to the South about what they believed was right and wrong, but, then, politics was a man's game. She felt uneasy getting into a discussion about any of it.

She closed her eyes and pictured Brennan Manor, the beautifully manicured grounds, the smell of azaleas and dogwood, the cypress and oak trees. The plantation was like a mother to her and Joey. So often she tried to remember her real mother, but there were few memories for a child of seven who took it for granted that mother would always be there. All she could remember now was a terribly thin, pale woman who lay in a bed groaning in death. Her face had no form. There was only the lovely painting of her mother that hung over a fireplace to help her remember the woman.

She turned away from the railing and sat down in a wrought-iron chair to rest her head in her hands. She was so homesick and so upset with Lee Jeffreys that she knew she would not be able to sleep tonight. She tried to fight the unwanted tears, but now they came again. She had nearly gotten over this intense desire to go home, until today. She let herself have a good cry, feeling enveloped in loneliness. It was only when she stopped to retrieve a handkerchief from the pocket of her night robe that she realized someone was standing near her.

"You all right, Miss Brennan?"

Audra jumped at the voice, looking up to see Lee Jeffreys watching her. She felt angry and humiliated that he, of all people, had caught her bawling like a baby. She quickly wiped at her eyes. "Do you really care? I should think you would *enjoy* seeing me cry. It is certainly obvious you don't much like me." She drew her robe closer around her neck, realizing then that he had not only caught her crying but had caught her sitting out here alone in her night clothes. It was highly improper. "Do you always sneak up on people this way?" She started to rise, but he caught her arm.

"No. I didn't know you'd be out here, but since you are, please stay. I'd like to talk."

There was something different in his eyes tonight, and she was amazed that she actually saw an apology there. His touch on her arm brought a rush of warmth to her blood, and it surprised her so that she sat back down without arguing. She thought of how good and kind this man's mother was. Maybe some of those good qualities ran in her son's blood after all, and she finally admitted to herself that deep inside she wanted Lee Jeffreys to like her. "Fine, Mr. Jeffreys. I think we *should* talk."

He knelt in front of her. "You can start by calling me Lee. May I call you Audra?"

Why did she suddenly have so much trouble turning her eyes away from his? "I suppose that would be all right."

The night breeze stiffened some, and it ruffled his dark hair. The grip of her arm had been firm, a big, strong hand, yet it had been gentle. She realized he looked even handsomer in the moonlight, and it struck her that she had been so concerned with her own problems and with the way he had treated her at first, that she had not really thought about how dashing he appeared when she first saw him come into the parlor. She remembered how strangely moved she had been at the way he had looked in that fine gray silk suit, smiling that brilliant smile. She had never seen a man with such blue eyes set in such a handsome face, framed with such nicely layered dark hair.

Now he wore simple cotton pants and a plain shirt that was partially unbuttoned, revealing a good deal of his bare chest in the shaft of light that came through the open doors of her room. There was dark hair on that chest, and she quickly looked away. What on earth was she feeling? A moment ago she hated this man, yet it struck her only now that she had actually been attracted to him. Was it because of the challenge he posed? Maybe it was because he was a lot like her father in some ways. He was not afraid to express his beliefs. He was a man who took charge, just like her father, and to her chagrin, she realized he had been right to chastise her earlier today. She had literally given him orders in his own house. After all, she was a guest. She must show these people how gracious and mannerly a southern lady could be, but she would not swallow her pride.

"I was walking around the veranda," he was saying. "Came to this side because I like to look at the ocean. I heard you crying, and I can't help feeling I'm probably the reason." He rose and pulled a chair over close to her and sat down. "I want to apologize. I was rude to you at dinner tonight, and I damn well know it. I don't generally judge people without even getting to know them, and your being so young and away from home and all—our guest here—I've been way out of line, and I'm sorry."

Audra sat a little straighter, looking out at the ocean, suddenly unable to meet his eyes for fear she would get the odd feeling again that made her shiver. "I accept your apology, sir, and I apologize in return. I should not have spoken to you the way I did. However, I know that you don't like the way we live in the South, but it is our way of life, just as you have your own way." She heard him sigh deeply.

"Audra, you must know deep in your soul that slavery is wrong."

She wiped at her eyes once more. "Of course it's wrong."

"What?" Lee frowned in surprise. "I don't understand—"

She glanced at him for just a moment. "Contrary to what you might think, Mr. Jeffreys, most of us in the South, especially the women, wish the whole practice had never been started." She looked away again. "But, you see, it is like . . . let me think . . . like a large stone rolling down a hill. Once it starts tumbling, it cannot be stopped. We have lived this way for so long that now our whole economy would come crashing down around us if we could not use slaves to work our plantations. Men like my father would be ruined." She looked at him again. "I am not ignorant just because I am a woman and young," she told him. "I have heard my father talk many times with his fellow businessmen. I understand the politics of it better than you think. The North knows that the abolition of slavery would ruin us, but they don't care. Each state should have the right to decide if it will continue allowing slavery, and neither the Federal government nor the President has the right to step in and cause our ruination."

Lee could not help smiling a little at the quick pride she showed. God, she was pretty, and that soft, southern drawl of hers somehow made her more enticing. He loved listening to her talk. "It can't go on forever, Audra. People like your father should begin preparing for that."

She wanted to look away from him again, but those blue eyes held her own. She caught the gentle warning behind his statement, felt a vague fear she could not quite name. "Each state will do what it must do, Mr. Jeffreys. People like you have to give us much more time. Our investment in slaves is very heavy. To set them all free and lose all that investment and have to pay our help on top of it would destroy us. Besides, it would be dangerous."

"Dangerous?"

Audra rose, walking closer to the railing again. "Perhaps you do not realize that there are nearly as many Negroes in the South as there are whites. If they were freed, where would they all go? Where would they live? There would surely be an insurrection, Mr. Jeffreys. They would murder us, take over our homes and farms. There have been uprisings in the past, my father tells me. You probably think it is cruel of me to be so stern with Toosie, but it is necessary, you see, to keep them in line. They can quickly become quite insolent. If one is not careful, it will be the slaves who run the household instead of the master. They must be constantly disciplined."

She heard his chair scraping the wooden floor as he rose, felt him move closer to her. There came that strange shiver again. She felt his presence, his tall frame standing close. Such a well-built man he was. Why was she noticing that? She had not much cared about any man's build before, had certainly never given Richard such thoughts. She kept watching the moonlight on the water, almost afraid to look at Lee.

"To the point of cruelty?" he asked.

Audra closed her eyes, thinking of March Fredericks, overseer of the cotton pickers. She hated March. "Sometimes."

"No human being can be owned, Audra, or whipped into submission like a dog. It's un-Christian."

She blinked back new tears. "Our slaves are well treated, Mr. Jeffreys. I know of only a couple of instances when our overseer had to use the whip. Actually, my father stopped him. He is good to his Negroes, and most of them need little reprimanding. Some are like friends to us." She quickly wiped at a tear that slipped down her cheek. "Yes, Mr. Jeffreys, I have read *Uncle Tom's Cabin.* I know what you are thinking but Miss Stowe gave a very distorted view of what slavery is like. The greater majority of us do not behave that way. We are simply caught up in a system that cannot change if we are to continue our present way of life." She finally turned and looked up at him. "Many of us wish it could easily be changed. The worst part is all the mulattoes, like Toosie, running about—the product of the abhorrent practice of white men . . . lying with Negro women. My father is staunchly against it."

She felt her face warming at the remark. She knew that "lying" with someone was somehow sinful, but she wasn't quite sure of all that happened when one did. She'd had no mother to teach her about such things, and her women friends just tittered and talked behind their fans about it. She wasn't sure if the things Eleanor told her were true, and besides, her cousin had never gone into full detail. Miss Geresy, her tutor and the woman responsible for teaching her manners and grace, as well as the duties required of the mistress of a plantation, never talked about personal, intimate matters.

Lee watched her a moment, wondering himself what this woman-child knew about sex. More than that, he wondered a little about Toosie. Maybe it was just his imagination, but when he saw the two together, he felt sure there was a resemblance. Had Audra's father ... oh, she'd never believe it. She probably thought he was the most perfect man in the world. "Who is Toosie's father?" he asked bluntly.

Audra walked back to her chair. "Some white foreman my father has long since fired. Her mother, Lena, has been in charge of the household staff for years. She answers to me, of course."

Lee decided not to press the issue. "Why don't you tell me about your brother? Seems like he would have stayed to help your father rather than come here with you. You said yourself summer is your father's busiest time."

Audra felt her defenses rising. If he ever made fun of or laughed at her brother when he finally heard him speak, she knew she could never like Lee Jeffreys. Joey had remained silent at the supper table tonight, and Lee had at least avoided coaxing the boy into talking. He had not been rude to him.

"My brother and I are very close," she replied. She moved away from him, toward her room, but she could feel him walking up behind her again. She wished he would keep his distance, because for some strange reason it was difficult to think with him so near. "I have been like a mother to him. My father ... he gets very impatient with Joey. I am afraid he is a little disappointed in him because he thinks Joey can't learn, but he is really quite bright; and in spite of how my father seems to favor me over him, Joey is my best friend and my biggest supporter. I understand him, and he understands me. Sometimes I feel like I have to make up for the attention he doesn't get from our father. I knew he wouldn't be happy at home alone. It is hard for him to be stern with the slaves because of his speech, and Father rather ignores him, so I asked that he be allowed to come with me. I thought it would be nice for him to see another part of the country."

She turned to face Lee, stepping back a little when she realized he was standing closer than she thought. "I really must go inside, Mr. Jeffreys. This is quite improper, me in my night clothes standing out here alone with you."

Lee glanced at the doorway, catching a glimpse of Toosie peeking at them from behind a curtain. "Oh, I don't really think we're alone."

Audra looked in the direction of his gaze and smiled a little when Toosie darted away. "She must have heard your voice. She keeps a good eye on me, you know. Her real name is Tuesday, because that is the day on which she was born. She has always been called Toosie." She lowered her voice. "I think she cares for me as more than her mistress. I care about her, too, if the truth be known, but I dare not let her know it."

Lee laughed lightly, strangely relieved that Audra Brennan was not as cruel and hard-hearted as he had first thought. Her tenderness and understanding toward her brother touched him. "This has been an interesting conversation, Miss Brennan. How about if I take you for a buggy ride tomorrow? We can talk some more. Might as well be friends as long as we're going to be seeing a lot of each other."

Audra dropped her eyes. "I would have to have an escort. My father expects your mother to see that I do not go out alone."

"So? We'll bring her along. She *is* my main reason for being here, you know. And bring your brother. I'd like to get to know him, too. We'll see some sights. Maybe it will make you feel a little better about being so far from home."

Audra felt her heart growing lighter. She had not expected this turnabout. "I would like that, Mr. Jeffreys."

Lee studied the deep pools of green that looked back at him. This young woman was stirring something in him he had not expected to feel. He could not help thinking that she must be naked under that robe and gown, every inch of her smooth and firm body untouched. "Call me Lee."

She nodded. "I really must not stand out here this way one minute longer." She turned and hurried to the doors, stopping once to look back at him. "Thank you for the invitation. I truly am sorry if I offended you earlier."

Lee smiled. "I'm sorry, too. We got off on bad footing. I'll make up for it tomorrow." He studied the lustrous red hair that cascaded down her back when she turned away again. It was brushed out long and loose, and he felt a terrible urge to get his hands caught up in it.

Miss Audra Brennan had spunk and pride, yet there was a gentle kindness about her, and she apparently had a great ability to love, considering how she felt about her brother. He was beginning to like her, a hell of a lot more than he would have thought possible a few hours ago.

"Until tomorrow, then," he said softly, thinking how beautiful she must look lying against silk sheets, how full her lips were, how green her eyes. By God, for a moment there he had actually wanted to hold her, and he'd gotten the distinct impression she just might have let him, or at least wanted to let him. Then again, she might have slapped his face.

3

"So, Joey, what do you think of Connecticut?" Lee turned to glance at the young man, who sat in the rear of one of Lee's father's finest English-made carriages. He gave Joey a smile and turned back around to guide the roan gelding that pulled them. The horse, named Belle, was one of the strongest and most magnificent animals belonging to Maple Shadows, and this particular buggy was the most elegant and comfortable. For some reason Lee found himself wanting to impress Audra Brennan.

"I like it j-just f-fine," Joey answered.

"Joey is excited," Audra spoke up. "He told me to thank you for letting him come along."

Lee glanced at her, thinking how perfectly lovely she looked today, wearing a white cotton dress trimmed with little green and yellow embroidered flowers. She wore a wide-brimmed silk hat that was tied under her chin with a green sash, and white gloves covered her delicate hands. Fourteen-year-old Joey was well built for his age, and a good-looking boy. He had Audra's auburn hair, but his eyes were brown rather than green. He had a quick smile, and Lee already liked the boy.

"You should let Joey speak more for himself," he told Audra. "He needs more confidence, that's all. You do too much of his talking for him." He looked back at Joey. "You say whatever you want, Joey, and don't worry about how slowly it comes out of your mouth."

The boy grinned again. "Are we going to a b-beach?" he asked. He was already learning to like Lee Jeffreys.

"Yes, we are, as a matter of fact. We could have gone just outside the house, I suppose, but I thought a buggy ride would be nice." Lee proceeded to point out some of the other elegant estates on Mulberry Point, where the wealthy of New York City, Stamford, and New Haven had built summer homes. "My father owns a canvas factory— makes tents and awnings and such," he told Audra. "He also owns a boot-and-shoe factory and an iron mill. Keeps him and my brothers pretty busy. I'm not really interested in the family businesses. I wanted something of my own—thought about staying in the army after West Point but decided to get my law degree instead. I've set up my own practice in New York, but unlike my father and brothers, I take vacation time once in a while. It's good for the soul. I love it here. Brings back good boyhood memories."

Audra studied the strong hands that held the reins as Lee guided the horse and buggy down a slope to a secluded beach. Today he wore dark pants that fit his muscled body well, and a white shirt but no tie. "Too warm for formal clothes," he had told her. There was a brashness about him that stirred her, a sort of rebellious, free attitude. He was so different from the men she knew in Louisiana, certainly unlike Richard. Lee was not quite so formal and gentlemanly, yet he was gracious and mannerly in his own way. There was a definite difference between Yankee men and the southern gentlemen to whom she had been exposed. Lee was livelier, more abrupt, and, she sensed, more daring.

She turned to watch the surrounding woods, and the way the sun filtered through the thick-leaved branches of oak and maple trees. The carriage rocked and bounced over a small lane that led down to a beach, where Lee halted the vehicle and climbed down, tying the horse. Audra moved to step out of the carriage, then blushed when Lee grabbed her about the waist and lifted her down as though she weighed no more than a feather. She liked the feel of his strength, and his hands on her. Something about the way he just grabbed her instead of politely taking her hand excited her.

"I would have brought Mother, if she wasn't having another one of her terrible headaches," he said. "I'm really worried."

"I feel so sorry for her," Audra answered. "She's had one other bad spell since I arrived. There doesn't seem to be much anyone can do for her when she gets that way."

"I know, and I can hardly stand to think of her feeling so ill. She doesn't deserve to suffer that way. I would have stayed with her, but she insisted she would feel better if we went off and tried to have a good day. The quieter it is around the house, the better." Lee helped Joey take some picnic items out of the carriage. He met Audra's eyes then, grinning. "Is this the first time you've gone off with a man unescorted?" he teased.

Audra felt the heat rising in her cheeks. "Joey is with us, so we are not exactly unescorted, Lee Jeffreys. However, I am trusting you to be a gentleman, and I am doing this because I am hoping it will make your mother feel better to know she has not ruined our day."

He leaned closer, and she felt a flutter in her stomach. "And your father doesn't ever need to know, right?"

She turned away and laughed lightly, totally confused by her feelings. She had not expected to like this man at all, let alone be excited about going for a ride with him. She had tried on three different dresses before deciding which to wear. Poor Toosie's fingers must be quite sore from buttoning and unbuttoning her clothes so many times.

Lee spread out a blanket on the sand, and they all sat down to sandwiches and lemonade that Tootsie and the kitchen maid had prepared for them. For a few minutes they did more eating than talking. Audra knew Lee was right about how furious her father would probably be if he knew she had come here with a man, a Yankee man, no less, with only Joey for an escort. Her father had trusted Mrs. Jeffreys to watch over her, but the woman was simply not up to it today, and for reasons she could not herself explain, Audra had dearly wanted this outing. If it led to Lee liking her better, it would be worth the risk.

She watched the ocean waves crest along the beach, shaded her eyes to study sea gulls flying nearby. A few landed near them, and Lee threw them a piece of bread. Several of the birds quickly converged on the morsel and began fighting over it. Audra laughed, realizing she felt more relaxed and less lonely today than she had since arriving here. It seemed strange that Lee might be the reason. He handed Joey a small basket that had contained their bread.

"If you walk along the harder sand out there where the waves come up, you'll find all kinds of interesting things," he told Joey. "Snails, seashells, what have you. You can use this to collect them if you want something to do."

Joey rose, taking the basket. "Th-thanks. I have a c-c-c—" He stopped and sighed, obviously very frustrated with himself. "C-collection at the house. I'll t-take them all home with me."

"Good." Lee began removing his ankle high, elastic-sided boots. "Take your boots and socks off first, young man. It feels good to squish the sand between your bare toes."

Joey eagerly obeyed. Not only was Lee not the least bit disparaging of his speech problems, but the man also just plain knew how to have fun. It had been a long time since he could relax and not be so self-conscious. Now that he was getting older, his father was constantly lecturing him that he couldn't ever be the man of the house and oversee the Negroes if he didn't stop his stuttering, let alone be able to talk with congressmen and the like, all requisites for a wealthy plantation owner. This was the most fun he had had in a long time, and he laughed at the realization that his sister was embarrassed that he and Lee were removing their shoes and socks, but he could not resist the feeling of freedom it gave him. His own father had never spent a leisurely day with him, not even when he was little.

"Have fun!" Lee told him.

Joey grinned and took the basket and left, glorying in the feel of the sand on his bare feet.

Lee turned to Audra. "Your father ridicules him, doesn't he?"

The remark made Audra forget her temporary surprise at Lee's removing his shoes and stockings without even asking if she minded. It seemed somehow improper to look upon the bare feet of a man she hardly knew. She glanced away from them to watch the sea gulls walk about on their spindly legs and pick at the sand, looking for food.

"I am afraid he does," she answered, "but not to be mean. He loves Joey very much. I just don't think he understands that his speech problem is something emotional—something from our mother's death, I'm sure." She met Lee's eyes then. "He never stuttered until after that, and he has a difficult time learning. That frustrates Father. Since Joey is his only son, Father seems to feel he has been somehow cheated, and I am afraid Joey feels very unloved. I don't think Father means for it to come across that way. He just wants so much for Joey to be able to take on responsibility. He worries about the future of Brennan Manor."

She watched her brother bend down to pick something out of the sand. "There is nothing Joey wouldn't do to impress our father and try to make him proud of him. He tries, but nothing works, and I can't help but try to make up for the loss of our mother and the hurt he feels over the way Father treats him. Sometimes when we are talking alone and he is relaxed, he hardly stutters at all. It's worse when he's around Father."

Lee followed her gaze to watch Joey himself. "He's heading for manhood, Audra. You can't be doing his talking for him, and you can't keep protecting him." He picked up a pebble and threw it, but it didn't quite reach the water. "Is there anything in particular he's good at?"

Audra paused to drink some lemonade. "Well, he likes

to carve. He has all kinds of figures in his room. Sometimes he sings when he is carving, and strangely enough, when he sings, he doesn't stutter at all. He is also a good marksman for his age. At home he goes rabbit-hunting."

Lee looked into the bigger picnic basket, taking out a fresh-baked cookie. "Well, then, maybe I'll take him hunting when you're having your lessons. He can't just sit around the house bored. Me, I've always got to be doing something."

A gust of wind blew at Audra's hat, and she retied the wide satin sash that held it under her chin. "Are you a good lawyer, Lee?" The question made him laugh, and Audra thought what fine, straight white teeth he had.

"How do you expect me to answer that?" he asked, still grinning. "Of course I'm a good lawyer. I wouldn't already have my own firm if I wasn't."

Again Audra was almost startled by a sudden rush of sweet desire she had never experienced before meeting this man. She turned her gaze from him again, and she pretended to be interested in watching her brother. "What is the name of your law firm?"

"Jeffreys, James, and Stillwell. We're already one of the most sought-after firms in New York City."

"I see. My father is acquainted with several lawyers in Baton Rouge, and even New Orleans. He is very well-known and respected, you know."

Lee kept his smile, realizing how proud she was of her father and Brennan Manor. "I gathered that," he answered. If she needed to believe her father was the most important man on earth, what was the real harm? He had once thought the same about his own father. He felt he understood Joey better than she realized. Joey was the outsider, the one who could never please his father. It was a lonely place to be. He decided he would have a good talk with the boy, make sure he understood that he could do whatever he wanted in life no matter what his father thought, or what the man tried to force him to do. His own situation was not the same as Joey's, but he knew about the pressures a father could put on a son.

"We don't live close enough to the Gulf to go to

beaches like this," Audra was saying. "Once when we visited my Aunt Janine in Baton Rouge—she's my mother's sister—we took a steamboat south to the Gulf. I enjoyed that." She looked back at him. "Did I tell you the Mississippi River runs right past the east end of my father's plantation?"

Lee caught her youthful excitement. "I've never seen the Mississippi. I guess the places where we live each have something unusual about them, don't they?"

"And pretty." Audra picked up a twig lying nearby and began tracing in the sand with it. "Oh, the Mississippi is beautiful, Lee. A river is so different from the ocean. It flows lazily along, making no waves. The river is part of the reason my father does so well. Cargo boats can come right up to our property to pick up loads of cotton. It saves my father from having to haul it by wagon first to a port. Brennan Manor produces tons and tons of cotton every year."

"Sounds convenient, being right beside the river like that." *How many slaves does it take to pick all that cotton?* he wanted to ask, but he didn't feel like getting into another argument over slavery, not today. They were just beginning to like each other and get along. He wondered if Audra sensed his thoughts, for she suddenly changed the subject as she threw more crumbs to the gulls. "Why didn't you want to work with your father and brothers?" she asked. "If that's too personal a question, you don't have to answer it."

Lee poured himself more lemonade. "I don't mind. Besides, I don't really have an answer. It's just something my brothers really seemed to want to do, but I hate the smell and the grime of the factories. I guess what I really hate is the sight of those poor workers sitting or standing at the same station twelve and fourteen hours a day, doing the same things over and over, freezing in winter and sweating to death in summer, breathing that dirty air, all for slave wages—" He hesitated on the words, giving her a sly glance. "Sorry. I just meant that the people in those factories don't earn much in return for how hard they work. I guess I just can't tolerate the wealthy lording it over the poor, exploiting them just to make even more money, whether they're slaves or paid." *Damn,* he thought, *here we are right back on the subject again.*

"A-ha!" Audra leaned down on one elbow. "Then you *are* admitting that the people who work in your own father's shops are hardly any better off than slaves." Audra also had not wanted to get into the subject, but she could not pass up the comparison and the chance to show Lee Jeffreys that slavery was not such a terrible thing, maybe not even as bad as people having to work in those dirty factories.

Lee smiled, chagrined. "In a way." He finished his lemonade and leaned closer to her. "One big difference—people up here aren't bought and sold like common chattel. They aren't whipped and forced to live in squalor, and we don't tear babies out of mothers' arms, or breed our help in selected pairs like cattle."

Audra scowled and sat up straighter, embarrassed at the last remark. Was this going to turn into another heated debate? Why didn't she know when to keep quiet? "Some slave owners treat their people that way, but we don't. It is true that my father's father was the first in the family to own slaves. He bought them from among some of the original captives brought here from Africa. My father has also bought and sold slaves, but most of those we own now are families, Negroes we have kept on and who have intermarried and had children, like Lena and Toosie."

Toosie, Lee thought. Again he wondered about the woman, but he was afraid he would offend Audra if he admitted his suspicions about her heritage. Besides, Audra seemed to be sure who the woman's father was.

Audra rested on her elbow again, both of them partially reclined on the blanket. "We will probably never agree on these things, Lee," she said with a hint of apology, "so why don't we go back to talking about your father and brothers. What are they like?"

He forced a grin. He didn't know her well enough to go into a family history and try to explain the hard feelings. "You mean my bragging mother didn't already tell you everything there is to know?"

This time it was Audra who laughed, and Lee drank in the sound of it. She had a lilting laugh that seemed to fit perfectly a beautiful young woman with an enchanting way of speaking and a voice that belonged to an angel.

"Yes, I suppose there is very little left that I don't know," she told him. "Let's see—you all look very much alike, except that you are the only one who inherited your mother's blue eyes. You are all tall like your father, you all have tempers, and so you don't always get along. You are the only one who attended West Point, but all three of you attended Yale. Carl handles the shoe factory, and he is thirty-three and has a wife and three children. David is two years younger and is also married but has no children. He is in charge of the canvas factory, and both are involved in the iron mill. Your father oversees everything, and he works *much* too hard."

Lee gave her a wink. "You see? I can't add much to that."

They both smiled, and for a moment their eyes held, neither of them saying a word, each suspecting the other was thinking something that was surely not possible, each feeling a building attraction. For a moment Audra actually thought he might lean a little closer and try to kiss her, and in that same moment Lee thought about doing just that.

Audra quickly sat up. "You are the only one who is not married," she added. "Surely you have someone special in your life, Lee Jeffreys. You are of an age when a man usually thinks about marrying."

When he did not answer right away, she looked back at him, saw the pain in his eyes. "I'm sorry if I said something wrong."

He sighed and sat up straighter. He bent his legs and crossed them, resting his elbows on his knees. "It's all right. I'm over it now, as much as can be expected anyway." He threw another pebble. "I was engaged to be married six years ago. Her name was Mary Ellen, and she was the daughter of one of my first clients. We were going to be married here at Maple Shadows, but she died of pneumonia."

"Oh, I'm so very sorry." Audra wished she had not brought up a subject that took away his handsome smile. She had enjoyed watching him laugh. She was amazed to feel so relaxed around this man. She could not remember laughing with Richard. Maybe a forty-two-year-old man just didn't have enough in common with a seventeen-year-old girl to find things to laugh about.

"Well, it was a long time ago," Lee went on. "Life goes on, and I decided I had to go on with mine. Besides, I was only twenty-three myself, and after two years at West Point and four at Yale, just getting started in my own law firm, I probably wasn't ready for marriage anyway. I am now, but there just hasn't been anyone else to come along who interested me that much."

Audra sifted some sand through her fingers. "I am to be married myself next summer, after I turn eighteen next April." Why had she told him that? A woman shouldn't discuss such things with a man she hardly knew.

The statement surprised Lee. She seemed so young, and she couldn't possibly know what marriage involved, either physically or emotionally. She hadn't had a mother since she was seven years old, no woman to teach her about men and sex and being a wife, as far as he could tell. Why did it disturb him to think about her being married to another man? He shouldn't give a tinker's damn what she would do when she went back home.

"I never have told your mother," she admitted. "I don't even know why I am telling you, of all people."

"Well, as long as you *have* told me, you might as well tell me more. Who is he?"

Audra kept toying with the sand as she spoke. "His name is Richard Potter, and he is twenty-five years older than I. He's a widower, the son of the wealthiest plantation owner in Louisiana. Other than my own father, of course. His plantation is called Cypress Hollow. Maybe you have heard of it."

"I don't keep track of such things," he said with a hint of sarcasm. Lee felt a little irritated, not only because she was surely marrying a man old enough to be her father, and for all the wrong reasons, but that she had an inflated notion of how important her father and his fellow plantation magnates were.

"Our marriage will make Richard the most powerful man in the state," she continued, "maybe in the whole South, especially once my father and his father are gone from this earth. I, in turn, will be the most important woman in Louisiana."

The statement irked Lee to the bone. "Is that the only reason you're marrying him? Do you love the man?"

Audra felt a rush of embarrassment at the question. Love? What did love matter in such a marriage? "It's what Father expects of me," she answered proudly, "and it would be good for Joey. He will probably never be able to take over our own plantation. It is important for me to marry someone who understands how to run such a place, who can control it, so that it can stay in the Brennan family. There are not many men capable of such a difficult job, Lee. I cannot marry just any old city man or even a small farmer. Richard would let Joey live with us forever. He would even agree to living at Brennan Manor, so that Joey and I can both stay on there in our own home. He is a good man. He will take good care of us."

Like a father, Lee thought. He let out a sigh of disgust. "For God's sake, there's more to marriage than just taking good care of someone, Audra. You have to have *feelings* for him. You have to *want* to be with him, especially—" He suddenly stood up. "Forget it. It's none of my business. Here comes Joey."

Audra said nothing for a moment, refusing to look at him for fear he would read her thoughts. For the first time since Richard had danced with her at her sixteenth birthday party, and in all the times he had courted her since, she realized something was missing. It had taken only one night's talk with Lee Jeffreys, and one picnic with him, for her to realize what that something was. The only name she could give it was desire. She did not desire Richard Potter, but no one had ever told her that might be important. She would never have thought that it was, until these last two days when she had become close to Lee.

She was shocked to realize how she felt. She desired Lee Jeffreys, desired his company, actually wondered how it would feel to have him touch her lovingly, take her in his arms. It was a forbidden thought, surely a sinful feeling. Of all the men besides Richard she could want, Lee Jeffreys was as far removed from a proper husband as he could be. Only yesterday she would have thought him the last man on earth who could make her feel this way. This was ridiculous! She felt engulfed in confusion, suddenly a stranger to herself.

"Do you want to walk along the beach?" he was asking.

She finally managed to meet his eyes again. "Yes, I would like that. Since I arrived, I have seen it only from the house."

He gave her a wink, his irritation seemingly disappeared. "Maybe we should go for a swim."

"A swim! I have no bathing clothes with me, and even if I did, I would not wear them in front of a man I hardly know!"

Lee shrugged. "I figured swimming naked would be the most fun. I do it all the time. Feels wonderful!"

Audra reddened deeply. "Mr. Jeffreys! Don't you dare begin removing your clothes in front of me!"

Lee laughed and held out his hand. "Come on. I'll help you walk through the sand. You really ought to take off those shoes and stockings."

"I declare! Now it's my bare feet he thinks he's going to see!"

"Feels good between the toes." He squeezed her hand. "Come on. I promise not to make you remove one article of clothing. We'll just walk."

Audra studied his handsome face, admiring the way his dark hair blew across his forehead. There was a daring recklessness about the man that attracted her. She let him help her to her feet, and she liked the feel of his strong hand grasping her own. He rubbed the back of her hand with his thumb. "Feeling better about being here now?" he asked.

"Yes," she answered softly.

"Good. Come on. Let's go out and meet Joey, see what he's collected." He turned, keeping hold of her hand as he led her closer to the waves. Audra hung on tightly, wondering how good it would feel to let the sand squish between her toes.

4

Audra's voice carried strong and clear, and although she was putting on her first performance before an audience, she was really singing only for Lee, who sat near the parlor fireplace. The room was filled with specially invited guests, neighbors whom Anna Jeffreys had invited for evening drinks and to listen to her latest protégé. She did not want to let Anna down, but, strangely, it seemed more important not to let Lee down.

Over a month had passed since Lee arrived. He had already stayed longer than he had intended. Was it because of her? They had gone for many rides, both in the buggy and on horseback; had frolicked on the beach. They had sat quietly together in the study, reading, discussing northern and southern culture. Lee seemed to be trying to understand her views on slavery, but most of the time they both tried to avoid the subject completely and talk about other things.

Inwardly she fought and argued over the reasons why she wanted to please him tonight, why she had fussed for hours getting ready so that she would appear more womanly. Toosie had rearranged her hair several times until it looked as close to perfect as possible, drawn up into a mass of auburn curls on top of her head. She wore a mint-green evening dress, the bodice cut low and off the shoulders, her slender waist accented by a wide dark-green sash that was tied into a huge bow at her back. Double-puffed sleeves fell from her middle upper arm to her elbow, decorated with narrow satin ribbon that matched the sash. The upper skirt of mint-green tulle fell over an underskirt of silk puffings, each puff tied, again with darker green satin ribbon; and the hemline was quilled in dark green.

Old Henrietta, her family's seamstress, had made the dress for her sixteenth birthday. Henrietta was just about the fattest woman she had ever seen, but nobody could sew the way she could. The woman had chosen green to bring out the green in her eyes, but when she tried the dress on for the first time, Henrietta had lamented that perhaps she had cut the bodice a little *too* low. Audra didn't mind. It had made her feel very grown-up at the time, daring to reveal the pale curve of her breasts.

As she got ready, she had thought about the grand ball her father had held to celebrate that birthday. Young men had lined up to dance with her, but Richard Potter had danced with her most of all. It was that night that the widowed plantation owner had suggested to her father the benefits of marriage between the two of them. Richard's first wife had never been able to give him children. Audra was young and could produce many offspring to rule one day the combined empire of Brennan Manor and Cypress Hollow.

She had not given much serious thought to marriage and children. Marrying Richard was something she had just taken for granted, and it had always seemed like something unreal, something that was always far in the future that she didn't really have to think about. She would still not be

thinking about it if not for the feelings she had begun to experience when she was with Lee. Neither Richard nor anyone else had made her heart beat faster or stirred new,
strange desires that made her ache.

Did Lee see her as a woman tonight? At her throat she
wore the diamond necklace her father had given her the
night of her birthday ball. More diamonds dangled at her
ears. She was no longer sixteen, but seventeen—going on
eighteen. She knew it was foolish to have these womanly
feelings for a Yankee man, and her father would be angry if
he knew how she felt about Lee.

Down in Louisiana and all over the south, the term
"Yankee" had come to represent the enemy. Lee hated slavery, and he still enjoyed irritating her by talking to Toosie as
though she were a neighbor from next door. He was the last
man she should be falling in love with, but she did love
him. She wondered if he knew how she felt. He was a
worldly man, experienced. He probably knew her every
thought and was laughing inside. If only she could find the
courage to tell him, to let him know she had written a song
just for him, a song she was too bashful to show him or sing
for him.

There was so much she didn't understand about men,
things that had never mattered until now. Lee had awakened something new and wonderful in her soul. It was as
though a woman she hardly knew was trying to break free
from her own body, a body she had begun to study at
times in the mirror, wondering what a man would think of
it.

She forced herself to concentrate on the forty or so
people who were packed into the spacious parlor. Anna Jeffreys had taught her to give her attention always to the
whole audience, whether forty people or a thousand. *Make
each individual think you are singing just to him or her
alone,* she had told Audra.

Before beginning, she had practiced the deep-
breathing exercises Anna had taught her to help relieve her
nervousness. There were so many "firsts" tonight—first true
performance in front of a real audience, first time singing an
aria from Italian opera. Mrs. Jeffreys had taught her how to

pronounce the words, explained their meaning so she could sing the song with real feeling. She prayed inwardly she would not stumble on the words or forget them. It didn't really matter what the others would think, but Lee was watching, listening.

She finished another song, and everyone applauded. Some rose to their feet, including Lee, and she felt the elation of having pleased an audience. She had never given much thought to taking voice lessons or performing before a crowd, but Anna Jeffreys had told her about her own career, and that she, too, could enjoy such fame if she wanted to work at it. All her life she had thought of nothing more than staying right at Brennan Manor, marrying, having children, living the quiet, genteel life of a rich southern woman.

Now her mind whirled with other possibilities. She could sing in the opera. She could turn down Richard's marriage proposal, which she knew would come formally soon after she went back home; she could think about a career instead. Or . . . she could fall in love with a Yankee man and stay right here in Connecticut. Still, in these restless times, it would not be easy to live here, surrounded by the "enemy." Many of these people had been cold and rude when first meeting her and hearing her accent. They had asked ignorant questions about plantation life, questions that hurt her feelings and her pride. Besides, there was her father to think about, Joey, and Brennan Manor.

She moved her gaze to Lee again. He was smiling, still clapping. Could two people so different fall in love and find happiness? Was that a hint of love she saw in those melting blue eyes, or was it just wishful thinking on her part? Part of the reason she loved Lee was his kind patience toward Joey. He had taken her brother hunting several times; and they had gone swimming, had studied together. Joey had changed dramatically over the past month, was becoming more self-confident. Lee had helped her see she was smothering her brother with love, was not allowing him to be his own man. Joey's speech had actually improved since Lee began working with him, and Joey practically worshiped the man. There seemed to be a special bond there, as though Lee actually understood how Joey felt. He had never told her his exact troubles with his own father, but she could tell from the way he usually avoided the subject or glossed over it that there was a rift between them.

Maybe it was that loneliness in his eyes that had made her love him even more. How quickly a month could fly by when one preferred that time stand still. Lee would be leaving soon for New York, and that would surely be the end of her short but sweet friendship with him. She was beginning to feel a desperate urge to blurt out her feelings, afraid he would go back without ever knowing, and maybe she would never see him again.

She finished her planned performance and began taking requests, singing more familiar songs for her audience, who seemed enraptured.

> *'Twas a calm, still night, and the moon's pale light*
> *Shone soft o'er hill and vale,*
> *When friends mute with grief stood around the*
>   *deathbed*
> *Of my poor lost Lilly Dale.*

"Lilly Dale" was the name of the sad song a woman had asked for, and she sang it with such feeling that the woman actually sniffled and wiped at her eyes. By the time Audra finished all the verses, several more women were dabbing at their eyes. She went on to sing several other songs, lighter ones, some with words that made people laugh.

"How about 'My Old Kentucky Home'?" one man requested then. He had a strange look in his eyes and was not smiling. It was Cy Jordan, another wealthy family friend here on vacation from New York. He had inquired if she was one of those "southern rebels" when he was first introduced to her, and even though he had laughed about it, Audra had caught the slight sneer in the remark.

"Fine," she answered, holding his eyes boldly. The room hung silent for a moment. Although "My Old Kentucky Home" was written by Stephen Foster, everyone knew it was based on a Negro spiritual. Cy Jordan was challenging her, and she was not going to back down from the challenge. She turned to Mrs. Jeffreys and asked her to play a few lines first. Audra thought how Anna had a way with the piano that made any song, even a most familiar one, sound like the greatest music ever written.

She glanced at Lee, who gave her a nod, as though to tell her to stand right up to Cy Jordan. She looked at Jordan then and began the song.

The sun shines bright on the old Kentucky home.
'Tis summer, the darkies are gay;
The corn top's ripe and the meadow's in the
   bloom,
While the birds make music all the day.

The young folks roll on the little cabin floor,
All merry, all happy and bright;
By 'n' by hard times come a knocking at the door,
Then, my old Kentucky home, good night!

She sang the chorus, the second verse, into the third verse.

The head must bow and the back will have to bend,
Wherever the darky may go.
A few more days and the trouble all will end,
In the fields where the sugar canes grow. . . .

Weep no more, my lady, oh, weep no more today!
We will sing one song for the old Kentucky home,
For the old Kentucky home far away.

The song brought back a longing for her own home, for the quiet elegance of Brennan Manor. She missed Lena and fat old Henrietta. She missed her father, and she realized then that Lee had taken up so much of her time and thoughts that she had not dwelled so much on them. The song brought it all back, and she felt a sudden urge to cry. She breathed deeply and forced back the tears.

"How about your own blackies?" Jordan asked her then. "Do *they* bend their backs in sugarcane fields, or is it cotton your father's slaves have to pick? How many Negroes does your father own, anyway? You ever see one whipped?"

"That's enough, Cy," Lee put in. "She is here as our guest."

Everyone was staring at Audra then, and she felt the old southern pride beginning to burn in her heart, a desire to defend her father, defend Brennan Manor, defend even the Negroes. "My father grows cotton, Mr. Jordan," she answered proudly. "He is one of the richest men in Louisiana, owns one of the biggest plantations. Yes, we own Negroes, but they are well treated."

"Oh, so that makes slavery all right, as long as they're well fed and not whipped? Tell me, Miss Brennan, what if someone put a price on *you*? How would you feel about that—stood up on a crate for people to stare at and decide what you're worth, not knowing what you'll be used for? How many of the pretty ones, like your own Toosie, does your widowed father take to his bed at night?"

Audra reddened, while others gasped at the crude remark and Lee rose from his chair. "Get out, Jordan!" Lee demanded. "Get out before I *throw* you out!"

Audra felt Anna Jeffrey's hand move into her own. The woman squeezed her hand lightly in support. "He's the one in the wrong, my dear," she told her quietly, while more gasps and whispers circulated among the guests.

"That was really quite uncalled for," Audra heard one woman say. Most of them seemed very upset with Cy Jordan, who rose and took his wife's arm.

"I'll gladly leave," he was telling Lee. "That girl might have a beautiful voice, but the fact remains she comes from a family who buys and sells human beings, and from a traitorous state that is already talking about seceding from the Union! Your mother never should have invited her here, or at least she never should have allowed the girl to bring her own personal Negro along with her. It's not right having a slave owner in your house, Lee."

"It *is* my house, and I'm telling you to shut your mouth and leave it right now! One more remark and that mouth is going to be bleeding!"

"Slavery is *wrong*, Lee!"

"I agree, but this is neither the time nor the place to discuss it, and one young woman isn't going to make the least bit of difference over whether or not the practice of slavery continues or whether her state secedes from the Union! And while we're at it, don't forget there are all kinds of slavery. Everybody knows how you treat your *wife*, Jordan, and I don't doubt some of Miss Brennan's slaves have it *better*!"

More gasps rushed through the audience, and Audra's own eyes widened at the remark. Lee was truly angry. Was it really just because Cy Jordan had insulted her? He was standing up for her! Defending her! Her heart literally ached with love, and she watched with fear then when an enraged Jordan stepped closer to Lee.

"If you weren't Edmund Jeffreys's son, I'd—"

"You'd what?" Lee was seething.

Jordan, a small, balding man, knew he was no match for Lee Jeffreys, whose hands moved into fists, ready for a fight. He could never win a physical struggle with the tall, powerful, and much younger Lee. He backed away, keeping a tight hold on his wife's arm. The rather plain, quiet woman stood there with a red face, and Audra felt sorry for her.

Jordan turned and stormed out, dragging his wife with him. Lee turned to the others, apologizing for the interruption.

"Please, let's all enjoy a few more songs and then we'll have some refreshments," he told them. He looked at Audra. "I apologize, Audra, for our rude guest."

Audra nodded. She wanted to shout *I love you, Lee Jeffreys*.

"Don't pay any attention to Jordan," another spoke up to her. "He's had too much to drink tonight."

"If it was ten in the morning, the man would *still* have had too much to drink," someone else put in, The others laughed, and things became more relaxed. Lee sat down, and someone asked Audra to sing "Home, Sweet Home." Mrs. Jeffreys began the tune, and Audra struggled to regain her composure. Did all these people think men like her father had harems of slave women? What horrible conception did they have of life in the South? She loved her home and her way of life. What was so wrong with it, and why did everyone think that all slave owners raped their Negro women and beat the men?

> *Mid pleasures and palaces, though we may roam,*
> *Be it ever so humble, there's no place like home!*
> *A charm from the skies seems to hallow us there,*
> *Which, seek through the world, is ne'er met with*
> *   elsewhere.*
>
> *Home, home! Sweet, sweet home! . . .*
> *An exile from home splendor dazzles in vain;*
> *Oh, give me my lowly thatch'd cottage again!*
> *The birds singing gaily that came at my call,*

She could picture Brennan Manor, the azaleas and dogwood in blossom.

> *Give me them with the peace of mind dearer than*
> *   all.*
> *Home, home! Sweet, sweet . . .*

She could not keep the tears from coming then, and she turned and ran out through the open doors onto the veranda and around a corner into the darkness. She could hear the wave of whispers that moved into louder talking then. Anna Jeffreys stopped playing.

"Audra is obviously upset by Cy Jordan's remarks," the woman told everyone. "I don't blame her. She is really just a child, you know, and she cannot be blamed for the entire southern culture. Thank you all for being here to listen to her sing. This gathering was strictly to give Audra some practice before an audience, and you have all been wonderful. You're welcome to stretch your legs and walk outside to the cool veranda. The servants will serve you refreshments. Please enjoy yourselves. I'll have Lee find Audra and bring her back."

Everyone clapped, and Audra moved farther into the darkness. A servant came outside to begin lighting lanterns, and she hurried away, walking toward the beach where no one would see her beyond the light from the house. She turned to see people filtering out onto the veranda then, and she wondered where Lee was. "Child," they had called her. "Girl." She felt like a fool now, too foolish and babyish to go back and face all of them. Jordan's remarks had hurt deeply, made her want nothing more than to go home to Brennan Manor and get away from these people who understood so little about how she lived. It had probably been silly to let the last song make her cry. If she had made any progress in getting Lee to look at her as a woman, she had certainly erased it all by dashing out this way.

The tears came then—tears of sorrow over a love she could never have, tears of homesickness, tears of humiliation over Cy Jordan's cruel words, tears of anger and pride. She must have disappointed Anna Jeffreys, behaving as she had. Now she was surely smearing her rouge, and she had no handkerchief with which to wipe her eyes or blow her nose.

"Audra?"

Her heart quickened at the sound of Lee's voice. Oh, the humiliation of it, having him find her bawling like a baby again! She hated crying. He was probably upset at how she had acted so childishly. She frantically wiped at her tears with her bare fingers, and in the next moment Lee was there, handing her a handkerchief.

"I thought this was where I'd find you. Once I got away from the lantern light and got used to the moonlight, I could see someone standing down here."

She took the handkerchief and blew her nose. "I'm so sorry I ran off that way," she whimpered. She felt his hand on her bare shoulder, felt his full arm coming around her then. "Audra." This time he spoke her name differently, almost reverently, and to her surprise he turned her and put both his arms fully around her, pressing her close.

"Go ahead and cry," he told her. "You have a right. If we hadn't been standing in my own mother's parlor, I would have knocked Cy Jordan clear across the room for what he said. The bastard!"

Audra rested her head against his broad chest, breathed in the scent of him, relished the comfort of his arms. He had never held her like this, and she wasn't quite sure what to make of it.

"Jordan is the attorney for my father's businesses, but that doesn't mean I have to put up with him. Mother and I both should have known better than to invite him," he said. "He drinks too much, and it makes him shoot off at the mouth. Part of the reason he made trouble was just to irritate me. He owns one of the biggest law firms in New York City, and he knows I'm fast catching up with him. He's jealous because I'm twenty years younger and already doing about as well as he is." He rubbed her back. "Besides that, people have seen bruises on Mrs. Jordan several times. The woman always has an excuse for them, but everyone knows her husband beats her. There's nothing I hate more than a man who would lay a hand on a woman or a child. I saw a man beating on his kid in an alley in New York once. By the time I got through with him, my own hand was broken."

Oh, yes, she did love him! She could just picture him defending that child. A man like Lee would defend not just those he loved, but even a stranger. He was brave and sure, intelligent and exciting. He was not a man to back down from a fight, yet he was so much the gentleman, so kind and considerate of people less fortunate than he, people like Joey. He had looked so handsome tonight in his black silk suit and white ruffled shirt.

The thought made her lean back. "Your shirt! I'll get rouge all over it!" she exclaimed, suddenly embarrassed that she had let him press her so tightly against his chest, more embarrassed that she might have soiled his shirt. She tried to pull completely away, but he only gripped her closer again.

"Don't worry about the damn shirt," he told her softly.

Something was different about him, the way he held her, the tenderness in his voice. She raised her face to look up at him, able to see him quite clearly in the bright moonlight. What was that in those blue eyes? Love? Some kind of adoration?

He kept one arm around her and with his other hand touched her cheek. "I have never laid eyes on anyone so beautiful as you look tonight, Audra." He moved his hand to touch her bare shoulder, and she wondered if she would faint. "Maybe it's this dress," he said, a slight tremor to his voice. "All I know is I don't want to let go of you right now, and I can't stand to see you hurting."

Her heart pounded wildly, and fire seemed to be rushing through her veins. "And I don't *want* you to let go of me," she said in a near whisper.

He crushed her even closer, one hand at the middle of her bare back, the other moving to her bottom. In spite of all her petticoats, she knew it was bold of her to let him press his hand there, yet she could not find the will to make him stop.

"You're supposed to marry someone else, Audra, and you don't love him. I know you don't, and for the life of me, I can't stand the thought of another man making a woman of you. *I* want to do it. I think I'm in love with you, Audra, and I know it's wrong. It's all wrong."

All the feelings she had been fighting flooded her body in uncontrollable desire. This was surely no mad crush. She loved Lee Jeffreys, Yankee or not, and she could not hold back for one more second. She flung her arms around his neck. "Oh, Lee, I love you, too! I think I loved you from that first day, when you got so angry with me. I love you for your kindness, and courage, and for how good you are to Joey—"

He cut off her words, capturing her mouth with his own. She felt the fire inside her build to explosive force when he parted her mouth, his tongue lightly running inside it. She returned the kiss eagerly, not thinking how inexperienced she was, how he might think her terribly childish by being suddenly so eager, but he did not seem to mind. He pressed her so close she could barely breathe, and his kiss grew hotter, deeper.

What was she feeling? She knew that at this moment he could do anything he wanted with her and she would not object. She yearned for him to touch her, to possess her, to hold her close to him forever. They didn't seem to be able to stop kissing. Over and over again he met her mouth, tasted it, licked at it, groaned her name whenever he took a breath. His breathing was as quick and heated as her own.

He was hungry for her, pressing his lips to her neck, kissing at her bare shoulder, drawing forth marvelous sensations she had never experienced. A little voice told her to be careful, warned her he was surely a man of experience, and she knew little about the extent to which a man and woman go when they are in love. Eleanor had said that kissing a man was most delightful. Now she knew what her cousin meant. This was wonderful! She could not get enough of Lee Jeffreys. He could not kiss her enough, hold her close enough, touch her enough.

"My God, if you weren't wearing such a beautiful gown, I'd lay you right down in the sand," Lee groaned.

And what would you do then? Part of her knew what making love meant, things Eleanor had told her about, but which had never made much sense to her until now.

She threw back her head, and Lee kissed her throat. His lips trailed lower, until he was kissing the whites of her breasts exposed by the cut of her gown. She sighed at the ecstasy he stirred in her soul. Was there even more? She wanted him to touch her everywhere, kiss her everywhere. He made it all so easy, seem so right. Could he so easily turn her into a woman who would allow him to do sinful things? Where was her common sense? She could not find it, not while Lee's arms were around her, not when his gentle lips were kissing at her breasts.

Lower he went, his tongue moving between the dress and her skin, searching for her taut nipple. When he found it, she groaned, totally stunned that she could not bring herself to stop him. Never in her life had she felt so wonderful, so alive, so beautiful, so much a woman. He kept one arm firmly pressed around the middle of her back, moving his lips to her throat and his other hand to the front of her to touch her breast, gently tugging it out of her dress. She whispered his name over and over as he fondled the breast, and his lips found her mouth again in a hot, penetrating kiss.

Her breath came in gasps when he left her mouth again to move back down to the exposed breast. He took it gingerly into his mouth, sucking gently, his tongue teasing her nipple. He moved his lips then to the very tip of her breast, pulling lightly at the pink fruit she offered. She nearly reeled with ecstasy, and new, wonderful, almost painful needs probed at her belly, pulled at private places suddenly awakened by this man she loved.

Oh, yes, there was much more to this, she was sure, and she wanted to know all of it. She wanted Lee Jeffreys to be the one to show her, just as much as he wanted it. Richard could *never* make her feel this way!

"Lee? Are you out there?"

It was Anna Jeffreys's voice. Lee stiffened. He had practically forgotten about the guests and the fact that his mother must be looking for Audra. "Damn," he whispered. "Fix your dress."

"I can't find Audra anywhere," Anna shouted. "Help me find her, will you? I'm worried about her."

"I've already found her," he called back. "Just give her a few minutes. I'll take her back to the house to freshen up. I think I've talked her into rejoining the others." He turned and grasped Audra's arms. "I'll take you back through an entrance where they won't see you. You can fix your face. . . ." He bent down to kiss her lightly. "And your dress."

Audra felt suddenly embarrassed and awkward, but still utterly on fire. "I want to stay out here with you," she said softly. She felt as though she were floating in some unreal world. Something wonderful had happened to change her into someone she hardly knew. Was she a woman now? Was this all it took? What more might have happened if Anna Jeffreys had not come along?

"I'm sorry, Audra," Lee was saying. "I had no right—"

She flung her arms around his neck again. "It's all right, Lee. I love you so much! And to know you love me . . ." She kissed his mouth again. "It doesn't matter that you're a Yankee," she said then. "Father will just have to accept it. You're a smart man. You can learn to run a plantation."

"What?" Lee did not miss the slight venom in the word "Yankee." And suddenly she had him being a slave master on a plantation.

"I could never leave Brennan Manor, you know. It would kill Father, and Joey, too. I can't take Joey away from there, and I have to take care of him. We will just settle at Brennan Manor. You could practice law at Baton Rouge. It isn't so far away. We'll get over our differences, Lee, you'll see. Love can change anything and anyone."

She kissed him again, and Lee was hit with the overwhelming reality of what he had just done. He had drunk too much tonight, that was it. If he'd been sober, he never would have allowed this to happen. Oh, yes, he loved her all right, but he had made up his mind he was never going to tell her. He was going to go back to New York and forget her, because it was best that way. God knew that in reality they could never last. Go and live at Brennan Manor? Never! And neither would she be happy living in New York. And what about Joey? He had reasoned it all out, his logical attorney's mind telling him it was best never to confess what he felt.

But tonight. Damn Cy Jordan! Damn her tears! Damn the liquor and the warm night! My God, what had he done? He pulled her arms from around his neck. "I've got to get you back to the house, Audra. We'll talk about all of this tomorrow."

Audra sensed the change in him. Had she said something wrong? She felt her cheeks growing hot with embarrassment. She had taken it for granted that he was ready to marry her! She had talked of his coming to live at Brennan Manor as though it were already decided! What must he think of her childish eagerness! Or maybe he thought she was giving him orders again. Still, look at how intimate they had just been. He surely intended to marry her, or had he just used her?

She pulled farther away, fastening herself back into her dress, suddenly feeling dirty, like a harlot. What did he really think of her after what she had let him do? Was that why she felt this sudden change in him? "I don't know what made me let you do that," she said, her voice still weak from a torrent of emotions. "I can imagine what you must think of me, but I swear, Lee, I have never—"

"Don't you think I know that? You've no apologies to make. I got carried away, and I had no right!" He took her arm and led her toward the house. "We both have a lot to think about, Audra."

She stopped and grasped hold of the front of his jacket. "You *did* mean it, didn't you, when you said you loved me?"

He just watched her for a moment in the moonlight. "I'm not a man to say such things lightly. Yes, Audra, I love you. But sometimes love isn't enough."

"I don't understand—"

He touched his fingers to her lips. "Let's not spoil tonight. We'll talk tomorrow, I promise."

He walked with her, keeping her out of the light until he could get her to a side entrance. "Go on upstairs and freshen up," he told her. "I'll be along in a little while."

"Where are you going?"

"I just want to walk alone for a while, to clear my head." Lee bent down to taste her mouth once more. God, he didn't want to hurt her, but how could he *not* hurt her? It was either going to happen now, or if they stayed together, it would happen later. One way or another, their differences were going to destroy the delicate love they shared. "Good night, Audra."

He turned and left, and Audra watched after him, wondering why, after the wonderful feelings he had stirred in her tonight, after discovering that Lee Jeffreys did love her . . . why did she feel this ominous dread? Her joy had lasted such a short while. Now something had changed. "I love you, Lee," she called out, but she could not see him.

Had what just happened been real? She touched her breast and could still feel a moistness left by his lips. Yes, it had been *very* real.

5

Audra buttoned her yellow dress up to the throat. This morning she would see Lee in the full light of day, and she was not sure she could face him after what she had let him do last night. Had they both lost their minds ... or just their hearts? It seemed important today to look as decent as possible. What must Lee think of her? She certainly couldn't appear at the breakfast table with her breasts billowing invitingly out of her gown again. He might think her a loose woman after all.

She didn't even know what to think of herself. Was he laughing at her this morning, or did he just think she was easily swayed by a man's touch? She fussed with her hair, asking Toosie to brush it out in back. She would wear it with the sides pulled into combs. She looked younger with her hair hanging down long, more innocent. That was good. That was how she must look this morning. She had wept half the night, and she hoped the powders she had used did a good enough job of hiding the circles under her eyes. The tears had not been over Cy Jordan's insults. They had been over the worry that the near-painful love she felt for Lee was hopeless.

Something deep inside told her she could never really have the man, yet never had she wanted anything so much in her life. She was used to getting what she wanted, but Lee Jeffreys was not something she could have at the snap of her finger, or buy with her father's money. Perhaps if she knew more about men, she would know how to snare and hold him, but already she had said or done something that would cause her to lose him. She had sensed it last night, after Anna Jeffreys had called out to them. Perhaps if his mother had not come along . . .

"I looked in on you last night and heard you crying," Toosie told her as she brushed Audra's auburn locks. "Miss Audra, you shouldn't let that Mr. Jordan upset you like that. He just doesn't understand."

Audra looked at Toosie in the mirror, surprised at the remark. "You *disagree* with Mr. Jordan? I should think you would have rejoiced at his attack on slavery."

Toosie lowered her arm and met her gaze in the mirror. "Mr. Jordan does not understand how it is for some of us. I have grown up at Brennan Manor. It is my home. If someone told me I was free to do as I wished, I would probably stay right there and keep doing what I have always done. I do not need my freedom, Miss Audra. I only need to know I will not be sold."

Audra rose, turning to face her. She was never quite sure how to feel about Toosie, who was an exceptionally beautiful woman of mixed blood. She was soft-spoken, surprisingly proud for her station in life, and very intelligent.

She was loyal, and sometimes she seemed to want to be friends. There were moments when Audra felt she would like nothing better, when she thought about confiding secret feelings to Toosie, who was seven years older than she.

She wished she could talk to her now about Lee. She suspected Toosie would understand. There had been a romance once, between Toosie and a field slave named Elijah.

She remembered some kind of argument between her father and Toosie's mother, remembered the day Elijah had been sold. Toosie had cried all day and remained on the verge of tears for many days after that. Had she loved the man? Did Negroes have the same feelings that way as whites? Ever since then, Toosie's mother had protected her like a hawk, always preaching that Toosie was meant for only the best, a man who had earned a higher station than tending stables or picking cotton.

"I should have allowed you to answer Mr. Jordan yourself," she told Toosie. "I would have liked for all those people to hear what you just told me." She wanted to reach out and hug the woman, but she held back. It was much too improper. "I would never sell you, Toosie. We ... we've been together too long. You know everything about me, how I like my things—and who on earth can do my hair better than you?" *Besides, we are very good friends, aren't we?* she wanted to add. "You are much too valuable to me ever to let you go, just like Father would never sell Lena."

Toosie nodded, wondering how Miss Audra Brennan would feel about her and her mother, if she learned the truth that only they and Audra's father knew. Perhaps then she *would* sell her, and insist her father sell Lena, just as fast as possible. The man would do it, if Audra insisted. Audra always came first, always would.

"Perhaps if things came to be that we Negroes were declared free, your father might *have* to turn us out," she told Audra. "He would cut his help because he would have to pay them."

"Father would *always* find a way to keep you and Lena. Besides, they might be able to keep us from buying or birthing *new* slaves, but the government cannot make us free those we already have. Father and the others will *never* let the Yankees tell us what we can and cannot do!" *The Yankees,* she thought. *Lee is a Yankee. How could I think he could come to Brennan Manor and be happy?* "Why, my goodness, the whole house would fall into shambles without Lena to run the place."

Toosie felt an odd foreboding, a silent fear she could not name. Things were changing. She had sensed it more since being here in the North, keeping to the shadows and listening to Lee Jeffreys talk about abolishing slavery, about how the Federal government was going to find a way to force the South to give up the practice. She knew men like Joseph Brennan, terribly stubborn and proud and defiant. A good deal of trouble was brewing, and she was afraid of where that would leave people like her.

Audra leaned closer to the mirror to clip on a pair of tiny sapphire earrings. "Governor Wickliffe and the governors and congressmen of the other southern states will make sure nothing changes, even if we have to secede from the Union and form our own country," she told Toosie. *And where would that leave me and Lee?* she wondered. They had argued about the importance of an undivided Union, about states' rights. Lee considered talk of secession as nothing short of traitorous. Never had she felt so torn and confused as she did this morning. Maybe, by some miracle, Lee had thought about how much they loved each other, and thought of a way they could always be together. . . .

Toosie was herself wondering if Audra's tears had been for Lee Jeffreys. She had not missed the way the two looked at each other. Audra's father would be furious if he knew how much time they had spent together, and she worried that Audra was heading for a broken heart. She knew the feeling. Her own heart had never quite mended after Elijah was sold. She had never seen him again, and she wondered if he had forgotten about her over these last three years.

"Is . . . is there anything else upsetting you?" she dared to ask Audra. She could not help feeling a little sorry for her. Audra had absolutely no female to whom she could turn for help and advice, except her cousin Eleanor, who knew only about lust, nothing about love. At home Audra was surrounded by Negro women, with whom no white southern woman would talk about intimate matters. She was sure that Audra's tutor, Miss Geresy, had never discussed men or sexual matters with Audra. Her only purpose was to teach Audra proper etiquette and how to run a household. There was no warmth to the woman, no concern for Audra's feelings. Perhaps she was stepping out of place even to ask Audra if she wanted to talk about anything else, but wasn't there at least some form of friendship between them after all these years? She saw a pleading look in Audra's eyes, but quickly it vanished.

"For goodness' sake, Toosie, if there was anything upsetting me, I certainly would not talk with *you* about it!" She straightened and studied herself in the mirror. "I have already said more than I should." She stood back, deciding she looked "respectable" enough to face Lee. "I'll be going for a walk with Mr. Jeffreys after breakfast, so I won't need you for a while. Do what you can to help the house servants, and don't go getting in anyone's way."

"Yes, ma'am," Toosie answered. She wanted to ask if Audra was again going off unescorted, wanted to warn her of the dangers of falling in love with someone of whom her father would highly disapprove; but she had obviously already overstepped her bounds. If Audra Brennan wanted to dive headfirst into trouble and heartache, there was nothing she could do about it. She thought she detected a look of sudden remorse in Audra's eyes for her abrupt remarks, but then the girl turned and headed out the door without another word.

How many times had she longed to tell Audra Brennan that she loved her, like a sister, like a friend? She saw beyond Audra's haughty attitude, knew she was fighting her own need to share and be close. She loved her for the way she looked after and defended poor Joey. Audra was a good person. If she had not been raised by Joseph Brennan, she would be free to show more of that goodness. Lee Jeffreys had brought some of it out of her, but her young and innocent heart was going to be broken by that man. Of that Toosie was certain.

"I think I'll be leaving for New York later today, Mother," Lee told Anna. He looked across the table at the woman, and from the corner of his eye he could see Audra slowly lower her fork, felt her eyes on him. "I have already stayed longer than I intended. I have some important cases that I have to get back to."

"Oh, Lee, I'll miss you so. I just wish you would visit when your father and brothers do."

"We'll manage it again somehow." He glanced at Audra, noticed the pale look about her. She was blinking back tears, and he hated seeing it, hated knowing he was hurting her. Most of all, he hated himself for having let his liquor and the magic of last night get the better of him. He had done a damned fool thing, and he could possibly never make up for it. "I'd like to take a walk later," he told her, "if you're up to it."

Audra nodded, looking down at her plate. She was no longer hungry. The slim hope that Lee was going to announce to the world that he loved her and wanted to marry her vanished, along with her appetite.

Lee glanced at Joey, seeing there, too, another disappointed look. "Joey, we've had some good talks. You remember what I told you about slowing down when you speak. Concentrate on each word. Pretend you're singing it if you have to." He gave the boy a wink. "We've had some good times together. You're a hell of a marksman, and your father will be proud to see how your speech has improved."

"Thank you, Lee. I sure will miss you." Joey spoke the words slowly, just as Lee had taught him. "Maybe we c-can write."

Lee nodded. "I'd like that. I'll give you my address before I go, and you can give me yours. You can keep me informed on the happenings at Brennan Manor." He glanced at Audra again, who was only toying with her food. "I'll want to hear from both of you."

Audra caught the affection in the words. She met his eyes, so very, very blue, framed by those dark lashes. He looked more handsome than ever this morning. Was it because he was going away and she might never see him again? Was it because she knew he loved her? Because he had kissed her last night, had tasted her breast? The memory brought fire to her blood, and a rush of crimson to her cheeks.

"I'm sorry about Cy," Anna was telling Lee. "I don't know why your father doesn't get rid of that man and hire you to represent him. It makes no sense at all."

"Cy's been with him a long time. It's hard to dismiss a man who has worked for you for twenty-some years."

"Just the same, I don't like him, and I intend to tell your father what he did last night."

Lee did not reply. There were things his gentle mother was better off not knowing. She liked to think she had a loving family and that he and his brothers and father all got along famously. Why spoil her pretty little picture?

Audra excused herself, apologizing for not having much of an appetite. Anna Jeffreys in turn apologized for Cy Jordan's verbal abuse of the night before, sure that Audra's hollow-eyed look and lack of appetite were due to Jordan's humiliating remarks. "I want you to put it right out of your mind," she told Audra. "We will go on with your lessons, and you will do another concert for our friends. Cy Jordan will not be invited, I assure you. You saw how kind everyone was to you when you came back to greet them last night."

"Yes, they were kind," Audra answered. She hated them all, but she could not bring herself to tell Anna that. They had smiled and apologized for Jordan and raved about her talent, but behind the smiles and cool handshakes, she had sensed the animosity, as well as the curiosity planted in their minds by Cy Jordan. She had defended Brennan Manor, her father, and her way of life, and it had all made her just want to go home; but not without Lee.

She left the dining room and walked out onto the veranda. It was a beautiful morning, sun shining, sea gulls calling, a warm breeze coming off the Sound. Fishing boats cruised far out in the water, and because the morning was so clear, she could see the vague outline of Long Island across the Sound. Somewhere to the southwest lay Manhattan, where Lee worked, but too many miles away to see.

Lee Jeffreys lived and worked in the middle of a city where she knew she could never be happy. Over a thousand miles farther to the south lay Louisiana, Brennan Manor, home, a place where Lee, in turn, could never be happy. It was very clear Lee was having the same thoughts.

She heard his footsteps behind her then, felt his hand at her waist. "Let's walk to the flower gardens," he told her.

Audra did not look into his eyes. She couldn't. She loved him too much to see what was there. He led her off the steps to the east side of the house and into the manicured pathways that led through a maze of flowering plants and bushes. He said nothing until they reached a gazebo shrouded in climbing roses. He led her inside and sat down on a bench, urging her to sit beside him.

"I already know what you are going to say," she told him. "I am so ashamed of last night—"

He grasped her arms and made her look at him. "Don't ever be ashamed of it, Audra. You only reacted like a beautiful woman in love, a woman who wanted nothing more than to demonstrate that love. I haven't felt this way about a woman since Mary Ellen, and even she didn't make me behave so foolishly. I'm a grown man who should have known better than to take advantage of your innocence that way, but something happened ... I don't know. I've never lost control of myself that way, and I'm sorry, but it wasn't just the liquor and the way you looked last night. It was all because I love you, and for a little while I wanted to pretend I could have you; but it would never, never work, Audra. You already know that, don't you?"

She glanced down at her lap, feeling entirely inadequate and inexperienced. What should she say that might change his mind? "It *could* work, Lee, if we tried really hard—"

He took hold of her chin and forced her to look at him. "Audra, when you're so young, you think love can conquer all things. I know that it can't. You think my mother is so terribly happy, but it's her sons that keep her going. I caught her crying one night a few years ago, and in a very vulnerable moment she told me that in spite of how much she loves my father, she has never been truly happy since giving up her singing career. It was a stipulation of their marriage. Father didn't want her traveling all over the world instead of being a wife to him. It eroded their relationship until the last few years they have really had nothing between them. If not for her sons she might even have left him, but by then it was too late to rebuild her career."

He moved his hand under some of her hair that hung

over her shoulder and pushed it back. "I don't want that, Audra. There is much more against us than a possible singing career for you. There is Brennan Manor. You *are* Brennan Manor. Can you tell me, honestly, that you could leave your father and Joey and your home in the South forever? I could never live there, Audra. That's what you expect, isn't it? You want me to go back with you and learn to love that life."

"But it's a wonderful life, Lee. We could be so happy—"

"No. *You* could be happy. *I* would be miserable. I would be living a lie, just as you would be to stay here with me." He studied her lovingly, kissed her forehead. "If things were different, if there wasn't this trouble brewing in the country, maybe it would be easier for us. But right now, people up here are cold to you. You're a southern girl, the daughter of a plantation owner who buys and sells slaves. Down South I would be a Yankee, and totally unwelcome. I would *hate* that way of life, Audra, all the talk of secession. It would come between us. I can't take you away from what you love any more than my father had a right to take my mother away from what *she* loved. They should have ended it before it began, as we have a chance to do right now. I don't want to end up arguing, to end up hating each other. Before this is all over, a *lot* of people are going to be hating each other. Friends are going to become enemies, Audra, even within families. I can see it coming."

She frowned, pulling out of his grasp, angry that he apparently did not love her enough to see that nothing could destroy that love. "I just cannot imagine things getting that bad. For heaven's sake, our government can surely work it all out. It's a simple matter of states' rights, which have always been recognized and must continue to be. I told you that we want to get rid of slavery as much as you northerners do, but we would be ruined in a day, if it was done quickly. The Negroes must be taught *how* to live on their own, or perhaps sent back to Africa. You cannot take millions of uneducated people who are totally dependent on their masters and just suddenly set them free, Lee. It would be a disaster for all of us, *including* the Negroes! I simply don't understand why you and others like you cannot understand that, or why things like that should matter when it comes to how much we love each other. Why, you could live a grand life at Brennan Manor." She rose and faced him. "It's so beautiful there. Once you got used to it—"

"Audra, I can't live there, don't *you* understand? You expect *me* to understand your side, but you don't want to understand *mine*. You want me to give up everything I have worked for and go running off to be the overseer of poor, overworked Negroes who have been bought and sold like cattle! I can't do it, Audra. And I know by the way you talk that you could never leave your father and Joey and stay here with me. It would eat at you, just like what happened to my mother. I can't be married to a woman who can't belong totally to me; and I know that no man marries you without also marrying Brennan Manor. I see it in your eyes, in the way you talk; it's in your blood, Audra, and it runs much deeper than even you realize. Not until you were taken away from all if it would you understand what I'm telling you."

She blinked back tears and turned her back to him. "Then why did you kiss me last night? Why did you tell me you loved me?"

"I *do* love you, but I never meant to tell you. I was going to go back to New York and never say a word . . . until I found you crying on the beach. I made a big mistake, Audra. I can never apologize enough, and I won't ever forget you; but it just can't work."

Oh, how she loved him . . . and how she hated him! It wasn't fair, holding her that way, taking advantage of her, building her hopes. "You damn Yankee!" she said, seething, then gulped in a deep sob.

The words pierced Lee like a knife. She had every right to hate him, but there was something deeper in the words than unrequited love. They were spoken with a vehemence that sprang from a longer, deeper hatred than one night's mistake. The words showed him her true feelings. He could just picture her father saying them. Multiply her father by thousands more who felt the same way, and the whole country was headed for deep trouble.

He wanted to reach out for her, but for the moment he knew she did not want him to touch her. "You just said it in your own words, Audra. I don't want to be married to you for three or four years and then hear those words come out of your mouth with such venom." He watched her shoulders shake in weeping, and his heart ached for her. "Audra, if the southern states start seceding, I will do whatever our government thinks is required to preserve the Union, *and* to end slavery. I don't think you realize how grave the situation has become. If this country ends up in war, I'll be a part of it, and I sure as hell won't be fighting for the South. What would I do then, with a true southern rebel for a wife?"

"*War!*" She whirled, tears streaming down her face. "For heaven's sake, Lee, you don't really think it would come to *war*! That is ridiculous!"

"*Is* it? You'd damn well better realize it *could* come to that. Your father shelters you from what is going on in the world, Audra, but I live with it every day. In case you haven't heard, the whole damn country is coming apart, and this sure as hell is not the time for two people who stand so firmly on different sides to be falling in love!"

"Well, I guess love just doesn't know about those things, does it?" She wiped at her tears. "Go on back to New York, Lee. I fully understand what you are telling me. I belong with someone like Richard Potter, after all, a true southern gentleman who understands my way of life!"

She saw the pain in his eyes, but anger quickly replaced it. He stood up. "Yes, I suppose you're right," he said, his voice calm and cool. "In the long run, you *would* be happiest. You and Richard will someday run the biggest plantation in the South, but by then there may not *be* a South as you know it today!"

She frowned, feeling a creeping fear. "What do you mean by that?"

He closed his eyes and sighed. "I hope you never find out, Audra. I hope neither one of us does." He ran a hand through his hair. "I didn't mean for our conversation to take this turn." He stepped closer. "Audra, it's killing me to let you go. It's just that it's easier this way than for either of us to face what is coming if we try to stay together. A small hurt now is better than a lot of real pain later."

"And you think I'm not in real pain now?"

He reached out to take her hand, but she pulled it away. He sighed deeply, hating himself for hurting her. "Once you get home, back to Brennan Manor, you'll know I was right. You'll know where you belong."

"I don't *want* you to be right," she sobbed, wiping wildly at her tears then, furious that anger always made her cry.

"I know," he answered, "and I wish someone could show us it *could* work. But you're young. The pain *will* go away, and you'll forget last night, or at least think of it as one little summer fling when youth and passion made you forget your senses."

Her whole body shook in renewed rage. "And what made you forget *your* senses, Lee Jeffreys? The chance to take *advantage* of that youth and passion? The chance to touch me sinfully? To steal a kiss?"

"You know better."

"*Do* I?" Her green, tear-filled eyes moved over him scathingly. "I should *hate* you. I *do* hate you! Go on back to New York and your Yankee ways. Just see how far you get trying to change *us* and *our* ways! You think you're so righteous and good, but men like your father treat their people no better than slaves, sometimes worse!" She tossed her head and moved past him. "And if there *is* a war, we will just see who *wins* it!"

She stormed up the pathway to the house. Lee had not intended for their conversation to end like this, but then how could he expect it to be any other way? She had a great pride, and he had hurt it deeply.

"Yes," he muttered, feeling sick inside. "We *will* just see who wins it." Already a literal war was raging in Kansas Territory, so much so that people were beginning to call it Bleeding Kansas. How long before the bitter fighting spread? Before leaving New York, he'd heard talk of a fanatic abolitionist by the name of John Brown who was gathering Negroes together to create a "country" of their own in the Appalachian Mountains. Men in Congress were getting into fistfights over states' rights, over how the country's banks should be run, and over tariffs, all issues that were hurting an increasingly angry South. This was no time to be loving Audra Brennan.

He headed to the stables, ordering Tom to hitch up a buggy. "I'm going back to New York," he told the man. "There's a new passenger-ship service out of New Haven every day at two. I have just enough time to talk to Joey Brennan for a few minutes and say good-bye to Mother, then I'll be ready to leave. I'll want you to drive me there so you can bring the carriage back."

"Yes, sir, Mr. Jeffreys. I hate to see you go."

"Yes," Lee answered with a sigh. "So do I, but much as I love this place, for more reasons than one I need to get the hell back to New York." He headed for the house, looking over at the big maples that lined the driveway. This vacation had not turned out at all as he had planned. He never dreamed there would be an Audra Brennan in his life, or that a man could lose himself in a woman as he had last night with her. A sudden chill moved through him, and somehow he knew nothing at Maple Shadows or in his own life would ever be the same.

6

Audra sang an Italian song about love, pouring her heart and soul into the music. During lessons Anna Jeffreys had commented on how much more passion she put into her singing now, and she wondered if the woman had any idea it was because she was thinking about Lee. She wanted to hate him, but it had been impossible.

It was already September, and her father would be coming soon. Lee had been gone over two months, and she would be going home, never to see her summer love again. Tonight at Maple Shadows she performed her last solo concert for friends and neighbors from Mulberry Point. Summer was ended. Maple Shadows would be closed up soon, and she would go back to Louisiana with bittersweet memories.

Among those who watched and listened were Lee's father and two brothers and their wives. When they had first come for their visit, Audra had felt even greater yearning to see Lee again, for his brothers looked very much like him, except for their dark eyes. Edmund Jeffreys was a tall, well-built man, very gracious but also arrogant. To Audra he appeared cold, except with his wife, to whom he was quite attentive, although his commanding nature told her Anna was expected to do his bidding.

The arrival of the rest of the family had brought back Audra's homesickness. Edmund was not at all pleased that Audra had a Negro slave with her, and he had lectured her more than once on the folly of her way of life. They were not gentle talks like the ones Lee had with her; it was more like preaching about sins, and the man had stirred Audra's defenses. Here was a true Yankee, the kind of Yankee her father would consider his worst enemy.

Even Lee's brothers and their wives had been rude, and she was not allowed to play with Carl's children, as though she might somehow contaminate them with her beliefs. Never had she been this lonely. She was more than ready to go home, but Anna had insisted on one last concert, and she realized that her singing was the one thing that could bring them all together in harmony. This was something she could share with everyone, no matter what differences they might have. Anna had told her that music was a universal way to bring all ages and races and beliefs together. Back home her father often allowed the house slaves and even some of those from the fields to come and listen to her sing. In those times it was as though they were all equal, and she enjoyed giving them the pleasure of her voice.

She finished her last song of the evening, and everyone rose and clapped. She curtseyed, and Anna Jeffreys took her hand. Even Edmund and Carl and David looked genuinely impressed. Anna's hand tightened over her own, and at first Audra thought it was just a reassuring squeeze, but seconds later people stopped clapping, and their faces took on a look of shock and tragedy. Anna Jeffreys began tugging oddly at Audra's hand then, and Audra turned to see the woman slump to the floor.

"Mrs. Jeffreys!" Audra leaned over her, but instantly Edmund Jeffreys was there, shoving Audra aside with such force that she nearly fell over. People began to whisper and mumble as Carl and David joined their father at Anna's side, David shoving the piano bench out of the way.

"It's those damn headaches!" Carl was saying. "There's something really wrong, Father. It's a hell of a lot more than nerves."

"Someone send for Dr. Kelsey," a man from the crowd shouted.

"He's delivering a baby," another answered. "That's why he couldn't make it tonight."

Audra, shaken and frightened, hurried through the crowd to Joey's side. She saw the fear in his eyes, and she took his arm, leading him into the hallway, where Toosie stood nearby. "What is it, Miss Audra?"

"Oh, Toosie," Audra whispered. The crowd had quieted, and Edmund Jeffreys groaned his wife's name as though in terrible pain. Carl rose, his face ashen. "It's too late for a doctor," he said, his voice quivering. "My mother is dead."

People gasped, and a wave of shock and grief engulfed Audra. She ran down the hallway and out to the gardens. How could such a thing happen so quickly? Moments earlier Anna Jeffreys had been playing the piano with more vigor and beauty than she had ever heard her play. In the next moment death had snatched her away, just as it had her own mother.

Lee! He would be crushed. It would be even worse for him because he would feel he should have been here with Anna when it happened.

Somewhere near the house she heard a woman weeping, and she could hear Edmund Jeffreys groaning his wife's name. A flock of sea gulls flew in and landed nearby, and the air was filled with their piercing cries, as though even the birds were suddenly in mourning. The scent of roses filled the air, borne by a gentle breeze that carried their lovely smell from the many bushes that bloomed throughout the grounds. Anna Jeffreys had so loved flowers.

•　•　•

Lee, my love,
Just as the sun shines
And the ocean wind blows wet and wild,
I love you as a woman loves,
But you see me as a child.

Audra studied the song she had secretly written for
Lee before she had ever voiced her love for him, before that
magical night on the beach when, as far as she was concerned, he had changed her from child to woman. She had
always meant to show it to him, sing it for him, but she'd
never had the courage. She certainly couldn't do so now, but
the song would always be special to her, the words forever
true.

Lee, my love,
When I am with you
I never want the days to end.
I love you more than life itself,
Yet to you I'm just a friend.

Lee, my love,
You stand before me
Tall and strong, your eyes so blue,
I long to feel your arms around me,
To hear the words, I love you.

Lee, my love,
We walk together,
We feel the sand and smell the sea.
I know we live in different worlds.
A life together can never be.

Not even Joey knew about the song. She had even begun composing music to accompany the words, and she
started to hum it softly when she heard a carriage clatter up
to the front of the house. She quickly folded the papers and
slipped them into a pocket of the lambswool sweater she
wore today against the cool air. Autumn was coming early to
New England, so people said, and she thought how it certainly had come early to the hearts of the Jeffreys men.

She knew that Lee should arrive today, so she had walked around the balcony to the front of the house to watch for him. She had not expected to see him again, certainly not under these horrible circumstances. All her animosity toward him over their encounter before he left had vanished. The fact remained that she still loved him, and her heart ached at the thought of how devastated he must be over his mother's death.

How many times had she wished over the past three months that Anna Jeffreys was her own mother? The woman held a genuine concern for everyone she knew, and her love for her family had caused her to give up her career. Lee had been the "favorite son," the child closest to her heart.

For the past four nights she had been unable to sleep. Whenever she managed to doze off, the nightmare returned to jerk her awake again. In the dream she was holding Anna Jeffreys's hand. The woman was hanging over a black pit, staring up at her, begging her not to let go; but always she slipped away, screaming Audra's name as she fell into the black hole and disappeared. The dream would awaken Audra in a cold sweat, and she had spent the past nights wrapped in a blanket and sitting out on the balcony most of the time, watching the stars, listening to the waves on the beach, weeping.

Each morning she was sure she had no tears left, but they always returned, her loneliness over Mrs. Jeffreys's death made worse by the fact that the rest of the family acted as though Audra didn't even exist. She had gone down to the parlor just once to view the woman's body, laid out in a casket and ready for the funeral services that would take place tomorrow.

Thank God Lee had made it home in time. The family had waited longer than they would have liked so that the youngest son could be present. Finally he had arrived. Audra watched him climb out of the carriage. Wearing a black suit and overcoat, he looked even handsomer than she had remembered. As he hurried inside, she wondered if he realized she was still here, if he even cared. If not for Anna's death, she would probably never have seen him again.

Now her worst fear was that Lee would somehow blame her for some of this. If not for her, he might have stayed longer, gotten to see more of his mother before she died. It must make him sick to think he could have had more time with her.

What a disaster this summer had been. She was glad that her father would be arriving soon. She could leave this place that had given her such a mixture of good and bad memories. Home! She could go home at last. Maybe there her heart could heal. Maybe once there was a good thousand miles between her and Lee Jeffreys, she would finally get over her love for him, for she knew she had no choice.

She moved to one of the patio chairs and sat down, thinking how, if nothing else, she had certainly grown up this summer. Joey came around the balcony then from his own room, and Audra noticed his eyes were red and swollen. Anna's death had been a traumatic event for both of them, especially hard for Joey, whose heart was tender and easily broken, and who had a terrible fear of death since losing his mother at such an early age. He often talked of his fear of losing his sister, too. Anna's collapse had only reminded him how quickly a loved one could be snatched away.

"Lee is here," he told her.

"I know. I saw him arrive." She had never told Joey of her feelings for Lee, although he probably suspected. There was no sense in building his hopes. He had grown to love Lee, and she suspected he would like nothing better than to see her marry the man; but how did you explain to a fourteen-year-old boy, whose spirit and emotions were even younger, the reasons why two people should or should not marry?

"He went right into the parlor and b-broke down. I was going to say hello to him, b-but I didn't. I wish he didn't have to come b-back just for this. I've missed him, b-b-but he won't want to go hunting or anything now."

"No, Joey, he won't. He's probably just here for the funeral and will have to go right back."

"I'm g-going to write him after I g-get home. He said I could."

Audra touched his hand. "I think that's a good idea. Lee is the kind of man who will always be your friend, Joey. He's a good man, even though he is a Yankee and against our way of life."

Joey sighed and ran a hand through his red hair. "I wish he wasn't. I b-b-bet he would even come and visit if we d-didn't live on a plantation. Sometimes I wish we d-didn't even have it."

"Oh, Joey, Brennan Manor is a wonderful place, and some day you and I will own all of it. By then it will probably be combined with Richard Potter's land, and we'll be the richest landowners in the South. That's very important to Father, and it should be to you, too."

The boy scowled, shoving his hands into the pockets of his tweed pants. "It doesn't matter. F-father thinks I'll never b-be able to run it."

"Of course you will. You just have a lot of growing to do yet, and Richard will certainly help you."

Joey sat down near her. "I'll f-find a way to make F-father proud of me someday. You'll see."

Audra touched his arm. "He's already proud of you, Joey. He's just a stubborn man who wants the best for you. He's afraid if he praises you too much now, you'll quit trying to do better. I know he seems tough and unfeeling, Joey, but he's just trying to make *you* tough. He knows what it takes to run Brennan Manor, and he's trying to mold you into a man who can take over for him some day."

A frown crossed the boy's freckled brow. "I just don't want you t-to marry Richard just b-because Father wants you to or b-because you think it's best for me. Richard is too old f-for you. He doesn't make you laugh like Lee does."

Pain stabbed her heart at the words. How right he was, yet how wrong it was, too. "Lee would never make a good husband for the daughter of plantation owner. And besides, he is just a good friend, certainly not husband material!" She forced a smile for him. "And don't you dare bring up such a thing in front of Lee! It would embarrass both of us. Besides, Richard is a very good man. We are very good friends. He is kind to me, and there certainly is not a man in all of the South better qualified to run both plantations.

I'll do just fine marrying him. Why, can you imagine the magnificent wedding we will have? Half the state of Louisiana will be there!"

Joey leaned closer. "Audra?"

She kept her smile, wanting him to believe she was happy. "Yes, Joey?"

"D-don't marry Richard just on account of me. I'll work hard to learn to run B-brennan Manor by myself. You don't have to d-do it through Richard."

Her smile faded, and she took his hand, squeezing it. "I promise I'm not doing it for you," she lied. "I'm doing it because it's the right thing all the way around, for father, for me, for Brennan Manor. The North is trying to break plantations like ours, Joey. If they manage to do it, we'll fall into ruin and be turned into beggars. Combining Brennan Manor with Cypress Hollow will give us the strength and power we need to fight anything the government tries to force us to do."

Joey studied her eyes. They looked sincere. "If you say so." His eyes teared anew. "It scares me to see how quick Mrs. Jeffreys died. What would I d-do if something happened to you?"

"Nothing is going to happen to me. You have to quit thinking about these things, Joey. Mrs. Jeffreys will be buried tomorrow, and soon Father will be here to take us home. You'll feel better when we're back at Brennan Manor."

Someone knocked on her door then, and Audra gave her brother one more reassuring smile. It seemed strange, with only three and a half years difference between them, that she could feel more like a mother to the boy than a sister. She rose and walked to her bedroom door, surprised to see Lee standing there when she opened it. Immediately she put a had to her hair, remembering she had left it very plain today, pulled into a bun at the nape of her neck. She wore a simple gray cotton dress. She had not intended to do anything today but stay in her room. Downstairs she felt like a complete outsider. Friends and family had come and gone in an almost constant succession that only made her feel in the way.

"I wanted to see how you are," Lee told her.

"Come out onto the balcony," she told him. "Joey is anxious to see you." Oh, those wonderful blue eyes! How full of sorrow they were today, red-rimmed from crying, yet she could see past the sorrow to realize the love was still there. The recent tragedy of his mother's death had apparently erased any hard feelings he might still have over the way she had talked to him before he left. Just as with her, it all seemed inconsequential at the moment. He tore his gaze from her and walked out onto the balcony to greet Joey, and Audra closed the door.

Joey hugged Lee. "I'm sorry," he told the man. "You're lucky, though. I was only f-four when my mother d-died."

"I know." Lee patted his shoulder. "Compared to you and Audra, I can't complain. But we were very close, Joey, and she was the best—" He could not finish the statement. He let go of Joey and walked to the railing, throwing back his head and breathing deeply.

Audra stepped closer. "Is there anything I can do, Lee?"

He cleared his throat and blinked back tears. "As a matter of fact, there is. That's why I came up here." He turned to face her. "By the way, you never answered my question. How are you? Father told me you were holding her hand when she— " He stopped and swallowed. "It must have been very painful for you."

She shivered. "I've had nightmares ever since, of trying to hold on to her and keep her from falling into nothingness." She felt her own throat begin to swell with a need to cry.

"My God, how terrible for you, being so far from home, after what happened between us. . . ." He hesitated, noticing her glance at Joey. "I imagine my father and brothers haven't paid much attention to you since it happened. You must feel like such an outcast. If you had known what this summer would bring, I'm sure you never would have come here."

She watched his eyes. "Oh, yes, Lee. I still would have come." *I would never have wanted to miss the chance of knowing you, loving you.*

He nodded, as though he understood what she was thinking. He turned to look out at the water. "All I can think about is the look in her eyes when she practically begged me to stay a little longer. I should have known, Audra. I should have stayed an extra week or so. She *knew*. My God, I think she knew then that she was dying!"

His voice broke on the last words, and Audra could not keep herself from going to embrace him. He hugged her tightly, wept into her hair. She clung to him, all the feelings of spite and hatred vanishing. She still loved him, and there was no arguing the fact. Whether he loved her or just clung to her as a friend, she could not know for now. This was not the time to talk about it. At least the friendship was still there, close enough that he felt free to come to her and let her hold him.

"I'm so sorry, Lee," she said softly. "I loved her, too. I knew her such a short time, yet it was long enough to realize what a wonderful, giving person she was. I know how close you were, how much she loved her sons."

Joey stood up and gave both of them a hug, then quickly left, sensing that it was best to leave his sister and Lee alone right now. Lee probably didn't want him to see him cry, nor did he want to cry in front of Lee. He would go back to his own room for that, though his tears would not be for the death of Anna Jeffreys, but because his father would be here in a few days. It would be time to go back home and face the problems that waited for him there. He wished Lee were going back with them.

Lee clung to Audra, thinking how strange it was that, though friends and family stood about downstairs, he had felt compelled to come up here and cry in Audra's arms. He had tried so hard to forget about her these past two months, had planned on never seeing her again. She was supposed to have left before he came back to Maple Shadows, but his mother's death had changed all of that.

His mother was dead. It all seemed so unreal. How could Anna Jeffreys be dead? Why did God take people like her, who had so much to give to the world, and leave behind people like Cy Jordan, and like some of the other bastards he'd known in business? Some of the wealthy men he represented would steal from their own grandmothers to line their pockets, yet they lived and his mother did not.

He released his embrace and pulled a linen handkerchief from his pocket. "I'm sorry. I didn't mean to do this."

Audra wiped at her own eyes. "What else are friends for?"

"Yes," he answered. "What else?" He took a moment to compose himself, and Audra waited quietly.

"You said there was something I could do to help," she reminded him.

"Yes. I wondered if you would sing at the funeral tomorrow," he finally spoke up. "My mother had two favorite hymns—'In the Sweet Bye and Bye,' and 'Abide with Me.' Would you do us the honor, or would it be too hard for you?"

Audra faced him and put a hand to her heart, loving him for asking her. "I would like that very much, but what about your father and brothers? Perhaps they would prefer someone else—"

"They know Mother would have liked nothing more than for you to be the one. She was very proud of you, enjoyed working with you. Besides, there isn't anyone in the whole state of Connecticut who sings like you do. It wouldn't be right to ask anyone else." He studied her beautiful face, wishing things could be different for them. "Mrs. Hartman from our Congregational church will play the piano. She's nothing like my mother at the keys, but she's good. It will be a Protestant funeral. I hope that's no problem. Because you're Irish, I suppose you are also Catholic."

"Yes, but that makes no difference. We have a little chapel on our plantation. The closest Catholic church is in Baton Rouge, but we don't get there often. A plantation is like its own little community. We seldom leave it, except for Father sending me here this summer, and trips to Baton Rouge to visit my aunt and cousin. We—"

She realized she had begun rambling on again about Brennan Manor. She could see by his eyes that she had only recalled for him the reasons they could not be together; realized that she always ended up talking about home, no matter how a conversation began. And she was Catholic, another difference they had. The Jeffreys family was very Protestant, she had learned from Anna Jeffreys, who, although she had been kind and understanding in every other way, had acted at times as though there were something wrong with being a Catholic. She and Lee truly did not have one thing in common, except that they loved each other. Other things had to go with that love, and those things were not there.

"The funeral will be at one o'clock tomorrow," he told her. "Do you know the hymns I mentioned?"

"I have heard them sung a few times. Do you have a hymnal that I can use to study the words?"

"We'll get one from the church." He grasped her hand. "I can't thank you enough, Audra. I know it won't be easy."

She smiled sadly. "I am beginning to learn that *nothing* in life is easy. I'll be all right because I will be doing it for your mother. I will pretend it is she playing the piano, urging me to sing my best."

To Audra's surprise, he bent down and kissed her forehead. When he stepped back again, his eyes moved over her strangely, and she wondered if he was remembering that night when he tasted her breast. The memory of it brought a tingle to her body and a flush to her cheeks.

"I'll have a lot of things to tend to after tomorrow," he told her, squeezing her hand, "family matters and such. I doubt that I'll see you alone this way again before you leave for home. Carl tells me your father is probably already on his way to get you."

She nodded. *I don't want to leave you, Lee. If only you would come with me.*

He closed his eyes and took another deep breath. "Mother was the center. She held us together."

"I know." Audra squeezed his hand. "I suppose Maple Shadows will never be the same without her."

"No, it won't," he answered in a near whisper. He turned away. "I've got to get back downstairs." He hurried out before Audra could say another word. She watched the door close and felt almost numb, too many wildly different emotions surging through her to allow any of them to surface for the moment. Now they would have to suffer another good-bye, and she was not really over the first one.

7

Audra opened the French doors and rubbed the backs of her arms against the cool breeze that came off the water. The weather had turned much colder, and at the funeral several people remarked that they could "feel winter" in the air. The leaves on the maple trees were already beginning to turn, and the change in weather had made Anna's funeral even more depressing. The life had gone out of Anna Jeffreys, and out of her grand piano. It had gone out of Maple Shadows, and would soon go out of the trees and the flowers. Winter would come not only to the land, but to the hearts of those who had loved Anna.

She knew she should close the doors, but the sound of the waves on the beach, the feel of the cool air, helped her feel more alive, and right now life was suddenly something to be highly treasured. How quickly it could leave a body! She wished she could get rid of the memory of the way Anna's eyes had looked as she stared up at her while clinging to her hand and sinking into death. She wished she could get rid of the nightmare that still visited her.

She had tried to sleep earlier, but again, all she could see was Anna, falling into that dark hole. Added to that was the fact that it had been such a very long day. So many people had come to Anna's funeral that they overflowed the house and spilled out onto the veranda and the lawn. In spite of the cool air, doors and windows had been flung open so that everyone could hear Audra sing Anna's favorite hymns. She hoped Lee was pleased. She had sung as she had never sung before, praying on every word that God would help her get through it all without breaking down. The only way she could do that was not to look at Lee and see the devastation in his blue eyes; and not to look at poor Joey and see the fear in his. Most important of all, she could not look at the closed casket.

She saw a movement then, and she gasped in surprise when Lee stepped into the light shed by a dim oil lamp in her room. His eyes looked hollow and vacant, and in spite of the cold air, he wore no shirt or shoes. She noticed dark hair on his bare chest and felt suddenly shy at seeing it. His arms and chest boasted hard muscles, and she wanted to stare at him, but she forced herself to meet only his eyes. "Lee! You must be so cold! What are you doing out here?"

He shrugged. "I couldn't sleep. Apparently you couldn't either." He glanced past her into her room. "I was just walking. I *wanted* to feel the cold air." He looked back at her and he could see the outline of her nipples through her gown. They were taut from the chill. "What about you? Aren't *you* cold?"

Audra folded her arms over her breasts self-consciously. She had not even put on a robe. "A little." How odd it felt, Lee standing there with no shirt, she wearing just a filmy gown. Why didn't it upset her more to be alone with him half-dressed?

"You'd better go inside," he told her. "I'm used to this weather, but you're more likely to take sick. Your father would have a fit if he came back to find you down with pneumonia." His eyes grew even deeper with sorrow, so deep that they actually looked a darker blue. "That's how Mary Ellen died, you know."

She caught a light scent of whiskey. He had tried to escape his sorrow with liquor. *Always be wary of a drunken man*, Lena had warned her once. *They have little control over themselves.* Still, he seemed very steady, not at all drunk as she considered the state to be. Besides, he had buried his mother today. He had a right to swallow a little whiskey. "I'll go inside if you'll come with me. You shouldn't be alone tonight," she told him, wondering if she had lost her mind. She stepped back, and he hesitated.

"That might not be such a good idea." He spoke softly, his face betraying his inner pain.

She watched how his dark hair played about his face as the wind ruffled it, and she wondered if a man existed who was more perfect physically. He reminded her of pictures of some of the Greek gods she had studied under her tutor back home. "No one will know you're here," she told him. "It's all right. You need to talk, Lee."

He rubbed at his eyes as though very weary, then looked around to be sure no one saw him before stepping inside. Audra closed the doors, remembering that he had also been drinking the night he got carried away on the beach. What was she doing, letting a half-naked, slightly drunk Yankee man into her room?

She hurried to a chair to pick up her robe and pull it on. When she turned around, Lee was standing near the bed, watching her. She stepped a little closer, tying her robe. "Maybe you'd like to wrap a blanket around your shoulders."

He shook his head, walking past her to pick up a small portrait of his mother that sat on a small stand. He kept staring at it as he slowly put it back. "You know," he said quietly, "when you get older, you don't really need a mother anymore as far as taking care of yourself; but you still need to know she's out there somewhere, thinking about you, loving you. It's kind of strange. You can go a whole year or more without seeing her at all, and it doesn't really bother you much, because you know you can *go* and see her whenever you want. But when she's dead . . . when you know you can't ever, ever see her again . . ." His voice choked, and he rubbed at his face.

"It will take time, Lee. That's just the way it is."

He turned to look at her, and his gaze moved over her lovingly. "You lost your mother so young. I sound selfish, don't I?"

Audra came cautiously closer. "No. You just sound like a man who loved and respected his mother very much and is mourning her death. There is nothing wrong with that. If it helps to talk about her, then you should."

He watched her green eyes, thinking how beautiful she was even when she wore no cheek color, no fancy hairdo. Hers was a simple, natural beauty, and in spite of all the arguments against having feelings for her, those feelings were still there. Carl and David both had wives to turn to. That was the way life was supposed to be. A boy becomes a man, and he takes a wife. The wife takes over the loving and nurturing that once came from the mother. He had been too absorbed in his career, in proving to his father that he could make it on his own without having to be a part of the family businesses, to give any more thought to falling in love and taking a wife after Mary Ellen died. It was not until Audra, this child-woman, had come to Maple Shadows that he'd thought of such things again, but this was one woman he could never fully possess. She belonged first to Brennan Manor, to her father and brother, to the South.

He had to look away from her. God, she was beautiful tonight, her auburn hair brushed out over her shoulders. He had not expected to find her standing there on the balcony with her nipples showing through the pretty gown she wore. He thought she would be asleep, behind closed doors. He wished he could forget the sweet taste of her mouth, her breasts, her smooth young skin. Was he fooling himself to think he had not wanted to find her awake, that he wasn't hoping maybe he would end up right here in her room?

She had drawn him here just as surely as if she had come to find him and put a rope around him. She had drawn him by the mere fact that she existed and was here in his house. When he looked at her, he saw youth and life, and today he liked seeing those things. He felt a terrible need tonight to experience life, to cast away the pall of death that hung over this house he loved so much. That need was fast manifesting itself in the form of Audra Brennan.

Get the hell out of here, he warned himself. He ignored the warning. He needed desperately to talk to someone, and Audra was so easy to be with, as long as they weren't talking about slavery or states' rights. He walked over to a chest of drawers and touched one of the ceramic knobs. "My mother refinished this when I was little. I remember watching her. There were so many things she liked to do." He sighed deeply. "Ever since her death . . ." He ran a hand through his hair. "Actually, it started the day I left here after you and I argued about war coming and all. . . . Ever since then, I have felt a change coming about, Audra, something dark and forboding . . . something I can't even name. I see now that nothing stays the same. My mother's dying is like ending a certain part of my life. It's as though God took her away so that she wouldn't have to be here to see what is going to happen next." He turned to face her, looking grim. "Maybe none of us should see it."

Audra put a hand to her stomach at the somber words that frightened her a little. "I don't understand—"

"Neither do I." He laughed bitterly. "But it's there all the same, like some evil monster lurking in the shadows, ready to pounce on us." He saw the fear in her lovely eyes, and he shook his head. "I'm sorry to sound like a doomsayer. I guess it's just the aftereffects of burying my mother today, combined with things that are going on all over the country."

He put his hands on his hips, looking around the room that had always been his until this summer. He could remember jumping on the bed as a little boy, could hear his mother scolding him for it. Even in anger, his mother always spoke softly and calmly. "Maple Shadows will never be the same without her, Audra. I may not even come back here next summer. She was the center around which we all moved and behaved. She held my family together. Now we'll all go our separate ways, and it tears at me inside."

He began pacing restlessly. "At the same time, I feel the whole damn *country* coming apart. The government is passing more and more laws to stop slavery, while at the same time the state of Georgia is passing laws to *preserve* slavery. Up here we're screaming about abolition, while our own factory workers are calling strikes, trying to get better working conditions and better pay. The country is falling apart; and at the same time my personal life is falling apart, too. My mother is dead, and my family, this place I love, will never be the same. Never."

His hands closed into fists. "All she wanted was for all of us to come here together. She wanted it so much, but we were all too stubborn . . . and my damn father . . ." He closed his eyes. "I should have swallowed my pride and made it a point to come here when the rest of them came."

"What is it about your father you aren't telling me?"

"It doesn't matter now. What's done is done." He came closer, his broad shoulders and big frame towering over her, and again she was painfully aware of his maleness, the bare skin of his torso, the dark hair on his chest that drew her eyes downward to that part of a man that she did not fully understand. She had seen Joey when he was little, knew that a man was different from a woman, that it all had to do with the mysteries of a man and woman "lying" together.

She averted her gaze, looking down at the floor and feeling a heat move through her at his closeness. An ache formed deep in her body when he reached out and touched her hair.

"I haven't stopped loving you, Audra," he told her in a near whisper, "in case you're wondering. But I know I can never have you, that it can never, never work in a million years; and that just adds to my frustrations."

She felt his power, sensed an odd danger, yet she was not afraid. "I *have* to go back to Louisiana, Lee. I have no choice." She raised her eyes then to meet his. "Please come with me."

He shook his head, his eyes tearing. "I can't. You know I can't. We would end up hating each other. I've had enough of love turning to hate right in my own family. Oh, I have contact with my father and brothers. I even work for my father's senatorial campaign because I believe in the same things he does when it comes to politics; but the hard feelings are there just under the surface. We just don't talk about them anymore. Mother brought some sense to it all, kept the spark of love and family unity alive. Without her . . ."

Their eyes held, and in the next moment he grasped the front of her robe and pulled it open. "I want to look at you," he said softly, "remember you always. I want to feel alive tonight, to drink deeply of life and forget about what is happening to this country. I want to pretend you and I can be together."

Never in her life had Audra felt literally possessed by some unnamed spirit. She did not stop him from untying the robe and letting it fall to the floor. The same unfamiliar desire she had felt on the beach, to let him ravish her however he chose, returned to take away all common sense. "We *can* be together, Lee . . . tonight," she answered, wondering where she had gotten the courage to say the words. "Maybe we owe it to each other . . . to our love. No matter what happens after I go back home, my heart will never belong to anyone but you."

His hand began to tremble as he touched her cheek with the back of his fingers. "You truly don't know what you're offering, Audra. You would hate me tomorrow."

She closed her eyes. Why was it suddenly all so easy; why did it seem so right? She wanted desperately to hold him, and even in her innocence, instinct told her that once she was in his arms, there would be no stopping what would happen next. Was it something terribly sinful, this secret that took place between man and woman? Her cousin Eleanor had seemed to know what it was all about.

Men can do the naughtiest and most wonderful things, she had whispered to Audra once. *Mother thinks a woman has to wait until she is married, but I don't see why. And I swear there are some old married women who never learned to enjoy it. I can't imagine why, unless their husbands are simply terrible lovers.* Eleanor had never bothered to explain what "it" was that some women never learned to enjoy, and she seemed to glory in the fact that she apparently knew more about "it" than Audra.

Audra wondered if "it" was the magical way she felt right now, the ache to taste Lee's lips again, the burning desire to have him touch her again, taste at her breasts as he had done that night on the beach. Whatever came after that, she wanted to share with Lee Jeffreys, not Richard Potter.

Part of her, the part that had become woman, wanted him because she truly loved him. Another part of her, the part that was still an innocent child, wanted him out of mere curiosity. She took hold of his hand, turned the palm to kiss it. She leaned closer, daringly resting her head against his chest, enjoying the feel of his skin against her face. He was hot to the touch.

"If we can't have forever, Lee, then let's steal tonight. I want to lie in your arms. We are each suffering our own grief, and we need to be touched, to know there is still life and love."

She looked up at him, and Lee searched the eyes that were wide with wonder and innocence. He knew full well he might hate himself tomorrow if he accepted her comfort tonight. All reason told him to leave, but instead he met her mouth savagely, and she flung her arms around his neck in youthful, fiery passion. That was all it took to be lost in her, to ignore all the wrong of it. The life had gone out of his mother in a few quick seconds. The line between death and feeling this alive was so terribly thin, and he wanted to stay on this side of it.

He left her mouth and bent down to taste her sweet neck.

"Oh, Lee, I love you so," she whimpered.

"Hush," he whispered. "We have to be quiet, if that's possible." He picked her up in his arms and carried her to the bed, laying her gently on it.

Audra watched him walk to the door and make sure it was locked. He did the same with the French doors. She felt as limp as the sheets on which she lay. Lee Jeffreys was going to make love to her. And how could it be sinful when she loved him so? Reason told her this was all they could ever have, but better this than nothing at all. She would want no other man to be the first one to show her what it meant to lie together.

He walked back to the bed and unbuckled his belt. He dropped his pants to the floor and stepped out of them. His knee-length long johns fit his hips and thighs tightly, and she wondered how much bigger a man was than a little boy. Again she wondered why she wasn't afraid. She moved her eyes to meet Lee's as he climbed onto the bed and knelt above her. Gently he ran a hand under the shoulder of her gown and drew it down, and fire ripped through her. Like that night on the beach, she was suddenly keenly aware of her breasts and nipples. She could feel her nipples tingle, felt a near-painful yearning for him to touch and taste them when he drew the gown to her waist. Without question, she pulled her arms out of the sleeves and reached up, weaving her fingers into his hair and urging him closer.

"I want you to taste them again," she said softly. "I like how it feels."

Lee watched the fascination and curiosity in her eyes. How could he let any other man be the first to do this? Maybe that man wouldn't be as gentle. It had to be just right, this first time. He didn't want to frighten her. He looked at her full, firm breasts, then leaned down and took one into his mouth, sucking on it as though it were a ripe berry.

She groaned, arching against him, pulling at his hair. He took more of the breast into his mouth, unable to hold back his own groan of ecstasy. There was no turning back now. Right or wrong, he had to have her. He flattened his tongue against the nipple, then circled it lightly, noticing how her breathing quickened. Since this was her first time, it was important to build her desire, to make her want him so badly she had no reservations at all.

Audra wondered who this woman was lying in bed with this Yankee man and letting him do these terrible, glorious things to her. He pressed his lips to her other breast, tasting it with pleasure. She moved her hands to his shoulders, wanting to feel the hard muscle of the man, relishing the feel of power and virility about him. He awakened in her something wicked and insatiable, and she had no desire to stop him when his lips moved downward as he pulled her gown farther away. He circled her navel with his tongue, lowered the gown even farther.

She drew in her breath in near-agonizing ecstasy when he kissed at her most private place. Then the gown was down to her knees and he was kissing at her thighs, telling her how slender and satiny and beautiful they were. Off came the gown, and he was kissing her legs, her feet, her toes, moving back up again, running his hands over her legs, her thighs. There was a demanding strength in those hands when he grasped her knees and forced her legs apart; but had it really been force? She wanted to open them, wanted Lee Jeffreys to drink in her nakedness.

Now it seemed she was the one with the power. His eyes were glazed with desire, and he seemed nearly to tremble as he moved his hands back and forth over the insides of her thighs. Her breath came in short gasps when he gently moved his thumbs to open that private place no man had ever seen or touched. Even she didn't know what mysteries lay there.

"My God, I've never seen a woman this beautiful," he told her.

She grasped his powerful forearms. "Lee . . ." It was all she could bring herself to say. Part of her felt she should press her legs together and push him away, but the curious, aching, wicked part of her let her lie there to be raked by his melting blue eyes. He leaned closer, and she gasped when his tongue touched her intimately, made her ache fiercely. She felt as though she were on fire, wondering where this brazen lust had come from. Never had she realized she had it in her to be this bold and wanton.

She twisted his hair in her fingers, pushed herself against him, succumbing to a great desire to give Lee all he asked and more. Oh, yes, Eleanor was right. Men could do such wicked and wonderful things to a woman, but it had to be just the right man. It had to be a man she loved with great passion the way she loved Lee. She had to have this desire to comfort and please him. What a wonderful way to show love!

For several glorious minutes he took her to the heights

of ecstasy, then moved his lips to kiss her belly while continuing to toy with that magical, intimate place with his thumb, and moving a finger inside of her. For a moment she thought perhaps her breath had completely left her. Her heart pounded wildly as he explored, building a fire that raged deep in her belly until she cried out with the ecstasy of her first climax.

He left her for a moment then, and she felt removed from herself as she watched him discard his underwear. Finally she saw him, naked and beautiful, and instinctively she knew how he would join his body to hers. He moved back onto the bed, and knelt over her. She met his eyes. "Will it hurt?" she whispered.

He leaned down to rest his elbows on either side of her shoulders. "Yes. But only at first." He kissed her hungrily, and she felt him probing at her belly, moving between her thighs. She felt him enter her then, just a little at first. He grasped her hips, and then came the pain. She pulled a pillow over her mouth to stifle her cries. He grasped her bottom firmly and was moving in a quick rhythm now, thrusting deep, filling her impossibly deep. The pain burned at her insides, but somehow she knew that he could not stop even if she were to scream and beg. His face was flushed with ecstasy, and his eyes had a wild look to them.

In moments her pain lessened, and soon she found herself moving to meet his thrusts. He bent closer then, meeting her mouth in a hot, savage kiss, thrusting his tongue deep as though to fill as many parts of her as he could. She felt a surging then deep in her belly, and Lee groaned her name over and over as his life spilled into her.

"Audra, my Audra," he whispered, holding her tightly in his arms. "I love you." His broad chest pressed against her breasts, their skin damp with perspiration. "There are so many ways to enjoy it," he said softly. "Let me stay here with you. I'll show you all the ways. Tonight we will share what it means to be alive. We will laugh in the face of death, and we will forget about all the reasons why we can't be together."

Before she could answer, he met her mouth again, claiming it hungrily. She moved her own tongue to meet his, ran her hands over his hard body, into his thick, dark hair. Yes, she would let him stay. Already she could feel him swelling inside her again, and she wanted him to be there. They had tonight, and no matter what lay in the future, nothing and no one could take this away from them.

8

A shaft of morning sun filtered through an opening in the curtains at Audra's bedroom window. Its brightness woke her, and she squinted as she stretched. For a moment her mind was blank, until the sudden memory of the night before startled her fully awake.

She sat bolt upright. "Lee," she whispered, realizing he was gone. In total disbelief that she could have done what she thought she had done last night, she stared wide-eyed at her rumpled bed, and she only then realized when she looked down at herself that she was still naked. Her robe lay on the floor where Lee had first let it drop, her gown lay half-on and half-off the bed; and a dull ache between her thighs sealed the memory. It had not been a dream.

There came a knock at the door then, and Toosie called to her, asking why the door was locked. Audra realized Lee must have left the way he came, through the French doors.

When had he gone, and what must he think of her this morning? Part of her was elated and bursting with love, but another part warned her not to get too excited. Had he just used her in his grief? Both of them had understood that last night was all they could ever really have. Had he agreed only to take his pleasure, or had he been sincere about loving her?

"Just a minute!" She got up and quickly pulled on her nightgown before opening the door. This was all so new to her. How did she look? Would Toosie know? What *did* Toosie know about these things, anyway? When she opened the door, Toosie immediately looked surprised and concerned.

"Miss Audra, are you sick? Your hair is a terrible tumble as though you've tossed all night." She glanced at the bed. Almost at the same time, Audra did, too, and both of them saw the spots of blood on the sheets. Toosie's eyes widened and she looked back at Audra. "Is it your time, Miss Audra? I thought only a few days ago—"

"Hush, Toosie!" Audra quickly pulled her inside and closed the door. "No questions. Just draw me a bath. And don't you dare say anything to your mother or anyone else when we get back home about the blood on the sheets. Do you understand?"

Toosie studied her green eyes. Something was changed. Audra Brennan was no longer an innocent. She knew the signs. After all, she had had her own tumbles with Elijah before he was sold; and she had changed Master Brennan's bedclothes many times after her mother had spent the night with him. That was the only innocence left about Audra. She thought her father was such a saint. "I understand," she answered, concerned for Audra's state, both physically and emotionally. She had no doubt Lee Jeffreys had been in Audra's bed last night. "Are you all right?"

Audra felt her cheeks growing hotter. "I'm fine. Please hurry with the bath. I need to wash. Have the Jeffreys men had their breakfast yet?"

"Yes, ma'am . . . all but Lee. He's sleeping in." She folded her arms, giving Audra a knowing look. "I suppose it's because the funeral and all yesterday was such a strain."

Audra raised her chin defiantly. "I suppose."

Toosie arched an eyebrow as she turned to walk to the bathroom connected to Audra's room. If Audra wanted to talk about what had happened to her last night, it was up to her to say something, certainly not Toosie. She shivered at the thought of what Joseph Brennan would say and do if he knew his precious daughter had lost her virginity, and to a *Yankee* man, no less! There would be hell to pay. She was certainly never going to say a word and be the reason for the tirade that would follow if the truth were known. She had to smile, though, at the thought that if Master Brennan owned Lee Jeffreys, he would sell him off quick enough if he'd found him with his daughter.

Audra watched Toosie disappear into the bathroom. She ached to talk to the woman, to *any woman*. She had so many questions. What happened physically to a woman when she lay with a man for the first time? She couldn't even remember how many times Lee had made love to her. And why had it been so easy to let him do it? Never had she known such utter ecstasy, and she wished it didn't have to end. Maybe it didn't. Maybe now, after what happened last night, Lee would go to Brennan Manor with her, help her face her father with the truth, and marry her.

She looked down at herself, put her hand to her belly. *Is it your time, Miss Audra?* Toosie had asked. She wished she could ask the woman if Lee was right about what he had said last night, when he asked her the same thing. He wanted to know when she had had her last monthly period. She had been embarrassed to death to talk about such a thing, but he seemed to think it was so important. When she told him it had ended only three days ago, he had looked relieved. *It's not likely I've made you pregnant then,* he had told her. She wished she could ask Toosie if she knew that was true. And how did a man know such things?

She knew so little about Lee Jeffreys's life beyond Maple Shadows. How did he conduct himself back in New York? Did he have a mistress in the big city? Had he visited whores? She would not know about such things herself if not for the indecent things Eleanor was always telling her, stories she learned from her many "suitors." Were such women better at pleasing a man than she had been last night? And now that she knew what "it" was, she was shocked to realize that Eleanor must be doing such things with several different men. How terribly sinful!

Still, was doing it with just one man any *less* sinful? Surely it was, for she had lain with Lee out of great love and passion and pity, not just for the physical pleasure of it. Oh, she had so many questions, and no one to ask! How would she face Lee this morning? It had been bad enough having to face him after that night on the beach, but this!

Her heart was more torn than ever, for she so longed to be back home, yet the thought of leaving Lee behind brought a terrible pain to her chest. It was going to be impossible now to forget him, equally impossible to marry Richard Potter. Never could she imagine letting anyone but Lee do such things to her. If Lee still felt they could not be together, would she never make love with a man again for the rest of her life?

She felt as though she was moving in a haze as she picked out her clothes, deciding she had better dress demurely. She chose a pale-pink linen dress with embroidered roses bordering the ends of the long sleeves and around the high neckline. Each little button up the front of the dress was shaped like a rose, and she decided to wear very tiny ruby earrings. Toosie came to tell her her bath was ready, and she gladly undressed and climbed into the brass tub, sinking deep, letting the hot water soothe her aching body.

Would Lee think her a wanton woman, like the whores? Was that how she had behaved? The whole night was a blur of ecstasy. She wondered if she had somehow been drugged, for until now she never dreamed she would be capable of such wildness. Surely he understood she had allowed his pleasure only because she loved him, and that love made her desire him so. And what would Joey think? She could not tell Joey. She would never tell *anyone* what had happened last night, even if Lee should decide to marry her.

She finished bathing and came into the room to see that Toosie had removed the bedclothes and rolled them up so that the maid would not see the stains on them. Toosie had not said another word, but Audra could feel the woman's unspoken questions and criticism. She helped Audra dress, and Audra sat down so that Toosie could brush her hair.

"Just roll up the sides and back and pin them. I want a very plain hairdo this morning." Audra looked into the mirror to see the hint of a smile on Toosie's face as she obeyed the order. The look in her eyes made her uncomfortable. "I happen to love Lee Jeffreys," she told Toosie proudly.

Toosie nodded. "I have known that all summer, ma'am. He seems like a man easy to love, for a Yankee, that is. I understand about love, Miss Audra. Just because I am black and a slave does not mean I don't have the same feelings as white women."

The opening had been made, and Audra could not help sharing her feelings. "What should I do, Toosie?"

The woman finished pinning her hair and set down the brush. She took extra hairpins from a pocket on her apron and laid them on the dressing table as she spoke. "You just have to follow your heart, Miss Audra. You have to choose . . . Lee Jeffreys, or your father and Brennan Manor. You will never be able to have both. I can't see Mr. Jeffreys coming there to live, and I'm not sure you can bring yourself to leave Joey there alone. He will never be able to run the plantation, ma'am. That's my opinion. When Master Brennan is gone, who will do it but you and your husband? Mr. Jeffreys, I figure, is very capable, but would he be *willing* to do it?"

Audra sighed. "Maybe after last night . . ."

"Maybe last night was just something that had to be, no matter what happens after that."

Audra rose and faced her. "I never thought you'd understand."

"I understand more than you know, Miss Audra, especially the hurt. You'd better know that the hurt will get worse. Mr. Jeffreys is part of the northern cause against men like your father. Ask yourself, Miss Audra . . . what if, because of last night, Mr. Jeffreys agreed to marry you and went back to Brennan Manor with you? And what if after that, Louisiana and other southern states seceded from the Union? It would tear him apart. If the North should take measures to stop the secessions, whose side would Mr. Jeffreys be on? He would be treated like an enemy at home, and life would be very unhappy for him. He would want to come back north, and he would bring you with him, take you away from Brennan Manor and your father and Joey. You would be up here, your heart and loyalties torn. Then *you* would be the unhappy one. You would blame Mr. Jeffreys for that. If something terrible happened to Brennan Manor, to your father or Joey, you would end up hating your husband; and if he stayed there with you, it would be he who ended up hating you. Isn't it better to part now, remembering your love, instead of learning to hate later on? By then there might be a child between you, and that would make all the deciding even harder. You know where you belong, Miss Audra, and Mr. Jeffreys knows where *he* belongs."

Audra blinked back tears. She should never listen to the advice of a Negro, but Toosie was smarter. She had been tutored right along with Audra and Joey. Education was generally forbidden to Negroes, but her father had allowed it for Toosie. She supposed it was because he wanted his daughter's personal servant to be better than the common slaves. Whatever the reason, Toosie was a well-spoken woman. Audra knew good and well that Toosie was loyal, that she cared about her. She should chastise her for offering advice to her own mistress, but she had asked for that advice, and she knew the woman was right.

She was too weary and confused this morning to worry about protocol. She felt emotionally shaky, physically unsure. "Do you think he still respects me?"

Toosie smiled. "Yes, ma'am, I believe he does."

Audra turned to study herself in the mirror before going downstairs. She looked so different than she had the day before. A tight feeling moved into her stomach when she realized she was most certainly not innocent any longer. Would everyone downstairs stare at her as though she were wearing a revealing gown and were wickedly painted, or would they treat her no differently than they had yesterday? "I have to talk to him."

"Yes, ma'am. And you look just fine. I am sure nobody knows what happened, and I am sure that Mr. Jeffreys loves and respects you enough that he would never tell. It will be your special secret that nobody can take away from you."

Audra turned to notice tears in Toosie's eyes. "The same thing happened with you and Elijah, didn't it?"

Toosie nodded. "Yes, ma'am."

"I don't know why Father wouldn't let you marry him."

Toosie turned away. "Your father and my mother did not think he was good enough."

Audra frowned. "For goodness' sake, Toosie, why on earth should it matter to Father who a slave chooses to love?"

Toosie ignored the harsh remark. She was used to Audra talking that way, and she knew she did not mean it the way it sounded. "I suppose he thinks I am special because I am your personal servant," she lied, "and because he thinks so highly of my mother." She faced Audra. "It might be best not to bring it up to him. He would know I had been talking to you about Elijah, and he would be angry with me, as well as angry with you for talking about personal things with me." She walked over to pick up Audra's soiled nightgown. "I'll wash your gown and bedclothes myself so that no one sees them. You had better go and have your talk with Mr. Jeffreys. Your father could arrive here at any time to take you home."

The words brought a sinking feeling to Audra's stomach. Yes, she must go home soon. Maybe it was best. She could not really choose between Lee and home until she was back at Brennan Manor, until she was home again. There was something about this place that had caused her to lose herself. Maybe it was not the real Audra who had shared a bed last night with Lee Jeffreys. "Thank you for your advice, Toosie. I don't think we should speak of any of this again."

"Yes, ma'am."

Audra was tempted to walk over and put an arm

around Toosie, comfort her, but felt it would be totally out of place. She turned and left the room.

Toosie heard the door close, and it was only then that she let herself sink into a chair. "Elijah," she whispered. She had not wept over him for a long time, but knowing Audra would suffer a similar pain awakened old memories. She covered her face and let the tears come.

Audra walked the winding pathway to the Jeffreys-estate cemetery. Grass around the pathway was trampled from the crowd that had gathered there yesterday for Anna's burial. Her plot was beside the grave of the child she had lost at birth. Lee's paternal grandparents were also buried here. Someday his father would rest beside his mother, and probably Lee himself would be buried here, for New England was where he belonged, just as she belonged in Louisiana.

The housemaid had given her a message that Lee was at the cemetery and wanted her to come to him. He must have known it would be difficult for her to join the rest of the family right away, as though nothing had happened, and she was glad she would have the chance to talk to him alone first. Still, she trembled inside, and she felt much too warm for the cool morning. She had started out with a shawl, but she had already removed it.

She spotted him then, sitting on a bench near the grave, which was on a rise overlooking Long Island Sound. A breeze rustled the drying leaves on the thick stand of trees that surrounded the little plot, and the sun made their colors seem more brilliant than usual. She came closer, then hesitated, aware that her face had surely turned a deep red the moment their eyes met. It took only that one look, that vision of him standing there in a fine tweed suit, so tall and broad and handsome, his eyes so blue, for her to want him all over again. She thought about her song . . . *There you stand, my love, so tall and strong. . . .*

He walked toward her, put out his hand. She took it, and when he closed his around her own slender fingers, she felt a warm reassurance. Yes, he still loved her. He still respected her. He led her to the bench and she sat down beside him. He took hold of both her hands then, leaning close. "Are you all right?"

She looked down at his hands. Last night they had touched her everywhere. He knew her intimately now, had claimed every part of her body, tasted every inch of her. "Yes. I'm just tired."

He smiled a little, aching to spend the day with her in the bed they had shared. Never had he enjoyed a woman so much. No wonder she was tired. She had responded so willingly and with such innocent passion. He had taken something he had little right taking, yet somehow he did not regret any of it. Deep down he felt a wonderful satisfaction that at least he had been the one to show her the way, to keep lovemaking from being terrifying and unsatisfying. He squeezed her hands.

"I love you, Audra. Always remember that. I would never have used you, and I never want you to think that I would."

"I know," she answered quietly.

Oh, the desire to kiss that sweet mouth again. But he knew that if he did, he would lose himself again, and he didn't want that this morning. Something had to be decided. "I'm willing to marry you and go to Brennan Manor," he told her.

She raised her eyes then, and he could see her surprise. What a lovely green those eyes were, like the sea. She studied him intently before answering. "Tell me honestly, Lee, if that is what you want, or if you just want to do the right thing by me."

He sighed deeply. "I *do* want to do the right thing, but not just because of last night. I simply love you and want you to be my wife."

"And you would give up your law practice for that? You would give up your whole way of life? You would come to Brennan Manor and learn to run a plantation full of slaves, to take second place to my father as master of that plantation? You would learn our way of life and would be perfectly satisfied and support us if we should secede from the Union?" Audra saw the look in his eyes change from tender love to anger and confusion. "No, Lee, you couldn't do that. In fact, I suppose I would not love you as much if you swallowed your pride and your honor and beliefs just for me. I don't want you that way. You love me now, but you would hate me so after a while." Her eyes filled with tears. "I don't think I could bear having you for my own for a year or two and then losing you. You said once that parting would be easier now than later. I know now what you meant."

He saw something new in her eyes, a maturity that had not been there before. Audra Brennan had grown up a lot since he first met her back in June. God knew he'd done his share in forcing it on her. Joseph Brennan would not be getting back the innocent daughter he had sent here.

"What about you?" he asked. "It goes both ways. Do you love me enough to stay here, give up Brennan Manor, to stand up for the Union and support me in my efforts to stamp out slavery?"

A tear slipped down her cheek, and she let go of one of his hands to wipe it away. "It is not a question of how much we love each other, is it, Lee?"

"No." He moved an arm around her and let her rest her head against his shoulder. "We know we love each other as much as anyone can love. It's a question of principles and loyalty. Much as it hurts, sometimes those things have to come first, don't they?"

She clung to his wool jacket and cried quietly. "Yes," she whispered.

"It's decided, then. I had to try at least." He gave her a gentle hug. "I'm going back to New York today. After everything that has happened, I can't stay while you're still here. You should go back home, regain your perspective of who you are, where you belong. I don't think you can decide what you really want until you go back, Audra."

She took a handkerchief from her sleeve and wiped at her eyes. "Promise me you will never tell anyone what we did; that you will never joke about it or say anything to take away from the beauty of it."

He kissed her hair. "You know me better. It's no one's business but our own; and it was right, Audra. I know in my heart it was right, no matter what happens."

"Do you really think it'll come to war?"

It made him sick to think of such a possibility. "I only know there are powerful men in the North who are already talking about using armed force if southern states begin trying to secede. There is already talk about what we can do to strangle the South into submission if necessary." He shifted, taking hold of her arms. "Audra, no matter how much you believe in your way of life and in states' rights, you have to try to make your father understand what could happen if he and others like him keep ignoring government demands. The North has all the industry, many times the greater population, all the resources necessary to destroy the South if that's what it will take to preserve the Union."

She pulled away from him, sensing for the first time the intensity of his beliefs. "*Destroy?* You would go along with such a thing?"

He closed his eyes and looked away. "If it came to that, yes, I would."

"Even if it meant killing men like my father? And Joey? Even if the Negroes would rise against us and murder us and burn us out?"

"Don't put it that way, Audra."

"What other way *is* there to put it?" she answered indignantly. She rose from the bench, walking to look at the water.

In the next moment he was standing behind her, resting his hands on her shoulders. "Let's not get into all that, Audra."

"We have no choice." She turned and faced him. "Would you really have married me if I had said yes a moment ago?"

He searched her eyes. "Yes."

"Knowing it could never last?"

The words stabbed at him. "Yes. I just didn't want you to think last night meant nothing to me." He grasped her hands again. "Audra, let's never let our differences spoil last night, how we felt. We loved each other, and we expressed that love. For one night we had no differences. For one night it was just Lee and Audra. There was no Maple Shadows, no death. There was no Brennan Manor, no Joey, no politics."

She let go of his hands, again walking away from him. She couldn't bear his touch, for it made her want him so, and it was useless to want him. She went to stand near Anna's grave, feeling cold again. She wrapped her shawl back around her shoulders. "But there *is* a Brennan Manor, and I have to go back there with Joey. There *is* the matter of politics. And the fact remains that you were so consumed with grief that you yearned to feel alive and needed to mock death, so you spent the night feeling as alive as you possibly could. But today we know such moments can never last."

"Audra—"

"Go back to New York, Lee. My father will be coming any day, maybe even today or tomorrow. I will go back to Louisiana, out of your life forever. I will be where I belong, and you will be where *you* belong, and that will be the end of it."

"I'll never stop loving you or thinking about you, Audra."

She turned to face him, love in her eyes again. *I wrote a song about you, Lee. I never showed it to you. I wanted to sing it for you.* "Nor I you," she said aloud. "Even if I should take a husband, you will always be first in my heart. Will it be the same for you, Lee, if you should marry?"

"You know it will."

She sniffled as an unwanted sob engulfed her, then took a couple of deep breaths, struggling to keep her composure. "Maybe some day . . . all the country's troubles will . . . be over," she said, forcing a smile through her tears. "Maybe you and I will still be unmarried . . . and somehow we'll find each other again. Maybe then it could be different."

She could tell that his own smile was forced. "Maybe," he answered.

You don't believe that, Lee, but we can pretend, can't we? "I'll go back to my room and we won't have to see each other until you're gone." Oh, what pain she saw in his sky-blue eyes!

"My brothers' wives will be staying until your father

comes for you. My father and my brothers are going back in a couple of days."

She nodded, glancing at the fresh grave. "She will be so lonely," she said in a near whisper. She met his eyes again. "What will happen to Maple Shadows?"

He quickly wiped at his eyes with the sleeve of his suit jacket. "As soon as you're gone, one of my brothers will come back here and close it up. We'll keep old Tom on just to keep up the grounds and tend to the stables. As far as next summer . . . I don't know. I'm not sure I can come back here anymore. Not only is the place full of my mother and memories, but now when I come here, I'll see *you* everywhere."

"She would want you to come back, Lee, *especially* you. It would break her heart to know no one is opening the house for the summer, letting in the sea air, the smell of her lilacs."

He closed his eyes against the pain. "I know." He bent down to rearrange some flowers on top of the grave. "I'll try to get my brothers to come back next summer. She'd like it if all of us were here at the same time. That was what she had wanted for so long, but we were always so busy. . . ." He had never wanted his mother to know the truth, to discover the extent of the discord between him and his father and brothers. That's what made it so hard to let go. Unlike his father, his mother had loved him unconditionally. She had been his rock, his peace. He could not get those things from Edmund Jeffreys. He touched the grave gently. "We take so damn much for granted, don't we?"

"Not everything, Lee."

He rose and faced her. No, not everything. Never had he taken for granted that he could have her for his own forever. It had been the same for her. "I could have kept all of this from happening," he told her. "I'm the one who should have had the common sense, the strength, the wisdom never to have touched you. If you end up hating me after all, I won't blame you, Audra."

She shook her head. "Never."

He smiled sadly. "It's easy to say that now. That's why we have to leave it at this. If we stayed together, it might

not be so easy later on to vow you could never hate me."
He came closer, and she could not make herself move away.
He touched her shoulders, and both of them knew they
must have one more kiss to remember the other by. She
closed her eyes and felt his mouth touch her own, lightly at
first, in a gentle kiss of good-bye. In the next moment he
was fully embracing her, and she had wrapped her arms
around his neck, returning the kiss with the great passion of
her youth. Oh, how she ached to make love with him again,
to feel his naked body against hers, to feel him inside of her.

He groaned, crushing her against his chest, then suddenly tore away. "Go on, Audra!" he said sternly. "Go back
to the house."

She hesitated, and he turned away. "Go, dammit!"

She touched her lips, and the pain was so bad, she
wondered if a woman her age could have a heart attack.
"Good-bye, Lee," she whispered. There was no sense in
prolonging the pain. She turned and ran.

A moment later Lee turned back to see her gone.
"Good-bye, Audra," he answered softly. A choking sob began to engulf him, and he angrily forced it back. He walked
over to a nearby tree and leaned against it for a moment,
fighting the urge to go after her. In rage and frustration he
formed a fist with his right hand and slammed it into the
tree trunk over and over, until his knuckles were scraped
and bleeding.

9

Audra had been home for only three hours, and already she knew this was where she belonged. She breathed deeply of the sweet, humid air as she moved through the gardens behind the house where she had visited her mother's grave. Flowers bloomed everywhere, and before her stood the stately Brennan mansion, fluted pillars encircling the entire house like sentinels, supporting the second-floor and third-floor balconies. Such a grand home it was, much grander than Maple Shadows. She had never seen the Jeffreys home in New York. She was sure it was quite spectacular, considering their wealth, but nothing could compare to Brennan Manor and its heavenly surroundings.

Now that she was again in her own realm, she hoped it would be easier to mend her broken heart. Her father had arrived the day after Lee left, and she had struggled to hide her feelings from him on the trip home. When their carriage pulled away from Maple Shadows, she had been unable to look back at the home where she had found and lost the love of her life, the place where Lee Jeffreys had changed her from child to woman.

She realized more clearly now that she and Lee had made the right decision. Brennan Manor was her center, her life's blood. There was a gentleness about life here that would never change, she was sure, no matter what happened in the world beyond her father's plantation. Here she could heal. She walked behind the house, and in the distance she could see some of the Negroes scurrying about, tending to the house and grounds. Past the flower gardens and beyond a thick grove of trees she could hear the squeals of Negro children playing near their quarters. To her surprise, she realized she had missed even those familiar sights and sounds.

She breathed deeply of the sweet smell that was Louisiana and Brennan Manor and southern warmth. If only Lee would come here and see how good life was, he would surely not be so quick to condemn it. She approached their gardener, an old Negro man named George, who had walked from behind a bush he was trimming. He nodded to her.

"Well, Miss Audra, it's good to have you back!"

"Hello, George."

"This place wasn't the same without you an' Master Joey," the man told her. "Your father, he be ornery as all git out when you is away. He frets that he never should have let you go. He be in better spirits, now you're back."

Audra smiled. "I hope so. It's a long trip, so we're all still very tired. We came by ship to east Florida, then took a coach across to the Gulf, then back on a ship to New Orleans. The North is like living in a whole different world, George. I don't care ever to go back." *I fell in love with a Yankee man, George. What do you think of that?*

"Yes, ah suppose it would be different," the man was saying. "Ah never thought your father would send you away like that, into that nest of Yankees. Mebbe he thinks it be good for you to know what them people is like. We hear stories about how they want to free us, but me, ah'm happy right where ah am. Ah don' need no freein'. Where would I go?"

Audra smiled. "Father won't let anything happen to you, George."

Someone rang the bell signaling supper, and Audra bade George good-bye and headed toward the house. It warmed her heart to see him, one of the few Negroes with whom she conversed like an old friend. Even the sound of the dinner bell was comforting. She remembered times when she was little and would be playing far out on the lawn or in the woods with Joey, when she would hear the bell calling her home ... home. Lee had said she should come home and find herself before she could know where she really belonged, and already she knew where that was, but she still missed Lee, ached for him.

She walked around the shady veranda to the front of the house, greeting more servants, who all welcomed her back. Lena was at the front door when she reached it, and the woman gave her a gentle smile. "I was about to come lookin' for you, girl. Your supper is ready, and your father and brother are at the table."

"Thank you, Lena. I'll bet you're glad to have Toosie back."

The woman nodded, and Audra thought how beautiful Lena was. She had a special grace and pride about her. "As glad as your father is to have *you* back." Lena let her inside with a smile. She loved Audra and Joey as if they were her own. She had been the closest thing to a mother they'd had since their own mother died, and often she had had to remind herself of her place in the household. She was still just a servant, bought and paid for, except for the nights that Joseph Brennan came to her room. Then she was someone very special.

Audra joined her father and Joey for supper, and Joseph Brennan carried on about how wonderful it was to have his children home with him again. "There are a few things I haven't told you yet," he said. "Oh, and we're going to a horse race that was going to be held in Baton Rouge soon. I'll take you both along. Richard Potter is coming, too. I told you on the trip home that his father passed away this summer. The man is even more alone now, and I have a feeling he will be presenting you with a ring soon, Audra, now that you're back. We'll have a grand engagement party for you, maybe around Christmas!"

Audra felt her appetite leaving her. What was she to do about Richard? She hated the thought of disappointing her father, but she was no longer sure she could marry the man. Before she could say a word, her father had already changed the subject, talking about things that had happened over the summer while they had been gone, what a good cotton harvest he'd had. "Tons of cotton means tons of profits," he commented as he finished his meal. "It's probably a good thing you were in Connecticut, though, at least you, Audra. It was a hotter than normal summer, and the cotton came in a higher tonnage than ever before. The heat caused some trouble with the Negroes, and I was glad you were gone. It might have been good for Joey to be here, though, to see how it was all handled."

The man leaned back in his chair and patted his full stomach. "Old Hannah is the best cook we've had in years," he said then, as though not quite ready to finish his story about the Negroes. "I bought her from that agent in Baton Rouge, Stu Bailey. She comes from a farmer down in Mississippi who went bankrupt and had to get rid of his Negroes."

"This certainly is fine pork, Father," Audra answered, finishing her last piece. "The Jeffreyses almost never ate pork. I missed it."

Joey sat eating quietly, always choosing to speak as little as possible around his father. He had missed the man more than he thought he might. It felt good to be hugged when Joseph first came for them to take them home. It was a rare moment when his father embraced him.

"There are probably a lot of things that seemed very different up North," the man was telling Audra. "I'm terribly sorry about what happened with Mrs. Jeffreys, especially your being right there beside the woman when she died. It must still haunt you, having it happen the way it did. I had hoped you would never get that close to death again, after losing your own mother."

Audra pushed her plate aside. "Mrs. Jeffreys was one of the kindest people I ever knew."

Joseph studied her a moment, sorry she had had to witness such a thing, let alone the way those northerners apparently treated her. "That story you told me about that man insulting you and our family at that gathering of neighbors Mrs. Jeffreys held should tell you what those Yankees are like, Audra. That's part of the reason I sent you there, to learn what we are up against."

"Lee J-jeffreys stood up f-f-for her," Joey put in. "He's a g-g-good man."

Joseph frowned, his ruddy complexion growing slightly redder at the remark. "Perhaps he is, son, for a Yankee; but the short conversation I had with his father while I was waiting for the two of you to get ready told me all I needed to know. Mr. Jeffreys is running for the New York Senate, and the whole family is friends with the governor of New York. Edmund Jeffreys made no bones about telling me how he felt about slavery, and it didn't take him any time at all to warn me that I should urge Louisiana legislators not to allow our state to secede from the Union. We almost got into quite an argument, but I held my tongue only because it was his home and he had just lost his wife. I knew I wouldn't be there for long, so I let it go. At any rate, his son, your Mr. *Lee* Jeffreys, feels just as strongly against southern politics as his father, or so Edmund Jeffreys told me. I am sure the man was defending Audra as a young woman who did not deserve such an attack, but he most certainly was not defending slavery."

Talk of Lee brought the ache back to Audra's heart, and she drank some water, hoping to feel better. *But I love him, Father.* Sometimes she wished she could shout it to the world, but what good would it do?

"Most Yankees are not as understanding and accepting as Mrs. Jeffreys," her father was saying. "Those damned arrogant northerners are so jealous of the serene, idyllic life they think we lead down here that they will do anything they can to change it."

"They just don't understand the economics of slavery,

Father," Audra put in, feeling that somehow she had to defend Lee, at least.

"They understand it, all right. The way they treat their help in those stinking factories in the North is *worse* than how we treat our Negroes! All they have is the filth of their cities, crime and despair, disease. Orphans run the streets and commit crimes or get murdered. They have no right to tell us *we* are living wrong! Let them clean up their own messes before they start telling others what to do!"

Audra's heart sank at the realization that Lee could probably not last more than five minutes in the same room with her father.

"Those arrogant fools think we get all our labor free," the man continued. "Don't they realize the cost of buying good Negroes? Don't they understand we have to house them and feed them and clothe them?" He took a deep breath to calm himself. "Well, you're both home now, where you belong. Your Aunt Janine can't holler at me about your not having a well-rounded education or not being well traveled. One thing I will *not* do is send you off to Europe as she did with Eleanor. As far as I'm concerned, Eleanor is 'well rounded' in more ways than one. She is getting her education from those men who court her, and it isn't the kind of education I would want *my* daughter to get!"

Audra felt her cheeks growing hot. What would he do if he knew about her and Lee? He would probably die of shame. How could she ever make him understand why it had happened, how right it had been?

"As far as your singing career, Audra, that's up to Richard and what he will allow. He's a fair man and knows how much you like to sing. I'm sure he'll allow you to sing for weddings and such."

Allow? The more he talked about Richard Potter, the harder it became for her to suggest she might not want to marry the man. Her father seemed totally set on it. "I . . . you said there was trouble with the Negroes this summer," she told him, wanting to change the subject again.

Her father sighed in lingering anger. "Yes." He glanced at Joey. "I wish you had been here to see how it was handled, son. You need to know these things." He looked back at Audra. "One of the field workers, that Henry Gathers, he got a few other Negro men together and demanded more food and fewer hours, or they wouldn't get the crop in. Can you imagine it? *Negroes,* making demands on the man who owns them!"

Audra glanced at Joey, who she knew hated seeing any of the slaves disciplined. She moved her gaze back to her father. "What did you do?"

The man poured himself a little more wine, and Sonda, the new girl, came into the room to clear away some of the dishes. Lena followed her with a tray that held plates of pecan pie. She placed a piece in front of each of them, at the same time giving Sonda orders in clearing a table without disturbing Master Joseph and his family.

"What do you *think* I did?" Joseph was telling Audra. Audra noticed how he glanced at Lena then, looking almost guilty when she returned a look of literal chastisement. It seemed to Audra that Lena had a strange hold on her father, perhaps because she had been such a part of the family for so many years. Joseph scowled at her and raised his chin defiantly. "I did what was necessary. Henry Gathers was properly whipped and sold. The others were also punished. It's been a long time since I've had to ask March Fredericks to use that bullwhip of his, and you know I don't like to do it." He glanced at Lena again. "Get this girl out of here!" he barked, referring to Sonda.

The trembling girl stepped back from the table, her arms full of dishes. "We will finish later," Lena told her calmly, casting a look of defiance at Joseph Brennan. The two women left.

"That damn Lena tries to make me feel guilty for chastising my own slaves," Joseph grumbled. "And she's one herself! She's been with me too long, that's what. You keep them too long, they think *they* run the place."

"You wouldn't sell her, would you?" Audra asked. She could not imagine Brennan Manor without Lena there.

"She's much too valuable to us. You know that. Trouble is, she knows it, too, so she takes liberties." Always he worried about how Audra would react if she knew the truth. "I keep her mainly because she's been like a mother to you and Joey," he added, "and because I know you wouldn't want me to get rid of Toosie. Where Lena goes, Toosie goes. I'm not cruel enough that I would separate them."

"But you have separated other families," Audra reminded him.

Joseph gave her a scowl. "Seems to me you've been listening too much to someone up North. Are you questioning the way we live, Audra?"

Audra picked up a clean fork. "No, Father. The only reason I asked is that I have always wondered why Lena and Toosie were more special to you."

Joseph felt an uneasiness. How much longer could he hide the truth? It had been easy when Audra was a child, but she was growing up now. In fact, he had noticed something different about her only hours after he had picked her up in Connecticut. She seemed more of a woman, but he could not quite put his finger on what made her seem that way.

"Your mother bought Lena, Audra. She liked her very much, and she made me promise never to sell her. I keep her to honor your mother's wishes."

Audra toyed with her dessert, thinking about Lee's feelings about slavery. "I wish you didn't have to have March Fredericks use that whip," she commented. "I don't like that man, anyway. Maybe if you had a kinder overseer, the Negroes would cooperate better."

"*Kinder!* Audra, haven't you learned *anything* in all these years? You treat them too good, and they get lazy and spoiled! You have to keep a firm hand, or you end up with a disaster like what happened in Virginia thirty years ago."

"You've told us a hundred times about Nat Turner's rebellion," Audra answered.

"That's because I want you to *remember* it!" Again his temper was rising. When he got angry, everything about him seemed red, from his face to his hair and even his ears. That red hair was peppered with gray now, and there were considerable wrinkles about his brown eyes. His short but powerful build seemed as rock solid as ever, making him a most formidable contender, both verbally and physically. Few people cared to argue with Joseph Brennan.

Audra was the only one who could talk back to him. "Those Negroes murdered fifty-seven white people, Audra, most of them women and children; and what they did to the women first would make you faint if I told you! Firm discipline by all slave owners ever since then is the only thing that has kept them in line. Our biggest problem now is all this talk about freeing them. Most of them don't have the slightest idea what is going on in Washington and the North, but when they do, they'll be harder than ever to control!"

The man paused and scowled before continuing. "I'm sorry, Audra. I shouldn't be losing my temper when we've only just got home. Lord knows I missed you this summer. Nothing is the same here without you. I was so worried someone up North would sway you, or some Yankee man would fill you with lies and take advantage of your innocence. I don't know what compelled me to allow the trip. It was mostly your Aunt Janine's nagging, I suppose. I've got to stop letting that woman influence me. I know more what's best for my own daughter than that woman. Lord knows she's done a pitiful job of raising her own daughter." He cut into the pie. "Now you can concentrate on your lessons with Miss Geresy. You'll be helping to run a very big plantation soon. You've got to be fully prepared."

Joey swallowed a piece of pecan pie, noticing that the man seemed to direct most of his attention to Audra.

Finally his father turned to him. "About this Negro trouble—you must understand how important it is to keep them in line, Joey," he said. "A lot of men like me never used to be so firm with discipline, but it has become a necessity, and there is no getting around it. You and Audra need to understand that."

Audra pushed her pie away from her. "The difference is, March Fredericks *enjoys* using that whip of his. It's his attitude that creates anger in the hearts of the Negroes. You should get rid of him and hire someone whom they can respect."

Joseph swallowed the last of his wine, surprised at his daughter's sudden interest and rather commanding attitude. Yes, she *had* changed. It really wasn't proper for southern women to interfere with or have an opinion on such things as disciplining the Negroes, but he rather liked it in his own daughter. She was smart and she cared, and that was good. When she married Richard Potter, the man would need a wife who was strong and knew how to take control.

"With Negroes you don't get cooperation out of respect, Audra. You get it from fear. It's the only thing they understand—fear and discipline." He glanced at Joey. "Tomorrow, son, we'll go out to the fields. You need to watch March work, see how he manages the Negroes. Even with Richard Potter running things, some day you will *have* to help take charge, whether you like it or not. God knows it's a battle just getting you to be firm enough and respected enough to do a good job of it."

"Father, Joey has grown this summer, not just in size, but inwardly. And his speech is improving. Be patient with him," Audra pleaded.

"I d-d-don't need you to speak f-for me," Joey said then, looking from Audra to his father. His cheeks were flushed with embarrassment. "I can run B-brennan Manor just f-fine." Damn! he thought. Why did he always stutter more in his father's presence?

Joseph studied his son sadly. "Not with that stutter. No one will respect an order that isn't barked crisply and firmly. You've got to work on that stutter, Joey. And can you order a whipping when necessary?"

Joey hated violence of any kind, hated bringing pain to anything, animal or human. "If I have t-t-to," he lied, wanting desperately to please his father.

"I have my doubts," Joseph grumbled. He picked up a crystal bell and rang it, then brushed at a crumb on the sleeve of his silk suit while he waited for someone to come. "If you want to go on with voice lessons, Audra, perhaps I can find someone who will come here to teach you."

"I'd like that, Father."

The man rang the bell again. "Where in hell is everybody?" He looked back at Audra. "I am letting you experiment with your talent only to your own heart's content. I would not push you into anything. It's really up to you and Richard what you do with your voice."

Lena opened the swinging door between the kitchen and the dining room. "Yes, Master Joseph?"

"You certainly took long enough! Have that girl bring me some tea, will you?"

"Yes, sir." Lena left, and Audra breathed deeply for courage.

"Father, I . . . I think you should know that Joey is right about Lee Jeffreys. He truly was very good to us. He befriended us when no one else would. He can be quite kind and wonderful, and he is as much against the labor situation in his father's factories as he is against slavery in the South. He is so much against it that he refuses to have anything to do with the family businesses. He has his own law firm in New York. He is very smart and accomplished, graduated from West Point and Yale both. Joey likes him very much. He even tried helping Joey with his speech problem."

"Well, that's all very commendable, but he's still a Yankee." The man squinted, studying her closely. "Are you telling me you had fond feelings for the man?"

Audra exchanged a knowing look with Joey, and she felt her cheeks growing hotter. Sonda came into the room then and delivered a silver pot full of tea, then quickly left when she saw the ornery look on Joseph Brennan's face. "Well?" he asked Audra, pouring himself some tea.

Audra poked at a pecan that topped her pie. "He was just a good friend." *I loved him, Father. I shared my bed with him. I gave him up for you, for Brennan Manor.* "I just do not want you to think of him in the same way as the others."

"Mmm-hmm. Well, you tell me one thing—how strongly does he feel about preserving the Union, about slavery?"

Audra continued to keep her eyes averted. "Very strongly. He hates slavery, and he is very much against secession. He feels talk of secession is the same as treason."

"And how do you feel about Brennan Manor?"

She met his eyes. "I . . . I don't know what you mean."

"Yes, you do, Audra. Your heart is here. If this trouble over states' rights and slavery grows into secession and perhaps even fighting, could you still call a Yankee man friend, a man out to destroy men like your own father? I don't think you or your brother realize how serious all this has become, Audra. There is terrible bloodshed taking place right now in Kansas. This is not something that is going to be fixed overnight, and above all else, you are a southern woman, born and bred. If it came to the point where you had to defend your home and your way of life, I believe you would do it with great passion, because you are a proud young woman who loves her daddy and the home where she was born. Brennan Manor is your life, Audra."

The man sipped his tea. "I suspect you are trying to tell me you could even have had feelings for this Lee Jeffreys that are stronger than friendship." He watched the flush in her cheeks grow deeper. "I am not a fool, Audra, and not so old that I don't remember what it's like to be your age. Young women your age think that love can conquer all, but that simply is not true, Audra. The direction in which this country is headed right now, it's best you both forget your feelings and each of you stays where you belong. This is not the time to be falling for any Yankee man. And I don't want this mentioned to Richard Potter—ever."

Audra struggled against a sudden urge to cry. "It never came to anything serious because Lee would not let it," she lied. "I just wanted you to know that he is a good man."

Joseph rose, coming to stand beside his daughter. "I think it's time you began seeing more of Richard now," he told her. "You're old enough. He is a fine southern gentleman, who knows how to run a plantation. He is the only kind of man a woman of your station belongs with, and he would be good to you. The man has loved you for a long time, Audra. He has just been waiting for you to grow up." He patted her shoulder. "You know you would never be happy with a Yankee. You do realize that, don't you?"

If only he were wrong. "Yes, Father."

"For the time being, you're better off not venturing any farther than Baton Rouge. If that damned Abraham Lincoln gets elected President, our troubles have really begun. You're safer right here at home until the whole matter is settled."

Yes, she thought, he was surely right. Lee would certainly agree, and now that she was home, it even felt right.

In spite of his sometimes harsh ways, she loved her father dearly. He had always made her feel as though she and Brennan Manor were all he lived for, and it was difficult to picture him growing old here all alone among the ivy and the willows without her at his side.

All that had happened in Connecticut was already beginning to seem like a faraway dream. She had experienced her first feeling of love with a man she could never really have, and that was the end of it. Lee would go on with his life, and she with hers. "May I be excused?" she asked. "I am really not hungry enough for the pie."

Joseph smiled, glad the subject of Lee Jeffreys was apparently put aside. "Of course. You must be very tired. You go upstairs and get a good night's sleep. In the morning you'll wake up in your own, familiar room and you'll know where you belong. This is the only place where you can be happy, Audra."

Audra kissed her father's cheek and left to find Toosie and finish unpacking. She hurried to her room and closed the door, deciding to wait before getting Toosie. She wanted to unpack alone ... to remember. She had worn this dress to the beach, that dress for her first solo concert. And here were the seashells Lee had gathered for her.

Yes, the memories were there, to be secretly treasured forever. She found some of the sheet music Edmund Jeffreys had allowed her to keep, opera songs she would continue to study on her own. It was the sheet music that brought a gasp to her throat when she remembered with disappointment that she had forgotten to pack the song she had written for Lee. She had left it at Maple Shadows, in the desk drawer in her room ... Lee's old room.

Would he find it? Probably not. After all, it would be months, maybe years, before he went back there again. What would he think by then if he did find it? Would he have forgotten all about her? She had never even had the chance to show it to him, sing it for him. Perhaps it would lie there forever now, forgotten ... like their brief love for each other. For some reason the thought of it brought on the tears she had been trying not to shed. She lay across the bed and let them come.

Downstairs Joseph Brennan took his seat again, glancing at his son. "You might have become friends with this Lee Jeffreys, but I want you to have no more contact with him, understand? No letters, nothing that might encourage the man to reconsider a relationship with your sister."

Joey swallowed a piece of pie. "B but I p-promised Lee I would—"

"No contact whatsoever! *Is that understood?*"

Joey knew when there was no arguing with Joseph Brennan. "Yes, s-s-sir."

Joseph drank down some more tea, a dark look in his eyes. "No Yankee will ever take my daughter from Brennan Manor."

PART
2

Who is to say which is the braver thing to do?
To sacrifice one's pride and beliefs for love?
Or to sacrifice love for one's pride and beliefs?
For each individual the answer is different,
But for all individuals, either answer can only bring
Pain, and the haunting wonder if he or she has made
The right decision after all. . . .

—AUTHOR

JANUARY 1860

"You did a great job with that railroad merger, Lee."
Bennett James approached Lee's desk and shook his hand.
"Thanks, Ben. Have a seat."
The short, balding man settled his pudgy body down in
a red leather chair across from Lee's desk. Even though he
had been practicing law for twenty years longer than Lee
had, he admired the young man's brilliant mind. Lee was
good at what he did, and a law firm that made money meant
more money for all its partners. Lee had used his personal
trust fund to get the firm of Jeffreys, James, and Stillwell off
the ground, and it was his intelligence and determination to
go after the biggest cases and win them that had made it
one of the most respected practices in New York City. Ben
had gladly left Cy Jordan's firm to join Lee. Jordan was a

greedy bastard who kept the best cases for himself and who gave little credit to his junior partners. He figured that in the four years he had been with Lee, he had made more money than in the most recent ten years he had been with Jordan.

"With the way the railroads are growing, convincing the B and O to dump Jordan's firm and take ours on is going to mean money in our pockets for a long time to come," he told Lee. He reached into a pocket inside his brown tweed jacket to take out a cigar. "Those railroad backers are swimming in money. There will be more mergers, and with this talk about maybe building a railroad west ..." He stopped and lit the cigar. "You think that will ever happen?"

Lee shrugged. "Never say never." He rose and walked to a liquor cabinet, taking out a bottle of his best whiskey and two small glasses. "How about a little celebration?"

"Fine with me."

Lee poured a small amount in each glass. "You know, Ben, this one was sweeter than most, and not because of the money we made from it."

He turned and handed one of the glasses to his partner. Ben grinned, his bright brown eyes glittering mischievously as he took the whiskey. "Because you stole the whole thing right out from under Cy Jordan?"

Lee chuckled with sweet victory. "Nothing makes me happier than to be one up on that man. Maybe some day I can run the son of a bitch right out of business."

Ben shook his head. "If anybody is smart enough to do it, you are."

"I'll do it out of sheer desire."

They touched glasses and drank down the whiskey. Lee closed his eyes and let it burn his throat, his gut. A little voice told him he had been imbibing a little too much the last four months ... ever since Audra disappeared from his life. It seemed a little whiskey every night was the only way he could get any rest without painful memories making sleep impossible.

"Tell me something," Ben spoke up. "I know Jordan's a bastard. I worked for him long enough to know some of the tricks he pulls. You told me that when you first opened up,

Jordan made a point of advising big businesses not to risk giving you a try, that you were too young and inexperienced—is that the only reason you're always after his ass? Hell, he's the attorney for your own family's businesses. What's this problem between you two, and why in hell aren't *you* the attorney for the family business? You figure you're just too close to it to do a good job?"

"That's part of it. Sometimes when it's your own family, you're better off letting someone else handle things." Lee walked to a window, looking down at the busy street below. At the moment it was clogged with horses and carriages, held up because a team of horses had apparently gotten out of control, probably startled by an unusual noise. The wheels of the wagon they had been pulling had crashed into and locked up with the wheels of a passing buggy. Both drivers were standing in the middle of the street shouting at each other. *There's a good little lawsuit,* he thought, but he was not interested in "little" cases—only the big ones, the kind that could run men like Cy Jordan out of business.

"I suppose the real reason is my father hates the fact that I'm doing fine on my own. He's a man who likes to have control not just of his businesses, but his wife ..." God, it still hurt to think of his mother lying in that lonely grave in Connecticut, never to play and sing again. "And his children," he continued. "We never did get along. Maybe we're just too much alike in a lot of ways. When either of us thinks he's right, he won't budge." *That's how I lost the woman I love,* he thought. *I always think I have to do what's right and logical. Are a man's principles really worth more than love?* "At any rate," he added, "my father was adamant that I join in the family businesses, but I never wanted anything to do with those stinking factories and the poor souls who sweat out their lives in them. It infuriated my father when I opened my own practice." He turned to face Ben. "I hate to admit it, Ben, but I suspect my father had something to do with Jordan trying to keep me from being successful."

"Your *father!*"

Lee sighed, walking back to the liquor cabinet to pour one more shot of whiskey. "Oh, he loves me, all right. He's just damn stubborn. He never wanted me to go to West Point, and when I finally went on to Yale, he figured I'd walk right into the family businesses like my brothers did. He's tried all kinds of things in an effort to make me do what *he* thinks I should be doing. I think he asked Jordan to do what he could to keep me from getting business, so I'd give all this up and become a part of Jeffreys Manufacturing. I've never really been able to prove it; I just know it in my gut. My father can be a real bastard." He slugged down another shot of whiskey. "But so can I."

Ben sighed, shaking his head. "If you were my son, I'd be proud as hell."

Lee smiled in appreciation. "Thanks. Too bad my father isn't more like you."

Ben puffed on the cigar for a moment. "You shouldn't hate your father, Lee. I've raised six kids of my own. I know there are times when a father just thinks he knows what's best for his child. He loves the kid so much that he can't see the forest for the trees; can't see that by trying to force the kid to do what he thinks is best for him, he's just making him unhappy and alienating him."

"Well, there comes a point when a father has to let go. You've probably learned that."

Ben nodded.

"My father hasn't," Lee added. He sat back down behind his desk.

"Don't hate him, Lee. It will only hurt more when something happens to him."

Lee picked up an ink pen and twirled it in his fingers, staring at it but not really seeing it. He was remembering the little boy Edmund Jeffreys had led through all the offices of Jeffreys Manufacturing once, proudly showing his son what he would inherit one day. Lee could barely remember the actual manufacturing side of it. All he remembered was the looks on the faces of the workers, men and women alike, even some children. "I don't hate him. I just don't agree with how he makes his money. Trouble is, it's that money that helped me open my own law firm, so I'm caught between when it comes to principles."

"Maybe you worry too *much* about principles."

Lee thought about Audra. "Yeah, maybe I do." He met Ben's eyes. "We're pretty close now, Ben. Can I ask you something personal?"

The man shrugged. "You're the brilliant one as far as handling the law goes. But I suppose I *do* have an edge on you when it comes to life in general. After all, I've raised a family, gone through two wives, and have been around twenty years longer."

Lee grinned, and Ben caught the hint of sadness behind the smile. He knew Lee's mother's death had been very hard on the man, but he had always suspected there was something more eating at him that didn't have anything to do with death or politics or his problem with Cy Jordan and his father.

"Last summer, when I visited my mother in Connecticut, I met a young woman," Lee told him.

Ben's eyebrows arched, and his round face lit up in a knowing smile. "Lord knows a woman can be a bigger problem than anything else a man faces," he said with a low chuckle.

Lee leaned back in his chair, a somewhat embarrassed smile on his face. "I suppose." He folded his hands across his lap. "I fell in love with her, Ben, and I mean really deeply in love. She's young, beautiful, talented, capable of loving with great passion. She's also a stubborn, spoiled brat, yet she can be very giving and caring. She's everything, all rolled into one small, perfectly shaped package with auburn hair and green eyes that cause a grown man to behave like a sixteen-year-old."

Ben chuckled again. "So? Why don't you marry her and get her into your bed and out of your system?"

Lee looked down at the desk. *I've already had her in my bed.* There was no sense in telling him. He didn't want to risk anyone thinking less of Audra, and it was his own damn fault he'd let it go so far. "On the one hand, for very logical, practical reasons," he answered. "Then again, I wonder if I'm an absolute fool." He leaned forward again, resting his elbows on his desk. "She's a first-class, spoiled, pampered, thoroughbred southern belle, Ben; the daughter of one of the biggest plantation owners in Louisiana."

Ben let out a light whistle. "Slaves and all?"

"Slaves and all."

Ben reached out to tamp some ashes from his cigar into a large ashtray on the desk. "Everyone knows how you feel about slavery," he said. "That's one issue on which you *do* agree with your father. You're even helping him in his race for Senator, aren't you?"

Lee rose. "That's one area where I have set aside my hard feelings." He walked back to the window. Several policemen were now involved in the row taking place in the street below. "Her name is Audra Brennan," he continued. "She's all I can think about, but we could never last. She's promised to a wealthy southern gentleman who understands her way of life, and she's where she belongs. She'd never be happy living here, and I'd never be happy living there. Brennan Manor is as much a part of her as the blood that runs in her veins. She won't leave her precious father, whom she practically worships. Her mother died when she was seven, and her father raised her to believe that nothing was more important than preserving the plantation and their way of life. She's actually been trained by a tutor on how to properly run a plantation household. She also has a brother who needs her. I met him when he came to Maple Shadows with her. Joey has a speech problem, and his father doesn't treat him too kindly—disappointed in him, I guess. He's a good kid, but a real innocent, good-hearted, the kind who could never properly take over something that big. Audra feels she has to live there so she can always care for Joey. She's been like a mother to him."

He turned away from the window. "At any rate, by her marrying this Richard Potter, the man's plantation will be combined with her father's into *the* biggest cotton farm in the whole South, or so she tells me. She's been too long influenced by her father to realize that those things aren't all that's important in the world. She has convinced herself that she can be happy marrying a man she doesn't love and running the huge plantation that would be created by their marriage. She thinks her father's happiness has to come first, and Joey's. She's very brave and giving in that respect, but I can't stand the thought of her being unhappy in any way."

"Most of all you can't stand the thought of some other man touching her," Ben added. "Right?"

Lee grinned sadly. "Right."

"And you're both afraid that if you should marry each other, no matter where you settled, you would end up hating each other."

Lee shrugged. "It's bound to happen. She won't leave Brennan Manor, and I can't really expect her to, not as long as Joey needs her, anyway. I sure as hell can't live there. I have a feeling her father and I would mix together about as well as fire and oil, and the slavery issue would be the match that would cause the explosion. We both figured it was better to end it now, while we still had sweet memories, before we were left to remember only the hatred. Do you think we made the right decision?"

Ben reached out to the ashtray again, this time to put out the cigar. He sat back in the chair and rubbed at his chin. "That's something only you can know, Lee. Sometimes love can overcome a lot of differences, but knowing how you feel about slavery and states' rights, seeing what is happening to this country, you're probably right that it can't work. Especially if she's as thoroughly entrenched in that way of life as you say. Hell, a man like you could never live down there and go along with what you feel is flat-out treason." He rose and walked over to the liquor cabinet. "Mind if I have one more shot?"

"Go ahead."

Ben opened the whiskey bottle and poured a little more into his glass. "You know, Lee, this is all going to get a lot worse before it gets better. Look at the blood that was shed when that fanatic, John Brown, seized Harpers Ferry. Now he's been tried and hanged, and the South is in a panic that Negroes everywhere will start rebelling." He swallowed the whiskey in one quick gulp and set the glass on the liquor cabinet. "Word is, southern slaveholders are clamping down even harder on their Negroes. And even though the North helped convict the man for attacking a Federal arsenal, I suspect a lot of people here secretly admired Brown's goal of arming the Negroes and helping them form a country of their own. Don't forget the note Brown left behind saying that 'only through shedding blood will the country be rid of slavery.' If this country goes to war, Lee, and you're married to a southern woman, where in hell would that leave you?"

Lee nodded. "I know. I told her all of that. She agreed. I just wish I could forget her."

Ben paced for a minute, his hands clasped behind his back as though he were preparing to give a closing statement to a jury. "Has she married this Richard Potter yet?"

"I don't think so. They aren't supposed to marry until summer, after she has turned eighteen. I thought I'd hear from Joey. I've written him a couple of times, but got no reply. He promised to write. I don't understand it."

Ben faced him. "When will Audra Brennan be eighteen?"

"April twelfth, I think."

"You *did* pick a young thing, didn't you?"

Lee grinned, feeling the ache all over again. "She's old enough."

"Mmm-hmm. Old enough to keep you awake at night." Ben smiled and paced again. "Well, maybe you should go down to Louisiana, Lee, just to see for yourself if you really could never live there. After all, she's had a taste of life here, but you've never given hers a try. You're taking May and June off, aren't you?"

Lee leaned back and put his feet up on his desk. "I had planned on it. Figured I'd go to the Republican convention in Chicago and help get Abraham Lincoln on the ticket."

"Well, why don't you go to Louisiana instead? Lincoln isn't going to win or lose just by the fact that you're there. Write this girl, or I should say, woman, a letter. Tell her to hold off on marrying this Richard Potter until you can come for a visit. Tell her you feel it's only fair that you come and see Brennan Manor and have a talk with her father, that maybe something can be worked out."

Lee shook his head. "I don't know. Why reopen old wounds that might just fester and get worse? It's too much to ask of her. Apparently she has decided where she belongs and what she wants, or she would have written to me by now. Even Joey, it seems, hasn't given me a lot of thought since he went back."

"And what about *your* side of it? Don't you have the right to see her once more, see how she lives, make sure she's making the right decision? After all, you do love each other. For all you know, she's still pining away for you. Maybe her father has forbidden her to write; Joey, too. I'm sure the man isn't happy about his children forming a friendship with a Yankee man who is a confirmed abolitionist. If they told him about you at all, he probably decided to nip it in the bud." He stepped closer to the desk. "I've never known you to give up so easily, Lee Jeffreys. You won't let your own father tell you what to do with your life, but will you let a man you don't even know keep you from the woman you love? For God's sake, man, love is so much more important than all this other stuff."

Lee leapt to his feet. "You're no damn help at all. First you try to talk me out of this, and now you're saying I should pursue it."

Ben grinned. "I'm only being a good attorney, my friend. I'm forcing you to weigh both sides and ask yourself which is more important. You of all people know that a lot of issues can be compromised. Maybe you could marry her and live there for a while. If things get hot, you can bring her north with you until they cool down again. As long as her father is alive, he can keep running the plantation. When he dies, you're free to sell it if you wish. I'm told some of these slave owners actually get attached to certain of their Negroes. If this is the case, once you own the plantation, you'd have the right to free the slaves, which would ease your own conscience, and they could come north with you and work for you as paid servants. The girl would have her favorite Negroes with her and could still live a grand life. You can certainly provide her with the kind of living to which she is accustomed. That gets you out of the plantation and slavery problem, but lets you keep the woman you love. You could bring her brother north with you. Maybe by then the boy will be more able to get by on his own."

"I don't know." Lee walked back to the window. Now

men were working at unlocking the wagons that had crashed into each other. "I might be busting right into a hornets' nest down there. You make it all sound simple, but you know better, Ben. And what about my practice? I've managed to build Jeffreys, James, and Stillwell into one of the best firms in New York. I can't just walk away from that."

"You'd be a success wherever you went. Stillwell and I would keep it going, hire the best. You could remain owner and pick it up again when you move back north. Is the practice more important to you than your love for Audra Brennan?"

Lee faced him. "That isn't a fair question, no more fair than asking her if Brennan Manor is more important to her. Neither of those things is the issue here. It's the rest of it, our beliefs, our very way of life, the slavery issue, her father and brother. She won't do anything that would mean hurting her father."

"Well, now you're the jury. You have to decide."

"Thanks a lot."

"Sometimes it helps just to talk about it. I appreciate your thinking enough of me to tell me. It won't go any further than this room, unless, of course, you go to Louisiana and come back with a wife on your arm." Ben walked to the door. "I'll leave you with your thoughts."

"And no real answers," Lee answered with a hint of sarcasm.

"You know your own heart, Lee. All I'm saying is, you're probably right in the decision you already made; but before this girl marries and you lose her forever, maybe you should go down there and make damn sure you both still feel the same way. Meet this Richard Potter and make sure he's someone who will love her and be good to her. Maybe you'll be better able to put it all behind you if you're convinced that she will be happiest right where she is. Maybe you'd see her in a different light if you went to visit her in her own realm. That might take some of the heat out of the fire. Back in her own little world she might see you differently, too."

Lee ran a hand through his hair. "I never thought of it that way, but you could be right."

Ben grinned. "One way to find out," he said. "You do what you think is best. And good luck to you. He gave Lee a pat on the shoulder and left.

Lee walked over and poured himself another drink, then studied the glass for a moment. Yes, by God, he *should* see her once more!

He set the glass down without drinking the whiskey and walked to his desk. He dipped his pen into a bottle of ink and started to write.

My darling Audra, he began, *I have been giving a lot of thought to our situation, and I am wondering if you would be opposed to my visiting Brennan Manor next June.* He had to be careful how he worded the letter. He wouldn't want her father or Richard Potter to know he had slept with her. This had to be a very formal, honorable letter. He crossed out "My darling" and inserted "Dear." Once he had it just right, he would redo it on clean stationery and send it off. It should reach her well before any wedding took place.

APRIL 1860

Audra walked through the gardens, trying to sort out her feelings. It frightened her to realize how ill her father had become. The doctor who had come from Baton Rouge had said it was his heart. *He'll be fine perhaps for many years yet,* he had told them. *He simply has to get a lot of rest and never overexert himself or get too upset.*

Not get too upset. That was what bothered her. It upset him that he could die before she married Richard Potter. The wedding was not supposed to take place until August, but her father dearly wanted to see it, to give her away, and to have the security of knowing everything was in order before his death.

The thought of Brennan Manor without Joseph Brennan was almost incomprehensible to her. Her father was always so strong and feisty, she had supposed he would live to be a hundred years old. But the still-vivid memory of how quickly Anna Jeffreys had died frightened her. The same thing could happen with her father. She had been putting off thoughts of the marriage, but now she had to face it. She wore a splendid diamond-and-sapphire ring on her finger that was a token of her promise to marry Richard. He had accompanied her family on a trip to Baton Rouge to visit Aunt Janine and Uncle John, and there her aunt and uncle had held a magnificent party to announce the engagement.

Richard was every bit the gentleman. In all his visits to court her, their rides together, their private talks on the veranda and in these very gardens, he had been kind to her. He had not touched her in any way, had not even tried to kiss her. Sometimes she wished that he *would* try, so that she could tell if she would even *like* him kissing her. She shivered at the realization that if she married him, he would want to make love to her as Lee had done. Why did that idea make her uncomfortable? After all, Richard most certainly did seem to love her, and he was a handsome man, for forty-three years old. He was the most eligible bachelor in southern Louisiana. Eleanor had told her that, not without a strong hint of jealousy, adding she was the luckiest woman in Louisiana. *You must tell me about your wedding night,* she had said then with a snicker. *If you want me to tell you what to expect, just ask. I know everything there is to know.*

Audra had been tempted to tell her cousin that she already knew what to expect, but Eleanor was a terrible gossip. She would make sure Richard found out the truth about Lee. He would consider her a soiled woman then and refuse to marry her. That would break her father's already-delicate heart, but she suspected Eleanor would be delighted.

She had convinced herself that she loved Richard. After all, how many women were there who would *not* find him easy to love, let alone the glorious life they would enjoy as the richest couple in Louisiana. Richard was even thinking about running for governor, but he was more concerned first about finding the best way to manage two plantations.

He was discussing the same with her father right now. She was sure they were also discussing moving the marriage to an earlier date, perhaps even within the next month. Her father had already brought up the subject again this morning when she sat beside his bed while he ate his breakfast.

She wished she could have readily agreed. What was holding her back? It was the most logical union possible, and it would mean Brennan Manor would forever be protected and strong. Richard was a good man . . . or was he? That was what disturbed her. He had been kind and generous and attentive. He had expressed his love for her. But there was something behind his dark eyes that sometimes frightened her. Everyone knew he was very stern with his slaves, that he ordered whippings much more often than her father or some of their other friends did. Her father told her it was because Cypress Hollow was even bigger than Brennan Manor, and since the attack on Harpers Ferry it had become even more pertinent to clamp down hard on the Negroes. The entire incident was still the most talked-about subject among people from her father's circle.

Because of her father's ill health, Richard had already taken over a good deal of the management of Brennan Manor. He worked with Joey, took her brother along on tours of the plantation. He was good to Joey, and that meant a lot to her. Still, no matter how good he was, she did not feel the same passion for him as she had for Lee. Sometimes she found herself hoping Lee would come for her. If only he would have at least written. Even Joey had not heard from him. Joey had told her that their father had forbidden him to write to Lee because he was a Yankee, and at first she had been hurt and angry. Now she supposed it had been a wise decision after all. After Harpers Ferry, it had become even more obvious that the slavery issue was going to draw more blood. Her father and others even believed that most northerners were actually secretly supportive of what Brown had tried to do. She did not doubt that Lee would have been one of those people.

Tension between North and South was growing stronger every day, just as it was becoming more obvious that the summer love she had shared with Lee was just that . . . a summer love that would always remain precious in her heart ... a secret she would carry to her grave. She had given something to Lee that no other man could have now, not even Richard. She had given him her soul, her virginity, her passion.

Had he just used her after all? What did she really know of men besides what they did to a woman's body? Was the Yankee Lee Jeffreys laughing about the little "southern belle" he had bedded? It hurt to know that even though she couldn't write him, Lee in turn had never bothered to get in touch with her either, when he was perfectly free to do so. He could at least have written Joey.

She leaned down to smell a rose when her thoughts were interrupted by a slashing sound, followed by a grunt. She straightened, concentrating on where the sound had come from. There it was again—a quick snap, another groan. It seemed to be coming from the area of the greenhouse, and she headed in that direction. She knew the difference between the sound of March Fredericks's bullwhip and the smaller whip he sometimes used for quick reprimands. He carried the small one in his belt at all times. It had a short leather grip that sprouted several strands of rawhide, each with a piece of sharp metal tied to the end of it, so that when it was used on human flesh, it left several bleeding cuts in one slash.

How she hated Fredericks! She understood the necessity of discipline, especially in these dangerous times; but she still felt that in some cases such severity was unnecessary. What disturbed her about March was the absolute pleasure the man seemed to derive from bringing pain to humans.

She rounded a hedge and saw him then, standing in front of the greenhouse. Old George was kneeling in front of him, his shirt off, his back bleeding badly. March raised his hand again. "Stop it!" she shouted to the man.

Fredericks hesitated, turned to see her standing there. There came that look again that made her feel ill. The man was never clean shaven, and his floppy hat and the underarms of his shirt were stained from sweat. His eyes were blue, but not a pretty blue as Lee's were. They were pale, and he had a way of looking at her that made her feel as though she were standing there stark naked. That was the other thing she did not like about him. He had absolutely no respect for his superiors. He did what he was told to do, but she suspected that if he thought he could get away with it, he would kill them all and be sitting at her father's table.

"Don't you dare hit George again!" she ordered, marching closer, "not now, and not *ever!*"

March slowly lowered the whip, and George remained bent over, half crying. March grinned as Audra came closer, and she felt savagely raked by his gaze. The sight of his teeth, stained from chewing tobacco, made her stomach feel queasy. "I caught him sleepin'," he told her. "He's supposed to be weedin' out the garden, and he was in the greenhouse layin' flat out like the lazy nigger that he is!"

"Ah . . . wasn't sleepin', Miss Audra," George told her, wiping at his nose and eyes with the back of his hand. "Ah got so hot . . . ah went in the greenhouse to get some tools, an' ah passed out on account of the heat."

Audra walked to where a bucket of water sat nearby. It truly was an almost unbearably hot day, even for Louisiana. The whole month of April had been unusually warm. She picked up the water and came over to pour it over George's head and back.

"Oh, that feels good, Miss Audra." George remained on his knees as he rubbed at his face. "Ole George does thank you. It's true, Miss Audra, ah passed out. You know ah don' sleep when ah's supposed to be workin'."

"I know, George. You go back to your shanty and rest."

The man slowly got up as Audra turned to March Fredericks. If looks could kill, she knew she would be dead. She also knew what he would like to do before he strangled her; but she was Audra Brennan, and the man didn't dare lay a hand on her. It struck her then how much more powerful and important she would be once she was Richard Potter's wife. Maybe she could even get Richard to fire this reprobate. "I mean it," she told him. "Don't you ever lay a hand on George again."

"He's a lazy nigger."

"He's an old man! Old men get weary, especially when

it is this hot! And you know good and well that George is different from the rest of the Negroes! He has been with this family since my own father was a little boy! We don't *expect* him to work hard. Father keeps him on because he doesn't have the heart to sell him at his age, nor would anyone want him; more than that, he keeps him on because this is the only home George has ever known and this is where he should be when he dies." She turned to George, who stood there hesitantly. "Go on, George."

The man looked from her to March, a little wary of leaving Audra alone with the man. He reasoned that Fredericks was too smart to dare touch Miss Brennan, so he finally decided he could leave. "Thank you, Miss Audra." The old man limped away.

Audra looked back at Fredericks. "I should have you fired!"

"Your father would never let me go," he sneered. "He needs me. I'm one of the best overseers in Louisiana."

"There are others."

He grinned, trying to look confident, but Audra saw the worry in his eyes. March Fredericks liked it here. He had a lot of power here, maybe too much power, and he was paid well. "You're just a female. It's your father and Richard Potter who make the decisions around here, and I'm tellin' you you ain't got no say in what happens to me."

Audra raised her chin proudly. "We'll just see about that!" She turned and stormed back to the house, furious over what she had just seen. She hated to upset her father with it, but something had to be done. She paraded past Toosie and Lena when she came inside, not even answering Lena when she asked what was wrong.

"Mr. Potter is upstairs with your father, if that's where you're going," Lena called out to Audra as she proceeded up the wide circular staircase that led to the second floor of the mansion.

"Good!" Audra answered. "I want to talk to both of them!" Her voice echoed from the stairway down to the grand, marble-floored great room beneath it.

"They asked not to be disturbed," Lena called up to her.

Audra did not listen. She marched into her father's bedroom, where Richard looked up from a chair beside her father's bed. Papers were strewn on the bed, some of them looking like some kind of legal documents. She supposed her father and Richard were discussing what would and would not belong to Richard once he married Audra. It had crossed her mind more than once that Richard might just be marrying her in order to have even more wealth and power, but what did it matter? It would be the same for her.

She walked closer to both of them, and they just stared at her a moment, surprised at her sudden entrance.

"Darling," Richard said then, rising. "You look terribly upset."

Audra watched his dark eyes. Why was it so difficult to tell if he was being sincere? He took hold of her arm gently.

"I *am* upset!" she answered.

"What is it, Audra?" her father asked.

She looked from him back into Richard's eyes. "I suppose Father has discussed with you the fact that he would like us to marry sooner because of his health."

Richard smiled. It was a handsome smile. Yes, he was certainly an attractive man, tall, still solid for his age, with dark, nicely trimmed hair and mustache, handsome dark eyes. He was gentle and mannerly. She could learn to love him, couldn't she, especially once she bore his children? Whatever love she believed was missing from her life by marrying Richard would surely be made up for through their babies.

"Of course we have talked about it," Richard answered, "and there is nothing I would like more. But perhaps you aren't ready—"

"I believe you will be going to the Democratic convention in Charleston the end of the month?" she interrupted.

Richard looked confused. "Why, yes, Audra. We want to be sure the party takes a pro-slavery platform. We have to keep Stephen Douglas from getting on the ticket. The man believes in popular sovereignty—"

Again she interrupted him. "I don't care about politics right now. I have decided, Richard, that as soon as you get back from Charleston, I will marry you. I have already been contemplating dates the last couple of days. How does Sunday, May thirteenth, sound to you? I want to be married in the Catholic church in Baton Rouge. While you are away, I can stay with Aunt Janine and let her help me with my wedding dress and wardrobe and in sending out invitations."

Richard's face lit up with pleasure, and when Audra glanced at her father, she could see he was thrilled. "Audra, I would be so honored," Richard told her. He took her hand and kissed the back of it, and she thought his lips felt rather cool. Perhaps it was because her skin was so hot from the weather and from her own temper. He squeezed her hand reassuringly.

"I agree to marry you earlier, Richard, but on one condition."

"And what is that, my dear?"

"I want you to fire March Fredericks!"

"Fire Fredericks!" It was her father who spoke up then. "Audra, I can't do that."

"Either you or Richard will *have* to, or I will not marry Richard. That is my stipulation."

"What brought this on, Audra?" Richard asked her.

She kept her eyes on her father, taking her hand from Richard's. "I caught March whipping poor old George. He accused him of sleeping in the greenhouse, but George says he passed out from the heat, and I believe him. March knows how we feel about George. I don't like the man, Father, and I have never trusted him. Deep inside he's a dangerous savage, and I want him dismissed. There are many times when Richard will have to be gone for days at a time because of all the things he has to manage. I will not have a man like March Fredericks running things while Richard is gone, nor do I care to be left alone to give the man orders. He has no respect for me."

Richard grasped her shoulders from behind then. "Audra, Audra, calm down. If it is that important to you, we'll make a compromise. March *is* good at what he does, but I agree he had no right to hit old George. What if I transfer him to Cypress Hollow? I am going to need the extra help there when I begin spending more time here with you. I'll hire a new man for Brennan Manor. Would you agree to that?"

Audra turned and looked up at him. "I will agree to anything that means I don't have to look at that man or talk to him again. Joey hates him, too. And I think March should be punished for what he did to George. He took advantage just because Father is ill. If you aren't going to fire him, you should at least reduce his pay for the rest of this year besides sending him away from Brennan Manor."

Richard smiled. "Then it is done." He took hold of her hands. "Is it really all that simple?"

No, she wanted to say. *I don't want to go to bed with you. I hope you will be patient. I hope your touch will come to make me feel the way Lee Jeffreys made me feel.* In spite of the night she had spent with Lee, she was still confused about sex, for that had been her one and only encounter with the pleasures and curiosities of it. When he touched her, something magical had happened to her. Was it possible that *any* man could do that to a woman, if he touched her in the right ways? She had to try to love this man, to enjoy his touch. She was going to be his wife, and once she married him, her father would be the happiest man alive, her brother would be protected, Brennan Manor would be preserved forever.

"Yes," she answered. "The only other thing I want is the assurance that Brennan Manor will always be called Brennan Manor, so that the name is always remembered, even after Joey dies."

"Of course, dear. Your father and I have already talked about that."

"And Joey and I can remain living right here, and Lena and Toosie and Henrietta and George will never be let go."

"Done."

"I want March Fredericks gone tomorrow."

"You will never set eyes on him again." Richard smiled reassuringly.

Audra felt a new power. It would not be so bad after all, being the wife of Richard Potter. She would have far more say in the plantation affairs as a wife than she did as a daughter. She realized that if she could not have Lee, then what did it matter *whom* she married, as long as he filled so many other qualifications, as Richard did. It might just as well be Richard as anyone.

"Then you can start telling people the wedding is set for May thirteenth," she told him.

He squeezed her hands. "I love you, Audra. You plan the grandest wedding you want to have! Money is no object. And as soon as the summer harvest is over, we'll take a trip to Europe. How would you like that?"

"I would like that just fine," she answered. Yes, Europe was a good idea. She would be even farther away from Lee. By the time she got home, she would be firmly settled as Mrs. Richard Potter. Maybe she would even be carrying his child by then. She would have babies. She would live at Brennan Manor, take care of Joey and her father, and life would be good.

Joseph Brennan smiled with great joy, already feeling better. Perhaps it had been his own alarm over the letter Audra had gotten from that Yankee man that had made his condition worse. Nothing could be harder on a southern man's heart in these times than the thought of his daughter marrying a Yankee. He had never shown Audra the letter, nor any of those Lee had written to Joey. Not even Richard knew about them. He didn't want to do anything that might cause the man to have second thoughts about marrying his daughter.

He had burned every letter. No children of his were going to become close with a Republican abolitionist! Lee's most recent letter had been to Audra, telling her he was coming to Louisiana in June to speak with her and her father. He knew damn well what that Yankee surely intended, and he hoped getting no reply would put a stop to it. Audra belonged with Richard, and by the time Lee Jeffreys arrived, she would be a married woman. He would deny any letters had ever arrived at Brennan Manor. Lee Jeffreys would be sent on his way, and that would be the end of him and any fond thoughts he might have entertained about Audra.

Richard kissed the diamond-and-sapphire ring on

Audra's hand. "May thirteenth, 1860, will be the happiest day of my life," he told her.

"And mine," Joseph added.

Audra wanted to say it, too, but the words would not come.

Lee walked through the house his mother had loved, shivering with memories. He had not meant to do this, knowing how much it would hurt; but he had been unable to resist the compelling urge to return once more to Maple Shadows. It seemed he had not really had the chance to say good-bye, to his boyhood, to his mother, to the sweet summers he had enjoyed here.

The house would not be opened this year. He had come here only for a last look, and maybe to find some answers. He had written to Audra but got no reply. He was probably a damn fool to think of going to see her, anyway, and somehow it seemed maybe if he came here first, he would know what to do. This was where he had fallen in love with her, and this is where he had told her good-bye.

He closed the front door, and a damp, musty smell met his nostrils. The stillness that greeted him was made more unbearable by not just his mother's absence, but Audra's. Sweet memories squeezed at his heart when he walked into the parlor and stood staring at the grand piano that his mother had so loved. The room was dark now, windows and French doors closed, curtains drawn to help guard against the drafts of the fierce, cold winds that had battered it the past winter. He could not help thinking of the house as having a soul, and though it seemed silly, he felt sorry for it. The place must be more lonely than ever, knowing Anna Jeffreys would never again throw it open in the spring and let in the smell of her lilacs.

He could almost hear his mother playing, and he could see Audra standing there, hear her singing. He remembered the parlor being warm and bright, with doors open to a summer breeze, vases of flowers perched on every possible flat surface.

He walked over and sat down on the piano bench, opening the cover and touching the keys. He played a couple of them, then shuddered with such overwhelming grief that he had to stop and put his head down for a moment and vent his feelings. He wept for several seconds before suddenly feeling a strange warmth move across his back. It was so warm, in fact, that it startled him. He sat up straight and looked around, almost expecting to see a sudden shaft of sunlight, perhaps, or to see that someone had come along and put a blanket over his back. May had been cold this year in Connecticut, and the house itself was still quite chilly.

He saw nothing unusual. There it came again, like a warm rush of air, this time over his face. He could swear he heard his name whispered. Again he looked around to see nothing unusual. He stood up, taking a handkerchief and wiping at his eyes, then moving away from the piano bench. He stared at it for a moment, dumbfounded over what he had just experienced.

Mother? He felt a strong presence, as well as a calming peace. The house remained quiet, but he felt a secret joy to think that perhaps Anna Jeffreys lived on here, that she still sometimes sat at that piano bench, and she was welcoming him again, as she had that day last year. He shivered as he closed the piano, still shaken by what had just happened, but glad he had come. He needed this time with his grief and his memories, and now it was easier to believe that his mother and her music lived on . . . somewhere.

He left the parlor, walked to the stairs, and looked up. Did he dare go back to that bedroom? Was there anything there that would help him know what to do about Audra? He was hoping he would find some kind of clue here as to whether he should try to see her once more.

He climbed the stairs and headed into the room where he had spent one glorious night with Audra Brennan. He stared at the neatly made bed, touched the bedpost. It was so easy to remember it all, the taste of her, the feel of her, the ecstasy of being inside her. Was there any explaining love? Why was it Audra for whom his heart yearned? Why did it have to be someone so forbidden, so impossible?

He felt an uncontrollable urge then to try to find something she might have left behind, something that was only Audra. He searched through the dressing table, hoping for perhaps a hairpin, an earring. Nothing. What in God's name was this sudden panic he felt? He tore through dresser drawers, realizing that if anyone saw him, they would think him perfectly mad. Still nothing.

He moved to the desk and ripped open the right top drawer, then hesitated when he saw some papers lying in it. His hand actually shook as he took them from the drawer, and he decided he must be working too hard, for he had surely lost control of his faculties. It was a good thing he was taking a couple of months off again.

He unfolded the papers to see that something was written on them. He walked to a window, drawing back the curtains so he could see better.

> *Lee, my love,*
> *Just as the sun shines*
> *And the ocean wind blows wet and wild,*
> *I love you as a woman loves,*
> *But you see me as a child.*

"My God," he whispered. She had written a song for him!

> *Lee, my love,*
> *When I am with you*
> *I never want the days to end.*
> *I love you more than life itself,*
> *Yet to you I'm just a friend.*

> *Lee, my love,*
> *You stand before me*
> *Tall and strong, your eyes so blue,*
> *I long to feel your arms around me,*
> *To hear the words, I love you.*

He went on to read the last verse. On the two other sheets of paper she had written musical notes. Apparently she had even been composing a melody for the words. Was this a sign he truly should go to Louisiana and find her? He read the song again, and he felt as though Audra had just walked through the door and was speaking the words aloud to him.

"Audra," he whispered softly. Had she simply forgotten to take the song, or maybe left it here because she was angry with him ... or had she meant for him to find it? She had never had the chance to show it to him, sing it for him. She probably felt there was no reason.

Should he throw it away? Burn it? Send it back to her? No. She would be embarrassed if he sent it to her, or maybe her father would see it and be angry. He certainly could not bring himself to destroy it. For now, somehow, it soothed him to read it. Maybe God meant for her to leave it by accident, so that he could find it in this time when he needed to hear the words, needed an answer to his dilemma of going to see her once more.

He folded the papers and shoved them into his breast pocket, then headed downstairs. He had already visited his mother's grave, and he did not intend to spend the night here. He had visited with old Tom. If he was going to get all the way to Louisiana and find out what lay ahead for him and Audra, there was no time to waste. It would be a long trip. He walked outside and locked the door, then turned up the collar of his overcoat against a cold spring wind.

He hurried to his rented carriage and untied the horse, then climbed into the seat. Maybe it was the craziest thing he had ever done in his life, but he was going to Louisiana and make sure he hadn't thrown away his only chance at real happiness. He felt light, free, alive. Coming here was the best idea he had had in a long time, and what he had found was like God giving him his answer.

He started to back the horse when he stopped for a moment, sure he heard the distant sound of a piano. He looked at the house, but only the sound of a spring breeze in the budding maples met his ears. "You're losing your mind, Lee," he muttered. He backed the horse and turned the animal, heading down the curved brick drive. If things went right, he could be in Baton Rouge by the end of May. He figured anyone there could direct him to Brennan Manor.

12

Audra gladly allowed Richard to keep an arm around her and help her up the stairs to the luxurious suite he had rented for their wedding night. She had deliberately drunk a little too much wine at the grand ball Aunt Janine had held in Baton Rouge for her and Richard after their wedding. She wanted to feel light-headed and gay, or was it that she didn't want to feel anything at all? Somehow she had to get through this first night with her new husband.

Grand, grand, everything had been grand, from her near-royal wedding to the ride in a white carriage pulled by a white horse, showing off the newlyweds to the general public of Baton Rouge.

She laughed, stumbled slightly. Richard chuckled and held her up. They were at the top of the stairs now. Yes, it had been grand! Aunt Janine's home was one of the biggest in Baton Rouge. She and Audra's own mother came from a wealthy plantation family in Mississippi, so both women had known the good life already before Audra's mother married into Brennan Manor, and Aunt Janine married Uncle John, who owned a bank in Baton Rouge. The house had a grand ballroom that was bigger than any other house in town. Audra had danced there with her new husband, watching his dark eyes, wishing they were blue. There would be another celebration at Cypress Hollow when Audra and Richard returned home, then another at Brennan Manor. Parties, balls, dancing, laughter. She had followed Miss Geresy's rules about how to conduct herself properly as the new first lady of both Cypress Hollow and Brennan Manor. Now the task would be fully hers ... Forever. Richard had already dismissed Miss Geresy, adamant that his new bride was ready for the task. The woman had been at her wedding, and that was the last Audra would see of her. Richard Potter had spoken, and that was that.

Richard was opening the door now. She didn't even know what hotel this was.. He was picking her up in his strong arms, carrying her through the doorway. Oh, what a wonderful day it had been! There would surely be a full page written up in the local paper, maybe even in papers in other parts of the country, about the wedding that had taken place today. After all, the wealthy Miss Audra Brennan had wed the even wealthier Mr. Richard Potter, and together they were Louisiana's most envied couple, rich, handsome, beautiful. Louisiana's princess had become Louisiana's queen, and with the combined plantations, Richard was surely a king.

Now her new husband was removing her veil and hat. He was telling her something, but his voice seemed distant, and she didn't want to concentrate, not on the voice or his touch. She would think about something else, that's what. She had to keep her mind occupied, because now Richard was unbuttoning the back of her wedding gown, saying something teasing about why women used so many buttons.

Think, Audra, she told herself. *Keep your mind active.* Politics. She was so tired of the subject, yet now she was beginning to understand the importance of elections and such. The wedding had come at a good time, because it made people forget about the troubles the South was facing, and the fact that the Democratic convention in Charleston had been a disaster. The proslavery platform was rejected, and the delegates from eight southern states had left. Richard had been among them. The convention was adjourned because no one could agree on a candidate. It was not a good situation for the South, which needed to be united.

United. Somehow it seemed that her marriage to Richard should help unite the South. Richard had power now, enough, perhaps, to talk to the right people and get something settled so that the southern states could get a proslavery candidate elected and show the North they were united and strong.

Richard was standing behind her now, removing her dress, pulling it off her shoulders, telling her how milky soft they were. His hands were touching her bare skin. She cringed when he moved them down the front of her to fondle her breasts, but she forced herself to pretend that she liked it. In time, she was sure, she *would* learn to like it. She had already enjoyed this once, but when Lee had touched her there, it had been because she wanted him.

Again she tried to think of other things, glad for the wine that made her thoughts swim. She thought how happy she was her father seemed to be doing better. He had been so proud to walk her down the aisle and give her away. Oh, yes, Father was pleased to see his daughter finally marry Richard Potter.

The rest of her clothes were being removed, and Richard seemed to be doing it rather roughly, but then he was anxious, as any new husband would be. He was carrying her to the bed now, laying her on it. He began removing his own clothes, and she turned away. Why had it been so easy to look at Lee? She had wanted to see him, all of him; she had wanted to touch him. Now she was embarrassed, not only for Richard to see her naked, but to look at him the same way.

She felt him move onto the bed, and she wished she had drunk even more wine. This was his wedding night. He expected his "prize." She might as well get it over with and learn to like it. If he made her pregnant right away, she could keep him out of her bed for a good long time, feigning complications of the pregnancy. And, after all, Richard *was* handsome, and he was a well-built man. He was kind and gentle. . . .

Why couldn't she open her eyes?

"I know it's your first time, my darling," Richard was saying. "Don't be afraid. In no time you will enjoy it immensely." She felt his hands moving over her, but he did nothing to make her want to open herself to him. He apparently thought her reluctance was because she was a virgin. Let him think what he wanted. She hated herself for not being as happy as she should be. Half the women in Louisiana would like to be in her place right now. Why did she feel like crying? If only he would go a little slower. Only minutes had passed and already they were both naked.

He was bending close, taking her breast into his mouth. He groaned her name, told her how beautiful she was, began moving over her eagerly, roughly. He pried her knees apart and positioned himself between them. "Quickly, Audra," he said. "We will do it quickly and get rid of the pain, and then all will be pleasure for you."

Audra gasped when he rammed himself inside of her without any further foreplay. His thrusts were hard and almost violent, and she wanted to scream at him to stop, but she was his wife now. She told herself to relax. Wine. She would start drinking more wine so that she never had to be any more aware than this of what he was doing. From now on she would keep wine in her bedroom, or perhaps drink as much as she could each night after supper.

He moved in quick jabs. It hadn't been like this with Lee. Such a gentle rhythm Lee had used, like music. And he had done such beautiful things to her first, so that she had wanted him desperately. Lee. She would think of Lee. Perhaps if she could pretend it was Lee doing this. Yes! That was it! She could always pretend it was Lee, and Richard would never know the difference! He would be satisfied that his new wife was responsive, and she would be satisfied, at least a little, with her memories. "Lee," she whispered.

Richard grasped her bottom and raised up, pushing so

roughly that it hurt. She opened her eyes to see him staring down at her like a conqueror, his eyes wild, a look of anger on his face. With one last thrust he buried himself in her, and she felt his life spill into her belly. She prayed it would take hold. Why did he still look angry? He should be quite satisfied. What had she done wrong? Had he expected her to cry? To protest? She drew in her breath then when he grasped her by the hair and jerked her head up, still breathing hard. "Who is he?" he growled, baring his teeth like a wildcat.

Audra frowned. Now she wished she *hadn't* drunk so much wine, for she could not think straight at all. "Wh . . . who?" she asked. The room was beginning to spin.

He held her face between his big, strong hands. "You were no virgin!" he sneered, bringing his face close to hers.

Audra's eyes widened. How on earth did a man know that?

"I've had my share of the nigger girls, broke in plenty of young ones. It was never this easy, wife of mine! I heard no cry of pain, nor did I see any in your face. I slipped into you like you were a greased-up whore! Somebody's had you first, and I want to know who!"

"I . . . Richard, I've never . . ."

The slap came quick and stung like fire. Audra cried out and shivered, part of her frightened, another part of her furious. How *dare* he hit her! Audra Brennan had never been hit in her life! She met his eyes boldly then, refusing to show fear, but realizing she was no longer Audra Brennan. She was Audra Potter, and her husband had just scaled the union. There was no changing any of it now.

"What difference does it make?" she seethed, her left cheek burning. "It's *you* I married!"

He slapped her again on the same cheek. This time he brought stubborn tears to her eyes, and a deeper fear set in.

"I'd do worse, Audra Potter, but this is our *wedding* night, and I wouldn't want the public to see my lovely new wife bruised the next morning!" He grasped and pulled at her hair so tightly that it hurt. "Do you think every nigger girl I take to my bed is willing at first? I *make* them willing, and you'll by God find out how I do it! I didn't want it to be this way, Audra. I intended to treat you differently, because I really did love you. But you've *betrayed* me! While I was lost in your pretty little body you whispered a name! A *name*, Audra! *Lee!* You were so lost in fantasizing about another man you probably don't even realize you spoke his name! Who *is* he, Audra? I want no more lies!"

She winced with fierce pain, wondering if a person could pull someone's hair out by the fistful. "He's someone . . . I'll never see again. It was a whole year . . . ago, Richard, and just once. Just once. I was . . . young and lonely and homesick."

"*Home*sick!" He let go of her but remained straddled over her. "It happened while you were up in Connecticut?"

She broke into tears, feeling more homesick at this moment than she ever had while in Connecticut.

He leaned close, his face only inches away. "A *Yankee* man?"

"He was . . . good to me. He loved me. . . ." She dared to meet his eyes defiantly. "And I loved him. But we knew . . . it could never work. I came home, and I have never . . . seen or corresponded with him again."

His breathing quickened with rage. "Joey has mentioned a man named Lee Jeffreys to me a time or two, seems to be quite fond of the man. Is *he* the one?"

She put a hand to her stinging cheek. "Yes," she answered, holding his eyes. She thought about the night Lee had stood up to Cy Jordan and later had told her about how Jordan treated his wife, how furious it made him. "And Lee Jeffreys would *never* hit a woman, no matter what she did!"

Richard straightened, then jerked her to a sitting position. "Well, I am not Lee Jeffreys! I'm so sorry to disappoint you, my dear!" He squeezed her arms hard enough to cause pain. "And as long as you are going to fantasize about my being someone else, I suppose there is no need to worry about being gentle with my new wife, is there?"

What did he mean by that? "Richard, I learned to love you. I married you because it was the right thing to do, and I have every intention of being a faithful wife, giving you children, making you proud."

He let go of one arm and put a hand to her reddened

cheek. "Oh, you will do all of those things, my sweet. I will have the most beautiful woman in Louisiana on my arm in public, and everyone will envy and admire us. But behind closed doors, my dear, I will *not* be proud! I expected a virgin, and I got a slut! It would have been bad enough if it had been a southern man, but a *Yankee!*" He moved off her legs. "Turn over, Mrs. Potter."

Audra frowned, the effects of the wine beginning to wear off. "Why?"

She gasped when he suddenly punched her in the chest. The pain was so shocking that he managed to grab her and yank her over and press her facedown against the mattress before she realized what was happening. She felt his hard shaft probing near her bottom then.

"*Learned* to love me? I don't need your love that badly, Audra, dear. You will learn a lot more things tonight, and they won't have anything to do with love! I will teach you things your Lee Jeffreys probably never thought of showing you, and if I can't be your first man one way, I'll be your first in another! By morning there won't be one inch of your naked body I haven't known intimately or got myself into, and tomorrow we'll do it all over again! I'll keep you here for days, if I have to, until you entertain no more thoughts of Mr. Lee Jeffreys."

He shoved himself into her then. The pain was excruciating, and Audra felt a darkness closing in around her.

Home. At last she was going home. Never had Audra longed for Brennan Manor and her own room more than now, so much more than when she had come home from Connecticut; yet she had been only a few miles away.

Ten days of hell, that was what she had just lived through. She had never dreamed that Richard Potter could be capable of such evil. She felt like a rag doll that had been thrown about, dragged around, kicked across the room. And like a rag doll, she felt like a limp piece of material, with no spirit, no soul, no heart. She struggled to think of a way to make Richard treat her with some little bit of respect, and she decided her only hope was to get pregnant. Maybe that would stop the abuse. He wanted a child more than anything else in the world. She would at least earn his respect as the mother of his son.

She knew now it would not be his first child. It would simply be his first *white* child. His first wife had never been able to give him children, but there were plenty of mulatto children running around Cypress Hollow, and Richard had made sure she knew who had fathered most of them. He had even dared to make her take another bedroom one night so that he could take a new Negro girl to his bed. She had been vaguely aware that slave owners sometimes lay with Negro women, but she had never given it much thought, for such things didn't go on at Brennan Manor. She had supposed that on some plantations it was just part of what was expected of a female slave. All her life she had given no thought to what the woman might think of it, that she might hate it. Now that she knew the uglier side of man, knew what it was like to have to submit because of pain, she couldn't help feeling sorry for them. The rumors had always been that Negro women were just naturally loose and eager. *Don't you know that mating is all the Negro women think about?* Eleanor had asked her once.

Audra was beginning to doubt that. Lena and Toosie certainly were not that way, and after ten days with Richard, she could not help feeling sorry for the plight of the Negro women, even sorrier for the near-children Richard took to his bed. They couldn't possibly be giving themselves to him willingly, and now she knew some of the ways he had of making them submit. She wondered where her own fierce pride had gone. It was as though Richard had squeezed it right out of her blood. She had never thought of what she had done with Lee as being quite so sinful and unforgivable as Richard had made it seem, and the things Richard had done to her had only added to her shame.

She never thought she would be grateful for the news that Abraham Lincoln had been chosen the Republican candidate for President. It meant she could be rid of Richard for a while. A messenger had brought the word yesterday, along with notification of a meeting of Louisiana's most powerful to be held in New Orleans in three days. Richard was being called to the meeting. Her father would also want to go, if he was up to it physically. Wealthy southern men all over the South would be getting together, planning their strategy, deciding where to hold another Democratic convention and how to nominate a proslavery man like Jefferson Davis, rather than the party's popular choice, Stephen Douglas.

Politics mattered little to her now, except as a means to be apart from Richard and have some peace. He was taking her home to stay at Brennan Manor while he was gone, and where they would live, as Richard had promised her father. Maybe after he had been away from her for a few days and had time to cool down, Richard would be kinder to her when he returned. And maybe at Brennan Manor, things would be different. He certainly couldn't beat her with her father around, nor could he go dragging little Negro girls into his bedroom.

Miss Geresy had certainly never prepared her for anything like this. Should she admit to her father how Richard treated her? The man probably thought she was the happiest woman in the world by now. Because of his delicate health, she was afraid to tell him the truth, afraid he would die of a heart attack. He would probably blame himself for urging her to marry Richard, and if Joey found out, he would do the same.

No. She would suffer this alone, find a way to bring some respect to her marriage and to keep Richard from abusing her. She wasn't sure how yet, and for the moment, getting pregnant was the only thing she could think of, so she submitted to Richard's lovemaking, if that was what it could be called. She lay there without objection, doing things that made her want to be sick. She did it all quietly and submissively, to avoid pain, and hoping, at least the times when they had "normal" intercourse, that his seed would take hold in her womb. She could only pray that the other things he did to her would not cause her to lose a baby if she did indeed become pregnant.

At last they reached the house. Richard had hardly brought their horse-drawn carriage to a full stop before she jumped out of it and ran up to hug Joey, who was the first to come out and greet her. He embraced her tightly, tears in his eyes at missing her. No, she must never tell Joey. It would break his heart to think he might be the cause of her misery. Next came Father, looking a little stronger, more color to his face. Another embrace. Her marriage had made him so happy. She could not tell her father. And here were Lena and Toosie. She hardly noticed Toosie's look of surprise when she hugged the woman like a long-lost friend. Lena would have expected a quick embrace, but not the clinging hug Audra gave her after finally letting go of Toosie.

She drew away, and Lena looked her over. "It's good to have you home, Miss Audra." *What has happened to you?* she wanted to ask. How could the girl have lost so much weight in just ten days? Why was there a weary, haunted look behind her usually bright eyes? This was not the way a blushing bride looked or behaved. She seemed ecstatic over being home, as though glad that for the next few days she would be away from her husband. And was that a faint bruise she detected beneath Audra's unusually heavy coat of powder and rouge?

She glanced at Richard, who was approaching the house then. She did not miss the way he looked at Audra, with a hint of disgust, not the look of a loving husband. He ordered two house servants to collect Audra's baggage, then turned to Joseph.

"We can leave yet today, if you like," he said to the man.

Joseph looked surprised. "Well, of course, if that's how you want it. I thought perhaps you would want another day or two with Audra first."

Richard looked at Audra and smiled, but Lena saw through the grin, sensed a kind of evil behind it. "Your darling daughter understands the importance of these things," he drawled. "Don't you, dear?"

Audra put on a smile of her own. "Yes." She looked at her father. "I think you *should* leave today, Father. With Abraham Lincoln running for President, we cannot gather our forces for the Democratic ticket any too soon. Everyone respects you and Richard." She glanced at her husband, and

Lena had a feeling Audra did not respect Richard Potter one tiny bit. "They will listen to you," she continued. She kept her eyes on Richard. "I will be fine while Richard is gone, as long as I can be here at home; but I will dearly miss him."

The pain that had eaten at Audra's stomach for days now grew worse at the lie. How long could she put on this act and save her own honor as well as her father's and Joey's? Richard stepped closer, bending down to kiss her bruised cheek.

"And I shall miss you, my sweet," he answered. "I look forward to coming home to my beautiful wife. When things calm down and we get a proslavery man into the White House, we will take that trip to Europe I promised you. And while I am gone, I would like you to plan a cotillion to be held right here at Brennan Manor. It will be another party to show off the newlyweds. You may even invite some of your favorite Negroes to come and watch from the veranda. Ask everyone from miles around."

How dare you mock me so! she thought. He knew she would have to play the happy, satisfied wife and how difficult it would be for her. And Europe! She could not think of a worse nightmare than to have to spend weeks alone with him on the ocean and in strange countries, away from Joey, away from her father and Brennan Manor. Perhaps she would be pregnant by then, and they would be unable to go.

The men went inside, followed by the Negroes who carried Audra's baggage. Joey followed them, wanting to hear the talk about politics, wishing his father would ask him to come along to New Orleans. He knew he would not be invited. Joseph Brennan would be too embarrassed to have the others hear the way his son stuttered. It felt good to have Audra back. Without her, he lived in a world of his own, and it was lonely there.

Audra remained outside on the veranda, glorying in just being here. She asked Toosie to draw her a bath. It would be wonderful to soak in a tub alone, without Richard being there to watch her every move, to insist on bathing her himself. She had not had a moment alone, her only privacy coming when she had to use the chamber pot. He had degraded her in every way possible, and she realized that she would have to be sure Toosie stayed away when she bathed so that the woman did not see the bruises on her body, bruises well placed by a man who knew how to hurt a woman without it showing. She had no doubt he had learned his tactics when raping the Negro girls he dragged to his bed. She wondered if he had one ounce of feeling for all the little mulatto babies he had fathered. The horror of the things he did was magnified by the worry that he might give her some kind of terrible disease. Eleanor had told her once that sometimes men who slept with lots of women got hideous diseases that killed both the man and woman, and usually they went crazy before their death.

Maybe Richard was already going mad. Maybe that was why he behaved the way he did. Would she be next? She shivered and looked at Lena. "It's good to be home, Lena. How has Father been?"

Lena's eyes drilled into her knowingly. "You've never been a good liar, Audra Brennan Potter," the woman told her. "Something is wrong. What has that man done to you?"

Audra looked away, wishing Lena didn't know her so well. "He is my husband. What's done is done."

"And your father is powerful enough to *un*do it, if necessary. He puts you above all things, Audra. If that man is mistreating you, he should know."

Audra shook her head. "Not in this case. It would mean he would have to know the whole truth, and that would kill him."

Lena frowned. "And what *is* the whole truth, child?"

Audra turned to meet her eyes. "I am far from a child, Lena. Richard has seen to that." Her eyes teared. "Lena, it isn't your business to go prying into the private lives of those who own you." *Help me, Lena!* How could she tell the woman the atrocious things Richard had done, and how could she explain the reasons why? She had slept with a Yankee man in Connecticut. She had not thought it so wrong, until now. Richard had shown her what a whore she truly was. Her father must never know. Joey must never know. Not even the Negro help should know that she had been so shameless with Loo Jeffreys, or know the hideous, filthy things Richard had done to her.

"Don't talk to me like I'm a common nigger," Lena told her, holding her chin proudly. "You know better, Miss Audra. You know that I love you like my own, and when I show concern for you, it is only because I care and want to help."

Audra closed her eyes. "If you care, then don't ask any more questions. And please don't say anything to Father." She met Lena's dark, knowing gaze. "I mean it, Lena. If you do love me, leave it be. If you tell Father and he raises a fuss, it will only make things worse for me. I am Richard's wife, and in the eyes of the law and the Church, that cannot be changed. Just help me make my situation as bearable as possible and don't do something to stir up Richard's anger and cause him to take me away from Brennan Manor. This is the only place where I am safe, Lena. Do you understand?"

Lena frowned with concern and sympathy. "I understand." She reached out and touched Audra's hair. "Come upstairs, child. Toosie will have your bath ready."

Audra followed her inside, not bothering to go into the parlor to say good-bye to Richard. She hurried up the wide staircase to her room, thinking how she even looked forward to seeing her dolls again. Tonight she would sleep with them instead of Richard Potter, and it would be the most blessed, peaceful sleep she had had since her wedding night. She would hold her dolls close and pretend she was a little girl again, blissfully ignorant of what it meant to be a woman. How strange that with one man it could be so beautiful and gloriously satisfying, while with another it could be a nightmare.

13

Lee halted the buckskin gelding he had rented from a livery in Baton Rouge. He had paid twice the normal rate for the animal, and he suspected the livery owner had deliberately overcharged him just because he didn't have a Louisiana accent. "What's a damn Yankee like you doin' down here?" the man had asked. He had carried on about how Lee was probably a "Lincoln man," and how "that goddamn Abraham Lincoln is going to destroy this whole country."

Lee could see there was no sense arguing with the man, either about politics or the cost of his horse. He had simply paid the still-grumbling livery owner and left, but he could understand better how Audra must have felt when she was in Connecticut. He almost felt as though he had left the United States and was in a foreign country.

So far everything he had seen and heard told him to turn around and go back home before he set eyes on Audra again, but here he was, at the iron gate of Brennan Manor and wondering how he had gotten this far. The gate stood open, inviting him to enter. His horse whinnied and shook his black mane, as though to warn him not to go any farther, and Lee took a handkerchief from his pocket and pressed it to his brow to catch a trickle of perspiration. He remembered his remark to Audra last summer about how much more pleasant the summers in Connecticut were than in the South. How right he had been. Maybe for those brought up here, this steamy heat didn't bother them; but right now he would dearly love to be lying on the beach at Maple Shadows, diving naked into Long Island Sound, or just enjoying the feel of a cool breeze off the water.

There was no cool breeze here, no wide, blue waters, and there were no sea gulls. There was, however, an estate so beautiful that it was like looking at a dream world. The house loomed at the end of a bricked drive that appeared to be a good quarter of a mile long, and heavy, humid air made the scene look like a misty mirage. A thick border of flowers of hundreds of species graced either side of the drive, a spectacular show of colors. Throughout the grounds brilliant deep pink and red azalea bushes bloomed, as well as white dogwood, and here and there Negro men and women tended the grounds, trimming, pruning, planting. The strong scent of jasmine and lilies engulfed him, so pleasant that it actually had a soothing affect on him.

He headed the horse up the driveway toward the house, and he was shaded by the great, gnarly branches of huge oak trees that draped themselves over the blooms of thousands of flowers and protected anyone beneath them from the afternoon sun. The trees, fat and old, led the way to the house, standing like guards over all those who might enter, and Spanish moss decorated their branches like green lace. There was no sound, other than the off-and-on singing of cicadas. In the heavy afternoon heat, even the birds were quiet, and the Negroes who were working in the lawn went about their chores quietly. A few glanced at him, but they immediately returned to their work.

Life was definitely different here. He had noticed that already, from watching people on the steamboat that had brought him from Chicago; even more apparent when he reached Baton Rouge. Compared to New York, it seemed everyone here moved more slowly, even talked more slowly. Some had such strong accents that he had to concentrate to understand what they were saying. He had yet to see someone who seemed to be in a hurry, and he supposed that people who lived in such heat learned to do everything slowly just to keep from passing out; then again, people never had to hurry or exert themselves, anyway, because they had their Negroes to do everything for them.

Negroes everywhere. He had never seen such a concentration of black people, and all of them had something to do. They were ordered around like trained dogs, and his irritation at what he had seen was giving him renewed doubts about coming here, yet his heart raced faster with a mixture of dread and hope and excitement as he drew closer to the house.

He had taken a train from New York to Chicago, reaching the Republican Convention in time to see Abraham Lincoln nominated for President. He had intended to skip the convention, but decided he could get to Louisiana just as fast by land as by sea, and the quickest way was by rail to Chicago and on to St. Louis, then take a steamboat down the Mississippi to Baton Rouge. He figured as long as he was going through Chicago, he would attend the convention, and as soon as Lincoln was nominated, he had got on the train to St. Louis. At last he was in Audra's territory, and already he could feel her presence. He had found a hotel in Baton Rouge, and the hotel manager told him how to find Brennan Manor.

"Anybody in town can tell you how to get there," the man had said. "That and Cypress Hollow north of it are the biggest plantations in Louisiana. You probably passed right by both of them if you came here by riverboat."

The remark had brought back the very vivid pictures of what Lee had seen from the deck as his boat had made its way lazily down the river, past huge fields of cotton. He had seen Negroes out in those fields, hoeing in the hot, merciless sun. The hotel manager had given him a look of distrust and disapproval. "Yankee man, aren't you?" he had asked, as though Lee had some kind of disease. After the tirade from the livery owner, Lee almost lost his temper, but he had managed to stay calm. He simply answered that he was from New York, being careful not to mention Audra. Yankees were about as welcome here as the plague, and if none of this worked out, he was sure she didn't need the whole town of Baton Rouge talking about how a Yankee man had come calling on her.

"I have business with Mr. Brennan," he had lied. "My father owns a clothing factory. We supply a wholesaler in New Orleans, and I just came from there. We need more raw material, namely cotton, and a gentleman in New Orleans told me Mr. Brennan is the man to talk to."

"Well, I'm surprised you didn't run into him down there. Him and some others are down there right now— some big political doin's. Could be they're on their way home by now. I just hope all this trouble with you Yankees don't ruin the cotton business. Mr. Brennan and other big cotton growers in the South are lookin' at markets overseas, you know, seein' as how some of you Yankee industrialists up North are threatenin' to boycott us if we keep talkin' about secedin' from the Union."

Again Lee avoided a political debate, which was beginning to be an almost impossible effort wherever he went, North or South. He was just glad to know he might catch Audra alone before having to confront her father. He had obtained directions to Brennan Manor, which was nearly a day's ride north of Baton Rouge, and he had brought a leather bag along with a change of clothes in case he could not get back to his hotel before it was too dark. He was glad he had thought of it. It was already late afternoon. He would never make it back tonight, but from the looks of the house ahead of him, there were plenty of spare bedrooms, but if Joseph Brennan was home, he would probably kick him out, and he'd be sleeping in slave quarters.

He studied the magnificent Brennan home as the horse carried him closer. Now he knew what Audra had meant when she said that Maple Shadows was "almost" as pretty as Brennan Manor. The house was white, three stories high, with huge, fluted marble pillars supporting a wide veranda and second- and third-floor balconies that encircled all four sides. The balconies and veranda were trimmed with a black wrought-iron railing, and all the windows were graced with black shutters. He noticed a Negro man washing the third-floor windows, and a Negro woman sweeping the veranda.

It was obvious that the house and grounds were beautiful and immaculate only because Negro slaves kept it that way. He wondered if Joseph Brennan would have people running around doing so much if he had to pay them all by the hour. He spotted a Negro woman coming out of the front door then. She carried a drink, and he watched her hand it to someone who sat at a table on the wide veranda. Was it Audra? He couldn't see her clearly enough yet.

Would this visit hurt both of them all over again? If he could just see her once more, look into those green eyes, and see that there was no longer anything there for him, he could start sleeping better at night, maybe quit drinking so much. Besides, he had written Audra that letter, fool that he was, and now he had to go through with this. He had said he was coming, so Audra and her father should not be totally surprised.

He felt as though he were riding into a lion's den, a Yankee man come to talk to one of the most powerful plantation owners in Louisiana, expecting to take the man's daughter away from him, expecting to keep her from marrying a man even more powerful than Joseph Brennan! Hell, they could hang him, and no one would ever know the difference. He had done his homework, and he knew that plantations like Brennan Manor were a world unto themselves, like little cities removed from reality, where they set their own laws, the owners ruling like kings. Whatever Joseph Brennan or Richard Potter wanted to do to him, they could probably do it and get away with it. It was men like that who were making trouble for the whole Union, proud, stubborn, southern men who didn't like anyone else telling them what to do, who were determined to set their own laws and to hell with the rest of the world, including the Federal government. He shook his head, realizing he was already arguing with the man, and he hadn't even met him yet!

Well, he was here now, and he might as well get this over with. When he saw Audra, he would know what he wanted to do; but, then, it was quite possible that if he never left this place, it would not be by choice; it would be because Joseph Brennan would make sure he was buried here!

He could see the person sitting at the table more clearly now. It was a woman, and she had auburn hair. . . .

Audra took a drink of lemonade, keeping an eye on the approaching rider. He didn't look like anyone she had seen from Cypress Hollow or the neighboring farms, and with her father and Richard both gone, she couldn't imagine what man would come visiting alone, anyway. He was apparently a stranger, and she started to call out to Lena to get the overseer or one of the Negro men; but before she could say a word, the man rode closer, and her voice caught in her throat. She quickly set down the glass, staring in disbelief. "My God," she whispered.

She felt suddenly dizzy, and she clung to the table as she slowly rose. A young Negro girl came out onto the veranda with a large feathered fan to cool her with, but Audra quickly sent her away with a sharp command. The girl scurried off, and Audra stood transfixed, staring at the intruder.

Lee? What in God's name was he doing here? How could this be? She saw a look of recognition in his own eyes as he guided his horse to a hitching post and dismounted, tying the animal before walking to the steps of the veranda. Never had he looked handsomer! Because of the hot weather, he wore no jacket, vest, or tie. His shirt was unbuttoned partway, and the sight of dark hair on his chest stirred memories better left resting. His black cotton pants fit him snugly, and he wore shiny black riding boots that came to his knees. He had removed his hat when he dismounted, and his dark hair looked damp from the heat.

Was this real? Had Lee Jeffreys really come to Brennan Manor? Why? And why had he waited until now, when she could not touch him; when she could not allow buried feelings to be resurrected? Didn't he know she was married by now? She watched his eyes, those blue, blue eyes she had so dearly loved once, had missed all these months. In return, those eyes studied her intently, and she saw there something she did not want to see—love. She had imagined that if she ever saw him again, everything would be different. The love and passion would be gone, and there would be only a casual friendship left behind. How could it suddenly seem that absolutely no time had passed at all since she saw him last? And after what she had been through with Richard, how could she hold that memory of being with Lee with such reverence and joy? Richard had made it all so ugly, yet here stood a man who made her forget the ugliness by the mere act of standing here in front of her.

"Hello, Audra," he spoke up, hesitating before coming a little closer.

In a few brief seconds Audra went from shock, to memories of love, to feelings of hate. Not now! He should not have come now! It was too cruel of him. She had managed to bury the memory, and it had to stay buried forever.

"Lee." She swallowed, still keeping her hand on the table for balance. "What . . . what are you doing here?"

Lee studied her eyes, saw something there he didn't like. Yes, she was angry, and God knew she had good reason to be. He had asked her to forget him, and now here he was; but there was something more there than anger and surprise. He saw tragedy behind those green eyes that had haunted him for a year. Had her father died? She looked ill, much too thin. "I . . . I needed to see you once more," he spoke up, feeling like more of a fool with each passing second. "I thought both of us needed to see each other once more . . . to be sure. I went to Maple Shadows not long ago, and I found something that seemed like some kind of sign I should come." He closed his eyes and sighed, closing his hands into fists from nervousness.

You're even more beautiful than I remembered, he wanted to tell her. But maybe he had no business. What had he done, coming here like this? And what had he walked into? She stood there as beautiful as ever, but her white linen dress hung on her loosely, and her hair was drawn into a plain bun. There were circles under her eyes, and the look in them was certainly not the look of the innocent girl he had fallen in love with last summer. Something was very different, and it was more than the fact that he had taken her to his bed all those months ago. He felt like an ass at the shock in her eyes, combined with something akin to a terrible remorse. "Audra, didn't you get my letter?"

She put a hand to her throat. "Letter?"

Lee frowned, coming even closer. "Audra, I wrote your brother twice. Didn't he tell you? And I sent *you* a letter, too, last January. I wanted to be sure you got it in plenty of time to give it some thought. When I didn't hear anything back, I wrote again. I got a little angry that you didn't bother to write back, and there are things we need to talk about, so I—"

"We never got any letters," she said, still staring at him as though he were a ghost. "Neither Joey nor I."

"But I—" No letters? Had her father kept them from her and Joey? A fierce anger began to brew deep in his soul. He could understand that perhaps the man wouldn't want Audra to see a letter from him, but his letters to Joey had been perfectly harmless, and he had felt it was so important for the boy to know he'd been thinking of him. "Audra, I *did* write. I wanted you to know that I had been rethinking some of the things that stood in our way. I had much more to tell, but I was afraid your father would get the wrong idea, so I left out the important things. I figured we could talk about them when I got here and had a chance to have a talk with your father. I just believed we needed to see each other once more, now that some time has passed."

She let out a little groan and turned away. Lee watched her grasp her stomach as though in pain.

"Audra, I'm sorry to shock you like this. I wrote you first so you wouldn't be so surprised, so you'd have time to think about things yourself before seeing me again. I don't understand why you never saw the letter."

Oh, how she needed him, but it was too late. Too late! The irony of his visit almost sickened her. "I never saw any letter," she said quietly. "And I thought I would never see *you* again." Her head was spinning. Was it just the heat, or was it the fact that her beautiful Lee was standing right there on her veranda, looking wonderful? She should turn and tell him to get off her property, scream at him for doing this to her; but if he had written first, this was not all his fault. If she had known, she would have written back and told him never to come; or would she? Maybe she would have begged him to hurry. Maybe she would have had the courage not to marry Richard, even though it would have broken her father's heart. Thank God neither Richard nor her father was here. There was time to send him on his way before either of them knew he had come.

Lee let out a sigh of disgust with himself. "It's obvious someone kept the letters from you. Audra, did you really think I would forget you that easily? That I had just dismissed you from my heart and never even bothered to write to Joey at least and see how you both were doing?"

She swallowed, walking even farther away to grasp the wrought-iron railing. "Yes," she answered. "You said once it was best we forget each other, Lee, and after all these months . . ." She squeezed her eyes shut. "You should not have come. You have no idea—"

"Audra—"

"Lee, just go home."

"What has happened, Audra?"

The front screen door opened, and Lee turned to see an older but exotic-looking Negro woman step out. Just as with Toosie, he was struck by this woman's unusually beautiful features. She wore a plain brown dress and an apron, and her hair was knotted on top of her head; but in spite of her unadorned appearance, she had an elegance about her. He nodded to her, feeling more embarrassed and confused with each passing second. "Hello, ma'am. My name is Lee Jeffreys. I've come here to visit Miss Brennan." He looked around. "Is Joseph Brennan here? I would like to speak to him."

Lena studied the man, almost gaping at him, for he was surely the handsomest white man she had ever set eyes on. So this was Lee Jeffreys! No wonder Audra had fallen in love with him. No one had told her so, but it had been easy to figure out; and now that she saw the look of devastation on Audra's face, she knew she was right in her thinking. She

moved her eyes from Lee to Audra and back to Lee. The
moment was terribly awkward. She wasn't sure what Audra
wanted her to say, or what had been said so far between the
two of them. What on earth was this man doing here? He
could not have picked a worse time.

"Lena," Audra finally spoke up. "Did you ever see any
letters from Mr. Jeffreys to me or Joey?"

Lena shook her head, already getting the picture. Lee
Jeffreys must have written to tell Audra he was coming, but
Audra, by the look on her face, had never seen the letters.
Had Joseph intercepted them? It would be just like him to
do that, but it was not her place to suggest that was what
had happened. "No, ma'am."

Before any of them could say another word, Joey came
bounding through the door. "Lee!" He put out his hand. "I
d-don't believe it! You came to see us!"

Lee brightened and took his hand and shook it hard.
This was the first warm greeting he had received since arriving in Louisiana. In the next moment he and Joey were
embracing and laughing. "You've grown, Joey! By God, if
you don't look like a full-fledged man!" Lee pulled away and
looked him over. "I thought maybe you'd write. Hell, I
wrote you twice!"

"You d-did?" Joey sobered, glancing at Audra.

"I told him we never received the letters," Audra said.

Joey turned to Lee. "Th-that's right, Lee. I never g-got
any letters." He was too embarrassed to tell Lee that his father had ordered him never to write him. "I f-figured you
got b-busy and maybe forgot all about me. I've b-been busy
with more schooling, and Father and Richard have b-been
letting me help run things some. I just never g-got around
to writing. I'm sorry, Lee."

"That's all right. I'm glad you're being given a chance
to learn to run the place." *Richard? Richard Potter?* So the
man was still a part of the picture. Audra was probably already formally engaged and planning a wedding. What the
hell was he here for after all? He would have to fake it now,
pretend he had just come to see Joey. He'd stay a couple of
days and get the hell out of here.

"Joey has talked about you often, Mr. Jeffreys," Lena

said then, stepping closer. "I feel as though I know you. Even my daughter, Toosie, talked about you. How kind of you to come visiting. Master Brennan is not here." *How sad,* she thought, *that Audra could not have been with this fine man, Yankee or not.* Audra had not told her anything about what had gone wrong between her and her husband, but the sight of the bruises she had seen on Audra's body left no explanation necessary. For some reason Richard Potter had wanted to break her spirit, and he had done a good job of it. Did it have something to do with this Yankee man? She had always suspected Richard could be cruel when he wanted to be, and the thought of his hurting Audra broke her heart. "He has gone to New Orleans with Master Potter," she continued aloud. "But since it is getting late, and you look very hot and tired, perhaps you would like to sit down and have some lemonade, then take supper with us. I am sure that Miss Audra, who is in charge while her father and her husband are away, will invite you to take a spare room for the night. Are you are staying in Baton Rouge?"

Husband? Her husband? The woman had emphasized the word, as though to make sure he knew Audra was married now. Lee felt as though the blood were draining from his head. "I . . . yes."

"Well, it's much too late in the day to think about going all the way back yet tonight. You sit down and have a nice visit." She put her hands on Joey's shoulders. "Joey, you can talk with Mr. Jeffreys all you want at the supper table. I believe he might want a few words alone with your sister."

"But—" Joey looked from Lee to Audra, noticed the stricken looks on their faces. They were watching each other as though both had just lost someone dear to them. He realized then the real reason Lee must have come. It was too bad he had not come sooner. Audra had not seemed very happy since coming home from her honeymoon at Cypress Hollow. He had wanted to ask her about it, but was too embarrassed to broach the subject.

"Come into the house, Joey," Lena urged. She looked back at Lee, but he was still staring at Audra. "I'll have more lemonade brought out," she said.

The woman hurried Joey inside, and Lee didn't even answer her. A sick feeling engulfed him. He was too late! "I'm sorry, Audra. You told me you wouldn't be marrying Richard Potter until at least August." Rage began to move through his blood. "Your father must have deliberately kept my letter from you so you wouldn't know I was coming."

"Father? He wouldn't do such a thing."

"Wouldn't he?" God, she looked so pale. How had her father and this Richard Potter talked her into marrying sooner?

Audra put a hand to her face, trying to weigh all that had been said in the last few minutes. "Your letters must never have reached us," she insisted.

Lee sighed in resignation. What difference did any of it make now that she was married, except that the thought of her already having been in another man's bed tore at his gut like a razor. How could it bother him this much? After all, he knew when he came here that it would probably all be for nothing. He just hadn't expected to feel this way when he saw her again. Maybe if she looked radiantly happy, it wouldn't be so bad, but there was a haunting sorrow in those green eyes that had not been there when she left Maple Shadows.

"What the hell is going on here?" he asked. "You look terrible. If you decided to marry Richard Potter, you must have loved him, at least a little. You look more like you *lost* a husband than just married one!"

Audra blinked, turned away. She had to think. *It's your fault,* she wanted to tell him. *Richard abuses me because I slept with you. Because of you I'm a soiled woman, filth!* Oh, but it had seemed so beautiful and right at the time. And part of her knew it had not been a terrible, sinful thing. The worst part was that seeing him again brought back all the feelings she had so cleverly buried. Dear God, she still loved him! After what Richard had done to her, she never thought she could have these feelings for any man again, not even Lee.

"I . . . I've been ill, that's all," she answered. She breathed deeply for control, deciding she had better look like the blushing bride. Lee Jeffreys had a temper. If he thought anything was terribly wrong, whether her fault or his or Richard's or her father's, he would try to do something about it. That was the nature of the man, and he was a Yankee man, a Union man, an abolitionist; he was in territory belonging to some of the most devout proslavery people in Louisiana. Besides that, Richard knew Lee was the man she had slept with. If Richard caught him here . . . She shuddered. A confrontation would be a disaster, particularly for Lee, who had unknowingly walked into a great deal of trouble, unless she could make him leave before Richard returned. He had been gone over a week already. He could come back any day.

She faced Lee, putting on an air of confidence. "What's done is done, and I am quite happy," she told him. "I'm sorry, Lee, about not getting the letter, but it wouldn't have made so much difference. I was promised to Richard for a long time, and once I got home, I knew this was where I belong. I also knew you would never be happy here. My marriage has made Father terribly happy, and Richard has helped Joey a great deal and is kind to him." She walked back to her chair and nodded toward another. "Sit down, Lee. It is so hot, isn't it? I remember your commenting to me last summer about how much more pleasant the summers were in Connecticut. I suppose you were right after all, but then the heat does not bother me so much as it probably bothers you."

Lee just kept staring at her as she took her own chair. She was making idle conversation now. My God, did she really think she was fooling him? His letter wouldn't have made any difference? He didn't believe that for one minute. And look at her! What on earth was wrong with her marriage?

He decided that for the time being he would let her carry on and put on a good show. She reached out her hand to show him her sparkling ring. "We were married May thirteenth. Oh, it was a grand wedding! We have clippings from the newspaper about it. I'll show them to you. In fact, Richard and I are holding a cotillion right here at Brennan Manor when he returns. The dance will be to celebrate our marriage with some of the local people. We were married in

Baton Rouge. Once the elections are over and a pro-slavery man is in the White House, Richard and I are going to Europe for a delayed honeymoon."

Lee came closer and took a chair, glancing at the ring. "Nice," he commented. "What are Richard and your father doing in New Orleans?"

She withdrew her hand before he could take hold of it. She would be fine as long as he did not touch her in any way. Oh, but she needed desperately to be held, protected! Lee would do it if she asked him, but he was the last person who should know about the hell she had been living in.

"There is a meeting there of the most powerful men of Louisiana," she said. "They are deciding what to do about getting a pro-slavery man elected to the Democratic party. The first convention was a failure, you know. No one could agree on anything. There will be another soon, this time in Baltimore. Father and Richard won't be able to go, but they want to do what they can beforehand to get the proper delegate on the ticket."

"It won't matter," he answered. "Abraham Lincoln is going to win."

"Never! The South will unite and keep him out of the White House."

What difference does it make right now? Lee thought. *Right now I am looking at one of the unhappiest women I have ever seen.*

Lena brought more lemonade and poured a glass for Lee. Joey returned and peppered him with questions. Lee mentioned he had been to the Republican convention, and both Joey and Audra wanted to know what it was like, what Chicago was like. Before long they were all talking like the old friends they had been back in Connecticut, and Lee thought Joey seemed a little happier. Maybe this Richard Potter was at least good to the boy. Maybe he treated Joey better than he treated his own wife.

He wished there was time to go back to Baton Rouge yet tonight and get the hell out of here. God, he still wanted her! Did he really have any business prying into her marriage? May thirteenth. Hell, that was only seventeen days ago. Something was very, very wrong here. She was carry-

ing on as though she were a nervous wreck. And thin—she
was so thin. Even if she did not love her new husband with
any great passion, if he was kind to her, gentle with her, she
should be at least reasonably happy. Maybe she *had* been
ill. Maybe she was pregnant already. He hated to think it
could be something worse.

Right now he felt like punching Bennett James right in
the mouth for urging him to come here. Never had he felt
so stupid and out of place. Hell, there were Negroes all
over the place, one out cutting the lawn with a scythe, another tending the flowers. Audra ordered another to take
care of Lee's horse and bring in his leather bag. A young
Negro girl came out to fan both of them, and he heard Lena
order someone inside to get started with supper.

"Why don't you have Joey show you around Brennan
Manor?" Audra was saying. "I would like to freshen up. I
just don't know what has been wrong. After our beautiful
wedding and our first several days of marriage, I became
quite ill and was unable to eat, as you can probably tell. My
clothes are beginning to hang on me in the most terrible
way. If I don't gain back some weight, I'll have to have Henrietta take in all my clothes. She will raise a terrible fuss
then! Oh, Lee, you must meet Henrietta. She is the fattest
person in the entire world!" She laughed then, and for a
brief second Lee thought the laughter was going to turn to
tears. Her mouth started to curve down slightly, and her
eyes watered.

She suddenly got up and walked away from him, taking
several deep breaths before facing her brother. "Joey, go and
put some shoes on. I want you to take Lee for a walk in the
gardens out back, and show him the house, too." Lee could
see real tears in her eyes, in spite of her smile. Joey ran inside, and she folded her arms in a show of pride and authority. "Of course, it would be impossible to show you the
entire plantation," she said.

In Lee's estimation she was stretching out her words
more than normal, as though to emphasize her southern accent so he would be properly impressed with their differences. "It would take a couple of days to see it all, and, of
course, I suppose you must leave tomorrow."

Was that a hint that he had *better* leave tomorrow? "I probably will," he told her.

She gave him a look that told him she was practically begging him to go. "Well, as I said, it would take days to see all of Brennan Manor *and* Cypress Hollow; and now I am in charge of both when Richard is gone. Why, I am the richest woman in Louisiana now, you know. You should have seen the crowd of spectators that turned out in Baton Rouge just to watch our wedding coach go from the church to my Aunt Janine's house. It was a white carriage pulled by white horses, quite romantic. Richard wanted everything to be perfect. And he agreed that I can live right here at Brennan Manor most of the time, so I can be close to Joey."

She walked closer to where Lee was still sitting, and her smile faded. "I truly am sorry, Lee," she drawled, "about not getting the letter. You must be so embarrassed, but you shouldn't be. I will always care deeply for you. You know that. And I dearly respect your coming here. If I had known, I would have answered the letter and told you not to come. We both know Richard is by far the best man for someone like me. I knew that as soon as I got home again. It was just like you said—I had to come home to know what I really wanted."

Lee did not remove his eyes from hers as he rose. "And you're the most miserable *liar* I've ever met," he told her bluntly, "as well as the most miserable-*looking* new bride! There is something wrong here, Audra, and I'm not leaving until I know what it is. I'm probably the cause of it, but maybe I can fix it before I go." He watched her eyes widen with something close to terror.

"No! You must leave in the morning, Lee, and never come back! I will talk to Joey and the house servants and make sure they never tell my father or my husband that you were here."

Lee felt the rage returning. "*Why*, Audra?"

Again a mask came over her face. "Because you're a *Yankee*. Why else? Right now Father and Richard would be outraged to know a Yankee man came visiting!"

"That isn't the reason, and you know it! I'll go make the rounds with Joey. I'll take supper with you tonight, and *maybe* I'll leave in the morning, because I can see by your eyes that you're terrified that I won't—and not because of what might happen to me. It's because of what might happen to *you*, isn't it! What have I walked into, Audra? What is going on?"

She stiffened. "It is none of your business anymore, is it? I am a married woman now, and that is that! You are the one who said it must be this way, and you should never have come here. Please just leave in the morning. We ended this once. You should never have started it again."

"It was never really finished. If you had gotten my letters, it might all be different."

"My God, Lee!" She raised her chin authoritatively. "It would have been the *same*. Look around you. You don't belong here. You might have tried hard, but it never would have worked. Why couldn't you have left it the way it was?"

He angrily reached into his pants pocket and pulled out some papers, slamming them down on the table. "Because of this! I found it at Maple Shadows, and I thought maybe it was a sign that I should try again, because no matter what our differences, I still love you, Audra Brennan! And you, by God, still love *me*!"

Audra stared dumbfounded at the familiar-looking stationery. With a shaking hand she picked up the sheets of paper, studied them a moment.

> *Lee, my love, Just as the sun shines, And the ocean wind blows wet and wild . . .*

"Dear God," she whispered. "I had forgotten that I left this there." No, no! She must not cry! "I . . . I was like a child when I wrote this, Lee. It was before we ever—" She felt the heat coming into her face, and it had nothing to do with the weather. "You should have burned it," she said, one tear finally slipping down her cheek.

Lee took the song from her and folded it, shoving it back into his pants pocket. "Never," he answered. "Apparently it is all I will have left of you." He ran a hand through his hair, turning away a moment to gather his thoughts. "It's no one's fault but my own. I failed you, Audra. I'm sorry."

"We failed each other . . . and ourselves, but we both know what had to be. This home, Joey, my father, they are all still most important to me."

"And that's why you married Richard Potter, to protect Brennan Manor and Joey." He turned to face her again. "Sometimes the things we hold dear are not always worth the price we pay for them, and if I had come sooner, I might have been able to find another way to convince you of that."

Oh, if only she could allow herself to let him hold her, just for a little while. How safe she would feel in those strong arms! "Promise me you will leave in the morning."

He reached out and brushed at the tear. "No promises, Audra. If you think I'm afraid of your father or Richard Potter, I'm not. But *you* are, aren't you?"

She could not take her eyes from his. Never had a more blessed sight met her eyes than to see him standing right here in front of her, but it was all for nothing now.

"N-no," she lied.

He leaned closer, grasping her arm. "I'm not leaving here until I know the truth about your marriage, Audra. You and I have some talking to do!"

Joey came back out then, eager and proud to show Lee around Brennan Manor. Lee let go of Audra, but he gave her a look that told her their conversation was not finished. He left with Joey, and Audra watched them, wondering how they both could have been so foolish as to think they couldn't find a way to work things out.

The song . . . she had left the song in the desk at Maple Shadows. Since that first day she arrived back home, she had deliberately put it out of her mind. Now she wondered if leaving it behind had been the worst mistake of her life, and if Lee's worst mistake had been letting the song bring him to Brennan Manor.

14

Lee swatted at a mosquito that buzzed near his ear, then sat up, wondering if it was the mosquito or the rumble of thunder that had awakened him. Brilliant flashes of lightning lit up the spacious bedroom like daylight, and in his sleepy state it took him a moment to remember where he was. He started to get out of bed to get himself a smoke when his feet got tangled in mosquito netting, and in a fit of anger he yanked it aside and rose.

Yes, he remembered, all right! He was in Louisiana, and he'd never had a more miserable night. The setting of the sun had done little to alleviate the heat, and now the air hung heavy and humid and still, waiting to be stirred by an approaching storm. The lightning hit again, and he could see his gear sitting on a nearby chair. He walked over to it and fished around for the box of thin cigars he carried in it, found one. He used the lightning flashes to make his way to the fireplace at one end of the dark room, where he found some long matches. He struck one and lit the cigar, wondering why in hell anyone in Louisiana would bother to put fireplaces in their homes. Did it really ever get cold enough down here to need them?

He took a drag on the cigar, wishing morning would come sooner, not even sure what time it was now. As soon as the sun was up, he was getting the hell out of here. He walked to the French doors that led out to a terrace, hoping to find a breeze, but there was none. Droplets of rain began pelting him, and he stood there and enjoyed it, letting the rain cool him until suddenly the heavens opened up and the rain beat on him so hard he had to go back inside. He closed the doors, and the wind finally picked up, blowing the curtains away from one window. He decided not to close it. It was too damn hot. Hell, let the floor get wet. What did he care?

He walked over and sat down in a chair near the window so he could feel the breeze. Part of him was glad he had come here, if for no other reason than to be able to see Joey again. The kid had grown, and his voice was deeper, but he still stuttered badly. He'd like to take him back north and send him to a special school where he was sure Joey could get help; but just as with Audra, he knew he'd never get the boy away from Brennan Manor. It was obvious by the way Joey proudly showed him around the sprawling mansion, and the way he talked about how big the plantation was, that the boy was solidly convinced this was where he belonged.

Lee suspected Joey really didn't care for the responsibilities his father and Richard Potter were putting on him, that his main reason for staying on and struggling to build himself into the "ruling king" he was expected to be was because of a need to do something, anything, that would make his father proud of him. He could not imagine the boy ordering a whipping or buying and selling human beings at auction blocks. Joey would never be the kind of man his father expected of him, and Lee wanted to tell him to quit trying. But what business was it of his anymore? Fact was, it had *never* been his business.

He shouldn't be concerned about Audra, either, but part of the reason he couldn't sleep was the haunting terror in her eyes. Seeing this place, seeing how she handled the Negroes, her elegance, her authority, all told him she was right to come back here. She did belong at Brennan Manor; trouble was, she did *not* belong with Richard Potter. She had put on one hell of a show to make him think she was fine, but he knew better.

Oh, how she had carried on at the supper table about all the "grand" things she and Richard had planned. She bragged about this and bragged about that, told him about Richard's valuable gun collection at Cypress Hollow, how the man had traveled to Europe and Africa and intended to take her to such exotic places some day. She did not doubt that some day Richard would be governor of Louisiana, which would mean that she would rule the governor's mansion.

Lightning flashed again, this time so close he heard a snapping sound. In almost the same instant thunder cracked in a mighty explosion that made him jump slightly. He stood up and began pacing, despising himself for not coming here sooner. He still loved her, dammit! And he knew by her eyes that Audra still loved him. For all her pretense at having done the right thing, there was a terrible sorrow in those eyes, and it came from something more than having seen her first lover again. The sorrow would not be there if she had married someone who was good to her, but no one could convince him that Richard Potter had been good at all. She had as much as admitted it earlier in the day, but then she had put on that front again, pretending all was well. If he thought for one moment that she was genuinely happy with her new husband, he could go home knowing that at least she would be loved and taken care of. Materially, she obviously *would* be taken care of, but a woman had more important needs that he suspected would never be fulfilled for Mrs. Richard Potter.

"You stupid son of a bitch," he grumbled to himself. "You should have come down here right away and had it out with her father, given it a try!" He wished there were some magical way a man had of knowing exactly the right deci-

sions to make in life. He and Joseph Brennan probably
would have had their share of battles if he'd come here to
live after all, but they might have been worth it if it meant
not seeing that awful loneliness and even fear in Audra's
eyes.

The storm outside raged on, just like the storm in his
heart. Thunder cracked nearby, muffling the sound of what
seemed like a knock at the door. He glanced at it, waited.
The rain poured down even harder. There it was again, a
light, hesitant knock. He took the cigar from his mouth and
went to the door to open it. Lightning flashed, and he saw
her in the light. It was so hot she hadn't even put on a robe.
Her hair was brushed out over her shoulders, and she
looked up at him with those exotic green eyes.

"Audra!"

She held up a bottle of wine and two glasses. "How
about a late-night drink?" she said. She stumbled inside before he could reply, and he realized she had already been
drinking. He closed the door.

Out in the hallway Lena had caught Audra's move-
ments in the lightning flashes. She had been up inspecting
windows because of the storm, saw Audra knock on the
door to the room where Lee Jeffreys was staying, watched
her go inside. Should she go and put a stop to it? She
thought not. She had seen Audra's naked body after Richard
brought her back from their "honeymoon." The poor girl
had been terribly abused, but she had begged Lena and
Toosie not to tell her father about what they had seen, and
she had refused to go into any detail about how or why it
had happened.

Lena had tried to decipher what had gone wrong, and
as soon as Lee Jeffreys came upon the scene earlier today,
she had her answer. She would never forget the fallen look
on Lee's face when he realized Audra was married.

Poor Audra. If only Joey and Joseph knew what the girl
had sacrificed for them, but Joseph's heart was too frail now
to know the truth, and Joey would probably shoot himself.
As for herself, Lena felt helpless to do anything about any
of it. In spite of her relationship with Joseph, she was still
just his Negro lover. It was not her place to tell the man

what was going on, nor was it her place to go into Lee Jeffreys's room and take Miss Audra out of there. Maybe Audra *needed* to be in there. Maybe she would finally open up to someone; and maybe, by some miracle, Lee Jeffreys would find some way to help the poor girl.

"Lord, help them both," she muttered.

Lee took the bottle and glasses from Audra's hands. "You're already drunk," he told her. "You don't need any more of this."

She puckered her lips in a pout. "Oh, but I do. Did you know that if you drink enough wine, you don't feel any pain, either emotional or physical?"

The words were spoken mockingly, her smile fake. Lee set the bottle and glasses on the floor near the door, lost her for a moment in the darkness. When the lightning flashed again, he spotted her wandering toward the French doors. He walked over and grasped her arms, turning her.

"I've used whiskey enough times this past year to know *exactly* what you mean," he told her, "but I decided that wasn't the answer, and it isn't the answer for you, either, Audra. What the hell is going on here! You're eighteen years old, and you're drinking like a damn sailor!"

They watched each other in another bright flash of light. Lee stood there bare-chested, wearing only a pair of knee-length long johns, and Audra could not get over the fact that in spite of his size and what she had been through, she felt none of the revulsion and fear she felt around Richard. She was actually still stirred by his physique, still felt warm and alive in his presence. She was safe here. As long as she was in Lee Jeffreys's arms, nothing could hurt her, not even Richard. "Hold me, Lee. Will you just hold me?"

He put a hand to the side of her face. "What is the pain you're trying to kill, Audra?" He felt her shiver.

"Please just hold me," she asked again.

With a sigh of resignation, he drew her into his arms, and she collapsed against him, breaking into bitter weeping that tore at his guts. He crushed her close, resting his cheek against the top of her head, stroking her thick mane of auburn hair. "It's all right, love. Somehow I'll *make* it all right."

He was glad for the storm that raged outside. It helped drown out her wrenching sobs, which he was sure the whole house would hear if it were a normally quiet night. He felt torn with emotion, a need to love and make love to this woman, a need to protect her, combined with the need to kill Richard Potter for whatever he had done to make her this way. The man had broken her spirit, shattered her heart.

Her crying was bordering on hysteria, and he picked her up in his arms and carried her to the bed, laying her on it and climbing in beside her. He pulled the mosquito netting back around it, and he just sat beside her and rubbed her back while she wept into his pillow.

"Just let it all out, Audra."

She curled up and he lay down beside her, putting an arm around her from behind. She grasped his arm, clinging tightly as though desperately afraid, digging into his skin with her fingernails until it hurt. He decided not to say anything for the moment. He would wait until she was ready to talk, and for several more minutes she just lay there weeping.

She seemed more like a frightened little girl than a woman, and he felt a fury building in his soul at how thin and withered she was. This was not the bratty, proud, feisty Audra he had left in Connecticut. He leaned over and kissed her cheek, gently stroked her hair back from her damp face. The breeze coming in the window had grown cooler, and the storm was abating. "You might as well tell me what's happened, Audra. There's no pretending anymore."

Her body continued to jerk in lingering sobs as her lungs struggled to get back into a normal breathing pattern. Finally she calmed down, and she rolled onto her back. "I don't know ... how to say it. It's ... too ugly."

Lee sat up and ripped the pillowcase off his pillow and handed it to her. "Blow your nose on it if you have to. Lord knows there are enough servants around here to get the damn bedclothes washed in the morning."

Audra obeyed, using the pillowcase like a handkerchief, then wiped tears and perspiration from her face. The storm was drifting away, and with it the clouds. Apparently a full moon was behind those clouds, for the room was much lighter now, and with their vision adjusted to the dark, they could see each other's eyes. Audra just stared at him for several long seconds, as though she were afraid that if she looked away, he would be gone.

"Am I bad, Lee?" she finally asked.

"What?"

"What we did," she sniffed. "Does it make me a whore?"

Lee already felt the temper he had been trying to train these past few months beginning to get out of control again. "Did Richard tell you that?"

Finally she looked away, turning onto her side. "Worse. Think of the ugliest things you can call a woman, and that's what he has called me."

Lee stretched out beside her again, pulling her close, bending his legs into the back of hers. "Why? How in hell did he even know about me?"

She shuddered. "You're a man. Wouldn't you know it if the woman you took to bed wasn't a virgin?"

Lee closed his eyes, wanting to kill. "Jesus," he whispered.

"I made it worse," she said, the tears wanting to come again. "That first night . . . he was so quick. I wasn't ready, and he didn't . . . do anything to make it nice. He was just . . . just there on top of me before I knew what was happening . . . and I'd drunk a lot of wine because I was scared. I wanted it to work, Lee. He'd been so good to me before that. I thought . . . if I could make myself get used to him that way . . . I'd be all right. Only I drank too much wine. I tried to make it better . . . by imagining it was you. I didn't realize it, but I whispered your name . . . He heard me."

"My God." Lee kept a tight hold on her when she shivered.

"When he was through," she continued, "he hit me . . . over and over. He called me so many names, and . . . he made me tell him who it was. I . . . I had to tell him. That's why you can't be here ... when he comes back. If he finds you here ... it will be all the worse for me. He'll take me back to Cypress Hollow. When he has me there, he can ... do whatever he wants with me. I'm safer here, near father and Joey."

Lee kissed her hair, feeling as though he would explode at any moment. He told himself he had to be calm for now, let her talk. "Has he hit you since then?"

She drew her knees even closer to her body. "He ... has ways of bringing ... pain ... without leaving any marks, except in places no one sees but him. That first night ... he said that if he'd married a slut ... then he'd use me like one. He made me lie on my stomach." She jerked in another sob. "He told me ... if he couldn't be my first man one way ... he would be the first in another way. I passed out from the pain of it ... but now it doesn't hurt so much anymore. I've learned not to fight it."

Lee felt a blackness closing in around him. He suspected it was a good thing Richard Potter was nowhere near Brennan Manor tonight. If he was, he would be a dead man! Rage rumbled through him with such force that for a moment he thought he might vomit. He sat up and breathed deeply for control. "Tell me all of it, Audra."

Lee had to keep reminding himself that for the moment he could not rant and rave. He could only listen, hold her, comfort her. He sat with his head in his hands as she told him more, the vile things her husband did with her, the fact that he raped young Negro girls right in their own bed.

"Joey doesn't know what he's really like," she said, wiping at her face again with shaking hands. "Neither does Father. Father has a very weak heart now. It would kill him if he knew."

"He *ought* to die, for keeping my letters from you and Joey! He's partly to blame for this!"

"No!" she insisted, rolling onto her back to face him. "Father wouldn't do that. Even if he did, it's still our fault, Lee, nobody else's. We never should have let it go so far, and after that, we should have found a way to be together. Father thought Richard was the best man for me. He thinks he's good to me. He can't ever know, Lee."

Lee could hardly believe her refusal to accept what her father had done, but he decided that, considering the state she was in, maybe she needed to keep thinking her father was incapable of reading and destroying her letters. It wouldn't do her any good to learn the man had apparently betrayed her, all to save his precious plantation. Besides that, she was probably right that Joseph Brennan thought he was doing what was best for his daughter. He apparently worshiped the girl. He would never give her over to such torture, not even for Brennan Manor. He surely had no idea the kind of man Richard Potter was behind closed doors.

"The only way to be together would have been for me to come here to live, and I was too damn stubborn and sure it was wrong," he answered. "The real one to blame is me."

She touched his arm. "I *wanted* to blame you, to hate you. But it was just as much my fault as it was yours. We made a mutual decision, Lee, and it's my doing that I'm already married. There was a problem . . . with the man in charge of the Negroes. I never liked him. I told Richard that if he'd fire March Fredericks, I would marry him sooner. I didn't think it would make any difference, and Father was anxious to see us married because of his heart problem. I was afraid he might die before he was able to give me away. And Richard was so kind and attentive. I thought I could be happy."

She sat up beside him, kissed his cheek. "You have no idea how I felt when I saw you ride up to the house today . . . the awful feeling of knowing you'd come too late. I wanted to run to you, to ask you to hold me and never let go, but I'm married to Richard now, and that can't be changed. For all I know, I am already carrying his child. A baby is my only hope of regaining his respect, as the mother of his children." More tears slipped down her cheeks. "I am hoping that after these last ten days or so apart, he won't be so angry when he returns; and if we stay here at Brennan Manor, he can't do the things to me he does at Cypress Hollow. But if he finds you here . . ."

Lee pulled her close, and she rested her head on his shoulder. "I understand. But I can't just ride off and forget you, Audra. I can't just leave you to answer to that bastard's torture. There must be something I can do."

"No, no, you mustn't try to do anything," she protested, shivering in another sob. "You don't understand, Lee. He's one of the most powerful men in Louisiana. If he catches you here, he could do whatever he wants with you and no one would stop him. It's too dangerous for you here."

"I don't give a damn!" He breathed deeply for self-control and gently laid her back down on the bed. He kissed her eyes, stroked her hair away from her face. "We won't think about it tonight." He thought how in his arms, the night he took her, she had seemed like a woman; but in Richard Potter's hands she had surely been nothing more than an abused child. He had tried to show her how beautiful and pleasurable lovemaking could be, but her husband had destroyed her trust.

He pulled her into his arms. "You remember who you are, Audra. Before you were Mrs. Richard Potter, you were Audra Brennan, a proud young woman, the daughter of one of the wealthiest men in Louisiana. You were full of spirit and pride, and you can't let that man take those things away from you. Don't you believe for one minute that what we did made you a bad person, or that what that son of a bitch does to you should make you somehow dirty and unworthy of respect. He's raped you, just as sure as he's raped those poor young Negro girls, and he's not going to keep getting away with it!"

"There's nothing you can do about it, Lee."

"I'll think of something. We can't do anything about the fact that you're married to him now, but by God, I can do something about how he treats you from now on!"

"Lee, you'll get yourself killed!"

"Don't you worry about me. Just because you're his wife doesn't give him the right to use you that way."

She curled up against him, feeling so safe and protected. Outside, the moon disappeared again, and thunder rumbled from a second approaching storm.

"Once a man marries," she said, "the woman and everything she owns belongs to him, to do with as he wants. You know that it's true, Lee. You're a lawyer yourself. With a southern man who has as much wealth and power as Richard, it is even more true. There is nothing you can do, and nothing I can do but find a way to make life bearable. Please, please leave before he finds you here."

Lee did not reply immediately. His head ached from desperate thoughts of how he could help her, and every muscle in his body ached to kill Richard Potter. Perhaps, for reasons other than he had planned, God had meant for him to find that song and feel compelled to come here. The least he could do now was help Audra out of this mess, if that was possible.

"I'll leave, all right. I'll leave Brennan Manor, but I'm not leaving Baton Rouge until I figure out how to help you. It's partly my fault you're caught in this, and I'm not going to let it continue."

She touched his face. "Lee, please let it be."

"I can't, Audra." Their eyes held as he took her hand and kissed it. "You just try to get some sleep."

"I should go back to my room."

"No. You'll stay right here in my arms so you aren't alone. You're safe here, from the storm, from Richard Potter and from your own nightmares. I'm not letting go of you, at least not tonight."

The thunder came closer, and she could not deny how good it felt to be safe and loved. Wrong as it was, she could not bring herself to leave his arms. "I'm a married woman now," she reminded him.

"You're a piece of property, apparently worth hardly more to your husband than one of his slaves. Married or not, you're staying right here. You know the house servants won't say anything if you order them not to, and as far as I know, none of them even knows you're here."

"Lena and Toosie will find out," she said, weariness beginning to overtake her. "They know everything that goes on in this house."

"Neither one of them would betray you. Don't forget you have full command of everyone in this house. If you tell them to keep quiet, they will. You remember who you are, Audra. Don't let that bastard destroy your spirit and pride. He can steal your body and your material possessions, but he can't steal what is inside of you, the love, the heart, the spirit that is the Audra I fell in love with."

Audra felt herself drifting into a much-needed sleep, her body utterly exhausted from her fit of tears. "You really . . . never stopped loving me?" she asked, slurring the words.

He kissed her hair. "I really never stopped loving you."

Moments later she was asleep in his arms. Rain began to pour again, but at least the room was cooler now, and Lee pulled a blanket over them. He fell into a fitful sleep of his own, unable to rest soundly for the vision of horrors that kept stabbing at him, imagining Richard Potter abusing her in such hideous ways.

Hours passed, and both of them lost track of time. Audra stirred awake in the wee hours before sunrise, and her movement woke him. He felt her kissing at his neck, stroking his chest. "I want to remember how good it can be," she whispered. "Show me, Lee."

He felt a fire beginning to creep through his veins. "You don't know what you're saying."

"I do," she whimpered. "I want to remember how gentle and beautiful you made it for me. No one else ever needs to know."

It was raining softly now, the raindrops pecking at the wide leaves of a rubber plant just outside the window. It was a warm, sweet moment, and it was a moment he could not resist capturing. If he could do nothing else for her, he could take away the ugliness she had known and replace it with gentle love. He met her mouth, wondering what it was about this woman that made him lose all reason. He was a man of education, a man who always thought logically, and until he had met Audra Brennan, he had been a man in full control of his faculties.

All that control was gone the moment he tasted her sweet lips once more. The thought of Richard Potter abusing her tore at his guts, bringing on a fierce need to possess her himself, to reclaim her, to remind her of the beauty of the act. She returned his kiss with sweet passion, but he felt her stiffen when he moved a hand under her gown to touch her bare leg.

"This is me, Audra," he said softly, kissing her eyes, her neck, her lips again. He gently rubbed his hand over her slender thigh, over her belly, noticing how her hip bones protruded from her loss of weight. "Look at me," he gently commanded.

She opened her eyes, and in the very dim light of early dawn she could see the sincerity and love there.

"I would never hurt you."

She let him kiss gently at her breast through her thin gown, but he did not tear it away. She felt him move between her legs, but there was no force. She shivered from ugly memories, but she kept watching his eyes. Yes, this was Lee. It was his face, his blue eyes, his touch. How could two men be so different? He reached down to unbutton his long johns, and she lay rigid and waiting, trying to tell herself this was wrong, but knowing it had to be. She had to know there was something more beautiful to this act than the things Richard had done to her.

"I'm not going to do anything but be inside you," he told her, as though to read her thoughts.

Yes, he knew she could not tolerate anything else for now. This was all she needed. In the next moment he entered her so gently that she gasped with the sheer delight of it. He found her mouth again, and his lips were so warm and soft, not cold and thin like Richard's. He didn't press her lips against her teeth until they hurt. He parted them, caressed them with his tongue while he filled her depths with rhythmic, gentle thrusts that were like strokes of love and adoration, as he cherished her body.

For this moment it didn't matter that she was married to someone else. In her heart she had married Lee Jeffreys first. No one could tell her this was wrong. It was as though with every thrust he put new life into her, renewed pride, as though he were filling her with life and determination.

Quietly it was done. His life spilled into her, and they both fell asleep again. When they awoke, the sun was a little higher. This time nothing was said. Their lips met again, he entered her again. He never touched her in any other way, as though to make sure she understood that a man didn't need to do all those other things to enjoy loving his woman.

Ho had done so much more that first time they made love, but that was before Richard had made it all so ugly. He understood that it would take time and patience to bring her back to the point where she wanted to please a man in other ways.

For Audra, this was enough for now. She was sharing her body with Lee Jeffreys, and Richard be damned. If he had not abused her as he had, she would not be needing this, and no one could tell her it was wrong, for she still loved this man with all her heart and soul.

15

Audra strolled about the ballroom on Richard's arm, greeting guests graciously. She must look the happy wife tonight, for that was what Richard wanted everyone to believe. He had not hurt her over the past three weeks since he came back from New Orleans; he had forced her to eat better and made sure she was rested and well for the cotillion that was planned to show off the newlyweds. He had even told her what to wear, had picked out the material and instructed Henrietta how to design the dress. It was a magnificent magenta silk-satin garment with a perfectly cut bodice that showed just enough of her bosom to let others know that Richard Potter's wife was a delectable, firm young treasure. Those were Richard's own words, followed by the remark that as soon as the cotillion was over, he would be taking her back to Cypress Hollow to remind her to whom that treasure belonged.

She could hardly keep smiling for the dread of thinking about going back to Cypress Hollow, but she put on a good show for others, who congratulated her and Richard, envy in their eyes. The women raved about her dress, the deep-magenta satin overlaid with pink lace flounces. Her silk lace stole was also a magenta color, and she wore white kid gloves and carried an ivory-and-silk fan. Diamonds graced her neck and earlobes, diamonds that Richard bragged to others were a gift he'd brought from New Orleans for his precious new wife. Toosie had styled her hair into a mass of auburn curls at the crown, with a diamond comb placed into the base of the curls. People commented that she had never looked more beautiful, and that marriage must certainly agree with her.

Audra knew that the past three weeks of relatively decent treatment from her husband were just a temporary reprieve, to put on a show for her father, for these guests. Richard wanted her to look healthy and happy. He had come to her bed only twice since his return, quick, rough ordeals during which he simply used her body for his pleasure. It could not be called making love, but at least he had performed his act the normal way and had done nothing disgusting. Even then she could see by his eyes that when he got her back to Cypress Hollow, life would again become unbearable.

Lee had said he would not leave Baton Rouge until he found a way to help her, but she had not heard from him since the night they had made love. He had asked to see the papers Richard and her father had signed just before the wedding. Audra had found the keys to her father's desk and had handed the documents to Lee, realizing her father would be furious if he knew, but desperate for Lee to find a way to help her. He had studied the papers most of the morning, then replaced them and left, with a promise that everything was going to be all right. She could not imagine what he had in mind, and she wondered if he had given up whatever he had planned and gone home.

Was he gone forever this time? She felt helpless and alone again, longed for the safety and protection she felt in his arms. The orchestra struck up a waltz, and the crowd of prominent and wealthy guests who had been invited to the cotillion at Brennan Manor insisted that the "happy newly-weds" dance alone first. Richard, looking very handsome in a gray silk waistcoat with satin stripes worn under a black silk knee-length suit coat, guided her out to the middle of the floor. He began whirling with her in even steps, a smooth dancer, his white pleated shirt and starched white bow-tied cravat making his skin seem even darker. Even in dancing there was a commanding air to the way he held her, the way he guided her through the steps flawlessly. Audra knew the people who watched were thinking what a wonderful, good-looking man he was, a prize catch for a young southern belle. If only they knew what an animal he could be.

"You are playing your role very nicely tonight," he told her, smiling for others to see.

"I intend to make you proud of me, Richard," she answered. "What I did last summer in Connecticut was because I was an innocent child who knew no better. Now I am a married woman, and I married you in faith and love."

"Did you?" He pulled her a little closer, while others watched in admiration. Both of them smiled as they spoke, pretending to be deliriously happy. "Perhaps you did," he continued, his eyes dropping to her bosom. "And perhaps I could forgive you, if I thought for one minute that you no longer cared about Lee Jeffreys. Can you honestly say that you no longer have feelings for him?"

She held her chin proudly. "In the end he was just a good friend. I will always care for him in that respect. I believe a woman should love her husband in a different way, and if you would treat me with the respect any man should treat the woman he loves, I could love you, Richard. I thought I *did* love you, but you destroyed that love on our wedding night."

"No, my love. *You* destroyed it, when you whispered that man's name." His grip on her hand tightened, and she knew that nothing she did or said was going to change his opinion. She had held a tiny bit of hope that time and talking might alleviate the situation. How much crueler would he be to her if he knew Lee had been there and that she had slept with him? If Richard had behaved as a normal, loving husband should behave, she would never have been untrue to her husband. There was a time when she couldn't have dreamed of committing such a sin, let alone feeling no remorse for it; but she had needed that night with Lee. It had given her a kind of strength, renewed her spirit. It was a wonderful secret she would carry with her, hidden from this man who harbored a surprising evil behind his handsome visage and his silk suits and his position of respect among the prominent people of Louisiana.

Others joined in the dance then, and cousin Eleanor whirled past them with the son of a cotton broker from Baton Rouge. She wore a great deal of color on her cheeks and lips and eyes, and huge diamond earrings and a diamond necklace decorated her face and neck—so big, they looked ridiculous. Her blue taffeta dress was cut so low that Audra wondered if her billowing breasts might jiggle completely out of the bodice with one wrong move. She understood so well now what Eleanor really meant by the suggestive things she had told her about men, and she wondered how the woman could lie with so many different ones and enjoy it. After being with Lee, and after what she had been through with Richard, Audra believed the only way to enjoy a man was to love him with every ounce of passion a woman possessed.

Eleanor had hardly spoken to her since her wedding, and she knew the girl felt a raging jealousy over the union. How ironic, for Audra would gladly give her husband to the girl if there were any way to do it. Maybe Eleanor would enjoy Richard's perversity in bed. Tonight her cousin seemed to be trying to prove that she was not the least bit impressed with Audra's fine catch. She had already danced with practically every eligible man at the ball, as well as some married men, and the night was still young.

"Your cousin has an affinity for anyone wearing long pants," Richard spoke up. "Does it run in the family blood, Audra?"

His fingers pressed a little harder into her back, and she met his eyes defiantly. "I am not like Eleanor," she answered. "Why can't you understand that, Richard? I was seventeen years old, lonely and homesick and ignorant about men."

He sniffed. "Well, thanks to me you're no longer ignorant, are you?" He smiled wickedly. "I think you should come back to Cypress Hollow for a while. After all, it *is* my home."

She felt her stomach churn, watched the look of victory in his dark eyes. "And mine is here. You promised Father we would live here."

"Most of the time, yes. He'll understand if I want to take you to Cypress Hollow three or four months out of the year."

"Fine," she answered defiantly. For some reason, ever since Lee's visit, she was not as afraid of this man. She dreaded his advances, she found him repulsive, but she was not afraid. Lee had told her not to let him break her pride, and she had decided to listen to that advice. "We can go whenever you wish," she told him, noticing a rather surprised look on his face. "You are my husband, and I have no choice but to go with you, if that's what you want. Cypress Hollow is your home, and I can understand that you need to be there."

Richard frowned, and Audra enjoyed a tiny victory. He probably expected, even wanted, to see horror and terror in her eyes, perhaps expected her to beg him to let her stay at Brennan Manor; but she would not satisfy his ludicrous wishes. The crying and begging were over.

The dance ended and another began. To Audra's relief Joey asked her to dance. Richard bowed to the boy and handed her over, and Audra realized that the one and only thing that made life bearable with Richard was the fact that he was good to Joey. Her brother had suddenly shot up in height this past year, so that now he stood taller than she. He turned her around to a waltz, and Audra smiled. "You have picked up quite well on my dancing lessons, little brother," she told him. "But I haven't seen you dance with any of the young girls here."

Joey reddened a little. "I'm afraid I'll begin to stutter and they'll laugh at the way I t-talk."

"Joey, you're the son of one of the richest men in Louisiana. It isn't going to matter to them how you talk."

He frowned, watching her eyes. "Is that why you married Richard? B-because he's rich?"

Her smile faded. "Of course not. It was simply the perfect match. I've known Richard all my life, and he is Father's best friend."

Joey had seen the fear in her eyes when she had begged him never to tell their father or Richard that Lee had come visiting and had spent the night. Until then he had thought she was happy with Richard, but she had been so sick after he brought her back from Cypress Hollow, and he noticed how she had brightened and gotten stronger after Lee's visit. There wasn't anyone he liked better than Lee Jeffreys, and he suspected it was the same for Audra. He could only pray she had made her choice because she truly loved Richard, and not sacrificed her heart just for him and for Brennan Manor.

You really love Lee, don't you? he had asked her after Lee left. She had insisted it was not true, that Lee was still just a very good friend; but she had warned that sometimes husbands didn't understand such things. He liked Richard well enough, but if the man made his sister as afraid as he suspected, then what had he done to put that fear in her? He could swear that first day home he had detected a faint bruise on her cheek, and she had done nothing but sleep for three days after Richard first left with their father for New Orleans, as though she were sick and exhausted.

"You sure look pretty tonight," he told Audra. "And you look happier. You seemed awful sick when you first came home. I'm glad you're better."

"I'm just fine, Joey. Thank you for keeping my secret about Lee. You do understand why I asked you not to say anything, don't you? After all, he is Yankee, bred and born, and with Father's heart condition, he would be terribly upset to think we were still good friends with someone like Lee. He won't be back again, so we just have to forget him. And Richard, with our marriage being so new and all, might misunderstand the purpose of Lee's visit."

"I won't say anything. D-do you think there really could be a war, Audra?"

She rolled her eyes. "Goodness, no! Men just like to talk about such things. Why, I swear, fighting and arguing are all they think about; but the arguments will never go any further than Congress. If things don't work out, we will simply secede from the Union and be on our own, and that will be that. Nothing else has to change."

"I hope you're right."

I hope I'm right, too, she thought. Secession, slavery, states' rights, the possibility of war, was on everyone's lips tonight. It was just about all anyone could talk about. There had even been a few arguments already over what should be done if Abe Lincoln became President, but right now Audra wished that politics was all she had to worry about. Her own husband had become a much more fearful adversary than the Yankees could ever be.

Audra glanced over at her husband and noticed he was dancing with Eleanor. She and Joey waltzed past them, and Eleanor was laughing, her crooked teeth showing, and batting her eyes as though she thought she was a raving beauty. She was twice as wide and twice as thick as Richard, a hefty lump in a beautiful jade-green gown that did nothing to help her look better. She gave Audra a haughty look of defiance, and Audra knew her cousin wanted her to be jealous to see her flaunting herself at Richard. Audra almost laughed at the thought. If only cousin Eleanor knew that for all she cared, Eleanor could take her place in the man's bed every night for the rest of their married life, if it meant he would leave her alone.

The waltz ended, and Richard left Eleanor to walk over to the raised platform that had been erected for the six-piece orchestra. He held out his hands to quiet the crowd, and everyone turned to listen. "I think my beautiful new wife should sing for all of us," he announced, surprising Audra. Others threw in their agreement, some clapping in support. Joey grinned, urging her to entertain them.

"I haven't heard you sing in a long time," he told her.

That is because I haven't had a song in my heart, she thought. It reminded her of the reason Lee had come here

. . . the song. She had left the song she had written for him at Maple Shadows, and it had brought him here. Why had God allowed him to find it, when He knew it was too late for them? She looked at Richard, saw by his eyes that his suggestion was more of a command. Her husband had spoken, and she must obey. She took a deep breath and walked up on the platform, taking requests. Yes, she would sing, but she would not sing for Richard Potter or any of these others. She would pretend that Lee was standing out there in the crowd, watching her, loving her. She would sing for Lee.

"Ain't she pretty tonight?" old George muttered to Henrietta.

On the third-floor balcony outside the ballroom, several Negroes watched the gathering of friends, neighbors, and dignitaries, beautifully dressed women, fine-suited men, glittering jewelry. As Richard had promised, Audra had been allowed to invite a few of the Negroes of Brennan Manor to share in the celebration and watch through the open French doors and through windows. They were not allowed to mix with the guests in any way, but just watching was enough of a treat for most of them.

They listened with delight to "Miss Audra's" beautiful voice. "Lawdy, she sure is the picture of her beautiful mama," Henrietta answered George. She fanned herself vigorously, the heat of the night harder on her hefty body than on the average person. She grunted as she lumbered over to a window where she could see better. "Master Potter, he sure knows how to pick material for a fancy dress. Ah ain't never seen a prettier color than that deep, deep pink. Ain't no other woman perty as Miss Audra in all of Loosiana, but to me she always be jus' a baby."

"That ain't no baby's voice," George told her. "Ah ain't never heard nothin' like that in all my days. Ah could listen to her singin' all day long."

Lena stood nearby, thinking how right Henrietta was. Audra was still a "baby" in so many ways, had married Richard Potter with such trust and hope that he would be good to her. The man had done a good job of ripping away her childlike innocence. She did not doubt that Lee Jeffreys had already stolen part of it last summer in Connecticut, but he had surely been loving and gentle, for Audra had returned home still full of dreams and hope and spirit. A whole summer in Connecticut with that Yankee man had not done the horrific damage that one week with Richard Potter had done. Her heart ached at the loneliness she knew Audra lived with. If only there were some way to help the girl, but there was not. If she told Joseph, it might be too much for his heart, and, after all, what could he *really* do? Partnership papers had already been signed, giving Richard authority over Brennan Manor. That could not be changed now, nor could the fact that Audra was legally married to the man, not just by law, but in the eyes of the Church. Nothing short of death would change the situation.

Richard owned her now, just as surely as any Negro was owned. How strange, that she and the other Negroes standing out here and watching Audra sing were slaves, with no hope of ever knowing the wealth and power someone like Audra enjoyed; yet right now they were all probably happier than Audra Brennan Potter. She was the richest, most beautiful white woman in Louisiana, but behind closed doors, she herself was no more than a slave to her cruel husband.

Lena's thoughts were interrupted when someone grasped her arm. "Get Toosie and come with me," a man said quietly.

She turned in surprise and confusion, looked up into the face of Lee Jeffreys. Her eyes widened in astonishment. "Mr. Jeffreys! What are you—"

"Do as I said. Get your daughter and come down to the second-floor balcony. I need to talk to both of you!"

He left her then, and Lena stared after him. She thought Lee had left Louisiana! Why on earth was he here at Audra's cotillion? She turned and hurried past George and Henrietta to find Toosie, taking hold of her hand. "Come with me."

"Where?"

"Downstairs. Lee Jeffreys is here and he has asked to talk to us."

Toosie followed her mother, her heart rushing with a mixture of fear and hope. Why on earth would Lee come on this of all nights?

Lee listened to Audra's singing, her beautiful voice drifting through the night air so strong and full that he could easily hear her from the floor below. Vivid memories engulfed him, memories of Connecticut, and the first time he had heard her sing. Her voice was just as beautiful as ever, and he wondered how he was going to leave Louisiana after tonight and never come back. He had no choice if he wanted to save Audra's reputation, but he also wanted to save her from further harm from her husband. The least he could do before he left was make sure Richard Potter never abused his wife again. He had been waiting three weeks for this, biding his time in Baton Rouge. He had gotten to know the city quite well, but few of its citizens treated him kindly. He had seen enough to know he did not belong in the South, and he was ready to leave; but not before meeting Richard Potter and setting the man straight in the matter of how he treated his wife.

It had been easy to get into the estate, passing himself off to servants as a business associate who purchased cotton for northern factories. He had purposely come late so that most guests would already be here. The more, the better. Outside, the driveway was lined with fancy carriages, and he supposed those who had come the farthest would be spending the night in the several bedrooms of Brennan Manor, as well as in a guest house nearby.

Negro servants were running every which way, tending horses, taking stoles and jackets, serving drinks, emptying ashtrays and chamber pots. It had been easy to talk his way past the Negro doorman, and because he was dressed as elegantly as the rest of the guests, no one else questioned him as he made his way to the third-floor ballroom. He had not actually entered the ballroom yet, but had stood on a side balcony, where no one else had seen him. He had watched Audra and the man he was sure must be Richard Potter step out to a waltz, urged by the guests to dance alone first.

Potter was handsome enough, well built for his age; but anyone could see the arrogance about the man, and considering his size, the thought of him abusing Audra only brought more rage to Lee's soul. The rage was combined with a burning jealousy at picturing Richard Potter using Audra's sweet, young body for his own sick gratification. His only comfort was noticing that Audra looked rested, healthier than when he had seen her last. Tonight she was absolutely the most beautiful woman he had ever set eyes on. Her gown was the most magnificent deep-pink color, her hair drawn up into a mass of curls and topped with diamonds. It irked him to see the way Richard Potter towered over her, his dark eyes drilling into her. He wished he could have heard their conversation as they danced. They smiled the whole time, but he knew it was a show for their guests. At one point Audra had held her chin in that way she had of showing defiance. What had the man said to her?

It was good to see that spark in her eye that told him she'd regained some of the spirit her husband had tried to beat out of her. By all outward appearances, he decided the man had not abused her quite so badly these past three weeks. He felt somewhat relieved to see she had put on a little weight, but he had a hunch Richard had just been "fattening her up" so his wife would look her best tonight. He would want everyone here to see her glowing and beautiful, not the thin, pitiful, hollow-eyed Audra that Lee had seen three weeks ago.

He could not think of anything more gratifying than to be able to tell Richard Potter that he had slept with his wife while he was gone, but he could not do that to Audra. It would be their secret, their last sweet good-bye. He had found it a hundred times more difficult to leave her this time, knowing the danger she was in. In some ways he felt as abusive as her husband, for he should have known better in the first place than to take advantage of her innocence back in Connecticut. If not for that act, Richard Potter might be a better husband to her, though Lee suspected that the man would have inevitably abused her in one way or another. He was a tyrant at heart, king of Cypress Hollow and now Brennan Manor—a man who clearly enjoyed the power he wielded over others. His own father was like that in some respects, and he suspected Joseph Brennan was also. They were not wife beaters, but they controlled people in other, perhaps less brutal, ways.

He hated being controlled, and he hated the thought of controlling others, whether a wife or slaves or the poor people who worked in his father's factories. Maybe that was why he was here, not just for Audra, but in part because Richard Potter and Joseph Brennan had destroyed his relationship with Audra. By doing so, they had controlled him, too; but after tonight, *he* would be the one in control. Audra might not be his, but he could at least protect her.

"Mr. Jeffreys!" Lena called out to him in the dark.

"Over here," he answered, spotting them in the moon light. They both came toward him, and Lee looked around to make sure no one was lurking nearby.

"What on earth are you doing here!" Lena scolded. "You will get Miss Audra in terrible trouble!"

"Get over here out of the light. I don't want anyone to see us talking." Lee took both women aside. "If my plan works, Audra will be a lot better off once I'm gone," he told Lena. "But I need your help, yours and Toosie's."

Toosie could not see the man clearly, as he kept to the darkness, but she smelled a stirring, masculine scent, and she could see his tall, broad outline in the moonlight. Lee Jeffreys was one handsome white man, with the bluest eyes she could ever remember seeing on anyone, male or female. She liked him better than any white man she had ever known, and she thought how happy Audra might have been with him if they had just tried to make it work. Now it was too late.

"Audra told me Toosie is educated," he was saying to Lena. "Is that right? Can she read and write?"

"Yes, sir," Lena answered, totally confused by this man's presence, more confused by the question.

"Good." Toosie watched him hand her mother a piece of paper. "This is the address where letters will reach me in New York. I know enough about you and Toosie to realize that you care very much for Audra. You must both be aware that things are not right between her and her husband. If he isn't stopped, he's going to kill her one of these days. I intend to make sure that doesn't happen."

Lena frowned and shook her head. "Mr. Jeffreys, what in the world do you think you can do about it? The man is her legal husband. I don't know if he knows about you, but if he does, and he finds out you was here while he was gone, that man could see to it that you're buried on Brennan Manor. You're a *Yankee*, Mr. Jeffreys! There ain't one person in that crowd tonight who would come to your aid if you was to get into a tussle with Richard Potter."

"Don't you worry about how I handle Potter." Lee kept his voice low. "Both of you must know how I feel about Audra. Toosie knows better than anyone, because she was with Audra in Connecticut. I might be taking a chance telling you this, Lena, but I'll say it flat out. I love Audra, and for the rest of my life I will probably regret not acting on that love. Now it's too late, but it isn't too late for me to help her find a way to live with this marriage. I can only pray I'm right in thinking I can trust both of you never to say anything to Audra's husband or father or brother, or any of the Negroes, about what I have just told you."

Lena straightened. "I love Audra like she was my own daughter," she answered. "I would never hurt or betray the girl. Nor would Toosie. She loves her like if she was her own sister."

Toosie glanced doubtfully at her mother. Certainly she loved Audra, but if Audra knew the truth, would she appreciate that love, or would she sell them off like the mere property they were, especially once Joseph died?

"I have a plan," Lee was saying. "It isn't necessary for either of you to know what it is. All I am asking of you is, after tonight, if you see any sign that Richard Potter is abusing Audra, I want you to write and tell me. Can you do that? Can you send a letter without Audra's father knowing about it?"

"I can," Lena answered. "There is a man comes by here every two weeks to pick up mail and take it to Baton Rouge. Joseph always goes through it first, then gives it to me to give to the man. I can easily put in another letter he don't know about."

"Fine. You have Toosie write me, but don't ever put a return address on the letter. We don't want it coming back here if for some reason it can't be delivered. Do you understand?"

"But what on earth could you do to stop Richard?" Toosie asked.

"You leave that to me. If I have to kill him, I'll do it, even if it means I'd be hanged. But I don't think I'll have to resort to that, and I don't want to create a scandal. I think I can settle it quietly, just between me and Richard Potter. After tonight I hope you won't ever have any reason to write me, and if you don't, I'll be out of Audra's life forever. I just pray her father won't sell either of you or cause you to be separated from Audra for any length of time."

Lena began to wonder just how much he knew about her relationship with Joseph Brennan. Lee was a smart man. Surely he suspected something. "That is not likely to happen, Mr. Jeffreys. I have been with Mr. Brennan for twenty-seven years, since I was just fourteen myself. I have been like a mother to Audra since her own mother died, and she would never want anyone but Toosie for her personal servant."

Lee grasped her hand and squeezed the piece of paper into it. "I want your solemn promise to write me if you see one sign of abuse."

Lena nodded. "Yes, sir. I promise. But I still don't understand—"

"You never talked to me tonight, either one of you," he interrupted. "God bless you both."

He disappeared around the corner of the house, and Lena looked at her daughter. "We had better get back upstairs. God knows what will happen tonight."

They both took another direction, Lena putting the piece of paper in her apron pocket. She had never told Toosie she had seen Audra go into Lee's bedroom the night he visited. Apparently he had been good for Audra, and that was just fine with her; but she had not expected him to come back. She hoped the little bit of happiness Audra had found that night would not now be destroyed by whatever Lee had planned.

She and Toosie made their way back to the third floor, where the guests stood transfixed, spellbound by Audra's magnificent voice as she sang "Shenandoah."

Audra herself was lost in the song, singing not about a ship or a river, but about her love for a man she could never have.

Away, we're bound away,
Cross the wide Missouri.

How she wished she could sail away with Lee, leave behind all the things that stood between them.

O, Shenandoah, I'll ne'er forget you,
Away, my rolling river!
Till the day I die, I'll love you ever,
Away, we're bound away—

The words caught in her throat, and she could not finish. She stared at the man who had just entered the room, wearing a black silk jacket and a gray satin waistcoat. How wonderful he looked, but what in God's name was he doing here, tonight of all nights! She should feel joy at the sight of him, but she felt only terror.

Lee!

16

All eyes followed Audra's gaze to stare at the stranger who had appeared in the ballroom. "Don't let me stop you, Mrs. Potter," Lee spoke up to Audra.

He gave her a smile that told her he was enjoying this, but he could see her terror, and he wanted to hold her and tell her not to be afraid.

"Since you are an uninvited guest, sir, perhaps you will introduce yourself to the others and explain your presence," Richard spoke up. "I am Richard Potter, and this gentleman beside me is Mr. Joseph Brennan, who owns this home."

Lee tore his eyes from Audra and faced Richard. Never in his life had he had to call on more reserve strength to control his temper than he did at this moment. He put out his hand. "Lee Jeffreys," he answered. "From New York City . . . and I have a summer home in Connecticut."

Audra wondered if she would faint. The room was still

quiet, as everyone realized that not only had Lee come here uninvited, but he was a northern man at that. She watched Richard's face grow dark, and her father's begin to redden.

Lee looked down at his empty hand, not at all surprised that Richard Potter had refused to shake it. He enjoyed the look of shock in the man's face. "Are all you southern gentlemen so rude?" he asked. "My mother gave your wife some voice lessons last summer. She was very fond of Audra. I heard Audra had married, so I came to give you both my best wishes. I have even brought a gift. My mother would have wanted me to."

Richard slowly grasped Lee's hand, realizing he had no choice at the moment but to pretend to be gracious. He reasoned that no one in the room knew that Audra had slept with this man. If he lost his temper now, though, what rumors might result? Rage seethed in his soul at the sight of Lee, much younger, terribly handsome . . . Audra's first lover. Lee Jeffreys would be lucky to leave here alive, and Potter's own desire to hurt Audra returned full force.

The two men clasped hands, and Richard winced when Lee squeezed his in a firm grip of warning. What did this man know? What the hell was going on here? He forced a pleasant look and nodded. "Audra told me a lot about your mother. A fine woman."

"They don't make them any better," Lee answered.

"I'm sorry for your loss." Richard let go of his hand and turned to the others. "Ladies and gentlemen, you recall that Audra took voice lessons last summer up in Connecticut, from Anna Jeffreys, a professional concert pianist and opera singer. Audra thought very highly of the woman, but I am afraid that Mrs. Jeffreys died suddenly before Audra left. Apparently Mr. Jeffreys here felt it was his place to come to our celebration in his mother's memory. Let us all show this Yankee what true southern hospitality is."

People began to relax and talk, some heading toward Lee to introduce themselves. Lee turned to Audra's father. "Mr. Brennan. I finally get to meet you. Audra talked about nothing but you last summer—you and Brennan Manor." Again he put out his hand, and Joseph shook it reluctantly. He tried to warn Lee with a look that told him he had better not do or say anything to embarrass Audra or Richard. Lee returned his grip as though he were himself angry, and Joseph realized Lee must know he burned his letters. The bastard! What the hell was he doing here now? Audra was married! He took a deep breath. "Welcome to our home, Mr. Jeffreys," the man drawled. "It is a long way from New York to Louisiana, quite a trip just to congratulate someone."

Lee grinned, a look of victory in his eyes. "I always thought a lot of Audra," he answered, looking back at Richard. The look that Richard Potter returned told Lee that if no one had been around, the man would have tried to kill him in an instant. *I wish you* would *try,* he thought. *Give me an excuse, Richard, any excuse to knock the hell out of you!* He already had that excuse, but this was not the place or time. The opportunity would present itself before the night was over. He would make sure of it.

Others gathered around him now, introducing themselves, some with such heavy southern accents that Lee had to ask them to repeat their names. He did not miss the wariness and animosity in their eyes, their southern pride causing them to distrust and dislike anyone who came from anyplace north of Kentucky. More trouble was coming, that was sure. Earlier, when he had stood outside watching, he had heard some of their conversations, bitter threats against the North, vows of what they would do if Lincoln became President. Southern pride was at its peak in this room tonight.

Audra managed to make herself move toward Lee, quickly intercepting Joey when he came into the room from outside. She saw the excited look in Joey's eyes, and she was afraid he would say something about Lee's first visit without thinking. She stepped in front of him. "Remember your promise," she quietly reminded him.

Joey frowned. He had gone outside to sneak a glass of premium wine to old George, whom he loved almost like a grandfather. He looked from Audra to Lee, confused. Audra had no time to explain, and she couldn't if she wanted to. She had no idea what Lee was up to, or what he expected her to do or say. She only knew she would be expected to join her husband and greet their Yankee visitor.

Joey walked with her and put out his hand to welcome Lee. He glanced at his father and greeted Lee as though he had not seen him for a year. "This is the man I told you about—Mrs. Jeffreys's son," he told his father.

"So we have discovered," Joseph answered, his cheeks still flushed. He was worried, too—worried about what Lee Jeffreys would say about the letters. If the man already knew Audra had married, why had he bothered to come here at all, he wondered, if not to make trouble for all of them?

The orchestra began playing another waltz, and Lee turned to Richard. "I wonder if you would allow me a dance with your beautiful bride?" he asked.

Richard did not miss the hatred in Lee's blue eyes, nor the warning that he had better oblige. Damn him! As long as all these guests were around, Lee had him right where he wanted him. "Of course," he answered. "I understand you and Audra struck up quite a friendship last summer. You were a great help in relieving her loneliness."

Audra walked over to stand beside her husband. "She was very homesick," Lee was saying.

"So I understand," Richard answered, the words spoken in a near growl.

He looked down at Audra, and she cringed at the threat in his dark eyes. Why was Lee doing this? Surely he knew she would only suffer for it. "Mr. Jeffreys would like this dance, love," he said. "I gave him permission. After all, you *are* old friends."

Audra looked from Richard to Lee, and Lee grinned. "You look absolutely stunning tonight, Audra," he told her. "Mother would be proud of you, and the way you sang tonight."

Audra could not find her voice to reply. Lee put his hand to her waist and whirled her out onto the floor, where a few other couples were already drifting in gentle circles to the music. For several seconds Lee and Audra just watched each other, fire moving through their blood. *Oh, for one more night together, naked skin touching, uniting in sweet love,* she wished.

"Why are you here?" she finally managed to ask, her voice almost squeaking in alarm.

He squeezed her hand. "Relax, Audra, and look happy. I'm here for one last look at you, and I brought you a wedding gift, went all the way to New Orleans to buy it. I left it downstairs on the piano in the parlor, wrapped in white. You can open it later, and every time you look at it, promise you'll think of me."

"You know I will."

He saw her struggling against tears. "Don't cry, Audra. People will wonder. And don't be afraid for me or yourself. I know what I'm doing." He leaned a little closer. "I love you," he said softly. "Always remember that."

He straightened and whirled her around while others watched with curiosity. Just how well did Audra Potter know this handsome Yankee man, her cousin Eleanor wondered, glowering at them. What had her supposedly innocent cousin Audra been up to last summer in Connecticut? She had never seen a man quite so handsome, and if she herself had gotten the chance to have an affair with this Yankee, she'd have done it in a minute, husband or no husband.

Audra paid no attention to anyone but Lee. She was oblivious to her cousin's sneering face, oblivious to the women who whispered behind their fans. She had rested her left hand on Lee's upper right arm lightly when he first asked her to dance, but now her fingers dug into it with growing alarm. "Lee, I don't understand. You shouldn't have come!"

"Didn't I tell you I'd make sure your husband never hurt you again?"

"Yes, but—"

"That's why I'm here. Richard Potter and I are going to have a little talk later, and after that you won't see me anymore. I promise to stay out of your life, but I also promise that your life will be better after I'm gone."

"But how—"

"Just believe it, Audra. Trust me."

He pressed his hand more firmly against her back, aching to pull her close, longing for one last delicious kiss, but their happiness had to end, here, tonight, forever, just as the waltz to which they danced was ending. He drank in the sight of her a moment longer. "Good-bye, Audra," he said softly. "God be with you." He bowed. "Thank you for the dance, Mrs. Potter," he said, loud enough for all to hear.

"And thank you for coming so far just to wish us well, Mr. Jeffreys." *I love you, Lee Jeffreys, just as the sun shines, and the ocean wind blows wet and wild . . .*

Lee started to lead her back to Richard and her father but was stopped by Eleanor and a man Audra recognized as Miles Farrell. Farrell, a married man with three grown children, owned several riverboats used to ship cotton up the Mississippi to St. Louis. His wife, who was ill, had stayed home that night, and Audra wondered if Eleanor realized what people must be thinking about the way she had been throwing herself at him all night.

Eleanor looked Lee over as though she were studying something delectable. "Why, Audra Potter, you never told us you met this handsome Yankee man while you were in Connecticut," she drawled. "Why ever did you keep it a secret?"

Audra did not miss the suggestiveness of the question, and she wanted to slap her cousin.

"We didn't really see much of each other in Connecticut," Lee lied, taking Eleanor's offered hand and kissing it. "I work in New York and met Audra when my fiancée and I visited Maple Shadows on a short vacation."

Oh, how Audra loved him! Lee saw right through Eleanor, and he was rescuing her from Eleanor's effort to embarrass her.

"Fiancée!" A look of enlightened surprise came over Eleanor's face, followed by near disappointment that she would fail to start a delicious rumor started here. "I see."

"Tell me, Mr. Jeffreys, what do you do in New York?" Miles asked.

"I'm an attorney—have my own law firm—Jeffreys, James, and Stillwell."

Miles looked him over as a few more of Louisiana's

wealthiest began to gather, including Richard, and Audra's father. Audra felt the tension building, saw the look of challenge and hatred in Richard's eyes. He took hold of her arm and pulled her away from Lee, pressing his fingers firmly enough to warn her he would deal with her later. All the while, though, he kept a smile on his face.

"Joey talked about you a few times," Richard was saying, holding Lee's gaze. Audra noticed Lee looked right back at the man without a sign of fear or apprehension. "Sounds as though you're quite successful. He says your father and brothers own several factories in New York."

"That's right," Lee answered. "Boots and shoes, tents, awnings. The family also owns an iron mill."

"Tell me, Mr. Jeffreys, what is the general feeling in New York—over this whole issue of slavery, I mean?"

The room quieted, and Lee could feel the lions gathering. "We feel that slavery must be ended—completely. We can't merely pass laws prohibiting the purchase of slaves; we must also stop the practice of breeding more Negroes on plantations. Human flesh should not be for sale or be exploited in any way, Mr. Potter, no matter the color of skin, no matter whether male . . . or *female*."

Audra's heart began to race, and she felt Richard stiffen. "Considering all the strikes taking place in the North by underpaid and overworked factory workers," he answered, measuring his words, "I'd say you should clean up your own backyard first, Mr. Jeffreys." Richard's voice was calm, but Audra could feel his rage.

Lee met his gaze squarely. "At least factory workers aren't bought and sold and bred like cattle," he answered.

"You weren't raised in our culture," Joseph Brennan put in angrily. "If you had been, you would understand there is nothing wrong with what we do, that none of our slaves is terribly mistreated."

Lee continued to keep his eyes on Richard Potter. "Aren't they?" He'd have liked to tell everyone in this room what he knew Richard Potter did with some of his young Negro girls! But he would not embarrass Audra that way. He simply enjoyed watching Richard squirm, watching his eyes grow darker with rage. "The northern papers tell stories of all kinds of atrocities being committed by southern slaveholders against their Negroes, ever since the incident with John Brown—whippings, rapes, even murders."

"The northern papers exaggerate!" Joseph insisted. "But you believe what you want. There won't be anything you Yankees can do about it if we secede from the Union and begin making our *own* laws. The North is out to destroy our whole way of life, Mr. Jeffreys, and we won't stand for it! What if the government suddenly told you that you had to increase the pay for your employees by ten times what they are getting now, while you get no more money for your product than you always have! Would that not ruin men like your father, Mr. Jeffreys?"

Others joined in, voicing their opinions but all with the same meaning. These men believed the South could survive only as slave states, and men like Lee and his father must understand that or face a broken Union.

Lee looked from Richard to Audra's father. "Louisiana and all the other southern states are a part of the *United* States, Mr. Brennan. To secede from that Union is nothing short of treason, and the President, *whoever* he is, will never stand for it."

Women whispered behind their fans, and the men grumbled. "Let them try to stop us!" one man muttered.

Audra watched Lee, and all other feelings aside, she saw that old Yankee determination in his eyes, just as strong and intent as Richard and her father could be in their own Southern pride. Yes, even if Richard were not her husband, loving Lee would have presented terrible problems.

"And I suppose you think that President will be Abraham Lincoln!" Miles Farrell challenged.

"Looks like a pretty sure thing to me," Lee answered.

"And just what will the Federal government do about secession?" Joseph Brennan asked.

Lee met the man's angry glare. "We'll come down here and *force* compliance and do whatever has to be done to hold the Union together."

"*We*, Mr. Jeffreys?" The question was posed by Richard. He looked down at Audra victoriously, as though he were about to show her how foolish she was to have gone to bed with this Yankee traitor. A sneer moved across his face. "Are you saying that if this matter should come to war, you would join in the fighting?" he asked Lee.

"That will never happen," someone in the crowd insisted.

"Of course it could," another replied.

"I'm a graduate of West Point," Lee answered. The rest of the crowd quieted. "Yes, if the Union needed me to fight a war, I would join the Union cause. They would need officers, men to help organize an army of volunteers."

Joey moved in to stand beside his father, wondering what kind of trouble this would lead to. Lee's glare at Richard never flinched when Richard responded. "An *army*?" Richard took a deep breath, a human volcano ready to explode. "You walk among us tonight, Mr. Jeffreys, come here to congratulate Audra and me, call yourself a friend to Joey; yet you would not hesitate to come down here as our enemy, and to kill men like Audra's father, young boys like Joey, just for the Union cause. Is *that* what you're saying?"

The room was hushed, all eyes on Lee. He stepped a little closer to Richard. "I'm saying I will do what I must. I hope it will never come to that; but there are *some* men I could kill very easily, Mr. Potter. I'm sure you feel the same way."

"Yes, Mr. Jeffreys, I certainly do." He pushed Audra's hand from his arm. "I appreciate your coming all the way down here to see Joey and to congratulate Audra, Mr. Jeffreys, but I think perhaps you had better leave."

"Damn Yankee!" someone whispered.

Lee gave Richard a bitter smile. "Gladly, Mr. Potter. I did not come here to make trouble. You southern *gentlemen* seem to be the ones intent on doing that. If my presence disturbs everyone so much, I'll leave, but first perhaps you and Audra and your father-in-law will be kind enough to come downstairs with me. I would like you to open the gift I brought you."

Richard frowned. What was Lee up to? "We will accept your gift, Mr. Jeffreys, with the good wishes in which I am sure it is intended. And we will all pray that there will never be war between us."

There will always *be war between us, Richard Potter,*
Lee thought. *And it will have nothing to do with matters of
North and South.* "I don't want war anymore than all of you
do," he answered.

Richard turned to Audra, his eyes so full of rage that
she felt like running away. She wondered herself what Lee
could have had in mind, coming here. So far he had only
made things worse for her. "Let's go downstairs, love, and
open Mr. Jeffreys's gift, shall we?" Richard grabbed her arm
even harder, nearly drawing tears. He forced a smile, ordering the orchestra to play more waltzes for his guests and
telling everyone to enjoy themselves. "Audra and I will re-
join you shortly," he told them. He looked at Lee. "Shall we
go downstairs?"

He turned and headed out, keeping firm hold on
Audra. People moved out of the way to let them by. Joseph
Brennan, his face beet-red with anger and hatred, followed.

Lee started to follow when he realized Joey was walking beside him. He turned to the boy, putting a firm hand
on his shoulder. "Stay here, Joey."

Joey looked almost ready to cry. "Why? I'd like t-to see
your gift, Lee."

The orchestra struck up another tune, so that no one
could hear what Lee said to Joey. "I don't *want* you there,"
he told the boy sternly.

"There's something bad wrong, isn't there, Lee?"

"Nothing that I can't fix. I'm going to do that right now.
You just promise me that you'll keep an eye on your sister
and make sure she's taken care of."

"You love her, don't you?"

Richard waited near the doors, his anger and irritation
building. What the hell was the man saying to Joey?

"How I feel about Audra doesn't matter now," Lee said
quietly. "All you need to know is, well, Audra and I—it
never could have worked out between us. But your new
brother-in-law hasn't been treating her right. I'm going to
set him straight, and then I'm going to get out of her life
forever. I trust that you and your father love her and will
make sure she's happy." He shook Joey's hand and squeezed
it reassuringly. "You're turning into quite a man, Joey. I'll al-

ways treasure our friendship, but it will have to be only a
memory. Do you understand?"

God, how he hated the look of despair in Joey's eyes.
He wished there were more time to talk to the boy, but it
was impossible. He had to have his say with Richard Potter
and get the hell out of there. He turned and left, Richard,
Joseph, and Audra following him downstairs.

Richard Potter closed the doors to the second-floor parlor, then turned to Lee. "Now," the man said, "suppose you
tell me and my father-in-law just what the hell you are *really* doing here! And talk fast, Mr. Jeffreys, before I decide
to gather some men and have you thrown off this property
by force, or *buried* on it!"

Lee did not flinch. "I'm not sure you want your father-
in-law to hear all of it, or that he wants Audra to know all
of it, but it's going to get said, and I don't give a damn if Joseph Brennan *does* have a bad heart!"

"Lee—" Audra started to interrupt.

"It can't continue, Audra!" Lee turned to her, sorry for
the helpless, frightened look on her face. "It isn't worth the
cost to you!" He looked at Joseph and noticed the man beginning to pale.

"What do you mean, *Audra's* cost?" the man asked.

Lee walked closer to him. "Are you *blind*, man? Didn't
you see the shape your daughter was in when this bastard,
your son-in-law, brought her home from Cypress Hollow?
Did you really think she was just *ill*? She should have been
happy! Glowing!"

"How in hell do *you* know what shape she was in?"
Richard interjected.

Audra put a hand to her chest, terrified.

Lee moved close to Richard. "Because I paid your wife
a visit already," Lee answered boldly. "Three weeks ago. I
didn't read about her marriage up North! I didn't know
about it until I came down here to see her, to see if she
might have changed her mind and decided *we* could be together after all!"

This time it was Richard who paled. "You get off this

property right now, you son of a bitch! And if I find out you fucked my wife while I was gone—"

Lee rammed a hard fist into the man's gut before he could finish, then kicked him in the groin. Audra gasped as Richard collapsed to the floor and curled up. Lee turned to a livid Joseph Brennan. "I visited Audra because I *thought* she had received a letter I sent her telling her I was coming!" he roared. "A letter she never received! Nor did she receive a second, more recent letter. Maybe you can *explain* that, Mr. Brennan!"

The man backed away slightly. "I . . . I don't know what you mean. Audra never received any letter."

Lee looked disgusted. "Go ahead and lie to your daughter," he said. "She believes everything you tell her. She loves you so much that she sacrificed her happiness, because she thought marrying Richard Potter was best for you and Joey and for Brennan Manor! The sad part is I went along with it! I agreed it was best, because we're too different to be able to stay together. I love your daughter, Mr. Brennan, and she loves me, but she came home because she knew this was where she belonged. I wouldn't have minded any of it, not even the fact that you kept my letters from her, if I had come down here and found her happily married. But what I found was a sick, thin, nervous wreck of a woman whose once-proud spirit was completely broken! Why don't you ask her what made that happen!"

Audra turned away, unable to speak. Lee told her father all he knew, while Richard kept struggling to get back to his feet. Outside the parlor doors Joey heard the awful truth, and he ran to his room, vowing to find a way to make up for all she had suffered.

Joseph Brennan turned to his daughter. "Is he telling the truth?" She collapsed into a chair and broke into tears. Joseph took a deep breath, looking down at Richard. "I was so proud to see my daughter marry you. I was so sure you were the right man for her. How *dare* you treat my Audra that way!"

"She *slept* with him, last summer in Connecticut!" Richard said viciously to a shocked Joseph Brennan. "When

I married your daughter, I expected a *virgin*. You gave me soiled goods, Joseph!"

Lee jerked him up by the front of his silk suit, and slammed him into a wall. "She was a young girl in love, homesick and alone. We *loved* each other, and there was nothing slutty or wrong about it! What Audra did had nothing to do with her honor. She married you in full faith that you would love her the way she *deserves* to be loved, and fully intending to be a faithful wife."

Richard shook with rage. "And *has* she been faithful? What happened while I was gone?"

"*Nothing* happened!" Lee lied. "And nothing ever will, because I won't be back after tonight. I came only to warn you, Potter, that if I hear you're mistreating Audra in any way, I'll be back. And by God, even if it costs me a hanging, I'll *murder* you! You can *count* on it!"

Audra looked shocked as, for the first time, she saw fear in the powerful Richard Potter's dark eyes. "You wouldn't dare—" he challenged Lee.

"*Try* me!" Again Lee rammed his knee into the man's groin, then slammed a hard fist into Richard's face, knocking the man against the piano. Richard grunted in agony and wilted to the floor, out cold. Lee started for him again, but Audra cried out for him to stop. Lee hesitated.

"He's still my husband!" she told him, her body jerking in a sob. "I'm vowed to him before God. I can't just stand here and watch you kill him! Please don't bring any more shame on me, Lee," she begged. "You've done all you can do."

Lee looked down at his bruised hands, then turned away from Richard's crumpled body. Audra turned anguished eyes to her father. "I'm sorry, Father. I didn't want you to know about Lee, or how Richard was treating me. I was afraid it would kill you—"

"This was the only way to make sure the abuse is stopped," Lee said. "I had to take the risk! You just make damn sure your daughter is treated right. If I have to come back here, I'll see that everyone in Louisiana knows what kind of brute you have for a son-in-law! I love Audra enough to risk my own life to make sure she never suffers at that man's hands again!"

Richard groaned and began to stir.

"He's a very powerful man," Joseph replied. "And he's Audra's legal husband and part owner of Brennan Manor now. How much can I do? I'm an old, sick man."

Lee took some papers from the inside pocket of his suit jacket. "You can file an amendment to the agreement you made with him when he married Audra," he answered. "I went to a local attorney's office in Baton Rouge and purchased the proper forms, wrote this up myself. It's a sworn statement that will be attached to your current arrangements for ownership of Brennan Manor."

Joseph looked at his daughter, and she met his gaze defiantly. "I showed him the papers. He said he could help me, Father. I was so afraid of Richard, I agreed."

"These say that Richard will share the profits of Brennan Manor, as in your original documents, but only under your approval, which he must get in writing at the end of every fiscal year. He will not actually own any of this place until your death, and then he owns only one quarter of it. Audra will own the other quarter, and Joey will own half. From then on Richard may still share half the profits, but only if Joey and Audra approve in writing, as you had to do. That approval will depend on how he has been treating Audra. If he still chooses to mistreat her and give up his share of the profits, I'll know about it, believe me. Richard believes his wealth and power make him immune to threats, but I have wealth and power of my own, Mr. Brennan, and *no* man is immune to death!"

Joseph looked down at the papers he held in a shaking hand, then sank into a nearby chair. He looked at his daughter, tears in his eyes. "I didn't know. . . . I thought marrying Richard would be best for you and Joey."

"You don't give Joey enough credit," Lee told the man. He walked over to Richard and yanked him to a sitting position. Blood oozed from the man's nose and a cut under his left eye. "I've got something for you to sign, you bastard!" Lee growled. You hear me? You be good to the woman who is going to be the mother of your *children*, or you're going to lose all the nice little extras that came with marrying her!" He looked at Audra. "Hand me those papers and get me a pen from that desk over there."

Audra obeyed, taking the papers from her father. Lee took a handkerchief from his pocket and pressed it against Richard's nose and face to help stop the bleeding. "Don't think I have any sympathy for you, you son of a bitch! I just don't want you to get blood on the papers you're going to sign." He took the papers from Audra, and laid them and the pen on the piano. Then he jerked Richard to his feet. "Sign on the dotted line, my friend!"

"What . . . what is . . . this?"

"Just sign, or I'll blacken your other eye and get rid of a few of your teeth! The handsome Richard Potter wouldn't want his looks distorted now, would he?"

Richard groaned, took the pen. "I don't understand. . . ."

"Your wife and father-in-law will explain later, when you're feeling better," Lee told him. "Just sign your name!"

Richard obeyed. As soon as he finished, Lee let him fall to the floor again, where the man lay groaning. Lee handed the papers to Joseph, keeping one copy for himself. "Make sure your attorney gets that. There's another clause in there I didn't mention—that Richard agrees never to sleep with his young Negro girls again. Any man who gets himself into that many women can end up with syphilis or worse. I couldn't care less if *he* died from it, but he's not going to give something like that to Audra. I just pray he hasn't already." He glanced at Audra, who stood beside her father. She looked away in embarrassment at the remark, and Lee walked closer, grasping her arms. "It's over, Audra. He won't hurt you again, he won't dare. Or I'll be back." He took her chin in his hands and turned her face to him. "I love you. You keep that spirit and pride, you hear me?"

"Yes," she replied in a near whisper, tears in her eyes. "I didn't stop you just for Richard's sake. If you had killed him, you would have been hunted down and hanged, and everyone would know why you did it. Adultery and murder are such ugly words, Lee."

He suddenly had to fight tears of his own, as he leaned

forward to kiss her forehead. "I understand." He backed away, holding her eyes a moment longer. "Good-bye, Audra." He turned and walked out.

Audra watched him go, tempted to run after him. She looked at Richard, then walked over to kneel beside him. She helped him to a sitting position and pressed the handkerchief to his still-bleeding wounds. "We have to go back to the ballroom and pretend everything is fine," she told her father. "We'll tell the others that Richard sent Lee on his way, that a messenger came to tell him there is some kind of trouble at Cypress Hollow. Get some of the servants and we'll take him to our room. I don't want anyone to see him this way."

Joseph looked down at the papers in his hand, still stunned by what had occurred. "Yes. All right." He shoved the papers into the pocket of his jacket and rose.

"Are you all right, Father?"

"Yes, child."

Audra looked up at him. "*Did* you hide Lee's letters from me?"

Joseph swallowed. "No. I never got any letter, Audra. Something must have happened to it. You know how easily mail gets lost, what with robberies and such. Just last month a riverboat carrying mail from Chicago had a boiler explosion. The whole thing blew up and all the mail was lost." He turned away. "I'll go get help."

He left, and Audra wondered if he was telling the truth. She had to believe him, didn't she? He was her father. He loved her. She took a cushion from a nearby settee and placed it under Richard's head. She wanted one last word with Lee. One last look, one last touch. She hurried to the second-floor balcony to call out to him, but she could hear the clattering of a horse's hooves on the brick drive as he rode away. *Let him go,* a voice told her. She wanted to scream his name, to run after him, but she couldn't, she was Mrs. Richard Potter.

She walked back into the parlor, and then she saw it—a big gift-wrapped box sitting on the piano. She had been so upset over all that had happened, she hadn't noticed it until now. She walked over to it, touched it lovingly, unwrapped it with shaking hands.

Inside the box were two sea gulls made of alabaster, set on top of wood carved to look like logs, and placed on a marble base. What a beautiful gift it was! She could almost see and smell the waves washing up onto the beach at Maple Shadows, could hear the cry of the sea gulls and feel the sand between her toes.

Found a man in New Orleans who makes these by hand, the note with the gift read. *They were made on the Gulf, but they reminded me of the good times we shared in Connecticut. Think of me whenever you look at them. God bless and protect you, Audra. Love always, Lee.*

Richard stirred, and she quickly folded the note and walked over to hide it in the piano bench. She was suddenly awash in tears. The man she loved was out of her life forever.

PART
3

January 3, 1861: Georgia takes over Federal Fort Pulaski.
January 9, 1861: Mississippi secedes from the Union.
January 10, 1861: Florida secedes from the Union.
January 11, 1861: Alabama secedes from the Union.
January 19, 1861: Georgia secedes from the Union.
January 26, 1861: Louisiana secedes from the Union.

MAY 1861

  Lee looked up at the ostentatious brick home that belonged to the Jeffreys family. Its several gables were trimmed with lace-design edging, and a turret at one end was topped with a concrete battlement, like that of a castle tower. It had been fun to explore the house with his brothers when he was young. He knew every nook and cranny of the twenty-room mansion, remembered once counting the arched windows and every separate pane, but he could no longer remember the total.

  The Jeffreys estate was in northern New York, past the Bronx, in an area where only the richest of the rich dwelled, nestled away from the grime and noise and smell of the city. Here lived the men who made their fortunes off the people who toiled for ungodly hours for equally ungodly wages in the city's factories. He could have built a home like this for himself, but it was the last thing he would ever want. His modest town house had been enough for him, and why his father hung on to this monster of a home now that his wife was dead and all his children were gone, he could not imagine. Fact was, his father had *never* needed a house quite this big. He had built it solely to show others how much money the family had. Lee had never thought about it when he was little, but now he understood that his mother had never liked it here. She had been truly happy only when she took the children to Maple Shadows in the summers. This house had a coldness about it, both outside and in. The rooms were just too damn big, so big that voices echoed inside them. It was a showplace, not a home, and in those years when his father was younger and building his empire, he was almost never there with the family.

He had not visited this place in years. Bennett James had talked him into coming. He tied his horse, wondering when he was going to quit taking Bennett's advice. He'd listened to the man when he'd told him to go see Audra, and what a disaster that had turned out to be! Thank God there had been no messages from Lena or Toosie over the past year. Apparently Richard Potter had taken his warnings to heart and didn't dared to abuse Audra.

He had felt so empty and alone this past year that he was almost glad President Lincoln had called for volunteers to help curb the "insurrection." So far eight southern states had seceded from the Union, and something had to be done. Now military duty would keep him plenty busy for a while, busy enough to put aside all thoughts of Audra, thoughts that he hoped would be gone for good once his stint with the Army was done. He feared that whatever was to come would affect Audra and those she loved, since Louisiana was one of the states that had already seceded.

South Carolina had dared to commit the first act of defiance by attacking Fort Sumter, and damned if the Union commander there hadn't surrendered! It was an embarrassment! The President had not actually declared war yet, but calling for seventy-five thousand volunteers was about as close as he could come to it. With his West Point credentials, Lee expected to join up as an officer, and help organize the hopelessly *disorganized* and pitifully inept Union Army.

He knocked on the door, hoping he wasn't making a mistake by coming here. James had suggested that if he was going to join the army, he ought to go see his father first, in spite of how he felt about the man. He'd heard from his brother Carl that their father had been feeling ill lately. Lee figured he had to be feeling pretty poorly to have left his offices in the city to come here and rest.

A butler answered the door, his face breaking into a smile when he saw Lee. "How good to see you, Master Lee! It's been such a long time. Come in!"

"Hello, Carter," Lee said, shaking the man's hand as he stepped inside. He tried to remember how long Carter Regis had been with the family, just about as far back as he could remember. The man had to be in his sixties, and he had never married. He seemed perfectly content to run the Jeffreys mansion.

"Your father will be so happy to see you. He hasn't been well lately, you know. It's too bad he lost his run for the Senate, but perhaps it was best, after all, considering his health."

"Is it that bad? I've never known my father to have anything that kept him down for long. I figured it was just a temporary thing."

"Well, that's what we all hope, and your father *has* been feeling better again the last few days. He is even talking about going back to work."

Lee handed the man his hat and overcoat, wondering if spring would miss New York altogether this year. It had even snowed a little this morning, but by late afternoon the snow had turned to a cold rain.

"I hope you have a good fire going in the parlor, Carter."

"Yes, sir. And that is where your father is sitting and reading, so you just go right in."

"Good." Lee rubbed his hands together. "The ferry ride through the East River and into the Sound on the way here was damn cold, let alone riding in an open carriage from the docks to here."

"Well, you go into the parlor and I'll have someone bring you something hot to drink. Will tea be satisfactory?"

"Fine. But bring me a shot of something stronger along with it."

"Of course," Carter answered with a knowing grin.

Lee left the man and walked through the huge two-story-high entranceway, beneath a magnificent chandelier. His footsteps echoed on the marble floor until he reached the parlor, which was carpeted with an Oriental rug. A fire burned brightly in the fireplace, and near the hearth sat his white-haired father in a black satin smoking jacket, a woolen blanket over his lap and a newspaper in his hands. He held a pipe in his mouth. Lee could not remember ever seeing the man without that pipe.

The minute Lee saw him, old, hard feelings enveloped him, but when his father looked up, Lee could not help a feeling of alarm at the man's appearance. Edmund Jeffreys was a tall, well-built man, who had always been strong and robust. He had never had a truly sick day in his life as far back as Lee could remember, but now he did look ill, much thinner, much older.

"Lee!" the man spoke up. "I got your message that you were coming. What brings you clear up here away from your work?"

Lee stepped closer. "I could ask the same of you, Dad. No one has dedicated more of his life to his work than you always have."

The man took his pipe from his mouth and set aside his paper. He rose, throwing the blanket over the back of his velvet chair. To Lee's amazement Edmund embraced him. "It's good to see you, Lee." He pulled away. "As far as myself, well, maybe old age and working too hard are catching up with me, I don't know. I probably should have listened to your mother all those years ago and started taking it a little easier a lot sooner." He sat back down in the chair, sighing as though weary. "God knows I should have spent more time with Anna. She would have liked that. It's hard to believe she's been gone two years already." He puffed his pipe for a moment, watching the flames in the fireplace. "It's a sad thing to realize too late that you should have shown someone a little more love and attention, Lee."

Lee was surprised at the remark. This did not sound like his father at all. He thought about Audra, how he'd decided too late to go to her; and his mother, who had begged him to stay a little longer that summer before she died. Yes, he had been too late himself in taking care of those he loved. "I know exactly what you mean," he answered, taking a seat across from the man. "I suppose if someone could predict our futures for us, we could all avoid a lot of mistakes."

Edmund met his son's blue eyes—blue like his mother's. There was a lot about Lee that was like his mother. "Yes, we could, couldn't we?" He took a deep breath. "I've made some mistakes with you, son. I didn't give them much thought until I began to suspect the meaning of the telegram you sent me. You wouldn't be paying me a visit out of any particular affection you have for me, now, would you? I know better than that. You've only come to tell me you're volunteering for the Union Army, which, by the way, does not surprise me."

Lee just stared at the man, dumbfounded at his insight, as well as at the simple admission that he had made mistakes. What was going on here? Was his father sicker than he was letting on? "How did you know?"

Edmund smiled sadly. "Because I know my son and how he feels about the Union. And, after all, I didn't get where I am without learning how to read people. You, my son, are like an open book. I've always known how you felt about most things."

Lee felt confused. He had expected no more than a cordial greeting and "good luck" from his father, but the man seemed eager to talk. There was actually warmth in his eyes Lee hadn't seen since he was a very small boy. "I'm heading for Washington next week. I figured my training at West Point could come in handy."

Edmund nodded. "And to think I was angry as hell when you told me you wanted to go to an academy first instead of Yale. I didn't see where it would do you any good as far as helping with the family businesses. It took your mother's death to make me sit down and take stock of a few things. It has taken my own illness for me to realize what is and is not important in life."

He sighed, setting his pipe aside. "For some reason you never wanted to be a part of Jeffreys Enterprises," he continued. "I couldn't understand that, Lee. Your great-grandfather started it all, and his sons carried it on, then their sons, except that I'm the only one left now. I expected all three of my sons to keep things going, but you were just never interested. I worked for years building the businesses so that I could hand my sons something even bigger and better than what my father handed me, and his father before him. But always I felt as if you didn't appreciate any of it."

A maid brought in a silver tray with a pot of tea and cups, as well as a small bottle of brandy and a shot glass. Edmund dismissed her as Lee leaned forward to pour himself a brandy. He gulped it down, then poured another. "It isn't that I didn't appreciate any of it, Dad. I'm just not cut out for that life. Carl and David are, and that's fine; but I wanted something of my own, and I'm damn good at what I do."

The man smiled knowingly. "Oh, I'm well aware of that. You think I tried to stop you, don't you? You think I deliberately tried to destroy you."

Lee frowned, amazed the man would admit such a thing. He had no idea how to react. He swallowed the second shot of whiskey, then set the glass down. "What else could I think when you didn't ask me to represent the family businesses, and when none of your close associates would deal with me? Why did you do it?"

Edmund leaned back, adjusting the blanket on his lap. "Someday, when you have sons of your own, you'll understand that fathers love their children so much that they will even risk losing their affection to do what they know is best for them. Pour me some of that tea, will you?"

Lee obliged. "Trying to hurt my business was best for me? I don't call that love."

"Well, son, let me put it this way. When a Jeffreys man

sets out to do something, he gives it all he's got. Nothing halfway. I decided that if what you wanted was to be a lawyer and make your own name and fortune without my help, then, by God, you'd *earn* it. I wasn't going to have people saying that my son got where he is because his father handed him his clients. I figured I'd test you, see just how damn bad you really wanted your own practice. You would either be a great success or fold and come crawling to me and ask to be brought into Jeffreys Enterprises. All this time you probably thought I wanted you to fold and come crawling; but what I wanted was to see you succeed in spite of anything I did to try to stop you; and you did. I'm proud of you, son. I celebrated inwardly when you stole that railroad deal right out from under Cy Jordan's nose. That was brilliant!"

Lee set the pot down on the tray. Was there something wrong with his hearing? He rose and walked to the fireplace. "Why in God's name have you waited until now to tell me all of this?"

"Because it *took* a long time for you to get where you are. Now I can honestly say my son is a successful attorney, and he did it all on his own. Why do you think I never asked you to represent Jeffreys Enterprises so I could get rid of that bastard Cy Jordan? You're ten times smarter than that man." Edmund chuckled. "Jordan fumed about that railroad thing for a long time." He breathed a sigh of satisfaction. "Lee, no father wants his son to suffer or not to succeed. You've done it right, and in grand style!"

Lee watched the flames, overcome with emotion, amazed at this revelation. He remembered Bennett James once saying that fathers often risked alienating their sons by choosing what they think is best for them over what everyone else expects them to do. "My God, Dad, I wish you would have told me all this sooner. You've had me practically hating you all these years." He ran a hand through his hair and turned to face the man. "I purposely made it a point not to be at Maple Shadows when you and Carl and David were because I didn't want any arguments in front of Mother, and because I could hardly stand being around you when I knew you had tried to practically ruin me before I even got off the ground."

"Your mother understood more than you think she did, Lee. She didn't always fully agree with what I was doing, but she went along with it because she trusted that a father knows best when it comes to his sons. Fact is, I meant to have a talk with you about it that summer, but then you went to Maple Shadows sooner than I could, and by the time I got there, you were gone, and your mother . . ." Edmund's voice choked up. "At any rate, grief kept me from talking about much of anything for a while, and then I got wrapped up in the senatorial race, and I heard you'd gone to Louisiana. One thing led to another, and we never got the chance to talk. I was thrilled when I got the telegram that said you were coming to see me, and I decided that if you were planning to march off to war, I'd better get some things said that needed saying." The man frowned and looked up at his son. "Why the trip to Louisiana, Lee? Did you go to see that Brennan girl?"

Lee returned to his chair and leaned forward to take one of his father's cigars from the table between them. "Yes."

Edmund watched him carefully. His son's eyes said more than they wished to, just as Anna's used to do. Lee was capable of loving deeply, like his mother. "Did you love her?"

Lee rolled the cigar in his fingers for a moment. He couldn't ever remember having such an intimate conversation with his father. "I fell in love with her that summer she was at Maple Shadows. For obvious reasons it never could have worked, but I couldn't resist going down there for one more try. She was already married to someone else."

"I'm sorry, Lee. She was a beautiful girl, but southern born and bred. I'm sure you were right that it would never have worked. With the North and South practically at war . . . I don't think this is going to be anything of short duration. I think it's going to be a bloodbath."

Lee lit the cigar and drew on it before meeting his father's eyes. "Bennett James said the same thing."

Edmund kept his gaze fixed on his son's face. "Those

southerners are a stubborn lot, Lee. You must know that. Seceding from the Union takes guts and resolve. We shouldn't take it lightly. Those rebels are in this for the long haul, count on it. If I were younger, I'd volunteer myself. I've lost the Senate race, son, but there is plenty left I can do with my money and power to help the cause." He paused. "I'm proud of you for volunteering. God knows the rotten excuse of an army we have right now can use a man like you. The minute Lincoln called for volunteers, I knew you'd decide to go. Maybe it will be good for you, a way to keep you completely occupied and keep your mind off losing that girl." He sipped his tea and watched his son for a moment. "What about the law firm? You could be gone for a year or two, Lee."

"James and Stillwell can keep things going. If I'm gone too long, I've told them they can take over completely. I'll just have to start all over again when I'm back. I can do it."

"I'm sure you can. I just pray you'll make it out of this alive and come home in one piece."

Lee frowned. "You really think it will be that bad?"

"There's nothing uglier than a civil war, son. Nothing. As an officer who will have to make decisions, you remember one thing. For the most part you'll be going into rebel territory to do the fighting. You'll be on their home ground, unfamiliar territory to you, but they'll know it like the backs of their hands. On top of that, they're used to the climate. The government may think this is going to be an easy victory, but we've already had our first defeat. I don't think folks in the North are taking this as seriously as the South, but they'll wake up soon enough."

"A blockade on the ocean side and along the Mississippi should shut them down quick enough. When they can't ship out their damned cotton and sugar cane, they'll be begging to get back into the Union."

Edmund leaned forward, resting his elbows on his knees. "It's like I said, Lee. These rebels are damned stubborn and resilient. We need to show our power, totally discourage them as fast as possible. This Confederate victory at Fort Sumter has only made them more confident and determined. Don't fool yourself into thinking it will end quickly.

The man leaned even closer, and Lee thought he detected tears in his father's eyes. "You understand something, Lee. If you join up, you're going to see fighting. You're going to kill men, and they'll be trying to kill you. Don't make the mistake of thinking this won't get nasty. I won't rest easy until both you and David are back home safe and sound."

"David? He's joining, too?"

"Yes. Carl would like to, but he's got his children to think about, and I need at least one of my sons to stay here and help me, especially with the way I've been feeling lately. I don't have the old energy anymore. Ever since your mother died . . . I don't know." He gazed around the high-ceilinged room. "I'm left with this big, useless house. I'm thinking of selling it. If I can unload it, I'll donate the money to the Union cause. I'll do everything I can on this end.

We should have more business than ever," he went on. "Carl is working on a deal with the government to make army tents using our canvas factory, and we ought to be able to get a contract to make boots for the soldiers. God knows there will also be more of a demand for iron. Railroads, iron ships, weapons to be made. At the same time, I'm losing employees. We've practically had to shut down temporarily because so many men quit to join up. They are flooding away from the factories by the thousands all over the North. President Lincoln has had no trouble getting volunteers. I hear Washington is swarming with regiments from every northern state. The newspapers say the capital is one huge military camp. Troops are stuffed into government buildings, warehouses, stables; tents cover every open piece of land. It must be quite a sight."

He looked resigned. "This raising of an army leaves me in a bind. I'll have to hire more women and children, more immigrants. It's one big mess, and I'm afraid poor Carl will be left to handle it all if I don't start feeling better, which means he'll end up just like me—spending all his hours on the job and neglecting his family when his boys are small and need him most."

Lee felt deep remorse at having misjudged his father

all these years. "How sick are you, Dad? Carter said you'd been feeling a little better the last couple of days."

"Oh, it comes and goes. I get pains in my right side that won't let up, then get sick to my stomach, then they're gone again. I expect it's just something I picked up in the city. I'm just glad you decided to come and see me before you go off to Washington. Will you be staying the night?"

Lee saw a plea in his father's eyes he had never seen before. It reminded him of the way his mother had looked at him that summer before he left Maple Shadows, but he hoped it couldn't be for the same reason. Edmund Jeffreys had always seemed so invincible. "I had already planned on staying over. I'm too damn cold to even think about going back out there. Besides, I don't think there's another ferry leaving until close to noon tomorrow."

"Is everything in order? Do you need me to do anything for you after you're gone?"

"No. I've rented out my town house, and James and Stillwell will handle office matters." Lee felt a dull ache in his chest, suddenly realizing that he had let pride and his temper cloud his image of his father. Finally he felt he could really talk to the man, and all he had was one night. It didn't seem right marching off to join the army now when his father was so changed. "Dad, I—"

"President Lincoln needs men like you, Lee. The *Union* needs you. These are dire times, and I'm just glad your mother didn't live to see what's happening." The man reached across and took Lee's hand. "You do the Jeffreys name proud, Lee. I wouldn't be surprised to see you come home a general, your chest covered with medals."

Lee smiled, feeling a little embarrassed at the words. "I'll do my best."

"You always have, Lee. I'm sorry for the misunderstandings over the years, son. I'm perfectly aware that I can be somewhat of a bastard at times. My own father was hard-nosed and demanding, and I guess I'm a lot like him; but I've let work rob me of a lot of good years when I could have been enjoying my family. I have a feeling that when the day comes you marry and settle, you won't be that way."

Audra. How was he ever going to find anyone to equal her? "I don't think that day is coming any too soon, Dad."

"Excuse me, sir," came Carter's voice at the door to the parlor. The man stood there holding a newspaper. "I have today's paper, sir, and I thought perhaps you would want to see it right away."

Edmund released Lee's hand. "What's so important, Carter?"

The man came inside the room, looking embarrassed at having to interrupt what looked like an intimate conversation between father and son. "Alarming headlines, sir." The man handed the newspaper to Edmund, and he opened it to scan it a moment.

"Damn," the man muttered. "More bloodshed already. It says here that a mob of secessionists stoned Union troops in Baltimore. Four of the men were killed." He sighed deeply. "Maryland has remained loyal to the Union, yet Union troops there get stoned to death!" He looked over at Lee. "It's getting ugly, son, just as I said it would."

"Excuse me, sir, but another article says that Mr. Robert E. Lee has resigned his army commission and has joined the Confederacy," Carter added.

Edmund sighed. "Which means the South is definitely building its army." He handed the paper to Lee. "I wish we had more time, Lee, but apparently you can't get to Washington any too soon. I'll wire Governor Morgan and have him contact the President himself to see that you get a decent commission."

Lee took the newspaper and scanned the articles. Audra, Joey and Brennan Manor seemed so far away. Surely, if this came to all-out war, it would be a long time before the fighting reached that far south. Maybe it never would. Northern Virginia was the battleground for now. Confederate troops were already positioned only two miles from Washington, with even stronger forces backing them at a place called Manassas Junction near a stream called Bull Run.

His father was right. He couldn't get to Washington any too soon. He was just glad he'd come home first. This time Bennett's advice had been right on target. Feeling closer to his father had removed a great weight from his shoulders, but he still had nightmares about Audra lying in Richard Potter's bed. That was a burden he would carry for the rest of his life.

18

Lieutenant Colonel Lee Jeffreys could see already that this war was going to last longer and be bloodier than even his father and Bennett James had predicted. The July heat was miserable, as were the thickly wooded hills of northern Virginia. It had been impossible to take troops and cannon through the thick undergrowth and dense forests, let alone over creeks with soft bottoms that bogged down heavy supply wagons. They had been forced to stick to regular roadways on their march to capture the Confederate stronghold at Bull Run, and most of those roads were nothing more than dirt tracks that allowed only one or two men to move through at a time. With several regiments totaling upwards of thirty-five thousand men headed for the area, the rough terrain and small footpaths made the going maddeningly slow, so slow that counting on an element of surprise to their attack was out of the question. That had become obvi-

ous when their first attack on Bull Run at Blackburn's Ford
had brought humiliating defeat.

All troops were camped at Centreville, the little village
where they had first gathered and to which they had been
forced to retreat. Lee's Twelfth New York Regiment and the
thousands of other men there were waiting for further orders from General Irvin McDowell, who Lee felt was totally
inept and whom few of the men even liked. Lee nursed his
own burned hands, full of anger as he recalled all that had
happened. Too many of the troops were still too green and
had been too confident. They had taken their sweet time
strolling toward their battleground, choking on dust and
groaning about the heat and humidity, which was almost unbearable. It had been difficult keeping the enlisted men in
order, as many would break rank to stop for a drink of water
or to chase some farmer's chickens. He'd even heard that a
regiment under Brigadier General Samuel Heintzelman,
which had marched in from another direction, had taken
hours to file one at a time across a narrow bridge over a
creek that was only knee-deep! Heintzelman was an honored veteran of the Mexican War and had fought in Indian
campaigns, yet even he seemed to be unconcerned about
the impending battle and how important it might be to
strike quickly.

This was no organized army. As hard as he and other
West Pointers had worked to train the troops, most of these
men had not been taking the war seriously. That first day
they headed into northern Virginia they had marched only
six miles. The Confederates had had plenty of time to become aware of their approach, and when they reached
Fairfax Courthouse on July 17, the rebels had already va-
cated the premises, so hastily that they had left behind
camp fires, some with food still cooking. It was reported
that Confederates had also had time to flee Heintzelman's
column to the south, and that the rebels had burned the
Orange and Alexandria Railroad bridge. If Heintzelman
had not gotten lost in the jumbled terrain, he might have
come upon the rebels before they had a chance to escape.
For a while General McDowell was not even sure where
Heintzelman's troops were located.

The Federals would try again, probably tomorrow, but Lee was convinced that if the battle was lost, it would be due to poor planning and misjudgment in the highest ranks.

McDowell had finally found Heintzelman that first day, but the maze of wooded hills and confusing footpaths had forced the general to rethink his strategy and move into Centreville, rather than take Sudley Springs first. Not long after that the real fighting had begun, when Lee was called in to back up Brigadier General Daniel Tyler, who had decided to charge across Bull Run at a crossing called Blackburn's Ford. Without McDowell's permission, Tyler had opened fire on the confederates with two twenty-pounders, and the Confederates were backing away. At first it appeared that that first skirmish would bring victory to the Federals, but hundreds of Confederates had taken cover along the tree-lined south bank of Bull Run. When the Federals came into the open past the stream, Confederates opened fire in a barrage of bullets that screamed and whistled and buzzed in every direction. Federal cannon exploded, rebels were yelling, and Federals were screaming their own war cries in return. Lee had never heard so much noise in his life. He had shot at several rebels, hitting many, never knew which were just wounded and which he had killed. It was a strange and terrible feeling to kill men, and he knew now that it was something he would have to get used to.

McDowell's adjutant had ridden into the melee to advise Tyler to withdraw, but Tyler smelled blood, and he was sure he could keep the rebels in retreat. Bullets had continued to fly into Lee's regiment in such numbers that their whirring and singing reminded Lee of a hideous kind of music. His ears still hurt and his head ached from the noise.

He dipped his hands into cool water again to soothe them, wishing he'd had more say in what had gone on, hating Tyler for being such a poor judge of the situation and sending so many men to pain and death. Tyler had finally decided to withdraw, but by then Lee and his Twelfth New York had been left stuck out in front of the fighting alone. They were caught in thick underbrush of pine woods, the trees and bushes seemingly alive with rebels, who opened up with a murderous volley that had forced Lee and his men to the ground. They had fired back at targets they could not really see, and soon the barrels of their guns were too hot to touch. That was when Lee had burned his hands. He and the others had simply to take whatever cover they could find and lie waiting for help, but help did not come soon enough. Lee had no choice but to order his men to retreat, while the First Massachusetts and Michigan regiments, who had joined in the Federal attack, were also so barraged that they were flat on their bellies, unable to fight back.

Eventually all the Federal forces were compelled to retreat. Lee found it humiliating, as did most of the other men. He could still hear the rebel yells, could still hear their curses and laughter and name-calling. The entire incident would never have taken place if Tyler had not disobeyed McDowell's original orders to scout the area, not fight. The scene at the rear of Tyler's command had been one of pure bedlam. Lee could not control his own troops, who panicked and ran in all directions. Some carried wounded comrades; other wounded men stumbled along alone, their uniforms soaked with blood. By the time Lee was able to get them organized again, several of his men were missing, most likely dead or captured by the rebels. McDowell marched all of them back to Centreville. The men were tired, angry, and frustrated, grumbling about poor leadership.

That first battle told Lee all he needed to know. These men were not fully trained or mentally ready for real war, nor had they expected such a slaughter. They were disorganized and dazed. Wounded men lay in a nearby clearing, and in the quiet of night Lee could hear their screams of dire pain. In this first day of battle he had seen enough blood and terrible injuries that he would never forget it. The war had truly begun.

Joey approached Audra, who sat in the parlor of Brennan Manor embroidering. It seemed that was all she did anymore. She seldom sang, and he thought he understood why. Without Lee in her life, there was no song left in her. He glanced at the sea gulls that sat on the fireplace mantel. Richard had never touched the gift, nor forbade Audra to keep it. In fact, the man was seldom there. He spent a good deal of time at Cypress Hollow without his wife, and Joey realized Lee must have said or done something the night of the cotillion to set the man straight. He had not stayed around to listen to all of it. He had heard enough that night, enough to know that his sister was a very unhappy woman. The next day he had seen Richard's face. The man had stayed in bed for days, allowing no visitors, ordering everyone who knew Lee had given him a beating never to tell anyone else about it.

Richard had been a changed man since then, quieter, more subdued. Joey was glad Lee had given the man what he had coming, and he loved him for it; but in the end poor Audra was still alone. She at least was no longer being abused by her husband, but the man she really loved was out of her life forever now, and her marriage was obviously not a marriage at all.

"Audra?"

She looked up and smiled. "Joey! I thought you were with Father in the fields."

"I was, earlier, but it got too hot for b-both of us."

"Yes, it is a miserable July, isn't it?"

The boy came closer. "F-father is going into B-baton Rouge tomorrow to see if there is any news about what's happening up in Virginia. I'm going with him."

"When Richard was here two days ago, he said that General Lee is calling up men from all over the South. I'm sure they'll end all of this quickly, Joey. Once Generals Beauregard and Johnston march on Washington like the newspapers say they will do, and show the Federals how strong and determined we are, the North will back away and leave us alone."

"D-do you really think so?"

Audra stuck her needle into the stretched fabric and leaned back in her chair. "We have to believe it, Joey."

The boy studied her a moment. She looked pretty today in a simple white linen dress, her hair drawn away from her face because of the heat. She had never really gotten back to her normal weight after that dreadful wedding night, and some of the sparkle was gone from her eyes. She was not the innocent, proud Audra who had spent the summer at Maple Shadows, but she was certainly still beautiful. It made him sick to think that he was part of the reason for her unhappiness. He had expected too much of her, had relied on her too heavily. He was man enough now to understand that, but it was too late. He ran a hand through his damp hair and walked over to take a chair beside her. "Audra, the reason I'm g-going with Father to Baton Rouge is b-because I'm joining up."

She paled. "What?"

"I'm g-going to volunteer in the Confederate Army."

Audra felt her stomach begin to ache. "Joey! You're only sixteen!"

"Sixteen is old enough. I already t-told Father."

"And he *agreed*?"

Joey looked down at a doily that decorated the arm of his chair and began tracing a finger over its design. "Sure he did. I knew he would. It g-gives him something t-to brag about." He looked at his sister again, unable to hide the tears of hurt in his eyes. "Don't you see, Audra? It's one thing I can do to make Father proud of me. Maybe I'll even be wounded and c-come home with a medal. It's for the c-cause, and it will make Father happy."

"Happy?" Audra set her embroidery aside and stood up. "Joey, you could be killed! Or you could be wounded and lie in terrible pain, without me to be there with you!"

The boy rose and faced her, standing several inches taller than she now. His body was filling out in a more manly way, and Audra could see less and less of the boy in him. There was even a new wisdom in his eyes. "That's just the t-trouble, Audra. I've depended on you way t-too long." Sorrow showed in his eyes. "I know about Lee, Audra, and about what Richard d-did to you. I heard—that night Lee came here. Part of the reason you married Richard was b-because you thought it was best for me, and now you're unhappy. It's p-partly my fault."

Audra closed her eyes and turned away, embarrassed

that her brother knew about her problems with Richard. "Joey, the decision Lee and I made had nothing to do with you. We had both simply decided it could never work. As far as marrying Richard, that's my own fault. I didn't feel right about it, but I really thought I could grow to love him. He seemed the perfect husband to help Father run Brennan Manor, and when Father got sick, it frightened me. Besides that, his dream was to see Richard and me married before he died, so I hurried the wedding myself."

She faced him again. "I've always had every confidence you could take over some day, Joey, but you were still so young, and I knew Father could die." She folded her arms and rubbed them nervously. "I really thought Richard would be good to me and it would all work out; but we don't always know what we are getting ourselves into in the choices we make in life, Joey, just like you don't realize what you're doing right now." She walked closer, her eyes misty. "Joey, what if the war doesn't end quickly? What if it turns into a long, drawn-out, bloody battle? I won't know where you are, if you're all right. From everything I've studied, war can be more terrible than you imagine. Soldiers starve and sometimes they're captured and imprisoned. All kinds of awful things happen." She took hold of his hand. "And you would have to kill men, Joey. Can you really do that?"

A tear slipped down his cheek. "You d-don't understand what it means to me to be able to d-do something that will make Father proud of me. I'll even kill Yankees, if that's what it takes. I'm a g-good marksman, Audra. They say the army will need sharpshooters, men who are extra g-good shots. I can make a name for myself." He quickly wiped at the tear. "I'm not afraid. This is something I can d-do all on my own, without Father, without you or Richard. I know Father has always been a little b-bit ashamed of me, and you have mothered me and sacrificed your own happiness for me. I c-can't let you and Father and Richard k-keep protecting me. I have to do this, Audra. Please don't b-b-beg Father to make me stay. He and Richard can run Brennan Manor and Cypress Hollow just f-fine on their own. If I don't do this, I'll never b-be of any importance."

Audra hugged him, breaking into tears. "That's not true, Joey. You'll always be important to me. You're my best friend. What will I do without you? I have no one."

"I'm sorry, Audra, b-but you have to let go of me and let me be a man."

Someone else had told her Joey needed that. Could it really have been two years ago, in Connecticut? Where was Lee now? Had he already joined the Union forces? He could die, and she would never know. She had never heard from him again since that night he had soundly whipped Richard into submission. Richard had hardly spoken to her since, nor had he made love to her. Toosie had hinted of rumors that Eleanor had visited Richard at Cypress Hollow several times and had spent the night. Her husband was apparently getting the sexual satisfaction he needed from her cousin, but it sickened her that Eleanor would do such a thing.

Her life was so empty now—no hope of children, no heart to go on with her music. Joey was literally all she had left, but maybe this was best for him, after all. Maybe the army would give him the self-confidence he needed. Maybe he would come home a decorated soldier after a Confederate victory. But she so feared the war. She hugged him even tighter. This was Joey, her innocent, soft-hearted brother. She didn't believe him when he said he wasn't afraid. She knew that having to kill the enemy would be terrible for him. "I'll be so lonely without you, Joey. It's always been the two of us."

Joey took her arms, gently forcing her to let go of him. "I know, Audra, but I'll b-be back. It won't be f-for all that long, and I'll write real often. I p-promise."

She nodded. How could she stop him? Making their father proud meant everything to Joey. She should hate the man for having brought so much heartache into his children's lives, yet she believed Joseph Brennan loved them and knew he'd meant well. He was still her father, and he had been so pitifully heartbroken over what had happened to her marriage that she did not have the heart to hold it against him.

"Maybe you and Richard will find some way to be

happy again, to f-fix things," Joey told her. "He's your husband, Audra. You should t-talk to him. I d-don't think he'll hurt you anymore."

She turned away. "I could have loved him once, Joey, but not anymore. I don't know what to do about Richard. We were married in the Church. If I divorce him, I'll have to resign my faith. Even then, in the eyes of God we'll always be married. I'm not sure I can go on this way, but I don't know what to do about it either."

Joey swallowed hard. "I'm sorry, Audra. When I g-get home, when the war is over, maybe everything will be d-different. Richard wants children. He has to patch things up sometime and b-b-be a husband to you."

Audra wiped at the tears on her cheeks, flushing at the remark. Her little brother understood more than she realized. "I don't know if *I* can ever be a wife to him again, Joey." She put on a smile for him. "Don't you worry about me and Richard. Just take care of yourself and watch out for those Yankees." She came over to him and touched his face. "Can't you wait just one more year, Joey? It might all be over by then."

He shook his head. "That's why I c-can't wait. I'll miss my chance." He put on a smile. "Besides, I'm excited about it! Wait till they see how good I can shoot! And F-father says he'll make sure I get into the b-best command. I'll make all of you p-proud of me. You'll see."

"I'm already proud of you, Joey. I always have been."

He sobered. "F-father hasn't. He will b-be, after this."

Audra hugged him again. "God be with you, Joey. You keep those Yankees out of Louisiana, you hear?"

"They'll never get this f-far. General Lee will make sure of that."

Weary. Audra felt so weary. How could she be only nineteen and feel so old? What was going to happen to her, to Joey? What was going to happen to the South? Could General Lee really keep the Yankees from getting this far?

For now she could take only one day at a time. Women were rallying in Baton Rouge, serving food and refreshments to volunteers who gathered there to ship out daily up the Mississippi, or by railroad to various gathering points.

Maybe she would take Toosie and go to Baton Rouge, help sew Confederate flags, organize fund-raising events to help the cause. She couldn't stay here, not with the situation the way it was with Richard, and not with Joey gone. She would go insane with loneliness.

"We'll win this war, Joey, and you will come home a hero. I can see it already." She drew back and met his eyes, praying she was right. "I love you, Joey. Always remember that. I love you more than anybody else on this earth."

He nodded, unable to answer, realizing just how true that statement was. He hated hurting Audra of all people, hated leaving her alone. Did she know that he was a lot more scared than he let her see? He didn't really want to leave Brennan Manor and his beloved sister, but there was something more important now. He was going to make damn sure Joseph Brennan never again had cause to be ashamed of his one and only son.

For two days after the disastrous fight at Blackburn's Ford, General McDowell contemplated a new plan of attack. To Lee's dismay, civilians from Washington began arriving at Centreville by the hundreds, following the Federal Army and expecting to see a firm thrashing of Confederates. They came in buggies and on horseback; some even walked—photographers, senators, congressmen, even women carrying picnic baskets. One Illinois congressman volunteered to fight as an infantryman, joining a Michigan regiment wearing top hat and tails!

Lee considered the whole situation ludicrous. These spectators did not belong there. They were making a circus out of the whole affair, and he feared they were not going to see the routing they expected to see. His confident superiors still were sure they could take Bull Run and push the Confederates well away from the capital, which was only twenty-five miles distant; but Lee was wary of the continuous sound of train whistles blowing intermittently over the last two days at Manassas Junction in the distant hills held by the Confederates. His superiors were sure those trains were bringing only a few unorganized rebel volunteers to join in the fight still to come, but Lee suspected the trains could be bringing many more men than the Federals surmised, building a rebel army that could give the Federals a thrashing.

What irked Lee the most was that the generals in charge were giving the Confederates all the time they needed to launch a stiff defensive, and he could not forget his father's words that the rebels were a stubborn, proud lot, fighting in their own territory, their own climate. They had already proved at Blackburn's Ford just how intimidating they could be, and there were several wooded hills to be crossed and conquered on their march to take Manassas Junction. All of them could be swarming with rebels.

Finally the orders came. Lee's units were to join General Heintzelman in a march on Sudley Ford, move through the area, and strike the enemy's left flank. McDowell would get behind the Confederates and drive them to the Manassas Gap line. The rebels would be surrounded and forced to surrender. An argument broke out between General Tyler and General McDowell. Tyler was still smarting from his humiliating defeat two days earlier and a berating from McDowell himself, and now he argued that McDowell might be underestimating the Confederate manpower that might be building up at Manassas Junction. He argued that the Federals might be facing two armies, one under southern General Beauregard, another under General Johnston. McDowell insisted that no matter what the buildup of Confederate troops, they had no choice but to attack and get the battle finished. They would take Bull Run, and they would march at two A.M. tomorrow morning, July 21, attacking at dawn.

Thousands of Federal troops lay in camp unable to sleep that night, including Lee. They watched the stars, listened to music from harmonicas and fiddles, watched the flames of their camp fires flicker. Many wrote letters home, praying those letters would not be the last ones received by their loved ones. Lee wrote to his father.

Dear Dad,
I am taking this time to write because tomor-

row we march on the Confederates at Manassas Junction, and I don't know when I'll be able to write again. I am afraid that you were right in saying this war will last a lot longer than three months. I have seen the determination of rebel resistance. I have heard bullets singing in my ears, have fired my weapon until it was too hot to touch. I have seen awful injuries that make a man sick to his stomach, yet we have fought only one battle. It was at Blackburn's Ford, and it was so poorly planned that we were forced to retreat, which took the fight out of a lot of the men. The troops are embarrassingly disorganized. I am doing what I can to get my own regiment in shape for what is to come and to buck up their courage. It is so easy to rally around one's flag and volunteer to fight for the "cause," but when a man gets into the reality of war, he quickly learns he has gotten himself into something that takes much more courage than he ever imagined possible.

I find that courage only in remembering why I am here. This awful hatred and division shows me what a terrible state this country will be in if the Union is not preserved. I am just afraid that the cost will be very high, and that it will be a long time before this country again finds union and peace. I have no idea when I will be coming home, so I send my love with this letter. Please carry it on to Carl and his family.

> *Always, Lee.*

One man nearby sat writing a letter to the woman he planned to marry. Lee desperately longed to know a woman waited somewhere for him, but the only woman he'd ever truly loved was the enemy now, and she belonged to someone else. Audra was gone from his life, yet for some reason he could not fully explain, he had brought her song with him into battle. He carried it in his inside breast pocket but never looked at it. Just having it close to his heart gave him an unexplainable comfort.

He folded the letter to his father and addressed it, handing it to a private nearby to get it mailed. He settled into his bedroll then, hoping to get at least a couple hours' sleep, if that was possible. Tomorrow they were to try to take Bull Run again. He had no doubt it was going to be one long day of hell.

19

NOVEMBER 1861

Audra poured punch from a crystal ladle into a glass, handing the drink to a young man she guessed to be close to Joey's age. His face was lit up with excitement at the prospect of going off to fight for the southern cause. Most of the men here in the ballroom of her Uncle John's home tonight were just as excited, including her uncle, who had decided that he, too, would lend his services to the Confederate Army. His age and wealth would ensure him of being appointed to a rank much higher than a common private.

Most of these young men seemed truly dedicated, willing to fight and die; but Audra suspected her Uncle John was only looking for glory. He was a pompous man who loved praise and attention. He and Aunt Janine believed that once the war was over and the Union was defeated, his having been an officer in the southern army would virtually guarantee John an important position in the new government, either on the state level or perhaps in the entire Confederacy. Aunt Janine was already talking about moving to Richmond one day soon. The woman did not seem the least bit worried that her husband might never come back at all.

Another young volunteer came to the serving table, and Audra offered him anything he pleased from the platters of sandwiches and fruits. She was glad she had come to Baton Rouge, even though staying with her aunt and uncle was often unpleasant. She had joined a circle of women who sewed flags and uniforms, and she felt as if she were truly contributing to the cause in some useful way. This was the third party her aunt and uncle had held for volunteers who had gathered here for a last farewell before setting off for Virginia, where it was reported thousands more were joining the Confederate Army. Although her aunt and uncle held these parties partly to show off their home and be the center of attention, she was nevertheless glad someone was doing something supportive for their brave southern boys, many of whom must be afraid and homesick.

Audra could not help getting caught up in the spirit of the times. From what she was hearing and reading, she decided perhaps she shouldn't worry so much about Joey. After all, according to newspaper reports, the Yankees had been soundly whipped at Bull Run, thanks to reinforcements led by General Thomas "Stonewall" Jackson. There had been more Confederate victories, at Wilson's Creek, Missouri, and at Leesburg, Virginia, where it was reported close to two thousand northern soldiers were killed.

That was the frightening part. The numbers of men killed and wounded were already staggering. She could not help wondering if Lee was involved in any of the fighting. Could she really have loved a man who was now truly her enemy? She hated the Yankees in general as much as any Louisianan; their blockade of southern trade was already beginning to strangle the South and affecting her father's business. Yet she could not ignore her feelings for Lee. He had risked his life to defend her, and there would always be a part of her that ached for him, a corner of her heart that held a special love for him. She dared not let herself think that he was most likely out there somewhere shooting at sweet southern boys like Joey, like those who ate and danced here tonight; such feelings would only tear her apart.

When she helped these young men, she felt as if she were doing something for Joey. Each young man heading for Richmond was given a small hand-sewn flag that represented Louisiana, along with extra pocket money. At the train station and on the docks, depending on which routes were taken to Virginia, Audra and other volunteer women provided the new soldiers with cloth sacks full of biscuits and jerked meat.

The entire project had helped keep Audra's mind not only off Joey, but also off Richard and Eleanor. Eleanor had been gone the entire two weeks since Audra had arrived in Baton Rouge. She was "visiting" Cypress Hollow, it was said politely. Audra was certain her aunt and uncle knew of the affair though all they would say was that Eleanor had "taken a liking to the country," and that Richard had been gracious enough to tell her she could visit Cypress Hollow anytime she chose.

Aunt Janine had haughtily chided Audra for "neglecting" her husband, telling her that her place was at Cypress Hollow with Richard, and Audra was glad for the excuse of helping the Confederate cause. She knew that Aunt Janine believed that Eleanor would have made the better wife, after all, and Audra supposed that no matter what the scandal, Aunt Janine hoped Richard might find a way to have his marriage annulled so that he could marry Eleanor. But Audra knew that would never happen. Richard would never drag his own name through the mud. He was using Eleanor for pure pleasure and that was all. She believed he cared no more for her than he might care for any of the negro women he slept with.

She shivered, realizing that as long as she was his wife, Richard could still send for her whenever he chose. Was it only a matter of time before Lee's threats wore thin and Richard considered them meaningless? And once her father died, if something happened to Joey, how much power would she have left according to the agreement Richard had been forced to sign?

A small orchestra struck up a waltz, and one young man asked Audra for a dance. She told him she was sorry, that she was married, and he walked away looking disappointed. She hated Richard all the more for putting her in this position—that of a married woman who really didn't have a husband at all. How long could she go on like this? She so wanted children, had once thought that having babies would fill her life with joy and help her tolerate her existence with Richard; but she just couldn't go crawling back to him, and that was the only way. Richard was cleverly getting his revenge. The man couldn't hurt her physically anymore, but he was punishing her this way, dooming her to a lonely, loveless life with no other men in it.

She served another glass of punch to a young man who smiled eagerly, but behind the smile she saw his fear. "God will be with you," she told him, "and He is on our side."

The boy nodded. "Thank you, ma'am."

"Your husband is here," one of the other women told her then. There was an odd tone to the woman's voice, and she had emphasized "husband." Audra looked across the room to see Richard entering the house with Eleanor on his arm! Humiliation filled her so thoroughly that she felt hot. How many people knew what was going on between Eleanor and Richard? The gossip must be intense. Did people blame her, think she was a bad wife? All the women she had met and worked with had treated her kindly, almost too kindly. Did they feel sorry for her?

Eleanor had actually lost some weight, and she was literally glowing as she left Richard's side and strode across the room in a lovely pale-blue taffeta gown. "Audra, dear cousin, I didn't know you were in Baton Rouge," she drawled.

Of course you knew, Audra thought. *That's why you walked into this room on my husband's arm.* How could a woman care so little about what others thought of her? Before she could say a word, Richard appeared at the table, all smiles, putting on his usual show for others. "My darling wife, you are working too hard. Come away from there and dance with me."

Audra chose not to make a scene here. She put on a smile of her own for the other women present, hoping to quell the hideous gossip that must be running rampant behind her back. "Of course," she answered. She looked at Eleanor. "Perhaps you will take over for me for a while? We *all* should do our share, Eleanor. You should not be off lounging in the country when there is so much to be done for the southern cause. It really is shameful."

Eleanor lifted her chin, her face flushed with jealousy and anger. "I am as ready and willing to help the cause as any of you," she answered.

Audra shoved a tray of sandwiches into her hands. "Good. Get to work, then." She moved from behind the table and waltzed away with Richard. She cared little for letting the man even touch her, but she intended to stop the rumors, if possible. It wasn't that she cared so much what people thought about Eleanor, and she cared not at all what they thought of Richard. What upset her most was that people might think she was at fault for Richard's philandering.

"Don't you care what people will say about your walking in with Eleanor?" she asked the man.

Richard's cold, dark eyes drilled into her as he whirled her in gentle circles to the music. "You are the only one who can put a stop to it," he answered. "All you have to do is come to Cypress Hollow, where you belong, and come willingly, and I will have no more need of your slutty cousin." He pasted on a grin as though he were enjoying himself. "In the meantime, she serves a purpose."

Audra felt her stomach turn. "Is that all I would be to you? A wife's purpose is more than just servicing her husband in bed and producing litters of babies for him."

"Really?" His eyes dropped to the soft crests of her bosom, revealed by the demure bodice of her russet-colored velvet dress. He thought her exceedingly beautiful tonight, far outshining any other woman present, certainly easier on the eyes than her plump cousin Eleanor. How he would dearly love to have her back in his bed, but he felt only contempt for her and was not about to apologize for his behav-

ior. She'd deserved every bit of what she'd gotten, and
more. He had enjoyed the look of hurt on her face tonight
when he first walked into the room with Eleanor. "I never
considered a wife good for anything else, except, perhaps, to
increase my personal fortune."

Audra held his eyes boldly. "Have you ever loved anyone, Richard? Did you love your first wife?"

He kept the phony smile on his face. "My first wife inherited a fortune that ended up in my hands, but she failed
in her duty of giving me children. Now my second wife has
also failed in that area." He pulled her a little closer, his
eyes smoldering. "I wanted to love you, Audra, but you betrayed me long before our wedding night. I will never forget it or forgive you for it."

"And you betrayed *me*, by pretending to be good and
kind, by taking Joey under your wing as though you really
cared, by fooling my father into thinking you truly loved
and wanted me and that you weren't marrying me just to
get your hands on Brennan Manor. Now you *still* won't!
Don't forget that both Father and I have to approve of your
annual take. If you keep humiliating me by blatantly carrying on with Eleanor, we will *not* approve! You cannot replace physical abuse with this outrageous behavior and
think you can get away with it!"

He snickered. "And what would your Yankee friend do
about it now? He's the enemy. If he dares to come back
here as he threatened to do, he's a *dead* man! We're at war
now, Audra, and no one will give a damn what his grievance
is against me. He's a *Yankee*. You wouldn't want these nice
folks to know you once slept with the enemy, would you?"

"He wasn't the enemy then."

"Well, he is now, my love, and that little act he pulled
to threaten me no longer holds much value." He leaned
closer, kissing her hair and breathing her scent. "But don't
worry, my dear. I don't intend to force you into anything. I
wouldn't stoop to it now. I can get what I want, whenever
I want it, from other women. In the meantime, you can live
your life of loneliness. You're the wife of Richard Potter, so
there isn't a man in all of southern Louisiana who would
dream of messing with you. If you start getting lonely for a

man, dear Audra, you will have to come to me. I am a patient man."

"I would not call our wedding night being patient, but that is beside the point now." Audra stopped to smile and nod at another couple, even though she knew they were gossiping about her and Richard. She met Richard's eyes again. "What you did to me *after* marrying me and promising in the eyes of God to love and cherish me was far worse than what I did *before* I married you. By the time I ever come crawling to Cypress Hollow out of some base need for a man's physical attentions, you will be too old and decrepit to be able to service me." She watched his face flush with anger. "And if the only way I will ever know physical love again is to come to you for it," she added, "I believe I can live out my life without ever again allowing a man to treat me like an animal! You took what was supposed to be a beautiful act of love and turned it into a hideous nightmare! And *I* shall never forgive *you* for it!"

The waltz ended, and Audra left Richard standing there to go back to the refreshments table, where Eleanor greeted her with a vicious look.

Audra moved beside her and began to serve punch.

"You must know by now, Audra dear, that Richard doesn't care for you any longer," Eleanor said with a smirk.

"Do you really think it matters to me?" Audra answered. "You don't know the whole truth, Eleanor, and I can't blame you for that; but no matter what the problems are between me and Richard, how can you so blatantly sleep with my husband? Have you no pride whatsoever?"

Eleanor turned to her, her eyes filled with hate. "Come into that little alcove with me, cousin dear, off the side of the ballroom." She marched away, and Audra asked one of the other women to take over for her. She felt several pairs of eyes on her as she followed Eleanor into the alcove, and she could almost hear the women whispering behind their fans. She moved behind a velvet curtain to see her cousin waiting with arms folded, her chin held high, her eyes full of bitterness.

"Say what you want, and say it quickly," Audra told her.

"I am not here tonight to talk about how you so flagrantly prostitute yourself, Eleanor. I am here to help the cause."

Eleanor sniffed. "You speak of pride! All my life I have lived in your shadow, Audra Brennan Potter! All I ever heard from my mother was how beautiful you are, and how I had to do this and that to keep up with you. All I have wanted since I can remember is to best you at something, and now I've done it!" She stepped closer, looking Audra over scathingly. "For all your beauty, you are a hopeless failure as a wife, especially in bed! Richard should have married *me*, and now he knows it!"

"He's *using* you, Eleanor! Can't you see that? He slept with his Negro women, even raped some of the young ones. Now he's just replaced them with you!"

Eleanor's face seemed literally to puff up bigger with anger. "Are you saying I'm no more to him than a nigger woman?"

Audra put her hands on her hips. "That is *exactly* what I'm saying! Don't let him use you that way! He isn't worth it, Eleanor, believe me!"

"I don't believe you! I love Richard, and he loves me! He's trapped in this marriage to you, so we're taking all we can get whenever we can get it!" She strutted past Audra, then paused, looking back at her. "As far as Richard sleeping with his Negroes—well, surely you know that most slave lords do it. And just as Richard loves me, some slave lords even fall in love with their *Negroes*. Better your husband picks another white woman to love than have an affair with a Negro woman, don't you think?"

Audra shook her head. "No white man would ever truly love a Negro woman."

Eleanor laughed wickedly. "Wouldn't he? Why don't you ask your father about that, or maybe it would be better to ask Lena ... or *Toosie*."

Audra could almost feel the blood draining from her face. "What are you talking about?"

Eleanor rolled her eyes. "Oh, Audra, you're such a dummy, and so naive. I swear, everybody at Brennan Manor and Cypress Hollow, probably everyone in Baton Rouge and maybe even New Orleans knows that Toosie is your half sister! Your father and Lena have been in love for *years*, since long before Aunt Sophia died. Why, my mother used to fret and fume about how terrible it was of Uncle Joseph to hurt her sister that way. I was always ordered never to tell you, but it doesn't matter anymore. It's time you knew the truth. You think that your father, that all you Brennans, are so pure and perfect! Mother says that her sister might have married a man with more money than my father, but at least *my* father has never slept with a nigger, let alone actually loved one!"

Audra fought back tears. She knew Eleanor wanted her to cry and be shocked, and she refused to do either.

"Why Audra, dear," Eleanor said. "You look positively pale!" She shook her head, clucking as though sorry to have had to tell her such things. "You must wake up to the real world, Audra. Everyone sleeps with everyone, and no one can be trusted! You slept with your Yankee man. Don't deny it. Richard told me." She shrugged. "Your Yankee man deserted you and probably just used you, anyway. Now he's the enemy. Your father still sleeps with Lena and was doing it for years before your mother died. I sleep with your husband, and you . . . well, I suppose that if you intend to remain true to your wedding vows, you will never sleep with another man again. If you want to enjoy such pleasures again, you will have to commit adultery, just as everyone around you is doing. You might as well join the crowd, Audra. It really can be quite fun." She laughed and walked away.

Audra sank into a satin-covered chair, her thoughts reeling with what Eleanor had just told her. Was it all really this ugly, then? She had imagined that her affair with Lee had been out of true love, a beautiful union between two people who wanted to express that love in the gentlest, most pleasurable, and giving way possible. Were all men just animals after something more exciting than their last conquest? And her father! Was Toosie really his daughter? In some ways it made sense—the way he'd protected her from the rest of the Negroes, the strange hold Lena seemed to have on the man, the reason he had promised he would never sell either woman.

"My God!" she whispered, putting a hand to her head. Her own father! She had always had a particular aversion to the thought of white slave owners sleeping with their Negro women. Richard had made the picture even uglier for her. Had her father forced Lena in the beginning? Even if he hadn't, could he actually love a Negro woman in that way? And with her mother still alive—that was the most hurtful part of all! How could he do that to her!

"Come, my dear," she heard Richard's voice then. "Now that I am here, it would look better if we were seen together more."

Audra looked up at him with tear-filled eyes. "I want you to take me to Brennan Manor right away," she answered. "Me and Toosie."

Richard frowned. "What did Eleanor say to you?"

"Is it true, about my father and Lena? Is it true that Toosie is my half sister?"

He snorted with amusement. "For heaven's sake, Audra, everyone knew. I always found it amazing that you never suspected, but your father made me promise never to say anything to you. He was worried how you would react."

"I want to see him and Lena and Toosie all together. Will you take me to Brennan Manor?"

Richard's face was still set in a scowl. "If that is what you want." He stepped closer. "Audra, most marriages *are* arranged, you know, just like ours was, and just like my marriage to my first wife. It was the same for your mother and father. They never truly loved each other, but they were happy enough, and Sophia gave Joseph two children. She knew long before Joey was born that your father was in love with Lena. She *is* a most beautiful and intelligent Negro woman. Surely you're aware of that." The man adjusted his cravat. "Sophia put up with it and was able to look the other way, as any good wife should do. There is the act of making love just to make babies, and the act of pure lustful pleasure. A man must have both. Your mother found happiness and solace in her children. Now, if you want our own marriage to look normal and happy to others, then you might as well allow me back into your bed so that you can at least have babies. I really think you could forget the past and get on with your life if you had little ones to look after."

Audra just stared at him. "I always thought that lustful pleasure and making love in order to have babies could and should be one and the same," she answered.

Richard shook his head. "And you are still the young dreamer. Your Yankee man took you out of pure manly desire to claim a virgin, nothing more. Lee Jeffreys can profess his love all he wants, but the fact is, he never intended to marry you, either before or after he slept with you. Maybe now you understand it all better and can let go of that ridiculous vision of Lee Jeffreys being your knight in shining armor. The man will end up marrying for the same reasons most men marry, to have the proper woman on his arm who most benefits his own future and who will give him heirs; all other women in his life are for pure pleasure. Sometimes, as in the case of your father, he can actually love the other woman, but she can never truly be a part of his life, just as you could never have been a part of Lee's life. He's a Yankee, Audra, and he'll marry a Yankee woman, and that will be that. Once I feel you understand that fully and have gotten that bastard out of your mind for good, I can be reasonable and treat you with more respect."

Audra did not want to believe any of it, but to learn this about her father shattered her vision of true love and her faith in mankind. She felt betrayed by everyone she had ever known, even her precious father. "Will you take me to Brennan Manor?"

"We would never get there before dark. I'll take you first thing in the morning." He glanced across the ballroom at Eleanor, who stood watching them. "If you like, we can stay in a hotel tonight. It might be a little awkward staying here at Eleanor's house."

Her eyes lit up with fire. "Yes, *wouldn't* it?" she answered scathingly. She shivered at the thought of being in the same room with him for one night. Angry, disappointed, and disillusioned, she wiped at her tears. "If you touch me tonight, I swear I'll scream and embarrass you to death! A lot of people in this town are already gossiping about you and Eleanor and what a miserable husband you must be."

He only grinned, smiling in a way that irritated her. "Maybe they're talking about what a miserable wife *you* must be." His smile vanished. "I won't touch you, Audra dear . . . for now. Gather your things and we'll leave this place and get a room." He handed her a clean handkerchief that had been tucked into the pocket of his elegant suit.

Audra took it and dabbed at her eyes. "Does Toosie know?"

Richard shrugged. "Of course she knows. She has known for years, but she had strict orders never to tell you. Why do you think your father forbade her to marry that Elijah fellow? He wants something better for her because he cares about her more than he does the others. Trouble is, in his mind *no* Negro man is good enough." He shook his head. "Your father made the grave mistake of allowing himself to have feelings for some of his Negroes. That is just not done, let alone caring about mixed-blood offspring. It's very dangerous for a man to allow emotions to come into the picture when it comes to his slaves. It's bad for business, you know."

Audra felt her heart harden. "Of course," she answered. "Go ahead and call our carriage. I will pack my things, and I want to pick up Toosie in the morning. She'll go back with us." She left him standing there and walked through the ballroom and its crowd of drinking, dancing guests; but she heard no voices, no music.

Eleanor continued to watch her, as Audra left the party, glowing with the satisfaction of finally besting her pampered and adored cousin, of having destroyed all her illusions.

20

Audra stood before her father, Lena, and Toosie in the downstairs parlor of Brennan Manor. Lena watched her with sorrowful eyes. Toosie was looking down at the floor. Audra had been unable to say one word to Toosie on the way home. She wished she knew how to feel about the woman, but right now it seemed she had no feelings at all.

"You should have *told* me, Father," she said then, looking at the man she had practically worshiped most of her life.

"Audra, how could I explain to my little girl that her father was in love with a Negro woman?" he pleaded. "Or that I had loved Lena even while your mother was still alive? How would you have understood such a thing? You *still* can't understand it, even at nineteen years old and after all you have been through yourself."

Audra watched his eyes. This man had been her whole

world for so long. She had thought him incapable of doing one wrong thing, and she had grown up believing her parents were very much in love. It was that vision that had made her want a perfect marriage of her own. "God knows I can understand a loveless marriage," she told him, caring little if her words might anger Richard, who stood at the fireplace smoking his pipe. "It's just that I always thought you loved my mother. You always spoke of her with such reverence."

"I *did* love her, child. Sophia was a wonderful, giving, caring woman and a good wife. But it was an arranged marriage. There was no passion there. We were good friends, and we respected each other."

"Respect! How could she respect you! It was bad enough that you loved some other woman more, but for that woman to be a household slave, a *Negro!*"

Lena drew a sharp breath, and Toosie turned away. "I thought you cared about me and Toosie enough to look beyond our black skin," Lena said. "I always loved you like my own, Audra. And Toosie loves you, too. She just could never tell you because you wouldn't understand unless you knew the truth. Your father always protected you from the realities of life, though over the years I have told him he shouldn't have. Now you have had to learn too many things the hard way. I know your father well enough to know how sorry he is about that. I know that he loves you with all that is in him, and that the last thing he would ever want is for you to hurt like this."

"Then he shouldn't have been sleeping with a Negro woman all these years! And he shouldn't have expected such perfection out of his children when *he* was so imperfect! Poor Joey is off fighting, killing Yankees and risking being killed or maimed himself—all to impress his father—all to try to find a way to make his father proud of him! I wonder how he would feel if *he* knew the truth!" She fought back tears. "I don't ever want him to know! Do all of you understand? I never want Joey to know!"

"Audra," Joseph spoke up, "it wasn't as though I hurt or betrayed your mother. She knew all about it for years. She cared very much for Lena, who had been her personal ser-

vant long before we got married. She brought Lena to
Brennan Manor with her, and after we were married a few
years . . . I don't know. Lena is a beautiful woman, easy to
love. I don't see her as a Negro. I only see her as a woman.
Sophia didn't like it at first, but she began to understand
and accept it. It was just something that was understood but
never really talked about. I was good to Sophia. I never denied her anything, never abused her in any way. She wanted
children, and I wanted heirs, so we . . . we were man and
wife in the fullest sense for the most part. I respected Sophia as a beautiful, gracious woman who was the mother of
my children. I truly grieved for her when she died, and so
did Lena. They were still close when Sophia passed away.
Lena was the last person she talked to, and she asked her
to take care of me always, and you and Joey, and to see that
Toosie married well."

"I cannot believe I am hearing this." Audra stepped
back. "Have there been others? Do *you* still take Negro
women to your bed for the pure pleasure of it?"

Lena stiffened, and Joseph's face reddened. "I don't believe that question deserves an answer. You know me better
than that, Audra."

"Do I? I am beginning to think I don't know you at all,
Father. It seems that everything I have believed about people I love has been dashed to the ground." She glanced at
Richard. "The man I married, a man I thought was gentle
and kind, turned into a monster." She stared at Toosie. "The
woman I have ordered about all my life and treated like a
common slave most of the time is my own half sister." She
looked back at her father then. "I gave up a man I love for
you, Father, for you and Joey and Brennan Manor. Now I
don't know what is right and what is wrong any longer. I am
beginning to see that anything that was supposed to be
wrong about my loving Lee Jeffreys *pales* in comparison to
what the rest of my family and my husband have been up
to! Everything I treasured and held honorable has turned to
something ugly and sinful, and my dreams of what marriage
should be have been destroyed."

She took a deep breath, walking past all of them to a
window, looking out at the slaves tending the lawn. "I am

not sure anymore what this war is about. I thought it was about honor, to protect our way of life; but you have no honor left, and I wonder if our way of life is so right after all." She faced her father again. "You say you love Lena just as a woman, that you do not see her as a Negro. What about the *rest* of the Negroes, Father? Why are they different?"

"There are a few, like Lena and Toosie, who are more intelligent than the rest," Richard answered for him. "The rest are ignorant savages who would slit your throat and take over this home if they thought they could get away with it."

Audra glanced at Lena, saw the hurt in her eyes. "I wonder," she answered. She looked at Richard. "Perhaps *all* humans have the ability to be savages when the circumstances are right. Men like you, who enjoy using their power over others who might be weaker or less fortunate."

"You have a power of your own, Audra," Joseph told her. "Can you tell me, in spite of everything you have learned, that you don't still love Brennan Manor, that this is not home to you? Can you tell me that if Yankees came here to take our home away from us, that you would not fight to keep it?"

Audra looked around the familiar room. Joey would come back some day, and Brennan Manor would be his. "Of course I would fight," she answered.

Her father came closer to her. "*That* is what this war is about, Audra. I agree that we need to change things, that slavery cannot go on forever, but to end it the way the Yankees expect us to end it would mean losing all of this, Audra! *All* of it! You and Joey and men like me and Richard would be left with nothing! It's the *principle* of the matter that we are fighting for! The Yankees are out to crush us, bring us to our knees. If that happens, they will come down here and rape the whole South, impose martial law, burn our cities, abuse our women! Places like Brennan Manor and Cypress Hollow will be no more! The slaves will be freed, and what the Yankees don't rape and burn and destroy, the Negroes will! We must be allowed to end slavery in our own way, our own time, but the Yankees want to force us with cannon and battles and blockades into coming back into the Union and destroying a way of life that has gone on for generations!"

"It surely won't go that far—"

Joseph took her hands in his. "It *could*, Audra, and you have to understand that! For now you must put aside family problems and think about what the war means. We all must work together to save Brennan Manor and Cypress Hollow, to save the South we love. The Yankees can yell all they want about preserving the Union, but they are using that as an excuse to come down here and take everything we have! Once we are ruined, wealthy men like Lee Jeffreys and his father can come here and buy up all that we have, and the South as we know it now will cease to exist. Where will that leave you and Joey? Where will that leave *any* of us! Homeless! Probably *dead*, murdered by our own Negroes! You have to realize we could be fighting for our very *lives!*"

"There are already going to be hardships by next year," Richard added. "If the North continues to build up its blockades, we won't be able to ship out our cotton. While you have been staying in Baton Rouge, I have been holding secret meetings with men willing to try to run the blockades and get our cotton delivered to ports in England. England is our biggest customer. If we can't get to them, we're all but doomed already."

Audra looked up at her husband, surprised that he had become involved in blockade running.

"It is time to set aside these little hurts and misunderstandings and begin working together for the bigger cause, which is to keep the North from destroying us and our way of life forever," Richard told her. "If you don't care for my sake or your father's, then care for yourself and Joey and those who will come after us. If we don't hold back the Yankees and force them to leave us alone to handle the South the way we know is best, boys like Joey will have risked their lives for nothing, because they will *have* nothing to come home to."

Richard took hold of her arms, pulling her away from her father. "You are Louisiana born and bred. That was part of my anger, Audra, that you had maybe forgotten that when you went to Connecticut that summer and had your fling with that Yankee trash. Now that we are at war, we cannot think in terms of the little things, whom we do or do not love, who is sleeping with whom. We all have to come together now, forgive and forget and remember who we are!" Richard paused, then, using all his skills as an orator, tried to convince her to agree. "We are *southerners*! We belong to our own Confederacy, and we are sending our finest men off to preserve that Confederacy against those who would destroy us! Whether slavery is right or wrong is not the issue. The issue is what will happen to the Negroes if they are instantly freed. Life would be worse for them, not better, Audra. If they were no longer owned and protected, fed and clothed and housed by men like me and your father, they would wander and starve. They have no education, no way to take care of themselves! They would kill people like us, not because they are bad, but because they would become desperate for food and clothing and shelter. Protecting our own way of life also protects the Negroes."

He let go of her then. "I don't pretend to have any special love for them. If there was a way to get rid of all of them without losing everything I have worked for all my life, I would do it." He glanced at Lena, seeing the pride and hatred in her eyes. How Joseph Brennan could actually love this black woman, he couldn't understand, but that was beside the point. "It's one vicious circle, Audra, and you are part of it. The South must fight to protect its way of life. Doing that will in turn protect the Negroes from almost instant starvation. By protecting the Negroes, we are in turn protecting ourselves from what they would do if they were freed too quickly. Any way you look at it, we must not let the Yankees win this war. And much as you might have loved Lee Jeffreys, that won't stop men like him from coming down here and destroying your home and the only life you have ever known. Get him out of your mind, and get rid of your notions of whether or not owning slaves is right or wrong. That is no longer something to be pondered. We have no choice but to continue to fight together for the southern way of life and the southern economy."

Never had Audra been so confused over what was right and moral. Everything she had been brought up to believe was a perfectly normal way of life seemed suddenly abnormal, yet now her personal battle over slavery didn't really matter. There was a bigger enemy at large, men who wore blue uniforms and threatened to tear apart everything that was dear to her. At the same time, her own father had sent her into emotional turmoil. In a twisted sort of way, she knew Richard was right about their reasons.

"Audra," her father said gently, "for now you must put aside your personal feelings and remember that you are a Brennan. Not only that, but you are also Richard's wife, and therefore you and your future children are heirs to a literal empire—but only if that empire is preserved against destruction by the Yankees. Part of the reason Richard married you was because he knew you were the kind of woman who would realize one day that, above all else, she is a southern woman with all the pride that comes with it, as well as a woman courageous and intelligent enough to handle the power that comes with being mistress of two plantations. No matter how you feel about what I or Richard have done with our personal lives, you cannot deny that you love Louisiana and Brennan Manor, or that you feel pride at also being part owner of Cypress Hollow. The only way we will be able to stand against Union forces is to be united ourselves, as a *family*."

Audra closed her eyes for a moment. "I need time away from all of this to think," she answered. She studied each one of them then, her gaze finally resting on Lena. "I am going to Cypress Hollow with Richard," she added. She could feel Richard's astonishment at the remark, but she kept her eyes on Lena. "Knowing what I know, I cannot have Toosie for my personal servant any longer. I am not even sure I can get used to the idea that a Negro woman is related to me. Part of me loves both of you, but part of me also hates what you've done. I will take Sonda with me to Cypress Hollow." She finally turned to face a surprised Richard. "And you will not touch her, nor any of the other Negro women. I want children, Richard, because the love between a mother and her children is the only kind of love that is innocent and pure, and apparently the only kind of love I will ever know in my own life. I do not want my children to discover what I have discovered today, that the little mulattoes running around their plantation are their brothers and sisters. I want you to sell all mulatto children who you know are yours, but you must sell the mothers along with them and not separate them. If you agree to do that, and agree never to take Eleanor to Cypress Hollow again, I will go home with you. Will you do that? And will you promise Father I will be treated with gentleness and respect?"

Richard's dark eyes moved over her, giving her the shivers. She told herself that it didn't matter anymore that they did not love each other. She wanted children, and Richard was the only man who could legally give them to her, but it was going to be on her terms.

"I agree," Richard answered. He stepped closer and touched her cheek. She felt like cringing, but she stood firm. "But only if you tell me one thing. Tell me that that Yankee bastard Lee Jeffreys is out of your life and your heart for good."

Lee! They would never recapture what they had shared at Maple Shadows. That had been another Audra, another Lee, another time. "Yes," she answered. "He is out of my life . . . and out of my heart." *Why did she feel like crying?*

Richard grinned. "Then I shall take you home, dear wife." He led her out of the room, and Audra did not give a second glance to Toosie, who was weeping quietly.

FEBRUARY 1862

Lee limped into the tent of Brigadier General Burnside and stood at attention, while the man studied some maps spread out on a makeshift desk consisting of a board laid across two barrels. "Sir?"

Burnside raised his balding head, and in the dim light of an oil lamp, Lee thought that their recent victory over the rebels at Roanoke had made the stern man look strangely aglow. "Lieutenant Jeffreys," he answered. "How's the leg?"

"I'll live." Lee was not sure how he was going to sleep well for a long time to come, if ever. While he lay in a makeshift Federal hospital on the island with a flesh wound to his left thigh, he'd had to listen to the screams of men having their own legs or arms sawed off, the sickening groans of other men with hideous head or gut wounds that meant slow, excruciating death.

Get him up here, he could remember one doctor ordering someone. Lee had felt himself being moved, remembered seeing a saw in the doctor's hand. He had pulled his revolver, which he still wore on his uniform belt, and pointed it at the doctor. *Cut it off and you're a dead man,* Lee remembered warning the man in his delirium. He waved the revolver and others stepped back while the doctor cut open his pants leg to announce it was only a flesh wound. *No shattered bone,* he announced. *I'll let you keep it.* He had poured whiskey into the wound and wrapped it, and Lee could only pray that infection would not set in. If it did, he'd already decided he would rather die before he'd let anybody take off his leg.

He could have stayed a few more days at the hospital, but the stench of old blood and the sight of arms and legs piled in one corner like the hind quarters of animals made him decide to leave sooner. He'd fashioned himself a cane out of a sturdy tree limb and gone back to his command of the Tenth Connecticut.

In one of the first onslaughts, Lee had originally been put second in command of the Twenty-fifth Massachusetts, still a lieutenant colonel. When the Twenty-fifth sustained massive casualties, it was ordered to pull back. That was when Lee took a piece of shrapnel in his leg. He'd yanked it out himself and tied it off with his own neckerchief. He had remained in the thick of battle, waiting while the Tenth Connecticut, under Colonel Charles Russell, moved in to take the place of his own regiment. The colonel had been killed, and Burnside ordered Lee to take over the Tenth.

Now Burnside finally broke into what could be called a smile. "I asked you to report to me, Lieutenant Jeffreys, for several reasons. First, you did a magnificent job of taking Colonel Russell's place yesterday. Because of that, I have requested you be promoted to a full colonel."

Lee's eyebrows arched in surprise. "I . . . don't know what to say, sir, except thank you."

Sighing, Burnside took a moment to light a cigar. "I'll see about getting you the winged-eagle insignia for your uniform." He paused. "We had a lot of men desert as soon as their initial three months was up, after that fiasco at Bull Run; but you weren't one of them. You're in this for the long haul, am I correct?"

"Yes, sir, unless something stops me."

Burnside smiled bitterly. "Yes. I know the feeling." The man took a bottle of whiskey from a crate sitting near him and offered Lee a drink. "By the way, I know that Hawkins's Ninth New York is taking credit for taking the island. Those Zouaves love glory, like to play the heroes. I'm grateful for their bravery and skill, but I know the real risk takers, and the ones who are truly responsible for this victory are men like your own Twenty-fifth Massachusetts and the Tenth Connecticut who came in first and took the worst of the attack. Don't get too upset with the Zouaves. We don't need disgruntled men among us. It's time to stand together. I'll make sure Washington knows who the real heroes were in this campaign."

"It makes no difference to me, sir, as long as the battle got won."

Burnside nodded, a troubled look in his eyes. Lee could not help wondering if there was another reason he had been called before the man. The general scratched his beard before continuing. "One of your men mentioned to one of mine that you had been to Baton Rouge, Louisiana. Is that right?"

There it was, Lee thought, the *real* reason he was here. A feeling of dread flooded through him. He had always hoped somehow that the war would never move as far south as Audra's home territory. "Yes, sir, I was there once, for about three weeks, close to two years ago." He swallowed the whiskey, suddenly wanting more. He had struggled not to think about Audra for a long time, and it irritated him that just the mention of a town near Brennan Manor could suddenly shake him. "I visited a friend of the family, a student of my mother's."

Burnside puffed on his cigar. "After three weeks, you must have gotten rather familiar with the city. Did you also visit New Orleans?"

"Yes, sir."

"Would the fact that this friend lives in the area affect your judgment in the case of an invasion of New Orleans and Baton Rouge?"

Lee met the man's eyes, seeing there the warning that this was not the time for personal matters to cloud the real issue. "No, sir." He meant it, didn't he? After all, he hadn't seen Audra for nearly two years. For all he knew, she had made a life with Richard, perhaps had a baby by now. He had told himself that a long time ago, realizing he must believe she was happy or else lose his mind.

"Good. I trust you mean that, Colonel Jeffreys, because I am advising Washington that you be put in charge of your own brigade as a colonel and be part of the troops sent to New Orleans under Flag Officer David Farragut. He will do his best to get his fleet up the Mississippi past Fort Jackson and Fort St. Philip, which in itself will not be an easy feat. Once that's done, you and the other land troops will be under Major General Benjamin Butler. When the two forts are taken, all army and naval troops will move in to take New Orleans, then Baton Rouge and eventually Port Hudson, a major stronghold on the Mississippi. Once that is done, we will have broken the Confederate defensive along the Mississippi, especially with Grant and other Union forces taking the Mississippi from the Tennessee-Arkansas end. We will have surrounded the South, and choked off the Mississippi. There will be no place for them to run, Colonel Jeffreys, except north, and I don't believe they'll want to run in *that* direction," he finished with a sly grin. "Hand me that shot glass, Colonel Jeffreys."

Lee gladly obeyed, his mind whirling with the fact that he would be in charge of a brigade, but wishing he was being assigned anyplace but Louisiana.

Burnside refilled his glass and handed it over. "This is, of course, between us for now. You'll stay here and heal while more troops are sent down from Washington, along with the naval ships that will take you to the Gulf. That will take a couple of months. I don't know yet just what regiments you will be leading, most likely a combination of several different states, like most of our brigades. You aren't prejudiced toward any particular state, are you?"

"I couldn't care less, as long as they're good fighting men that I can depend on," Lee said, then downed the drink.

"Good." The general paused. "Your promotion and the planned invasion of New Orleans was the good news, Colonel. Now for the bad news."

Lee frowned. "Bad news?"

The general sighed deeply, a look of sorrow in his eyes. "I got word three or four days ago, but with the impending siege of Roanoke, I couldn't tell you. There was nothing you could have done about it, anyway. Now you'll have some time to rest . . . and grieve."

A tightness filled Lee's chest. "Grieve, sir?"

"Your father is dead, Colonel Jeffreys. It happened over three weeks ago. It took your brother Carl a while to find out where you were. He may still be searching for your brother David. I have no idea where he has been assigned. I'm sorry, Colonel."

Lee struggled against showing too much emotion in front of the general. The news was so sudden. The fact that he had spent only that one night in true closeness with his father stabbed at his gut like a bayonet.

"It was some kind of cancer," Burnside added. "I'm to tell you he was buried at a place called Maple Shadows, beside your mother."

Maple Shadows. It was the only place where he had known any kind of real happiness. Was that the only way his family would ever gather together there again, in death? Oh, what he'd give for one more day of togetherness, with both his mother and father alive . . . to be young again, climbing those big trees with his brothers . . . and if only he could share one more summer there with Audra. He blinked back tears, handing the shot glass back to the general and rising. "May I go now, sir?"

"Of course. Get rid of your grief, Colonel while you let

that leg heal. You'll need to be at full readiness when you head for New Orleans."

Lee nodded. "Yes, sir."

Burnside shook his head. "Again, I'm sorry. I promise you, this hell will all be over one day, Colonel, and we can get back to a normal life."

What would a normal life be for him now, Lee wondered. By the time the war ended, he would have to start all over again. His father and mother were dead, Audra was lost to him. What dreams were left to him? What was he fighting for?

He limped off into the darkness to be alone.

APRIL 1862

Audra rearranged a turquoise comb in her hair, wondering if Sonda would ever be as talented at doing her hair as Toosie had been. Secretly she missed her half sister, but she still felt a bitter hurt. Although she and Richard had traveled from Cypress Hollow to Baton Rouge several times in the past five months to help with the volunteer work for the war, she had not been back to Brennan Manor.

Richard had behaved surprisingly well, and she had been a "dutiful" wife, allowing him to her bed just often enough to try to have a child; but so far her efforts had been a failure. She wondered if the deep hatred of him she had tried to bury was affecting her ability to conceive. Each coupling brought back ugly memories, but she was determined now to have a baby, to have someone to love with all her heart.

She had learned to shut off all feeling when she was with Richard, as though the body he slept with were not her own. She felt hard and wicked, and now when she looked at herself in the mirror, she was no longer sure who she saw there. She had decided she had no choice but to accept her life, to accept a loveless marriage, as she'd come to believe many other women did. If they could survive it and even bear children, she could, too. She would love a baby with all that was in her, love that for now was buried somewhere in her soul. There were no feelings left for anything else, except Joey . . . and lingering dreams of Lee; but Joey might never make it home, and to allow herself thoughts of Lee was too painful.

She opened a dresser drawer and took out Joey's last letter to her, written just last February. When he first joined up nearly ten months ago, he had been sent to Florida, and it had warmed her heart to read his letters. Although the Confederate troops with whom he fought had failed in an attempt to take the Yankees at Santa Rosa Island in Florida, Joey was still proud of the fact that he was indeed among the honored few who called themselves sharpshooters. Because his stuttering would have been an obstacle to his giving orders, he was still just a private, but he had told her he was well treated by the other men, and that the officers had a great deal of respect for his prowess with a rifle.

Still, his latest letter worried her. He was in Tennessee now, and she could tell that the glory of war was becoming something ugly for him. It had already changed him, she could tell. *We have been fighting against the Union General Grant and his Yankees in Tennessee,* his last letter read. *I tell myself it's okay to kill Yankees, because they are the enemy, and they want to kill me and take our home. But it gets harder, Audra. The other day I ran past a man I had shot, and he was holding a picture in his hand of a woman and a baby. I'm pretty sure it was his wife and child, and I got sick. He was a Yankee, but up close he just looked like any other man.*

I thought at first that the war would end quickly, but

now I can see we all were wrong about that. I will stay with it as long as God keeps me from being wounded or killed, because as Southerners we have no choice, and because I would not shame Father by quitting too soon. In fact, my commander has told me he might promote me to corporal.

Don't be sad for me, Audra. In spite of the ugly things I have seen, and how hard it is for me to kill other men, I have learned a lot about life and about myself. I have found I have courage, and I can make decisions all on my own. I have earned the respect of others who care nothing about the fact that I am Joseph Brennan's son. Most of them don't even know my father is a rich plantation owner. They just know me as Joey, and I like to leave it that way.

I worry about how Richard is treating you, and about the Yankees coming into Louisiana. My commander says there are rumors the Yankees will invade New Orleans. I am afraid for you, and I will pray for you and Father and everybody. I love you, Audra. I'm okay—not even any wounds yet—so don't worry. Just take care of yourself and Brennan Manor, and before you know it, I'll be home again. Joey.

Audra refolded the letter and put it back in the drawer. Poor, sweet Joey. What would she do if he never made it home? She could not imagine life without her brother. She shivered at the possibility, and pushed the thought away, telling herself she must not dwell on such things. God would not take Joey from her. She had lost too much already.

Joey's letter had been closer to the truth than he realized. According to newspaper reports in Baton Rouge, the Yankees were indeed on their way to invade New Orleans. Everyone was praying that the Confederate strongholds at Fort Jackson and Fort St. Philip could stop the Union naval ships from ever getting past the mouth of the Mississippi. She and Richard were planning a trip to New Orleans to witness whatever was to come.

At times she was almost glad for the diversion of war. It had helped her set aside her unhappiness, had kept her and Richard both occupied with fund-raising events and travel to Baton Rouge and New Orleans. Weariness from her hard work and from so much traveling had given her excuses to keep Richard out of her bed on the nights she could not bear him there, and the war itself had given them something to talk about besides the emptiness of their marriage.

They were back at Cypress Hollow now. It was planting time, and Richard told her he needed to keep an eye on the fieldwork. The Negroes had grown more restless, some of them becoming outright lazy and belligerent. A few had run off, and Richard had hired men to hunt down the runaways. There was an unsettled feeling lately throughout the Negro camps of both Cypress Hollow and Brennan Manor. Richard said it was because the Negroes knew that the Yankees were getting closer, that the Union soldiers were coming to "free" them. Audra wondered if many of them had given thought to what they would do if they *were* freed—how they would live, eat, survive.

More and more she was beginning to understand why Richard said that fighting the Yankees was as much for the Negroes as for themselves. *If you think most southern whites hate the Negroes now,* he had told her just a few nights ago, *just see what happens if they are freed. They will be more of a burden than ever, and if the South loses this war and we lose all we have, it is the Negroes who will get blamed for it, Audra. For most of them, life on a plantation will seem like a wonderful thing compared to how they will suffer if they are freed.*

At first she had thought he might feel sorry for them, and she had been heartened to think he cared, but then he had shocked her by saying that if they were freed, they could all go to hell. He vowed he would never pay Negroes for work or help them in any way. *If the niggers want their freedom, let them find out the hard way that it is not as sweet as they think it will be,* he had promised her. *"I will enjoy their suffering."*

She left the room and headed downstairs to direct the kitchen help in preparing supper. Richard would be back soon and would be hungry. Tomorrow they were to leave for New Orleans. March Fredericks would take over, as the planting was finished, and there would not be a great deal of work for the slaves until harvest time. She had learned to tolerate March, as he very seldom had reason to come to the house. The few times that he had, he had given her nasty looks that told her what he would like to do to her if he could get away with it. She had no doubt the man hated her for getting him fired from Brennan Manor and having his wages reduced when he was assigned to Cypress Hollow. He had never forgotten the incident over old George.

She decided to walk around to the back of the house by way of the veranda. It was a beautiful spring day, and she wanted to enjoy it. The temperature had been so pleasant, and the azaleas and dogwood were in full and splendid bloom. When she was able to put aside the horrors of her first days spent here, she realized that Cypress Hollow was as beautiful as Brennan Manor. The house was even bigger, as was the acreage. Richard had half again as many slaves as her father, and since his own father's death he had done an excellent job of running both plantations. That was one thing she had to give him credit for, although she could never accept some of his methods. He had stopped abusing the young Negro girls, as far as she was aware, but she had no idea what went on when he was in the Negro camps or out overseeing the field hands. She knew the kind of man March Fredericks was, knew Richard could be frighteningly stern. She stayed away from the fields and camps, deciding she was perhaps better off not knowing everything that went on there.

Somewhere nearby she heard a pigeon coo, and she thought what a peaceful day it had been. Everything seemed so quiet and serene. She had stepped off the veranda to smell a nearby rosebush when the silence was suddenly broken by the sound of a carriage. She could hear the hoofbeats of the horse pulling it pounding against the ground at a frantic pace, accompanied by the clattering sound of carriage wheels rolling at breakneck speed. She looked up to see Richard's carriage come flying up the road from the Negro camps a half mile away.

Her heart tightened in alarm when she realized March Fredericks was driving the carriage, whipping the horse into a lather. As he came closer, she saw that his face was twisted with fury and even a little fear. Then she saw Richard's body lying on the floor of the carriage by March's feet. She ran to meet him as March brought the vehicle to a dusty halt in front of the house. "What happened?" she exclaimed.

"That goddamn nigger, Henry Gathers!" March swore, jumping down from the carriage and quickly tying the horse. "The one who gave your father so much trouble a couple of years ago! He escaped from the man we sold him to, and he's been hidin' out here in the Negro camps! Richard discovered him, and the nigger stabbed him with a pitchfork!"

"My God!" Audra leaned over Richard and saw that the front of his vest and suit were covered with blood.

March called for a Negro man standing nearby to help him carry Richard into the house. When the man hesitated, March pulled his revolver. "Get over here and help me or I'll shoot you right between the eyes, you stinkin' nigger!" he ordered. The man hurried over and the two men carried Richard into the house. Audra directed them to lay him on a bed in a downstairs guest room rather than carry him all the way upstairs. Richard groaned as she and March quickly ripped away his jacket, vest, and shirt. Blood oozed from four punctures just below his ribs, and Audra felt suddenly sick. In spite of how she felt about the man, this was a hideous wound no one should have to suffer. She looked at March. "I don't know what to do for him!"

March looked pale himself. "There ain't much you *can* do except keep cold rags against the wounds. I'll organize some men to help you get him to the doctor in Baton Rouge." His pale blue eyes were sullen and bloodshot. "You'll need several men along to guard you. The Negroes are in an ugly mood, and some have run off and could be in the woods along the roadway. You get your husband some help, Mrs. Potter, and give me your permission while you're gone to handle this *my* way! We can't let the niggers get away with this, or that will be the end of Cypress Hollow, maybe Brennan Manor, too."

Audra put a hand to her forehead, trying to think. The realization of what March Fredericks was capable of doing sickened her, but when she looked down at Richard again and saw his suffering, she was frightened. Was it true that the Negroes would go on a rampage, would rape and murder and pillage if they got a taste of freedom? Such a hideous attempt at murdering Richard could not go unpunished. For her husband's sake alone she had to give March permission to right this wrong.

March sensed her hesitation. "They're gettin' cockier, Mrs. Potter. That Henry Gathers has them all worked up. I've got to hunt the man down and hang him in front of the rest of them. If I don't, they'll overrun us for sure, and you'll lose everything."

Audra felt sick, but at a deep groan uttered by Richard, she looked at March with tear-filled eyes. "I don't want the innocent ones to suffer, especially not any of the women or children."

"Don't worry. I know *exactly* who to go after, and there is no time to lose. The guilty ones are most likely already scatterin' themselves. I'll need all the men I can get, as well as the hounds."

She knelt beside Richard, while a few of the house Negroes stood in the background, shivering with fear at what might happen to all of them because of this. Sonda started to cry, and old Henrietta, whom Audra had brought with her to Cypress Hollow, clasped her hands in nervous agony.

"Lawdy, Lawdy," the woman quietly exclaimed.

"Hush, Henrietta," Audra ordered her. "Go get a pan of cold water and some compresses. Quickly!" She looked back at March as the woman lumbered away. "Do what you have to do, but I meant what I said. I want no innocent Negroes to suffer for this!"

A look of satisfaction came into March's eyes. "You have my word," he told her. He moved past her, and she could smell his perspiration. "I'll have the men get a wagon ready for Mr. Potter right away."

The man left, and Audra touched Richard's damp hair, smoothing it back from his face. "You'll be all right, Richard."

He opened his eyes, and she saw the terror in them, but he said nothing.

•   •   •

For nearly two weeks Richard had clung to life. He lay in a hospital in Baton Rouge, and when the doctor told Audra he was full of infection and there was no hope, Audra had brought him home to Cypress Hollow. Whatever her feelings for him, she knew that the man had loved this place, and he had begged her to take him home to die.

She stood staring now at his fresh grave, through the dark veil that hid her face. She wished she knew how to feel about his death. She had forgiven him for mistreating her, because in one of his moments of consciousness he had asked her to. Impending death had had a humbling effect on the man, and there were times when he'd clung so tightly to her hand that she thought he might break it.

Tell me you're with child, he asked her in one of his more lucid moments. *Tell me I have left an heir to Cypress Hollow.* To ease his agony, Audra had told him yes, she was pregnant, but it had been a lie. There would be no heir to Cypress Hollow, and after loving and losing Lee, then going through so much hell with this man, she had no desire to think about loving anyone else. Some day everything would belong to Joey. He was all that was left. Maybe he would find a woman to love him. Maybe Joey was the one who would have the happy marriage she had so longed for. Joey would not marry someone just because she was the perfect wife for a wealthy plantation owner. Joey was the kind of young man who would marry only for love.

She wept, as much for what she and Richard could have had as for the hell the man had put her through, and the hell he had himself suffered in the end. It didn't seem right that any man should have to die such a slow, agonizing death. Richard Potter had been a cold, calculating man, a tyrant, but, then, he had been brought up by a man just like himself, taught that the only thing important was holding his land. She wondered, if he had lived, would she have learned to understand him? Could she have touched whatever heart he kept buried deep in that tall, forbidding frame, behind those dark eyes that made her shiver? Why did he have to wait until he was dying to show that he could be vulnerable, that he had feelings and dreams, that he needed her? It wasn't fair of him, for now he had left her with a terrible guilt, wondering if there was something she could have done to touch his soul, to make him truly care about her. Was their miserable marriage all her fault, after all? Maybe if she hadn't been such an ignorant, frightened child, she would have known how to behave on that first night.

There were no answers to her questions. She told herself she had no reason to feel any guilt at all. Across from the grave Eleanor stood, weeping openly, also veiled, as though *she* were the poor, grieving widow. Her cousin had been furious when she had come for another visit several months ago, only to find Audra at Cypress Hollow. Richard had sent the woman back home to Baton Rouge, and Eleanor had immediately gone off to New Orleans. She had returned home just last month with a bewildered-looking new husband the woman ordered around like a pet dog. Albert Mahoney was ten years older than Eleanor, a widowed hotel owner Audra suspected had been roped and led down the aisle before he knew what was happening to him. She figured that Eleanor was out to prove she could get a decent husband, but she'd had to go to New Orleans, where the men did not know her, to find one.

Albert had hurried back to New Orleans at the news that the Yankees were indeed about to invade the city. He had to see that his hotel was protected. Eleanor had stayed in Baton Rouge, and she and Aunt Janine had come to Richard's funeral. Because of the impending invasion, and because so many men Richard had known were at war, Audra had held a small, simple funeral at Cypress Hollow. Joseph Brennan was among those who mourned, as were Lena and Toosie. Audra had not seen any of them in months, and part of her wanted to run and hug all of them, to be held and comforted, but pride and a lingering resentment kept her at a distance.

Behind her stood Henrietta and Sonda, both in tears. They were surrounded by several other Negroes, from both Brennan Manor and Cypress Hollow, but only a handful compared to how many slaves Richard owned. Audra knew that for most of them, there had been no love lost for Richard Potter. There was still a feeling of unrest among slaves and owners alike. Hard times were obviously at hand, for several slaves had run off and could not be found. A prominent white slaveholder had been murdered, and they all feared for their lives. March Fredericks had hunted down and hanged Henry Gathers and several of his cohorts, and Henrietta had told her there had been several cruel whippings. Audra had been too wrapped up in caring for Richard to find out all the details, and she was not even sure she wanted to know.

Now her biggest concern was survival. Luckily the planting had been completed, but with so many Negroes having run off, who was going to pick the cotton once it was ready at the end of summer? Even if it got picked, how would they get it to any market? The Yankees had choked up every outlet, and now they lurked at the only exit to the Gulf. To Audra they were like a dark cloud, hanging over the plantation, ready to swoop down and destroy everything.

If not for the Yankees, Richard would probably still be alive, and their help would not have run off and left them to fall into poverty, which would surely happen if they could not sell their cotton. Her father had a good deal of money set aside, but how long would it last with so much land and buildings and equipment to take care of, so many mouths to feed? She was a widow of means now, but she knew that with hard times coming, she would have to be very careful how she used Richard's money.

The land could always be sold, but she had promised Richard she would not do that, nor would she want to. What was all the fighting for, if not for the land? And who was going to buy such a huge farm right now, with the South in such turmoil, and not knowing if slavery would continue? How much would it cost to hire enough people to care for so much land and harvest the cotton if all their Negroes ran off?

Questions and guilt and confusion plagued her mind and heart. She told herself she could not decide everything at once. Today she could think only about the fact that her husband was being buried on a wooded hillside that overlooked his Cypress Hollow home. A priest from Baton

Rouge had come to the plantation to conduct the funeral, but Audra barely heard anything the man said.

Now the priest threw dirt onto the casket, and Audra knelt to scoop some into her gloved hand, then did the same. "I love you, Richard," she said quietly, deciding that the least she could do was appear to grieve for him, and quell any remaining rumors about their marriage being less than perfect. Would God strike her dead for such a display? She had *wanted* to love her husband, but he had not allowed it, and after the way he had treated her, it seemed that just forgiving him ought to have been enough. She had done all she could to comfort him, had never left his side. In the end the proud, pompous Richard Potter had been like a frightened child, clinging to her, telling her he was afraid of death. In that last moment of life, her heart had gone out to him, and she had seen a glimmer of what they could have had. She knew he saw it, too, and that was the saddest thing about his dying.

She longed for someone to cling to, just for a little while. But she felt desperately alone.

When the funeral ended, she heard her aunt telling the guests to come to the house for refreshments, adding that those who had come from far away could stay the night. Joseph Brennan came to her side, tried to comfort her, but she pulled away. If not for her father, she might never have married Richard in the first place. All her pain and humiliation could have been avoided.

"Audra, dear—"

"Leave me alone, Father."

Lena joined him in trying to comfort her, but Audra asked them both to leave her. Joseph wiped his eyes and walked off with the others, and Audra stayed beside the grave for several minutes. She did not realize until she turned to leave that someone else was still there. Toosie stepped in front of her, holding her chin proudly, her eyes showing their sorrow. Audra knew that Toosie understood the real reason for her deep grief. Audra started to walk past her when Toosie touched her arm. This time Audra did not pull away.

"None of this was ever my fault," Toosie told her. "You

can't hate me like you think you hate your father and my mother."

Audra reached under her veil to wipe at her eyes. "I don't hate anyone, Toosie. I don't know *how* I feel about anything anymore."

"Things are going to get a lot worse, and we will all need each other," Toosie told her. "I miss you, Audra."

Audra wanted to embrace her, but part of her still felt that such things just were not done with Negroes, and she held back. "I'm sorry. I just can't come home yet."

"You won't have to. Your father feels it's too dangerous for you, both here and at Brennan Manor, right now. There is a lot of resentment and hatred in the Negro camps. You have been so involved with Richard that you probably don't know everything that happened. I think you *should* know."

Audra frowned, seeing a grief in Toosie's eyes that went much deeper than Richard's death. "What don't I know, Toosie?"

Toosie blinked back tears. "March Fredericks went on a rampage, raided the Negro camps both here and at home. I don't doubt that some of my people that he beat and hanged deserved it, but not all of them. Your father was scared the Negroes would rise up and murder the whole household, including me and my mother. They all know your father sleeps with my mother and that I am his daughter." She took a deep breath, holding Audra's gaze. "Your father gave March Fredericks full rein, and Fredericks used it as an excuse to get back at poor old George for that time you stopped him from whipping the man. He hanged old George right along with some of the others."

Audra gasped in sudden grief and anger. "George! He would never hurt a soul! He was a good man!"

"We all know that. By the time your father found out, it was too late. He was furious. He fired March. The man threatened your father . . . and he said he'd get you, too. That was almost two weeks ago, and nobody has seen him since. Your father wants you and me to go to Baton Rouge. Even with the Yankees coming, he thinks we'd be safer there, staying at your aunt and uncle's house, than on the plantation. Between the angry Negroes still left there, and

March Fredericks out there somewhere thinking about revenge, it's too dangerous."

"But what about my *father!*"

Toosie smiled to herself. Yes, the love was still there. Audra would embrace her father again ... someday. "You know Joseph Brennan. He will never leave Brennan Manor, and my mother will never leave *him*. They will both stay there." She turned to watch Joseph talking with his sister-in-law, Janine. "Don't worry. He has plenty of good men guarding the grounds." She looked back at Audra. "As long as he can keep paying them well, they'll stay."

Audra wondered how long that could be, if there was no cotton harvest this year. And how many of those men would run off if the Yankees made it all the way to Baton Rouge?

"You're thinking you should stay with your father, but it's best you do as he says and go to Baton Rouge, Audra," Toosie advised. "I know it's not my place to be telling you anything, but I care about you. If Union soldiers come swarming into Louisiana, people on the remote plantations will be in a lot more danger than in the cities. There have already been stories of farms being burned and southern ladies being raped by Yankee rabble. Your father will tell you the same. I just ... I wanted you to know about George, and I wanted you to know I don't hate you for the way you feel about me. But we are going to have to set aside the hurt and be strong and brave. Your father heard just today that the Yankees have broken through the two forts at the mouth of the Mississippi and are right now taking New Orleans. That means they'll be coming this way."

Audra shivered. Too many things to think about at once. "I'm so worried about Joey. It seems we're suddenly losing the war, Toosie."

"We don't know that yet. We have to have faith."

Audra turned and met her eyes. "Poor George! He must have been so afraid." New tears came. "Do you think it's terrible ... that I feel more grief over George's death ... than my own husband's?"

Toosie shook her head. "No. George was a far better man, even if he *was* a Negro."

Audra did not miss the meaning of her words. George had been just as deserving of respect and love as any white man. At times Audra had not even thought of him as Negro. He was just a sweet man who had always been good to her . . . and she suddenly saw it was like that for her father and Lena. Joseph saw past the color of Lena's skin. Why couldn't it be that way for everyone?

"I'll go to Baton Rouge, if that is what Father wants," she said. "But first I want to visit George's grave."

Toosie nodded. "I knew that you would." She reached out, and Audra took her hand. In the next moment they embraced, and Audra began to cry bitter tears. Everything was so twisted and wrong—Joey off at war, George dead, her being estranged from her beloved father, Richard dying at the hands of a Negro, the Yankees coming to Baton Rouge. What would happen to Cypress Hollow and Brennan Manor? What was happening to the whole South? The only person she could turn to for strength was a sister she had never even knew she had until these last few months.

She felt literally weary from the battle going on in her soul over how she should feel about the Negroes. Richard had been killed by a Negro, but there were good, loving Negroes like George, and like Toosie and Lena and Henrietta. She had taken it for granted all these years that they were perfectly happy with things as they were. "I am so confused. I don't know who to trust anymore, what to believe is right or wrong. I just want Joey to come home and for things to be like they used to be."

Toosie kept an arm around her waist and began leading her toward the house. "I don't think they can ever be exactly the same," she said. "We just have to take one day at a time now, Audra, and be glad when that day brings us peace."

Audra looked back at the grave once more, wishing it held March Fredericks. Poor old George! He must have been so terrified, felt so alone! The thought of it made her sick, and she vowed that if March Fredericks ever showed his face at Cypress Hollow or Brennan Manor again, she would shoot him.

MAY 1862

Audra sat in a porch swing on the veranda of her Aunt Janine's house, watching the cone-shaped tents spring up like mushrooms. From the hillside mansion, she could see the Yankees settling into Baton Rouge as though here for a holiday. Hundreds of white tents were being erected across a wide expanse of flat land east of the city, and only a quarter mile from the McAllister home. Audra thought it was a good thing Uncle John was off to war himself and not here to see what was happening to his own home town.

She wished she could set fire to every single tent. The Federals had come into the city as if they owned it, their boats berthed in the harbor, troops marching through the streets unchallenged. She supposed she should be relieved that the occupation had been peaceful. Their own Confederate Army had withdrawn to the countryside—many, she was sure, having gone to help shore up Port Hudson, a strategic stronghold on the Mississippi that everyone knew was next on the Yankees' list.

Audra felt ashamed that there had been no resistance. Even in New Orleans, Confederate General Duncan had been unable to put up a decent defense. According to reports, half of his men had literally fled before the Union forces, which drove right through Fort Jackson and Fort St. Philip with their mighty gunboats. It had been the citizens of New Orleans who had tried to defend their city, angry mobs who had supported city officials in their refusal to surrender, until so many Yankee troops landed that there was no hope.

Union troops had surged through areas surrounding New Orleans and routed the remaining Confederates. New Orleans had finally fallen, but not before the Confederate General Duncan had ordered the Confederate ship *Louisiana* to be set afire and directed at the Federal gunboats, hoping that the ironclad, her magazines full of powder, would plow into the Federal ships and destroy them. To the humiliation of the citizens of New Orleans—indeed, of Baton Rouge and all of Louisiana—the Confederate boat had exploded before ever reaching the Federal ships. None were damaged, but the *Louisiana* was lost.

State and Confederate flags had been hauled down by Federal soldiers, and now the same was happening in Baton Rouge. The Yankees had shown such superior force in New Orleans that the citizens in Baton Rouge had put up no defense at all. In fact, some seemed literally excited about the flood of Yankees that had come to town. Fear had presented itself in the form of a quiet welcome, people running into town to watch the Yankees march through the streets, some actually opening their homes to them, merchants figuring to make some money, at least, off the Yankees. Audra found the entire event ludicrous and humiliating. She was not about to go into town to make a fool of herself the way Eleanor and Aunt Janine were doing right now.

Even Toosie had been anxious to go and watch, and Audra had allowed it. She could no longer bring herself to order Toosie around like the other slaves, and she had brought Sonda along to do most of the work, with Toosie only helping her dress and doing her hair. Aunt Janine fumed that she was spoiling Toosie now, reminding her that, although Toosie was her half sister, she was still a Negro and a slave.

A lot of southern women are related to mulattoes, the woman had added. *They do not choose to treat them any differently from the rest of the Negroes. Most, in fact, white and Negro alike, consider the mulattoes of an even lower class than the full-bloods. It looks bad to show favoritism, Audra, and it creates hard feelings among the rest of the Negroes under your control.*

Audra cared little for what Aunt Janine or anyone else thought. The fact remained that Toosie was her half sister and just about the only friend she had. In spite of how Audra had treated her before then, Toosie had remained loyal and seemed to harbor no resentment.

Things looked very bad, and the sweet life of wealth and luxury Audra had always known was already changing. The Yankees had nearly all ports closed off, and hiring blockade runners took a great deal of money. With none coming in, and valuable slaves running off, surely nothing but hardship lay ahead. Southern banks were collapsing, and Confederate money was losing its value. In Audra's mind every terrible thing that was happening was all the fault of men like those who pitched their tents in the fields below.

She did not trust the gentlemanly manners of these Yankee invaders. She had learned from living with Richard that power did something to a man, and she knew from stories of atrocities that when men were full of victory and feeling power over their "conquered foe," they often turned into animals. They could choose at any time to raid and plunder, steal and rape and destroy at their will, for they had the citizens of Baton Rouge at their mercy now, and they damn well knew it! No, she was not going into town to greet them with a smile as though they were long-lost friends!

Damn Yankees! They must all be laughing at the Confederates, even joking about how easily they had taken over New Orleans and now Baton Rouge. Slavery was no longer the issue now, nor the economy. It was obvious the Federals were cocksure they were winning this war, and the biggest loss here was the damage to southern pride.

Now here they were, boastful and victorious, probably thinking the Confederate soldiers were weak cowards. It made her want to cry, knowing boys like Joey were still out there risking their lives to keep the South alive. Joey would be heartbroken if he saw this. The only thing to be glad about was the fact that there had been no bloodshed . . . yet—but the scene below reminded her of dry tinder just waiting for a spark. Everyone whispered about the possibility of Confederates planning a sneak attack after the Yankees settled in. If that happened, Baton Rouge would become a war zone, and a lot of buildings would be destroyed, a lot of lives lost. Audra had read and heard too many stories about bloody battles everywhere, like the horror at a place called Shiloh in Tennessee.

Reading the reports had made her shiver. Estimates of the dead and wounded came to thirteen thousand for the North, nearly eleven thousand for the South, staggering numbers that had made people gasp when they had heard or read them. She still lived in constant fear that Joey might have been there, and every day she had Toosie go to the newspaper office and check the names of lost loved ones that were posted there. So far Joey was not among them, but she would not rest easy until she heard from her brother that he was all right.

She rose when she saw the three-seater carriage that belonged to Uncle John coming up the road to the house. The driver, a slave named Henry, who belonged to her aunt and uncle, kept her uncle's fine black mare at a modest trot, and Eleanor and Aunt Janine rode in the second seat, their parasols twirling as though they had just returned from a holiday picnic. Audra noticed that Toosie had been relegated to the backseat. As they came closer, Henry's face was unreadable. He was one Negro who she suspected was not any happier to see the Yankees here than most whites.

Henry liked his job, had been owned by John McAllister for years, and appeared to harbor no desire to be "set free."

Eleanor and Aunt Janine were excited and chattering like magpies. In spite of being a married woman whose husband was still in New Orleans trying to protect his businesses there, Eleanor flitted about in the prettiest dresses she could find. She had not seemed the least bit worried about poor Albert when the Yankees invaded New Orleans, and she had seemed almost disappointed when she received a telegram from him telling her he was all right. Audra supposed that maybe her cousin was hoping the man would be killed so that she could inherit his hotel and other businesses, live like a queen on the money, and go on to pursue other man. Eleanor had done her "duty" of marrying and making herself appear a proper woman. Who would blame her if, as a widow, she fell into other men's arms in her loneliness? Audra continued to find Eleanor's attitude and behavior disgusting, and she did not care to be seen with her in town.

Eleanor and Aunt Janine climbed down from the carriage, and Audra noticed Eleanor seemed to be in a hurry to reach her first. She walked swiftly toward her, while her mother unloaded some packages and spoke with the driver. Audra did not miss the look of contempt in her cousin's eyes. Since the day Audra had come to Baton Rouge, Eleanor had treated her rudely. Audra knew Eleanor all but hated her for keeping her from Richard those last few months, actually resented her now for being the one who got to play the role of the beautiful, lonely widow.

"Oh, you really should go into town, Audra!" the woman exclaimed when she got closer. She wore pink today, and Audra decided that the color made her look even heftier. "I never dreamed that there were so many handsome Yankees, and they are being ever so kind and gentlemanly. If this is war, I can't imagine what all the fuss is about!" She smiled wickedly. "And with most of our own men gone . . ." She twirled her parasol. "My, my, a town full of lonely men who haven't been with a woman in months . . . how utterly tempting!"

Audra kept her eyes on the camp below. "Don't trust them, Eleanor."

"Oh, you're such a prude and a worrier, Audra."

Audra turned then to look at her. "How can you betray our own boys who are out there fighting for the cause, and men like your own father, by greeting those Yankees with open arms! You should be ashamed, Eleanor. You shouldn't even be in Baton Rouge. You should be in New Orleans with your husband."

Eleanor sniffed, then turned and smiled at her mother, who had reached the veranda.

"Hurry inside, Eleanor, and we'll try on our new hats," the woman told her daughter.

Audra was dumbfounded that they had actually shopped! With the banks collapsing and Uncle John's own bank in danger, every penny was important. How could they think about buying hats at a time like this!

Eleanor waited for her mother to go inside the house before resuming her conversation. She leaned closer to Audra then, her puffy eyes full of animosity. "You're just jealous because you're still in mourning and will be for months! A recently widowed woman can't go flaunting herself, now, can she? Poor, lonely Audra, having to wear that ugly black," she sneered. "If only everyone knew that you probably *rejoiced* at Richard's death!"

Audra clenched her fists. "No matter how I felt about Richard, *I'm* the one who had to sit and watch him die a horrible death! I would not have wished such a thing on my worst enemy. You're a selfish, cruel-hearted woman, Eleanor." She held the woman's eyes boldly. "But then I suppose you know that and are proud of it!" She watched the hurt and anger in her cousin's eyes and enjoyed it. "I might add that a lonely widow on a manhunt would at least be more acceptable than a *married* woman whose husband is still alive! What would Albert think?"

Eleanor laughed. "Albert thinks whatever I *want* him to think. I'll go join him a time or two, and that will keep him happy. In the meantime, Baton Rouge is full of gentlemanly Yankees who are starved for a woman's affection. If I want to show some of them a little of our . . . southern hospitality

. . . that is *my* business." She looked Audra over. "You really shouldn't waste yourself in this fake mourning, Audra. After all, *you're* the one who has already slept with a Yankee man!" She tossed her head and stomped into the house, and Audra fought for control, telling herself there was never any sense in arguing with Eleanor. The woman still behaved like a selfish, spoiled child, and she felt sorry for poor Albert, a nice enough man who truly seemed to care about Eleanor. She turned and walked down the steps of the veranda to greet Toosie, then noticed the woman looked ready to cry. "What's wrong, Toosie? Are you afraid of the soldiers?"

Toosie shook her head. Was it best to tell Audra what she had seen, or to let it go? Surely the woman had a right to know. "I saw him, Audra," she said quietly.

"Saw whom?"

Toosie swallowed hard. "Lee Jeffreys."

Audra froze, and she just stared at Toosie. "You must be mistaken," she said finally. "It has been two years since—"

"I would never forget that man. It *was* Lee! He's some kind of important officer. I don't know what the different uniforms mean, but his was decorated with fancy patches on his jacket, some medals, too. He rode a horse beside a big group of marching soldiers and was giving them orders."

Audra put a hand to her chest. "Dear Lord! Did he see *you*?"

"No. He was too busy to notice. I kept to the crowd, followed along behind as far as where the soldiers are pitching those tents. He ordered some men to search through that school building in the clearing and make sure there were no Confederates hiding inside. I think he means to make the school his headquarters while he is here. I hurried back to find Eleanor and Janine, but he's probably still at the school. If you want to see him, I think you'd find him there."

Audra turned away, feeling almost faint. "I have to sit down."

Toosie helped her up the steps and sat down beside her in the porch swing. "I didn't say anything to Eleanor or your aunt," she said quietly. "They never saw him. I'm not sure they would even recognize him—they saw him only that one night at the cotillion—but even so, I wasn't sure you'd want either of them to know."

Audra rubbed her temples. "I don't know *what* to think, or what to do." She looked at Toosie, then took her hand. "Are you really, really sure?"

Toosie nodded. "I'm sure. It was Lee." She smiled. "I hate to say it, his being a Yankee and all, but he was handsome as ever, especially in that uniform."

Audra gazed again at the tents below. Lee! She'd been so sure she had gotten over him, but just the mention of his name, knowing he was not more than a quarter mile away from her . . . after all this time . . . Why did God keep sending him back into her life? "Did he look all right? I mean . . . not wounded or anything?"

"He limped a little when he got off his horse, but he wasn't using a cane or anything like that. Will you go and see him?"

It still didn't seem quite right to be talking to Toosie about these things, but who else could she turn to? And Toosie was the one person she knew she could trust. Her heart was pounding wildly, her thoughts swirling with sweet memories. But everything was different now. "It would seem so shameful, me still in mourning over my husband, him being the enemy now."

"He was your good friend first, and he did love you dearly."

Audra rose, wrapping her arm around a column of the veranda. "Yes." She watched the activity in the distance. One of those men riding through the city of tents could be Lee. Cannons were being brought in, and she could hear the distant voices of men shouting orders. "If I don't go, the whole thing will be left ended, as it should be."

Toosie came to stand beside her. "They say some of these soldiers could be camped here for a year or two. They are here to hold the city until this war is over, Audra. Can you really imagine living here that long with Lee Jeffreys so close? Even if you went back to Brennan Manor, you would still know he is here. And after his risking his very life to come and defend you two years ago, he deserves to know that Richard Potter is dead and you're all right. He gave me and my mother instructions to write him if Richard kept abusing you. He was willing to come back down here and kill the man if he had to, and I think he would have done it, even if it meant he'd be hanged."

"He told you that?"

Toosie nodded. "He should know you're all right. And maybe he should know where you are staying. Lord knows how long all this peace is going to last. If the Confederates attack and the Yankees go on a rampage through the city, it might help for him to know where you are so he can make sure nothing happens to you. It can't hurt to have at least one of those Yankees down there looking out for us."

Audra wiped at a tear that slipped down her cheek. "It seems so traitorous, as if I was consorting with the enemy; and here I am wearing black on top of it all! I can't, Toosie. Can I? It's men like Lee who could be responsible for Joey lying dead or wounded somewhere, or in one of their prisons! It just isn't right for me to go and see him."

"You don't know what he's been through himself. Maybe he'd be happy to see a friend in the middle of a town full of people who hate them so much. Maybe he has suffered something you don't know about and needs an old friend to talk to. Joey loved him, too. Joey would say you should go and see him—in spite of the fact that he is a Yankee."

Audra smiled. Toosie was right. Joey would never hate Lee, even though he was supposed to be the enemy. "I don't know. What about Eleanor and Aunt Janine?"

"They might as well know. Lee might come here asking about you. You have the right to see him. Lee Jeffreys was your good friend and he loved you. Even though he's the enemy, he's worth a lot more than Eleanor *or* your aunt!" She touched Audra's arm again. "Besides, Eleanor seems to think it's perfectly all right to mingle with the Yankees. But, if you want an excuse for going to see him, you can tell your aunt that since you know Lee, you're doing this to keep her and Eleanor safe, that in case of trouble, you're asking Lee to make sure no harm comes to them or to this home."

Audra looked back at the camp below. That summer at

Maple Shadows seemed like such a long, long time ago now, much longer than three years. And she was such a different woman now, a far cry from the innocent seventeen-year-old who had loved so openly and with such passion. Could she ever recapture that feeling? And even after the horrors of those first days with Richard, a few hours in Lee's arms had made it so easy to give herself again. Did he think often about that night they had shared a bed when she belonged to another man? Would it all be different now, because of the ugly war?

Everything Lee had predicted when they'd argued at Maple Shadows had come true. Something much bigger than their love had torn them apart, something not over yet. She would go and see him because it was the right thing to do for now, and because there was probably no getting around it; but the past could not be reawakened, could it? Nothing could ever be the same again.

"Tell Aunt Janine that we are just going for a walk. I want to wait until I have talked to Lee before I tell them I've seen him. If he isn't going to be here for long, there is no sense telling them at all."

"Yes, and I'll get your veiled hat and your gloves."

Audra wondered what it would be like to see Lee again. What terrible things had he been through? Would he hate her now, just because she was a Confederate? There was only one way to find out. She drew a breath and tried to be calm. "God help me," she whispered.

23

Audra found most of the Yankee soldiers well mannered, but she could not quell the uneasiness she felt being surrounded by hundreds of the enemy, any of whom might have shot her without hesitation if the citizens of Baton Rouge had resisted. Although most were polite and tipped their hats and seemed respectful of her black clothing and veil, she did not miss the looks in some of the men's eyes. There were obviously good men among these troops, but there were also those who enjoyed playing the conqueror, and who, if not for superior officers to keep them in line, would feel they had every right to take whatever they could, including women. A few were all-out rude and made comments about the "spoiled southern belle and her nigger."

"You can stay with us, honey," one man offered Toosie. "You don't have to go traipsing after some white bitch anymore."

These men were supposedly here to help free the slaves, yet she sensed that, for the most part, they didn't have any more respect for Negroes than someone like Richard had. She could not recall ever hearing or reading about any Northerners who had opened their arms to the Negroes or made them an offer to come North, where they would be welcomed, trained, educated, housed, given wage-paying jobs. She wondered how surprised and disappointed the runaways and freed slaves were going to be when they reached the North and found they were no more welcome there than they were in the South.

She couldn't help becoming angry about the irony of the situation. People like Toosie and Henrietta and their driver Henry were going to suffer, no matter how this war turned out, and she was feeling more and more responsible to do something about it. The war had awakened something in her she had never experienced before, had made her realize she cared about the Negroes in a way she had once never thought possible. She suspected that for the most part, she cared more about them than did most of these men who had come to "free" them.

A wagon clattered past, hauling a cannon. The sight of the big gun brought a tight feeling to Audra's stomach. Men marched everywhere, horses whinnied, orders were shouted. This was a fully armed camp, men ready to move at the slightest hint of aggression. No one had any doubts that Port Hudson was next, and Baton Rouge would probably be their home base for planning the next siege.

"Did you check the lists of dead and wounded this morning?" she asked Toosie.

"Yes, ma'am. Joey's name was not there."

Audra jumped when a nearby gunshot startled her. She turned to see a man holding a rifle, and a pigeon plopped to the ground not far away. "Just shootin' at birds, ma'am," the man said with a wink. He and those around him broke into laughter, and Audra felt a flash of fury. Only one of them did not seem to think it was so funny. He stepped away from the others and apologized. "Some of these men have been through a lot, ma'am. They need to shoot off a little steam, find ways to relax."

"And I suppose you think *we* have *not* been through any hardships!" she asked.

The man studied her black dress and veil and apologized again. "Can somebody do something for you, ma'am?"

Audra held her chin up proudly. "Yes. I am looking for Lee Jeffreys. I was acquainted with him a few years ago, and I am told he is among you. I have no idea of his rank or—"

"Colonel Jeffreys is right over there, ma'am," the man interrupted, "in that school building. You came at a good time. He's just finished his supper and he's ordered everybody out, wants to write a few letters and such. He's alone right now."

The man looked her over, and Audra knew what he was thinking. It was useless to explain herself, so she simply thanked him and walked on, her heart pounding faster with every step. After two years and thinking she would never see him again, it seemed so strange to realize Lee Jeffreys was just a few yards away. When she and Toosie reached the schoolhouse, Toosie touched her arm and said she would wait outside on the steps. "You should see him alone."

Audra closed her eyes and took a deep breath, sorely tempted to turn around and go back home, but now that she had come this far, she decided she might as well get it over with. "All right." She climbed the steps, and a private standing outside the door stopped her. "Your name, ma'am?"

"Audra Brennan Potter. I am an old friend of Colonel Jeffreys."

The man looked her over. "I'll need to search you for weapons, ma'am. We can't let just any southerner in to see an officer alone, even a pretty widow woman like yourself." He touched her waist, and Audra knocked his arm away.

"You tell the colonel I'm here, and he'll tell you I don't need searching!"

The man looked surprised, then shrugged and went inside. Audra felt a fierce desire to kick him squarely in the rear end. She smoothed her dress, wishing she could calm her heart better. What was she doing here? This was ridiculous! Lee was one of the damn Yankees now! How many innocent people had he killed, how many buildings and farms had he ordered burned? And how puffed up had he become from all his grand victories and his rank as colonel?

Then the door opened, and he stood there, looking more handsome than ever, just as Toosie had said. His blue eyes were still gentle and loving. In one quick moment every bit of anger and fear had left her, replaced only by memories that rekindled a fire deep in her soul, a fire that had never gone out.

At first he just looked at her, and she saw his pain, knew he had suffered the same as she had. If not for this war, they might have been so happy. Now everything they were feeling was said in that one first meeting of the eyes. "Audra," Lee said softly. "Come in."

He stepped back to allow her inside, but Audra turned to see several of his men staring at her. "I am not sure it would look right for either of us."

"You men get back to whatever it is you're supposed to be doing!" he ordered. "And you had all better know right now that I'll take a whip to the man who shows this woman any disrespect!"

A few grinned and some muttered among themselves as they returned to their duties. Lee noticed Toosie sitting on the steps and he smiled. "It's good to see you again."

"Hello, Mr. Jeffreys," Toosie answered.

Lee took Audra's arm then and led her inside the schoolhouse, ordering the private who guarded the building not to allow anyone in except in an emergency. He closed and locked the door, then turned Audra to face him. Part of her wanted to pull away at the thought of a Union soldier touching her, but the greater part of her still belonged to this man, and she owed him so much. At first neither said a word. They just studied each other, feeling a secret happiness at seeing one another again, but struggling not to show all they felt.

"I couldn't believe it when Private Dillon told me who was out here. What in God's name are you doing in Baton Rouge?" he asked. "Wouldn't you be safer at Brennan Manor?"

She pulled away. "Perhaps *you* can answer that, Colonel Jeffreys," she replied. "How safe *are* places like Brennan

Manor, with all you Yankees milling through the towns and countryside like a bunch of army ants?"

She turned and faced him again, lifting her veil. Lee grinned at the old haughty air that had irritated him when he first met her. "I don't know what you've heard, but I am not among those who order innocent people killed and homes destroyed. You know me better than that, Audra."

He folded his arms, and Audra thought how they looked even more powerful than she remembered. It was warm inside the school, and he had removed his uniform jacket and was wearing a plain white shirt and blue pants that fit his hips snugly. Long-buried desires swept through her with surprising force, making her turn away. She sighed, giving up her pretense at anger. "I suppose I do. That's what made it all the more difficult for me to come here. I should hate you as much as the rest of those damn Yankees out there." She turned to face him again. "I almost didn't do this, but I knew I had to. I have to be careful, Lee, or my own friends and neighbors will begin calling me a traitor."

His blue eyes moved over her, bringing the old shiver that only Lee Jeffreys could stir in her. His smile was as warm as ever, and his thick, dark hair hung past his shoulders. He was in need of a haircut, and his face showed a shadow of a beard, but none of that detracted from his good looks. "How did you know I was here? I didn't see you in the streets when we came through town."

She turned away again, strolling toward a desk at the front of the room. "I was not about to come into town and welcome your men as some kind of saviors, and I am furious at those who did. People should have stayed inside and locked their doors."

There was that southern drawl that had always charmed him. . . .

"Toosie saw you," she said. "She had gone to town with my aunt and Eleanor. I've been staying with them. For the time being."

Lee frowned, dropping his arms. "What's happened? Why are you dressed like that?"

She met his eyes. "Richard is dead. Since the war, the Negroes have become more belligerent, just as we predicted. One particular troublemaker who had been sold off escaped his new owner and came back to pay us a visit. Richard found him hiding in the Negro camp at Cypress Hollow, and the man stabbed Richard with a pitchfork." She looked away. "It was a slow, terrible death. Richard lived almost two weeks." She heard a deep sigh, and the room hung quiet for a moment.

"I'm sorry for the way he had to die, but I can't say that I'm sorry the man is dead," Lee finally spoke up. "It must have been a terrible thing for you to go through."

Audra walked to a window. "I never learned to love him, Lee, but I tried being a wife in the fullest sense, because I had no other choice. It was either that, and try to have children, or live a life of total emptiness."

Why did those words stir such hot jealousy in his soul? He wasn't supposed to care anymore, was he? He wanted to grab her, remind her that he had claimed her long before she'd belonged to Richard Potter. In just these few minutes he could not help thinking she'd never been any man's but his.

"It wasn't easy to ... be with him ... and there certainly was never any love lost between us. But in spite of how I felt about him, it was awful to watch him die. Now I feel such guilt—not being able to mourn him the way a wife *should* want to mourn her husband. I am afraid I feel grief only for how he suffered, but not for the loss of the man. Mostly, I feel ... relief." Her voice broke on the last couple of words.

"You shouldn't feel guilty about that," he told her, moving close behind her. "No one could blame you for not being terribly sorry that he's gone. How long ago did it happen?"

Audra took a handkerchief from her handbag and dabbed at her eyes. She paused before answering him. "He died hardly a month ago. Father was afraid there would be more trouble with the Negroes. . . ." She moved away from him. "He sent me and Toosie here because of an irate overseer he fired. He was also worried we could be attacked if the Negroes turned on us. So far everything seems to be quiet, but then, there aren't many slaves left to worry about.

Most of them have run off. Another year of being unable to harvest our cotton and unable to find a market for it, and we will be ruined! I hope that makes you happy." She felt her throat begin to tighten.

"Audra, it doesn't make me happy at all, and you damn well know it. I'm just doing what I have to do, what I know is right—"

"You don't know *anything*!" She whirled back around to face him, her eyes wet with tears. "You don't know how hard my father worked to build Brennan Manor, and his father before him! I even have to respect men like Richard for that much. Can't you understand we had every intention of ending slavery, in our own way and time! None of this was necessary, Lee! *None* of it! And if Joey dies, it will all have been so stupid and useless, and I will have *no* one! *No* one!" She began to shake, and in the next moment Lee was holding her, and she was letting him. Her tears came harder then, from a torrent of mixed emotions. The Yankees were responsible for her situation, and here she was turning to one for comfort! She wanted to hate him for it, but she still loved him, loved the feel of his strong arms around her. It had been such a long, long time since anyone had held her this way, allowed her to lean on him and weep to her heart's content.

"Please don't cry, Audra. It seems as if all I'm ever able to do is make you cry."

"It's just . . . all so wrong and unnecessary. I am losing everything that was . . . dear to me . . . Joey . . . father . . ." She leaned back and looked up at him. "Oh, Lee, Joey went off and volunteered for the Confederate Army. He was in Tennessee last time he wrote, and then I read about . . . Shiloh, and I'm so terrified he was there! The reports that came back to us were awful! Thousands killed. Men losing their arms . . . their legs. I haven't heard from Joey since. What is it really like, Lee? What happens in battle? Have you seen so many men dying at one time? Are they . . . getting their arms and legs cut off without anything for the pain? I've seen a few in Baton Rouge, men with bloody stumps for legs and . . ."

"Don't, Audra!" He pulled her tighter again. "Don't

picture the worst for Joey." *My God,* he thought, *Joey joined the rebels! What if he was at Shiloh!* He had heard what had gone on there, and from what he'd seen and experienced himself, he could just imagine what an ungodly hell Shiloh had been. Poor Audra had lost so much already. Her whole life had been turned upside down. There was no sense in giving her even worse visions of what might have happened to Joey.

"He's probably all right, Audra, or you would have heard by now, I'm sure." He led her toward a bench at the side of the room. "Sit down." She obeyed, and Lee pulled a pin from her hat and removed it, drinking in the beauty that had hidden beneath the veil. "My sweet Audra." He wiped at tear on her cheek with his fingers. "I never thought I'd see you again, even when I found out I'd been given the assignment to come to New Orleans. I figured you'd be at Brennan Manor and I'd be too busy to go there and see how you were. I'm glad you're here, glad to know you're all right and out from under Richard Potter's control."

She looked away. "I shouldn't be here," she murmured. "Everything is so mixed up now, so different. I don't know how to feel about you as a Yankee. How can I consider you a friend when any of those men out there that you command would kill Joey or my father in an instant if they put up resistance?" She shook in a sob. "It's all . . . just like you predicted, Lee. All the hatred, the bloodshed, friends turning into enemies, innocent people dying." She looked up at him with tender curiosity. "What about you? You're walking with a limp."

He sighed and leaned back, keeping a hand on her shoulder. "I took some shrapnel in my left thigh at Roanoke Island. I keep thinking the damn thing is healed, and then it flares up again and hurts like hell." He studied her a moment, thinking how someone who looked like Audra should not be wearing black. She was meant for pretty spring colors. God, those eyes, still green and exotic as ever, those lips still just as inviting, especially when they were slightly pouted like they were now. Her hair glinted red in the sunlight that came through the window. "I got my promotion to colonel at Roanoke because I took over for an officer who'd been killed, and because I kept up the fighting in spite of my wound." He turned away from her then and rested his elbows on his knees. "I've been through some hell of my own, Audra. It's been bad for both sides. I've seen the things you talked about, heard men screaming. . . ." He closed his eyes. "I have also had my own losses. After the battle at Roanoke, my commanding officer told me he'd gotten word my father had died."

"I'm so sorry, Lee."

He stared at the floor. "It wouldn't be so bad if I hadn't just gotten closer to him. I went to see him before I left for the army, and we shared things we had never shared before. I never told you everything about the problems between me and my father." He met her eyes again. "No sense going into all of that right now. I *am* worried about my brother David. He also joined up. I haven't heard where he is or if he's all right. It's a lot like what you're going through with Joey, except that I'm out there seeing the hell of it all the time, which makes it even worse." He took her hand in his. "All you can do is pray for Joey, Audra. That's all *any* of us can do, pray that this hell will end soon. Do you know what regiment he's with?"

She shook her head. "Not anymore. They keep moving him around because he's a sharpshooter."

"A sharpshooter!" He smiled, hoping to make her feel better. "That means he's one of those who gets to stand back and shoot from behind barriers instead of having to throw himself on the front lines. That should keep him safer." He squeezed her hand. "I'll bet he's proud. I was always surprised at how good he was with a rifle when we used to hunt together up at Maple Shadows."

Their eyes held at the words, memories pouring in, a warmth filling them both. Audra could not help wondering if he often thought about that first time they made love, with such utter passion and boldness. She was almost embarrassed now to remember the things she had let him do to her, and yet it had all been so gentle and right and sweet. Much as she fought it now, the memories stirred womanly needs she had not allowed herself to recognize for three years now ... except for once ... just that one night when Lee Jeffreys came to visit her at Brennan Manor, when she had dared to let him possess her body, even though she was another man's wife. "Lee—"

"I know." He kept hold of her hand. "We're stuck with this, Audra. I don't blame you for how you feel about those men out there, and you really can't blame me for doing what I'm doing. You're the last person in the world I would want to see hurt. I'll do everything in my power to make sure nothing happens to your father or Brennan Manor, or you and your aunt; but I command just one brigade. There's a whole division here under General Butler. There will be upwards of seventeen thousand men here before we're through."

Her eyes widened, and she drew her breath in a quiet gasp. "Dear God!" Seventeen thousand Yankees, all swarming into Baton Rouge! Who would be safe?

"Audra, I'm not going to let anything happen to you. Where is your aunt and uncle's house?"

Could she really trust him? Of course, this was *Lee*. "It's the big mansion about a quarter mile from here, up the hill behind this school building. I have been sitting on the veranda all day watching the soldiers pitch their tents." She closed her eyes. "Lee, you can't promise to protect us or put a special guard on us. It would look bad to your commander, and at the same time it would make *us* look bad to our own friends. People would say I was consorting with the enemy, and it would go hard on Aunt Janine." She rose. "Uncle John also went off to join the army." She shook her head. "It's all so crazy and wrong. I feel I should be with Father, but I've been so angry with him. Never in my life have I been so torn and confused about everything." She faced him. "I found out Father is in love with Lena. A *Negro*! I knew some white men slept with Negro women but never knew they really *loved* them. He was sleeping with her for years before my mama even died! Toosie is his child, my own half sister."

She watched his eyes, expecting to see his shocked expression, but he just shook his head. "I always suspected it, from the very first day I met Toosie and noticed how much some of her features resembled yours. I couldn't believe you didn't see it, Audra, but you were so damn trusting, and so sure your father could do no wrong. I tried to tell you he isn't perfect, but you wouldn't hear of it. And I still think he burned those letters I sent you. Your father has totally controlled your life, Audra. Joey's, too. The reason Joey is out there right now risking his life is probably because he thinks it will make his father proud of him. It's the one thing he can do to earn the man's respect."

She sighed. "I know. He told me before he left he was doing it to make Father proud." She turned away. "I feel so betrayed, Lee, by everyone. I just don't know what to think of anything anymore, what is right and what is wrong, how to feel about my father . . . about the Negroes. Ever since I learned about Toosie and the affair between Lena and my father, my thinking about Negroes has begun to change."

She watched out the window again. More tents were going up. "I never did hate them, you know. I simply thought they were far less important than people like us. They had their place, and that was how it was supposed to be. But now, knowing what I know, I can't treat Toosie like that." She sighed, turning to look at him. "I still believe what the North is doing is wrong, Lee. After the war, it will be just as bad for the Negroes as if they were still slaves. They won't know where to go, how to live. No matter what course this war takes, it's going to be bad for them. Down here you will find that a lot of men who tolerated them and at least gave them shelter and food are going to end up hating them and treating them worse than they were ever treated when they were slaves. And how many of your Yankee friends in the North are going to welcome them with open arms?"

She walked past him, letting out a little hiss of disgust. "This war will solve nothing. A lot of men and boys will be killed or maimed, the South as we know it destroyed, and for what? We will have a whole nation to rebuild, and the Negroes will be left out of all of it. They'll still be a poor, ignorant, depressed race who have lost the only protection they had."

"You may be right, Audra," he told her, "and it's a miserable state of affairs; but we're both in it up to our necks, and that's the hell of it. We've got to stick it out now, each of us loyal to our own cause. There is no going back."

No going back. How right he was. They could never recapture what they once shared. He was such a beautiful man, inside and out. How she wished it could all have been different for them. "How long will you be here?" she asked.

"I'm not even sure. Just telling you how many men are on their way is more than I should have done. I'm trusting that you haven't come here as a spy."

She laughed bitterly. "I have enough problems without getting into such things." She walked closer. "I suppose that may be what your commander might think, though, isn't it? Is it dangerous for me to have come here—dangerous for you, I mean?"

He ran a hand through his thick hair. "Just don't make a habit of it, much as I would love to see you every day. This one visit might bring me up before General Butler for an explanation. We probably shouldn't see each other at all again."

Pain rushed through her chest with a stabbing force. "I know."

"Maybe some day . . . when all of this is over . . ."

She blinked back tears. *I still love you, Lee!* "Maybe. It depends on what has happened to my family . . . to Brennan Manor . . . to Joey." She turned away again. "I'm not sure how I would feel about you if something happens to Joey. It just can't ever be the same, can it?"

He rose and came up behind her, putting his hands on her shoulders, wishing he could tell her that he still loved her; but not here, not now, maybe not ever. "It's like I said—we can't ever go back. I'll pray for you, Audra, and for your father and Joey and Brennan Manor; and I'll do my best to see that nothing happens to you. But I am only one man with just so much power. The outlying area is going to be full of Yankees in a couple more months, bound to clear the countryside as they head North."

She nodded. "Maybe you could just . . . hold me again . . . for a little while."

I would like to hold you forever. He turned her, and she

fell into his arms again, remembering that first night he held her on the beach, remembering how safe she felt in this warm shelter, his heart beating close to her own, his strong arms reassuring her that she was loved and protected. Neither of them spoke. They savored the feel of being close again, allowing themselves a moment to draw strength from each other, to remember another time, another place. Both of them felt a powerful, painful desire, yet both knew it was impossible to explore it. How easy it would have been for their lips to meet—but the moment was shattered by a gunshot followed by a Yankee yell.

Audra pulled away. "God be with you, Lee."

"And with you," he murmured, his gaze confessing the love that still echoed between them. He took her hand and walked her over to the window ledge where he had laid her hat. He placed it gently on her head and replaced the hat pin, and his closeness was torture. He took her hand, pressing it reassuringly, his own eyes growing misty for what might have been. "I'm glad you came, and I wish we could see more of each other. There is so much to talk about." He leaned down and kissed her cheek, then pulled her veil over her face. "Good-bye, Audra."

Audra could not find her voice. She turned and walked to the door. Lee studied the slender waist, remembering the feel of her, the sweet smell of her, the taste of her. Every muscle in his body screamed with wanting her, but everything had changed. He was a Yankee, and she was a woman of the South, and this was war. She never looked back before closing the door gently behind her.

24

The first explosion gave Sonda such a start that she dropped a tray of tea she was serving to Audra, Eleanor, and Aunt Janine on the veranda. China cups crashed, and hot water spilled over the wooden veranda floor.

"My God, what was that!" Janine rose, and contrary to her normal nature, she did not scold Sonda for the accident. There came another boom, and the roof of a building in the town below exploded in a spray of shrapnel.

"They're shelling the city from the gunboats!" Audra exclaimed.

"But why?" Eleanor gasped.

There came more thunderous booms, more explosions. From where the house was perched, they could see most of the city, but it was difficult to tell just which buildings were being hit. The only building they all recognized was Uncle John's bank building, which still stood intact.

"Yankee bastards!" Eleanor exclaimed. "And here I was so nice to some of them! Everyone in Baton Rouge has been courteous to them!" She turned to Audra. "I thought you said your Yankee lover wouldn't let something like this happen," she sneered.

"He is *not* my lover!" Audra answered, furious at the accusation at this horrible moment. "I saw him one time, and the only thing he could promise was that he would keep an eye on this house and try to make sure nothing happened to us."

The big guns began firing in more rapid succession, and all over the city rooftops were exploding. They could hear a few screams now, could make out a few people running in the streets. "Lee wouldn't have anything to do with this," Audra said. "It's all coming from the gunboats. He might not know himself what this is about."

Several of the Negro servants came running out onto the veranda then, exclaiming over the noise. Henrietta screamed and ran back into the house when a shell hit a building no more than an eighth of a mile away.

"My God, why are they doing this?" Aunt Janine groaned.

Audra looked at the Yankee camp below, where men seemed to be moving in every direction. Some were marching in formation around the east side of the town toward the docks. Now she saw a rider heading up the hill toward the house. He sat tall on the big horse that carried him, and as he came closer, she saw he was in full dress uniform and well armed. It was Lee.

"Stay inside!" he yelled when he got closer. "If you have a cellar, get in it and stay there!"

"What's going on?" Audra demanded.

"I don't know myself yet, but I'm going to find out. I think this house is far enough away that the guns can't reach it, but stay inside, just in case. Out here you're exposed to flying shrapnel."

Aunt Janine let out a chilling wail then, as she stared at another rooftop that went up in a spray that resembled fireworks. "The bank! John's bank!" She looked at Lee. "You Yankee bastards!" she screamed at Lee. "We've been good

to you! Why are you doing this? You've no right! No right!"
She ran off the porch toward Lee and began pounding at his
left leg with her fists, screaming and cursing at him. Audra
saw Lee wince, and she remembered it was his left leg that
had been injured. He grabbed Janine's arm and turned his
horse, half dragging the woman back to the porch.

"Goddamn it, somebody get her off me before I hurt
her!"

Audra ran off the porch and took hold of her aunt about
the waist, hanging on for dear life while the woman kicked
at Lee's horse and kept reaching for him. Lee backed the
horse away, and Audra could tell by his eyes he was as confused about what was going on as the rest of them.

"Get in the house now! I said I would protect you, and
I will, to the best of my ability. I've got other men watching
the house."

"We don't need your protection, you stinking Yankee!"
Eleanor screamed. "How dare you bomb my father's bank?
How dare you kill innocent people who have been good to
you?"

Lee just glared at her a moment before turning to
Audra. "I'm going to find out what this is about. Get them
inside like I told you to do!" He whirled his horse and rode
off, and Aunt Janine withered into a sobbing hulk, falling to
her knees.

"All our money! They'll loot the bank! We'll be ruined,"
she wept.

Audra knew her uncle was probably already ruined before the bank was hit by a Federal shell. His business came
from the wealthy plantation owners like her father and
Richard and with the plantations also falling into ruin, there
was no money for any bankers to handle. She knelt down
and touched her aunt's shoulder. "Come on, Aunt Janine.
We have to go inside."

Below, building after building was exploding. Some had
caught fire. She looked for Lee again, but he had already
disappeared into the mass hysteria and destruction taking
place below.

•   •   •

The honeymoon between the Yankees and the citizens of Baton Rouge was over, just as Audra feared would happen. They learned that Confederate guerrillas had conducted a sneak attack on Federal sailors along the docks, wounding three of them. The Federals had retaliated by shelling the city, and now half the buildings in town lay either in full ruin or with gaping holes in their rooftops and walls. Because of the Federal barriers, no food or other supplies could get into the city, and people began rationing, skipping meals, letting pets fend for themselves. Some livestock were turned loose to graze in the countryside. Merchants closed their doors, trying to keep their supplies from Federal hands but managing to sneak food and clothing to their own citizens who needed it.

It was near evening, August 5, and Audra clung to a sack of food she had daringly come to town to forage for her aunt. Janine had remained a withering, weeping, useless woman after watching the family bank explode into ruins. Eleanor refused to go into town at all, too afraid now of the Federals who occupied the town, afraid of more shelling. *Besides,* she had told Audra, *this is all the fault of your Yankee lover and his men! He promised to protect us, and look what happened! If anyone should risk her life getting supplies, it's you. It's the only way to prove to us that you haven't been a traitor after all. Everyone thinks you have been, Audra Potter! You went and visited that damn Yankee colonel of yours. I almost wish this house had been damaged, so people wouldn't think we have special favor with those Yankee bastards!*

Audra was not about to argue with the woman. They needed food, and that was that. It was Eleanor's own fault that people thought what they did. The woman had blabbed all over town that Audra knew one of the Yankee commanders quite well. In her efforts to make herself look better, after her own very public flirtations with Yankee soldiers, Eleanor had made Audra seem to be a traitor, which made life harder on all of them.

More and more, Audra's only friends were among the Negroes. Hatred and bitterness and distrust were growing among the town's citizens, and Audra was not the only one ostracized. Others whose buildings were left untouched were accused of some kind of collusion with the Yankees, and Audra thought how sad it was what fear and loss of security could do to people.

Federals were stationed everywhere throughout the town now, and every trip into the city was dangerous, especially for young women, who took the brunt of crude remarks and threats. Lee had offered Audra around-the-clock protection, and guards to take her to town, but she had refused, realizing how bad it would look to other citizens of Baton Rouge. She was first a Southerner, a part of the Confederacy and a woman of Baton Rouge and Louisiana. She would not accept special favors from a former friend who was now the enemy. She knew her decision upset Lee, but she also knew he understood why she refused his protection.

Aware of how bad things were in town, her father had sent word that she and Toosie should come home. Brennan Manor had remained relatively peaceful, and with all that was happening in Baton Rouge, he believed they would now be safer at the plantation. The messenger from Brennan Manor had also brought the news that Lena had apparently had a stroke, which was part of the reason Joseph had not come for Toosie and Audra himself.

Audra hated to leave Eleanor and Aunt Janine alone, in spite of how they treated her, so she had refused to go back. She had sent Toosie home to be with her mother, and had also allowed Henrietta to go, since the woman was afraid to stay in Baton Rouge. She told Toosie she would come home as soon as she knew Aunt Janine was safe and well, in spite of the fact that the woman now refused even to speak to her. She acted as though the shelling of Baton Rouge was all Audra's fault.

Eleanor herself had made crude remarks about her "privileged status," about her being a lover to the enemy; but Audra knew she was simply jealous. She had not even been back to see Lee after that first visit, and her only other contact had been when he rode up to the house the day of the shelling, then returned a few hours later to explain why it had happened. She had not seen him since, and now she worried that once she went back to Brennan Manor, she would lose track of him forever. Deep inside she knew part of the reason she stayed in Baton Rouge was Lee.

She knew her father would be angry with her, and worried, but staying in the city for the time being seemed best. The important thing was that Toosie could be with Lena, while Audra could not only help her aunt and cousin, but could continue to check the daily roster of dead and wounded Confederates, as well as get her mail sooner. She still had not heard from Joey.

She clung to the sack of bread, potatoes, and carrots, thinking that at Brennan Manor they could at least continue to grow some of their own food if worst came to worst. God knew they had enough land for it. Her thoughts were interrupted then when she heard gunshots not far away. A man cried out, and when she turned in the direction of the sound, a Federal soldier who had been standing guard across the street fell forward. Then came more gunshots, and she realized she should not have come to town so late. It was already getting dark.

"Rebels!" someone shouted.

More gunfire. Audra backed against the wall of a building in an alley, and she could hear a barrage of yips and yelps and chilling war cries as the town suddenly came alive with battle. She had heard stories of the way Confederate soldiers whooped and yelled when attacking, something the Yankees called the "Rebel yell." For the first time in the war she was seeing real fighting close up. She realized that somehow Confederate soldiers had suddenly swarmed upon the city in a surprised attack, and she had been caught in the middle of it!

The whole town broke into a bedlam of yelling and shooting. Regular citizens caught in the melee were running every which way, screaming women dragging their children indoors, a few male citizens stepping outside and taking potshots at Federals. Audra ran through the alley to another street, but everywhere she went, it was the same mass confusion. She heard a startling, loud boom then from one of the gunboats in the harbor, and she knew that because of the rebel attack, more shelling would take place. A building two doors away exploded into a million splinters of wood, and Audra screamed and ducked, feeling something skim across her upper back.

She crouched back into the alley, not sure which way to run. It was impossible to know where a shell might hit next, and as night fell, it was also impossible to tell a Federal from a Confederate, unless they were under the direct light of a street lamp. She decided for the moment to keep to the darkness of the alley and pray that no one would see her, that no more shells would hit close by. A few men charged past her on horseback, and she caught sight of a yellow stripe down the side of one man's pants.

Federals. A real man-to-man war had come to Baton Rouge, and she knew some Federals would say that gave them license to loot at will. How was she going to get home safely? More explosions hit nearby, and she forced herself not to scream, for fear of being found. She stared wide-eyed as another volley of shots rang out and a soldier's body landed on the nearby boardwalk under a street lamp. She could see he was a Federal, and she could also see that his back was littered with bloody holes. Two Confederate soldiers ran up to him and began rummaging through the dead man's pockets, laughing when they found some money. They threw papers and pictures aside, and she grew sick at the sight of her own kind doing such a thing. She stayed quiet, thinking how ironic it was that she should be afraid of Confederate soldiers.

One of them let out a rebel whoop, and they started to leave, but more gunfire cut them down. Audra backed away as one fell, dead, into the alley. Wounded, the second man had begun crawling for shelter when a Federal soldier rode up to him and fired point-blank at his head, obliterating the man's face. This time Audra could not quell a cry of revulsion. The Union soldier peered into the dark alley, and Audra turned and ran. She heard a horse bearing down on her, and when he got close, she turned and swung the sack of potatoes as hard as she could, landing them against the surprised man's chest and knocking him from his horse.

Audra then ran in the opposite direction, nearly reaching the street when someone grabbed her. "You little rebel wench!" the man snarled. "What are you doing hiding in this alley, huh? Have you been shooting at us, or are you just some whore walking the streets and got caught in the middle of this?"

Audra screamed, but there was so much shooting and shelling and shouting going on around them that no one noticed. The soldier dragged her back into the alley, and she kicked and scratched at him until he landed a fist into her jaw. The blow stunned her, and she felt herself falling into the dirt. Instantly the man was on top of her, tearing at her dress. "You got money on you, woman? Jewelry?"

Audra could feel the weight of him. "No," she squeaked in terror.

His mouth was close to hers now. "Well, then, I'll just get somethin' else out of you. With all that's goin' on right now, nobody is ever gonna know we're here."

He tried to kiss her, but Audra grimaced and turned her face away, trying to push him off. Their struggle was interrupted when the building beside them suddenly burst from a shelling. The explosion was so loud that for the next few minutes Audra was literally deaf. She felt the man's body fall heavily against her, and she literally huddled under it while wood and bricks came crashing down around them. A fire broke out and lit up the alley so that when she finally pushed the man's body off her, she could clearly see the piece of wood embedded in his neck.

Audra groaned and crawled away, then looked down at herself to see she was covered with his blood. She wiped at it frantically, gasping and crying, wondering if she would go insane before this night was over. The fire roared brighter and closer, and although she had no idea where to run, she knew she had to get away. She shook her head, her ears still ringing, and looked around, then ran into the street, which was alive with fighting. In her panic she ran for several blocks, not even sure in which direction she was going, until suddenly she stumbled right into a troop of Federals making their way toward the heaviest fighting. "Get her!" someone shouted. "Jesus, her dress is all tore. I can see her tits!" someone else yelled.

Men let out chilling cries of excitement, and their

hands grabbed at her. She screamed and fought, and to her surprise her attackers suddenly backed away. "Get hold of her and put your jacket on her!" a familiar voice shouted somewhere nearby.

Audra heard the sound of a whip, and a man's scream. "You goddamn sons of bitches came here to fight soldiers, not women!" a voice shouted. "I want your names, rank, and regiment! I'll see that you're all whipped within an inch of your life!"

Audra shivered as someone wrapped a jacket around her. "It's all right, ma'am," came a man's voice. He tried to help her up, but she hit at him and curled up. Suddenly there came another explosion, more gunfire. A horse reared and whinnied.

"Get yourselves around the north side!" someone ordered. "We'll trap them inside the city. And stick to fighting the rebels and keep your hands off the women!" Audra looked up to see that the man giving the orders wore a blue uniform and sat on a horse which was whinnying and prancing with fear from the noise and conflagration around it. The soldier pulled a rifle out and raised it, aiming and firing twice. She heard men cry out, and a Confederate fell from the roof of a nearby building. The man on the horse whirled, shouting an order to another officer to see that "the woman" was safely escorted to wherever she needed to go. In the light of the fire she could see his face.

"Lee!" she cried out.

He turned, horror in his eyes when he realized who she was. "Audra! What the hell—"

More shots rang out, and Audra screamed when one hit Lee's horse. The animal reared and came down, landing on Lee's bad leg. Rebel soldiers attacked, and Lee's men got into hand-to-hand combat with them. Lee squirmed out from under his horse, and Audra rolled into the shadows and watched as Federals and Confederates fought wildly, grunting like animals, shooting and stabbing. Lee managed to get off two more shots, but then a Confederate lunged at him with his bayonet. Lee leapt out of the way at the last minute, and Audra could see that he was having trouble with his leg. He turned and charged directly into the man, and they rolled on the ground. Lee landed a big fist into the Confederate soldier's face, and the man lay sprawled on his back, unconscious.

The rest of the Confederates took off running, and several of the Federals ran after them. Lee, dirty and panting, stumbled over to Audra, kneeling close to her. "Come on. I'll get you to safety myself."

She recoiled from him, seeing only a hated Yankee soldier.

"It's all right, Audra. It's *me* ... Lee. Let me get you away from here."

She wrapped the jacket close around herself. "He ... made me lose ... the bread and potatoes," she whimpered. "We needed ... that food."

"Bread and potatoes? Who are you talking about?"

She gasped in a sob. "In ... the alley ... a Yankee attacked me! The building exploded ... killed him." She turned away. "Don't touch me!"

Lee grabbed her close and forced her back, out of the light. "Audra, it's all right. You're just confused right now. Let me take you to your aunt's house."

She was cradled in familiar arms again. He was the enemy, yet when his arms were around her, he was just Lee, and Lee would never hurt her. She curled up against him, and he rose, picking her up in his arms. "Take over for me, Lieutenant Armstrong," she heard him shout to someone. "God knows there won't be much you can do with all the confusion here tonight."

"Yes, sir."

"I'm going to take this woman home to safety. I'll come back soon as I can."

Audra felt herself being carried. "I wish I had my horse," she heard Lee mutter.

She could feel that his gait was uneven, and as she began to think more clearly, she realized how difficult it must be for him to carry her when his leg must be bothering him badly. "I can walk," she told him. "I'm all right, Lee."

"Here. Someone left a horse tied."

Audra was not sure where they were, but the fighting seemed to be farther away. Lee lifted her onto a horse and untied the animal, then grunted with pain as he mounted behind her. He rode off into the darkness, and Audra could only trust he knew how to get her back without more trouble.

What irony there was in this war. At first she had been afraid of her own Confederate soldiers, sensing that the ones who had so disgracefully rummaged the pockets of their dead victim would have abused her just as savagely as the Yankee. Yankees had attacked her, and they were killing Confederates back in town, setting fires. Yet she was leaning against the chest of a Yankee man, trusting him to help her. She wondered sometimes who the enemy really was in this war, and if any of these men even knew anymore why they were fighting.

She heard more explosions, each one becoming more distant. Lee kept one strong arm around her so she wouldn't fall, and minutes later he headed his horse up the hill toward her uncle's mansion. She heard someone screaming and wailing then, and she could see her aunt running back and forth on the veranda, carrying on about the conflagration below.

"Who's there! Who's there!" Aunt Janine screamed as Audra and Lee approached.

"It's Audra, Aunt Janine."

Eleanor stood inside the doorway, apparently helpless to calm her mother.

"Audra, be careful!" Eleanor yelled to her. In the next instant Janine turned, pointing a revolver straight at them.

"You!" Aunt Janine screamed. "Traitor! My own niece a traitor! My own sister's daughter! It's a good thing Sophia is dead!"

"Aunt Janine!"

"Get off my property!" the woman screamed. "Get off, or I'll shoot you!"

"Aunt Janine, don't do this!"

"Mother, stop it!" Eleanor yelled. "It's just Audra!"

"She's with her Yankee lover! Get out of my sight!" The woman fired the gun, and Audra screamed when the bullet whizzed past her so closely that she could almost feel a brush of air.

"She's goddamn crazy!" Lee shouted. He turned the horse and rode off.

"My God," Audra wept. "What will I do! Where will I go? I have to get back to Brennan Manor, Lee!"

"Not tonight, you won't. I'm taking you to the schoolhouse. You can stay there until I figure out how to get you safely home. You should have gone back a long time ago. Baton Rouge might have been safer once, but it isn't anymore."

"I can't stay at the school," she wailed. "What will people think!"

"What does it matter anymore? You have no choice for tonight. Just do as I say, Audra. Promise me, dammit, or I'll be so worried about you, I'll end up getting myself killed."

She shouldn't care what happened to him. Down the hill she could see several buildings still on fire. What were the Yankees doing to Baton Rouge? It had been such a pretty, peaceful city. Still, Lee Jeffreys was one Yankee she couldn't bear to see lying dead, and right now he was her only refuge. "I promise," she said resignedly.

They reached the schoolhouse, and Lee got her inside, leading her to a back room and lighting a lamp. It was sparsely furnished . . . Union Army blankets, more guns and ammunition, a canteen, a blue uniform hanging on a hook. On a nearby table sat a wash pan and razor under a mirror mounted on the wall.

Lee turned up the lamp. "My God, look at you!" He removed the jacket a soldier had given her. Audra was still so confused and upset, she didn't even notice that part of her torn dress hung open enough that one breast was revealed. Lee tried to ignore it, fought to keep back memories better left buried. "You've got to get these clothes off," he told her. "I can't tell if that blood is from the man who attacked you, or if some of it is yours." He started to unbutton her dress, and Audra went rigid, wrapping her arms around herself.

"Don't!"

Lee gently touched the bruise on her face. "Audra, this is me. Please let me help you. It's all right."

She watched his eyes, those blue, blue eyes that always

had a way of breaking down her resistance. Pain seared through her upper back, and she knew she needed help. "What is going to happen, Lee? When will it all end?" She broke into tears, and he pulled her close.

"I don't know, but we can't worry about it tonight."

She wept quietly and offered no more resistance as he removed her dress. She took her arms out of the sleeves and stood so he could pull it down along with her slips. She stepped out of it, grasping at her torn camisole.

"Here." He reached over to a chair and grabbed a shirt from it. "Put this on." He started to help her when he saw the cut across her upper back. "Wait a minute! Jesus, you've been wounded," he muttered. "I'll get something to dress it with."

He tossed the shirt across the bed and rose. Audra watched him pour some clean water into the wash pan. He was himself filthy and bloody from fighting, his uniform torn. He was limping badly, and his eyes looked tired. He had cut his hair, but not very neatly, and she knew how much he hated having to be here; but he was a man bent on preserving the Union in whatever way necessary, and she had to admire him for being willing to fight and die for that, just as her own people were willing to do the same in order to be able to govern themselves. How strange, the lengths to which people would go just to prove they were right.

Lee wet a rag and knelt in front of her. He gently washed her face, and their eyes held for a moment, both of them wishing they were anywhere else, not at war, and that the last three years had never happened. He washed the blood from her throat and chest, and Audra clung to her camisole, part of her wanting to let it drop, wanting to feel Lee's lips at her breast again. How could she feel this way, after what she had just been through, and after what she had suffered at Richard's hands?

She reddened at the thought, and she suspected Lee had read the desire in her eyes, something he had always seemed able to do. "Take that camisole off and lie down on your stomach. I'll clean the wound on your back," he told her. "I'll put some ointment on it, and you can put that shirt on. I want you to stay here then, get some rest. I'll have to leave again for a while. I'll find some clothes in town somewhere and bring you something to put on."

Audra did not object. She winced with pain as she removed the camisole and lay down on her stomach. Lee leaned over her, gently washing her back, and she thought for one brief moment about the horrors Richard had visited upon her while he made her lie facedown like this. Lee would never hurt her that way.

Lee gently smeared some kind of ointment over the cut, a thousand memories of what it was like to lie with her surging painfully through him. Her back was so pretty, her skin so soft and pale. He glanced at the roundness of her bottom, so enticingly outlined in her ruffled bloomers. He sighed with unrequited need and put the ointment away, then emptied the dirty water out the door and poured some more into the pan to wash his own face.

"I've got to go find another horse," he told her. "Put that shirt on and lock the door that leads from the main room back here. Lock the back door, too. Keep the shutters closed and turn out the lamp. Just get under those covers and rest here until I come back. No one will bother you." He turned away and brushed at his uniform, then put his hat back on. He removed a pistol from his belt and checked it to be sure it was loaded.

Audra sat up and wrapped his shirt around herself while he was turned away, and when he finally looked at her, she felt a warmth surge through her blood at the way his blue eyes moved over her. "Be careful, Lee."

"Sure," he answered. "I'll try to stay out of the way of those damn rebels."

Their eyes held, and she managed a weak smile. He returned a bitter smile of his own. "If this is ever over . . ." he muttered. He walked out and closed the door behind him.

Audra rose and walked over to hook the door from the inside, then moved to a window, opening a shutter just enough to see him ride off and quickly disappear into the darkness. In the distance the sky was alight with a dozen fires.

25

Audra slept restlessly, jerking awake with nightmares. She could still feel men pulling at her clothes, hear them laughing. She saw dead bodies lying riddled with bullet holes. Fire surrounded her. Those visions were mixed into the nightmare of her aunt screaming at her. She could see the spit of flame at the end of the pistol barrel when the woman fired at her. The shooting pain that kept stabbing at her upper back only added to her inability to sleep soundly, and each time she stirred awake again, it took her a moment to gather her thoughts in the dark, warm room and remember where she was.

Lee. What if he didn't come back? Where was she to go? How could she get herself safely back to Brennan Manor? She didn't even have a decent dress to put on, and her Aunt Janine was apparently not going to let her back into the house to get her things.

What an ugly turn of events. She was not sure how many hours she lay there, trying to sleep, before she finally got up and felt her way back to the window. When she looked out, she could see the glow of lingering fires in the distance, but she heard little in the way of gunfire now. The shelling from the bigger guns seemed to have stopped. She decided that at least until daylight she had no choice but to stay here as Lee had directed. She went back to the cot and lay down, breathing deeply of the scent of Lee Jeffreys on his pillow and sheets. How odd that she felt so safe in this bed where a Yankee soldier slept. She was in the center of the enemy camp, yet she was not afraid here.

She drifted off again, losing all track of time. Finally someone knocked gently on the rear door. "Audra? It's me."

Audra rubbed at her eyes, holding the shirt around herself as she found her way to the door. It was still dark. "Lee?"

"Let me in. The worst is over."

She unlocked the door, and he came inside. "Light the lamp."

Audra obeyed, and Lee turned and latched the door again. Audra looked at him, seeing blood on his right arm. "You're hurt!"

"Nothing drastic. I told my commander I'd tend to it myself. He doesn't know you're in here, and I don't want him to know just yet." He threw a bundle of clothes on the small table on which the lamp was sitting. "I looted those out of a clothing store like a common thief. I don't know your size. I just took a guess. You've got to have something to wear when you leave here."

Audra touched the bundle, thinking how war could make looters out of men like Lee, who had been a respected, wealthy attorney before all this started. More contrasts. More hideous absurdities the war had created.

Lee removed his jacket and boots, then began unbuttoning his shirt. "It's a madhouse out there. Most of the men have chased the rebels back into the countryside, and they're looting through town like crazy men. It's practically impossible to keep any of these men in line. They aren't regular army, just civilian volunteers, for the most part, come here to teach the rebels a lesson. They don't know a damn thing about real military conduct or how to obey orders." He glanced at her. "I still intend to have the bastards who attacked you whipped. How do you feel?"

She sat back down on the cot, suddenly self-conscious now that she was more rested. She had removed her shoes and stockings and wore only the shirt and her bloomers. "Just terribly tired and . . . I don't know . . . numb, I guess. It's all so ugly and unreal."

"That's war, Audra, ugly and unreal. You asked me once what it's like. Now you know." He peeled off his blood-stained shirt, and Audra found herself studying his muscular arms and the familiar broad chest, the dark hair that lightly dusted that chest and led downward in a V shape past the belt of his pants. He walked to the stand that still held a bowl of water and he poured some fresh water into it, then wet a rag and held it to the cut on his arm, which was already scabbing over. "Some rebel tried to stab me with his bayonet. Missed what he was aiming for by a long shot, but he didn't miss me all together, obviously."

"Let me help you."

"Don't worry about it. It isn't bleeding anymore." He washed his face and neck, dried off, then picked up a flask of whiskey. He opened it and poured some over the cut, grimacing at the sting of it. Then he swallowed some of the whiskey straight from the flask. He lowered the bottle, studying her for a moment. "I've been hitting this stuff pretty hard for a long time . . . ever since I said good-bye to you at Maple Shadows, in fact." He took one more swallow, his eyes never leaving hers for a moment. "They say whiskey is supposed to help ease pain," he said then. "It does, but only physical pain. It doesn't do a damn thing for the pain in a man's heart."

She looked away. "Lee, don't—"

"Why not? In a couple of days you'll go back to Brennan Manor, and I'll go on with what I have to do, because I'm bound to do it and it isn't in me to be a deserter, no matter the reason. You have to stay near home because it's the only way you're going to know what happened to Joey, and you'll want to be there when he comes home, God willing. Who knows what will happen when all this is over? In the meantime I've found you again, and I need to tell you I love you, Audra. I never stopped loving you and I probably never will."

She just stared at her lap. He seemed a little angry, very determined. His attitude reminded her of that night after he buried his mother. He'd had a little whiskey then, too, and he was thinking about the reality of death and how quickly it could come, how every moment was precious and had to be taken advantage of. But why was he saying this now, when it was impossible for them to be together? Everything had changed. They were not the same people as they'd been that summer at Maple Shadows, and besides that, it was wrong to be sitting here half-undressed in front of the man she'd slept with while married to someone else, wasn't it? It was wrong to care this much about a Yankee. *All* of this was wrong, but then, what was right anymore?

She heard him set the flask down on the table. "This might really be it, Audra; the end for you and me. But we have tonight."

She met his eyes, her own full of tears. "Why is it always that way for us? It was like that at Maple Shadows, and that one night you came to visit. All we ever have is one night, Lee, never knowing what will come tomorrow. I can't do that again. It hurts too much, and it's wrong."

He stood up and removed his belt, unbuttoned his pants, and took them off. Audra looked away. "Please take me somewhere, Lee, anywhere away from here."

He came over to kneel in front of her, grasping her wrists. "There *is* no place to take you, not tonight. And it's *not* wrong, Audra. It was *never* wrong, and you know it. And this time it isn't just tonight. When this is over, I'm coming back, and we're going to be together, do you hear me? I'm not going to live like this the rest of my life. I want you, Audra, and, dammit you want *me*! We've both known it since that first day you came here to see me, widow or not! Maybe this *is* the last chance we'll have to be together, but as God is my witness, if I don't get killed or so badly wounded that I can't come to you, I'll be back to find you, and we're going to put this war behind us!"

She looked at him pleadingly "That's impossible now," she said in a near whisper.

"That isn't true. You just don't want to *believe* that it's possible, because it makes you feel like a traitor." He leaned closer. "Well then, *I'm* a traitor, too! Because while my men are out there chasing and killing rebels, I'll be in here making *love* to one!"

Why couldn't she object, argue, remember why she should say no? Why was she never able to resist this man she should have hated? Wasn't he indirectly responsible for just about every bad thing that had happened to her?

"I never said anything about making love," she whispered.

He searched her green eyes, eyes that had told him all along how much she wanted him again. "You didn't have to," he answered. He leaned closer, and his lips were suddenly tasting her own. Oh, how sweet and delicious his kiss was. How long had it been since a man kissed her this way, his lips warm and inviting and sweet? His tongue slaked into her mouth, and she whimpered with the ecstasy of it. It had been such a long time since she truly wanted to give herself to a man and take pleasure from him in return. Surely this was the way it was supposed to be, enjoying sex because she loved the man with every ounce of passion and devotion she was capable of feeling. She needed this more than anything right now, and she gloried in reawakened passions and womanly desires she had refused to acknowledge for more than two years.

She wrapped her arms around his neck, and the kiss grew deep and wild, both of them groaning with need, both of them forgetting their bruises and pain, all so easily ignored for this great need to love and *make* love, to relieve another kind of pain, one that burned hot as fire deep in their souls and seared through their loins like white lightning. She wanted to object when he pulled her arms away then and opened the shirt she wore, slipping it off her completely, but all she could do was whimper his name. Just like that first night he took her at Maple Shadows, he was in complete command of her, body and soul. His eyes raked her breasts, and his breathing quickened.

"My God, you're still so beautiful," he groaned.

He told her to stand, and she blindly obeyed, letting him jerk her bloomers down to her ankles. She stepped out of them, and he remained on his knees, leaning close to kiss softly but hungrily at that private place that had truly always belonged only to Lee Jeffreys. She grasped at his thick hair and pressed herself against him, shivering at the glory of it.

"Audra, my sweet Audra," he muttered, his lips moving over her belly then, and higher, taking a soft, pink nipple into his mouth. He gently laid her back on the cot, which was hardly big enough for one person, let alone two. Tonight it didn't matter. Two people this desperate could make do, and Lee Jeffreys intended to be on top of her most of the night, not beside her.

Was this so wrong? She simply could not find the strength to stop him, and she knew she didn't really want to. She groaned as he tasted her breasts, as though he was literally hungry for her. There was no waiting this first time, no putting off the inevitable. Somehow he had gotten off his long johns, and she'd wrapped her legs around his waist. He found her mouth again, kissing her savagely between words.

"I have to have you, Audra," he groaned. "I have to be inside you again or go crazy, but I don't want to hurt you or frighten you like he did."

"It could never be like that with you," she whispered, realizing he was talking about Richard. She gasped then when he pushed himself inside her with one hard thrust. He buried himself deep, and she welcomed the hot hardness that made her feel more alive and in love than she had imagined possible. Their lovemaking when he had visited her two years ago had been quiet and powerful, but this was different. This was total wanton desire, mingled with a love so strong and demanding that there was no stopping it.

Lee moved in wild rhythm, groaning her name, thrusting his tongue deep at the same time, totally reclaiming the woman who he had always felt belonged to him in the first place. He felt as though he could not get enough of her, could not love her deep enough, claim her thoroughly enough. It had been so long since he had been with any woman at all, and to finally lie with Audra was the most glorious thing he had experienced since that first time he took her at Maple Shadows. He had not intended to do this, but after bringing her here earlier, helping her undress, remembering how it had felt to make love to her, she had haunted him after he left again. Knowing she was here had made him ache with the need of her, and he was almost glad for his arm wound. It had given him an excuse to come back, and no one ever needed to know the truth. She was as beautiful as ever, sweet and tight and soft and willing, and his want of her was so intense that his life spilled into her sooner than he would have liked.

He shivered, raising up and kissing her eyes, then bending down to taste her breasts again. God, how he hated the thought of Richard Potter groveling over her, forcing her to do hideous things, pretending he owned her. Audra Brennan would never belong to anyone but Lee Jeffreys.

"I'm sorry," he told her, wishing he could have made it last longer. "Stay until sunrise, Audra. It's only two o'clock in the morning, and no one knows you're here. I want you in my arms for as long as I can have you."

A tear slipped out of her eye and down her cheek. "You know I'll stay. It will be like that first time, at Maple Shadows. It's just like you said. We both knew that first day I came here to see you that we would end up lovers again."

He pulled her close. "I'm sorry it always has to be this way. One night full of promises, never knowing when or if we'll see each other again." She could feel his tears on her neck.

"I'm sorry, too, Lee, my love, my enemy . . . my friend, I don't even know what you are anymore." She sniffed back more tears. "I only know that when I lie with you, beneath you, I forget everything else, all the things that draw us apart."

They clung together for several quiet minutes, until Lee finally pulled away and sat up. "Look at us, and me a colonel in the United States Army." He wiped at his eyes, and she smiled at how tender and vulnerable he could be.

Lee rose and poured some fresh water into a deeper pan for her. "You can wash with this one. I just wish we were someplace where we could sit in a nice, hot tub together." He walked to the door and threw out the other pan of water, refilling it for himself. "I must smell like perspiration," he commented, handing her a bar of lye soap. "Here."

"You smell wonderful," she answered, first washing her face with the damp rag. "You're one of those men who always smells good, even when he needs a bath," she drawled.

Lee smiled and washed himself, while Audra did the same. He turned to see her standing naked before him, and her eyes moved over him with a hunger that instantly reawakened his desire. It had been so long since he had enjoyed such pleasure.

Audra knelt in front of him, touched him gently. She stroked that part of him that had been so ugly on Richard, but was beautiful on this man. His magnificent shaft grew hard and hot again as she caressed him. He groaned her name and she gently pressed the velvety softness against her cheek, then moved her lips to kiss the scar on his left thigh, glad he had not been one of those who had lost a leg to this hideous war; but if he had, she knew she could still have loved him.

She moved back then to that most intimate part of the man, kissed and caressed him until he took hold of her arms then and drew her to her feet.

"I want it to last longer this time," he warned, a teasing look in his eyes. "You aren't helping me any." She smiled wickedly, and Lee thought how this Audra was a full, lusty woman who knew what she wanted, not the timid young thing he had first made love to a lifetime ago. He captured her mouth again, and she reached around his neck, returning his kiss with a hot passion that made him wonder who was the aggressor this time. Their lips never parted as he laid her back on the cot and moved inside her again, more slowly this time, hoping he had not hurt her back that first time. She had not complained, and he supposed that like the pain in his own leg and arm, she had forgotten it in the midst of her need to be one with him again.

He raised up to drink in her naked beauty while he grasped her hips and drove himself deep, imagining that somehow he could touch her very soul. He invaded her with rhythmic thrusts, enjoying the look of utter pleasure on her face as she arched up to him in total abandon.

Audra in turn allowed herself to enjoy how beautiful the act of love could be when it was with the right man. In spite of having been with Richard, she felt as if she had not been intimate with a man at all since Lee visited two years ago. When she had lain with Richard, it had been as though she were a total stranger to herself, but with Lee this was real and right and the most beautiful thing she had ever done. She ran her hands along his powerful arms, over his chest, shivering with the ecstasy of being Lee Jeffreys's woman again for at least this little while.

Both of them knew they were facing another good-bye, and this one would be more painful than the others. Outside this room they were enemies, but here, in each other's arms, they could be lovers again. She had never believed he was just using her for his own pleasure. The love in those blue eyes was too apparent, and he had cried real tears, right along with her. No one outside this room would understand what they were doing, how they felt about each other; and no one needed to know.

For four hours they made love, sometimes almost violently, other times just a sweet, gentle, rhythmic joining of bodies. Fulfilling long-neglected needs, man and woman joyfully giving each other pleasure. They gladly forgot the ugly war just outside the door. Each was risking everything—reputation and respect—for one night together, Yankee and rebel, enemies and lovers.

There was no sleep for either of them, except for a little while just before dawn. Audra had the nightmare again, and Lee held her close. She snuggled against his shoulder, lying half on top of him because of the size of the cot. "How will I go on without you after today?" she whispered.

"No easier than my having to leave here and go finish this war without you." He kissed her hair. "I'll go crazy worrying about you, Audra. I'd like to find a way to send you north."

"Where would I stay? I wouldn't be happy there, not while this is going on. And I'd never know about Joey. My father's health is poor. I can't leave him, either, not the way things are now. Lena has had a stroke. Toosie went to be with her, and I have to go, too. I can't desert Brennan Manor now, Lee, or leave without knowing what happened to Joey."

"I know." He gently stroked her hair. "I'll come back, Audra. I swear it. It will all be different when the war is over. We'll find a way to just be ourselves, to be together. Where we live will depend on what has happened here, what has happened to Brennan Manor, how things are with my brother in New York. I'll have to start over myself somewhere."

"Those are decisions we can't make right now." The sun was coming up, and Audra heard a bird twitter outside, a stark contrast to the cannon and shooting and screaming of the night before; but the sound was overcome then by louder noises, someone shouting an order, a wagon clattering by. Lee sighed and got up from the cot.

"I'd better get washed and dressed and get out there to see what's going on. I don't want anybody to know you're here. You get cleaned up after I leave and put those clothes on I got for you. Go out the back door and make sure nobody sees you, then come around to the front of the building and make like you're just coming in. Tell me you've come to find protection getting yourself to Brennan Manor." He sighed, studying the green eyes that always made him feel so helpless. "I'm sorry to have to do it this way, but it's just as much for me as you. If my commanding officer knows I've slept with a Confederate woman, I'm finished."

Audra watched him wash, drinking in the sight of him, wanting to remember . . . forever. He shaved and combed his hair, then put on a clean uniform, pulled on his boots and his weapons, took his hat from where it hung on a chair. He turned to look at her, hat in hand, and he gave her a sad smile.

God, he was handsome in full dress, yet there he was, now looking like the enemy again, a Yankee soldier like the others who were out there looting and destroying Baton Rouge. In the light of day, the reality of the war and all that had happened to her town, she began to wonder if it was really possible for him to come back when this was over, and for both of them to pretend this had never happened. Here she sat on the cot with a Union Army blanket wrapped around her—and she felt like a true traitor.

Lee saw the doubt in her eyes, and he came over and knelt in front of her. He kissed her eyes, her lips, this time gently. "Don't forget my promise. Whatever happens, I'll find you, Audra. Do you believe me?"

She watched his eyes, outlined by dark lashes and brows. His dark hair hung in disarray because of his clumsy attempt at cutting it, but he was still her handsome Lee. "I believe you," she told him.

He walked to his torn uniform and took something from an inside pocket, showing her the folded paper. "Your song. I still carry it."

Her eyes teared at the words, and he shoved the paper into a pocket of his clean uniform.

"I don't know how many times I was going to tear it up or burn it and just quit thinking about you, but I never could. War or no war, I'm still crazy in love with you, Audra Brennan, and somehow we're going to find each other again. There will be no more war, no more reasons not to be together."

"I want so much to believe that."

He took up a pen and dipped it into a bottle of ink on the table, then took a piece of paper from his gear and scribbled something, handed it to her. "Believe it. That is my brother Carl's address. If you don't hear from me after the war, write him. He can tell you what has happened to me. If I'm dead and you need help, he'll help you—send you money, whatever you need."

"Lee, I couldn't—"

"Just do it, Audra, do it for *me*. I need to know you'll still be all right if something happens to me. Our family has plenty of money. Carl will know it's what I would have wanted."

She took the paper. "I'll keep it."

"Good." He leaned down and kissed her lightly. "I love you, Audra. God willing, I'll come for you myself." His eyes were misty, and she knew he hated all of this as much as she did. "I have to go." He kissed her once more and left through the door that led to the main schoolroom.

Audra quickly washed herself and put on the clothes he had brought her. The camisole fit fine, but the yellow linen dress was a little big. Still, it was good enough, though wrinkled from being folded. She studied herself in the mirror, pulling her hair back and smoothing it with her fingers, as she had no brush for it. She twisted it into a bun and pinned it with the combs Lee had taken from it the night before. What time had that been? The whole night seemed like a strange dream.

She decided she looked terrible, but after last night, no one would think anything about it. She doubted there was one person in all of Baton Rouge who would look rested and well groomed this morning. It had been a horrible night for everyone. Poor Aunt Janine had apparently lost her mind, and Audra had actually felt sorry for Eleanor.

She realized that in last night's melee she had also lost her handbag and gloves. She pulled on her socks, buttoned her shoes, then smoothed her dress before carefully opening the back door of the schoolhouse. There was nothing behind the building but an outhouse and a stand of scrubby trees. She quickly stepped out and closed the door, then headed toward the front of the building, glancing up the hill at her aunt's home.

She drew in her breath then at what she saw. There was no house, only smoke and several tall brick chimneys. Sometime during the night her aunt and uncle's home had burned! "Dear God!" She immediately forgot about going to see Lee. Eleanor and her aunt might need her! She began running up the hill, her heart pounding with dread, her mind reeling with guilt. While her aunt and uncle's house was burning down, she had been sleeping with the enemy! Did Lee already know about this? After all, he had come back so late!

She ran hard, uphill all the way, and by the time she reached the mansion, she felt dizzy and nearly passed out. It did not occur to her that she had not eaten in hours, or that the traumatic events of the night before might have affected her nerves and strength. She had given no thought to anything but being with Lee, and now she had awakened to this! She ran around the house, screaming for Eleanor, for Aunt Janine. The house was still burning in some places, and the ruins were too hot to go into them to try to find any bodies. She was hardly aware of the presence of neighbors, who had come to help put out the fire, but there were so many other fires in the city that not enough people could work on any one of them.

A man grabbed her and pulled her away when she tried to climb the veranda steps, steps that led nowhere. "Come on away from there now, Mrs. Potter. Your cousin is all right. She got out and is down in town at Mary Tyler's house. Your Aunt Janine never made it, though. We tried to get her out, but she kept screamin' that it was her home and she wouldn't leave it."

No! This could not be happening! Audra did not even stop to see which neighbor had spoken to her. She tore away from him and ran back down the hill. Lee! This was his fault! Before she reached the schoolhouse, she saw him riding toward her. He called her name in a panic and rode up beside her, dismounting before his horse even came to a stop. He tried to grasp her arms, but Audra fought him.

"You knew! You knew!" she screamed at him, pounding at his chest. "All the while we were together, Aunt Janine was burning up in the fire!"

Lee shook her hard. "Stop it, Audra! I *didn't* know! I just now learned myself that General Butler ordered buildings burned to give a clearer view of the countryside, give the Confederates fewer places to hide! Men are cutting trees to build barriers. A lot of prisoners were taken last night, and some have said there are a lot more Confederates out in the hills, threatening to attack again!"

"Damn you! Damn you!" she screamed, jerking away from him and turning her back. "My God, what have I done! I should have been with them. I might have been able to help save Aunt Janine!"

Lee threw his head back and cursed the war and everything about it. He wanted to touch her, hold her, but the beautiful moments they had shared the last few hours were shattered. When she hadn't shown up at the front of the school building, he had gone outside to see the mansion smoldering, and he knew where she had gone.

"Audra, the woman would have shot you," he tried to reason. "There is nothing you could have done."

Audra stood shivering, and she looked out over the city. It seemed as though everything were on fire. She went to her knees then. "Aunt Janine," she said, sobbing.

"Let me help you, Audra. You're going to be sick. You need food and rest." Lee touched her shoulders, and she screamed at him to leave her alone. "Audra, don't do this."

"Damn, damn Yankees!" she sobbed. "How can you do this! You're burning down our whole town!"

"Audra—"

She whirled, her face red with rage. "We were crazy to think we can be together after this war, Lee! It's *impossible*! Nothing can ever, *ever* be the same, don't you see? I can never be with you and feel good about it, right about it! I did a terrible thing last night, sleeping in the arms of the enemy while my aunt burned to death in her own home!"

"Audra, I never knew anything about this, and I couldn't have stopped it if I did! You *know* that!"

"I only know that you're a *Yankee* first! I only know men like you are shooting at Joey somewhere right now, that Brennan Manor will fall into ruin, our slaves all run off or ready to kill us! My aunt is dead, maybe my uncle, too, their home and business gone! All of Baton Rouge is burned to the ground. Yankees tried to rape me last night, and I ended up in *bed* with one! People have every right to call me a traitor, because I *feel* like one!"

Lee stepped closer. "Dammit, Audra, keep quiet, for your *own* sake! Let me find someone to take you to Brennan Manor."

"No! I'll find my own way! There are still people left in this town I can trust!"

"It's too dangerous!"

"It doesn't matter anymore! Just go, Lee! Go do your soldiering and your killing and your burning and looting! Go, and don't ever come for me, do you hear? Don't *ever* come for me, because it's wrong and will *always* be wrong!" She tore the paper on which he had written Carl's address from her dress pocket and threw it on the ground, then turned and ran back up the hill. Lee started after her, then grunted when a large stone hit him in the back.

He whirled to see several young boys and girls and a few adults moving in on him, all of them holding stones. "Get out, Yankee!" one of the boys hollered. "Get back to your damn camp below and leave us alone!"

Another stone was thrown, this one glancing off his right knee. The pain was excruciating. Another stone hit Lee's horse, and the animal whinnied and backed away. Lee mounted up as more stones began to shower upon him. He had no choice but to ride back down to camp. When he got away from the angry mob, he looked back, trying to see Audra, but he could not spot the yellow dress. An ache moved through him unlike anything he had ever experienced. He felt almost as though he had just buried the woman he loved more than his own life, for he could probably get her back no more easily than if she were dead.

"Colonel!" someone shouted.

Lee turned his horse to see a lieutenant approaching on another mount. "The general is looking for you. Your brigade is moving north to rout a few thousand Confederates in the way of taking Port Hudson—says you're to join General Sherman after that. He wants to know if you're physically ready to move out."

Lee looked back up the hill. How could things change so drastically and so quickly? Never had he been so tempted to say to hell with it all, but he was a colonel, and he had a duty. He had not expected to move out for a couple more weeks yet, giving him time to see Audra again, to make sure she got home all right. Now he was apparently expected to leave Baton Rouge before nightfall, and as things were, Audra Brennan Potter was not about to look at him, let alone talk to him or let him take her home.

He felt as if a sword were buried in his heart. "I'm ready," he answered.

"Sir, the general says to hurry it up."

Lee gave the man a scowl.

"Sorry, sir. Those are the general's words, not mine."

"Just tell him I'll be there in five minutes."

"Yes, sir." The lieutenant rode off, and Lee sat on his horse watching the mansion a moment longer.

"I *am* coming back, Audra, whether you like it or not," he muttered. He closed his eyes at the searing memory of the hours of passion they had just shared, all changed in one morning of hideous reality. The only thing that could possibly heal this rift was time . . . and maybe if Joey came home alive and unscathed. It seemed incredible that this much horror could result from an argument between a few men in government over the right and wrong of slavery.

He remembered General Butler telling him not long ago that the war could go on for two or three more years. Where would Audra be by then? How would he ever find her again if she had to leave Brennan Manor? Where would she go, and who would watch after her, especially if something happened to her father and Joey? Her Uncle John would certainly never take her in again.

It wasn't fair that he was put in this position, having to chose between the woman he loved and his duty as a soldier. It seemed he had always had to make this choice, even before the war, and now it was Audra who was making the decision for him. She had told him to go and never come back, and maybe she was right this time. This was a hurt that might never go away, and she felt she had betrayed her own people. Why was it that he always seemed to find ways to make her unhappy, when all he wanted was to love her?

He rode back to the school. Behind him Baton Rouge lay in smoldering ruins, and somewhere amid those ruins was the woman he loved, alone and in danger, and he couldn't do a damn thing about it. His orders were to head north. What if Audra *did* come back for his help? He would be gone, and she would think he had lied about everything, all the more reason never to forgive him.

He walked into the back room to pack up his things, not even going to General Butler first. He hesitated at the sight of Audra's torn, bloody dress, then picked it up and hugged it close. When shouted orders outside brought him back to reality, he gathered up the dress, slips, and camisole and carried them outside, throwing them onto a fire so that no one would find a Southern woman's clothes in a Yankee colonel's quarters.

PART 4

Like the ghost of a dear friend dead
  Is Time long past.
A tone which is now forever fled,
A hope which is now forever past,
A love so sweet it could not last,
  Was Time long past. . . .

——PERCY BYSSHE SHELLEY,
      "TIME LONG PAST"

26

AUGUST 1864

"What will happen to Brennan Manor, Audra?"

Joseph Brennan reached out his hand, a movement that
took great effort. Audra took hold of it, remembering a time
when her father had a bull's strength. Now his grip was
weak as a child's. He lay thin and pale against the pillow.

"Joey will come home," she assured the man, although
she had not heard from her brother in six months. "Together
we'll find a way to hang on to the farm, Father." The last she
knew, Joey was somewhere in Georgia, and oh, how she
missed him. To see her brother again was the only hope left
for any happiness in her life. Surely he had grown and
changed immeasurably. He was nineteen now.

Lena sat on the other side of the bed, holding Joseph's
other hand in her right one. Since her stroke, her left side

was weak and almost useless, although she could walk with a cane. Audra saw the agony in the woman's eyes, and as her father had become sicker and weaker, she had begun to understand just how much Lena had loved the man. She almost never left his side, nursed him faithfully in spite of her own affliction. Audra had come to accept Lena again, and she was learning to love her and Toosie both.

Nearly all the other plantation Negroes had run off, including Sonda. Brennan Manor was becoming overgrown. No cotton had been planted or harvested for three years, and there were only a couple of Negro men left to tend to the lawn and flowers; but most of their time was spent planting and hoeing the vegetable garden behind the house. Just surviving and eating were all that mattered, and Audra did not doubt that the Yankees shouldn't have to do any more fighting. All they had to do now was sit back and wait for the entire South to starve to death.

She watched her father, whom she had long ago forgiven. The man had suffered so tragically over what was happening to Brennan Manor that she did not have the heart to give him more pain. He was still her precious father who had raised her the best he could, and who would never have pushed her into her tragic marriage if he had known what the consequences would be. There was no use in blaming him for loving Lena, for there was no room for hatred and blame when a man was dying; and Joseph Brennan *was* dying, slowly, quietly, just like his plantation.

"Audra, my . . . beautiful Audra," he moaned. "What . . . will happen to . . . my daughter?"

"I'll be fine, Father," she reassured him. "Nothing is going to get the better of me. Joey will come back and we'll at least have each other. And I still have my voice. Mrs. Jeffreys once told me I could sing in the opera, and with a little practice, I could still try."

It didn't seem possible that it had been five years since she took those lessons at Maple Shadows . . . five years since she first lay in Lee's arms. . . . She drew a deep breath and forced back the memory. She had meant to put Lee out of her mind and heart for good the day she saw Aunt Janine's home burned to the ground, taking her aunt with it.

She would never forgive herself or Lee for what they had done that night; nor could she forgive men like Lee for what was happening to her home, to her father, to the South. She had never told her father about that night, and she had never seen Eleanor again. As far as she knew, her cousin had gone to New Orleans to be with her husband, and if the man could hang on to what he owned, they would probably be all right; but she vowed she would never go to Eleanor for help, no matter how bad things got.

What *would* happen to Brennan Manor? Could she keep it going until Joey came home? Was there really anything they could do together to hang on to it? Cypress Hollow was already as good as lost. There was no money to pay the overseers. They had left, as had most of the Negroes. Jonathan Horne, the last remaining overseer at Brennan Manor, had told her that the Negroes left at Cypress Hollow were actually living in the mansion itself.

Audra supposed that in a sense those poor Negroes probably deserved to live in the mansion and get something back from the man who had mistreated them, but it saddened her to think of how grand and elegant Cypress Hollow used to be, in spite of the unhappiness she had known there. She still owned the plantation, but it did her little good. With no way to farm it, she was practically as poor as the Negroes. Most of the investment of both plantations had gone into the Negroes and planting cotton. Now there was no way to sell the slaves and get any money out of them; and there was no cotton. Her father and Richard both had converted most of their cash into Confederate money, which now was practically worthless. God only knew what would happen to the big landholders who were bound to go broke. If the North won this war, who really owned any of the land? Would wealthy Northerners come down here and claim it for themselves? Men like Lee?

She was not sure how much more she could take. She was torn as to what she should do about Lena and Toosie if she ever had to leave her home. She could not imagine not having Toosie with her, but she also could not support both of them, or Henrietta, who had also faithfully stayed with her. She supposed that eventually they would all have to go,

and she could never stay here alone. It was far too dangerous now. More than that, she could not bear to walk these
rooms, remembering a time of elegance, luxury, happiness,
a time when she innocently thought her father the most
wonderful human being who walked the earth.

Joseph gripped her hand weakly and muttered Joey's
name. "I . . . have to see him . . . once more," the man
groaned. "Have to tell him I love him . . . proud of him. I
should have told him more when he . . . was here, shouldn't
I?" A tear slipped out of his eye, and Audra wiped it away.

"He knows, Father," she assured him. "Don't blame
yourself. He went off to war as much for himself as anyone.
He needed to prove something to himself, to know he could
do something on his own and do it well."

"You tell him . . . tell him I love him."

Audra looked over at Lena, who just shook her head
and looked away, struggling against tears. "You'll tell him
yourself when he comes home," Audra answered, leaning
over to kiss her father's forehead. "Because you'll still be
here, and Joey is coming home soon. I feel sure of it, Father."

She felt her own tears fighting to come, and she did
not like crying in front of her father. She quietly left the
room, going downstairs to the parlor and asking Henrietta,
who had converted herself from a seamstress to a maid of all
uses, if she would fix her some hot water. Tea had become
a wonderful luxury, and she did not want to waste what little was left. Plain hot water was often all she needed to
soothe her.

Henrietta, herself near tears over the knowledge that
Master Joseph was dying, gave Audra a hug and went to
heat the water. There was no other kitchen help left, and
Lena was too crippled to take care of the house any longer.
It was up to Toosie, Henrietta, and herself to keep the home
cleaned and presentable, and she was determined to do that
for as long as possible.

She looked at her hands, not quite so soft and perfect
anymore. There would be no more balls and fancy gloves.
Scrubbing floors, washing dishes, hoeing gardens, and the
like were no longer work for the slaves. It was work she did

herself, and to her surprise she actually enjoyed it at times. She supposed it was mainly because it kept her busy, and that seemed to be her primary goal now . . . just keep busy, don't think, don't remember how things used to be, how grand and luxurious life was, how robust and powerful Joseph Brennan had been. Most of all, she must not remember Lee Jeffreys.

Five years it had been since that summer in Connecticut. She looked at the fireplace mantel, where the mounted sea gulls still sat. She should get rid of all memories of Lee, put him out of her mind forever now, for she had told him never to come for her, and she had meant it. That had been two years ago, and God only knew what had happened to him. Surely, if he was even still alive, he knew as well as she did that she was right. She could never look at him again and see anything but a Yankee, one of the men who was putting her through this hell, taking away her father, her brother, her way of life, her home, her dignity.

She walked over to the mantel and took down the sea gulls, stared at them a moment, touched them. Why did it have to be this way? Why had God brought Lee into her life in the first place? It wasn't fair. Nothing that was happening was fair, and she wondered how much longer she could bear this loneliness. If not for Lena and Toosie, and the hope that Joey would come back soon, she would end her life. She began to shake, and her stomach ached fiercely, but she knew what she had to do. She had to get rid of the memories, for there was nothing for her now but day-to-day existence, and the worry of what to do about tomorrow. Yesterday's happiness would never visit her again.

Her tears dripped onto the sea gulls, and after hugging them to her heart for a moment, she threw them, one by one, against the brick backing of the fireplace, feeling literal pain when each one shattered. She forced herself then to walk over to the piano bench, where she remembered putting the note Lee had given her with the gift. She wiped her teary eyes as she took the note from the bench, glancing at it once.

Found a man in New Orleans who makes these by hand. They were made on the Gulf, but they reminded me of the

*good times we shared in Connecticut. Think of me whenever
you look at them. God bless and protect you, Audra. Love
forever, Lee.*

She wadded the note into her palm. *Think of me ...
Love forever ...* No, she could no longer allow herself to
think about him or to admit she had loved him more than
her own blood. To love him was to betray her own people,
many of whom were suffering beyond human endurance.
For Joey's sake, she must not remember, and she deserved
to suffer this way, for sleeping with the enemy while Baton
Rouge burned and people died.

She walked back to the fireplace and struck a match,
holding it to the note. As soon as it flared up, she threw it
into the hearth and watched it burn ... burn, then disappear, just like her love for Lee Jeffreys.

Lee sat on his horse watching the orange flames and
black smoke as Atlanta, Georgia, burned ... burned ... like
most of the South. He had once hated watching things like
this, but he had seen so much of it that he had managed to
build a shell around his heart, no longer allowing emotion
to enter into what he had to do. He started building that
shell the day he left Audra behind at Baton Rouge.

In the flames of Atlanta he could still see her face, still
hear her shouted words for him never to come back. That
southern pride was the one thing he was convinced the Federals had not been able to defeat, no matter how much destruction and bloodshed they brought to these people.
Audra was full of it, and it was the primary reason he could
not go back. It was that pride, that love of their homes and
cities and their refusal to hand them over to the Federals
that made them set most of these fires themselves. These
people knew Sherman was coming, and they were determined to leave nothing behind of value for the Yankees.

When he thought about how painful it would be for
him to set a torch to Maple Shadows, he understood that
pride, and how determined these people still were that they
had been in the right. He did not doubt that by now
Brennan Manor must be all but lost, and he could not bear

the thought of what Audra must be suffering. The only way
to live with it was to try not to think about her at all, but
that was impossible, especially now. On his march to Savannah with General Sherman, in every building he ordered
torched, every warehouse with dwindling supplies, in every
farm their horses trampled over, every starving face of
woman and child, he saw Audra.

Just this morning they had seen a string of refugees
climbing a distant hill, the last brave souls who had stayed
behind to set more fires before fleeing with what they could
carry on their backs. Men burned their own businesses,
women their own homes, and the only way to live with the
nightmarish memories was to keep telling himself they had
brought this upon themselves. All they'd had to do was
agree to end slavery, stay in the Union, work together in
Congress to bring this all about peacefully; but that damn
southern pride had brought them to this. It had destroyed
the love he and Audra had shared; but then, his own pride
had been just as responsible. Was it so important to be
right, after all? What good would it do to bring these states
back into the Union now, when so much hatred was bound
to continue for years to come? The South was not about to
forget this, maybe not for generations. Neither would
Audra, and that was why, no matter what their own deep,
personal passions and needs, he had to stay away, even
though it meant never knowing what had happened to her.

He headed his horse down the hill toward the place
east of town where his men were camped, resting for a day
before going on. Some were calling this Sherman's "march
to the sea." It was the Federal government's way of cutting
one mighty swath through the heart of the South, a final
push to defeat and take over every southern state and end
this hideous war. In these last three years since first joining
the Union Army, Lee had seen so much blood and horror
that he felt numb to it. He no longer got sick to his stomach
when he heard a man scream while his leg was being sawed
off without anesthesia. He ordered piles of arms and legs
buried as though they were nothing more than so much
garbage. He had become used to the smell of blood and
gunpowder, was able to watch men die of infection or

dehydration from diarrhea because of bad water or rotten food. These things were common, everyday occurrences, all part of the horrors of war that a man either learned to live with or go crazy.

He was also learning to live with the loneliness. The war kept him busy, kept him from having to think about what the hell he was going to do when it was over, how he was ever going to find any happiness. Last year he'd gotten word that his brother David had also been killed. The loss was just one more blow in a series of losses. It sickened him to think how most of his family was gone now. He had no idea how his law firm was doing, but it didn't matter anymore. When this was over, there would be no mother or father to go home to, and thank God his mother had not lived to see all of this.

Below him, on the road out of Atlanta, several Federals herded along a group of Confederate prisoners, the remnants of a handful of rebels who had tried to defend Atlanta out of sheer stubbornness, even though they knew it was a lost cause. They staggered along, looking thin and hungry, some of them wounded, their uniforms worn.

"Keep moving!" he heard one of the Union soldiers order as he nudged one of them with the barrel of his rifle.

These captives would be held in temporary prison camps until Sherman took Savannah, at which time they would all be marched to waiting Union boats on the Savannah River and shipped out to the ocean and up the coast to Federal prisons, there to rot until the war was over. Lee supposed whatever they suffered, they probably deserved it, considering what he'd heard of the suffering in Confederate prison camps. A Confederate captive of their own had told them of the horrors of a prison camp in southwest Georgia in Andersonville, men living on salt and beans, dying at a rate of close to a hundred a day and being buried in mass graves. He wished Andersonville were one of the places they were set to invade, so that those poor souls could be freed, but Sherman's troops were marching east, not southwest. He had learned that conditions in other southern prisons were as bad or worse, men turned into walking skeletons, drinking filthy water, dying horrible deaths from disease and stomach ailments.

His thoughts were interrupted when the prisoners below turned and began an attack on the men who had been forcing them to march to the Federal camp.

"We ain't goin' to your stinkin' Yankee prison!" one of them shouted.

To Lee's surprise, weak as they were, and unarmed, the Confederates managed to pounce on the Federals and put up an amazing struggle. Two of the prisoners were shot instantly, but the rest managed to overcome the four guards, and some managed to wrestle away the Union soldier's guns. Two of the Federals were shot down before more troops noticed the fracas and began moving in.

It had all happened in a matter of seconds. The Confederates clearly had no chance, but Lee imagined they had decided they would rather die fighting than starve in a prison camp. Two of them began running up the hill, right toward him, one still carrying a rifle. Lee raised his own weapon, praying the man would not try to use the gun. The prisoner was weak and frightened, but this was war, and when the rebel stopped and took aim, Lee fired.

The man staggered backward and landed flat on his back without making a sound. Blood oozed from a hole in his head. By then the second man reached Lee, and Lee leveled his rifle again. "Stop!" he ordered. The young man kept coming, his long, unkempt hair partially hiding dark eyes bright with determination when he grabbed at Lee's rifle, never even looking into his face. Lee didn't want to shoot the unarmed man, and it struck him that the rebel seemed terribly young, but the crazy kid kept twisting and yanking at his rifle. Lee's right hand was still on the trigger, and the weapon went off.

The young man staggered backward, finally looking up into his face, his eyes growing wide with surprise. "Lee!" he muttered. "I d-didn't know. . . ." He fell to his back with a grunt.

Lee sat frozen, still on the horse, staring at the bleeding young man. A bright stain of blood began to spread at the left side of his chest, but he appeared still to be alive, his fingers digging into the ground. Of all the nightmares Lee had seen and experienced in this war, none could match the horror that filled him at that moment when the rebel called his name and spoke in a stutter. This couldn't be! He shoved his rifle into its boot and climbed down from his horse, his legs feeling like heavy iron. He literally forced himself to walk over to the body. He could see the boy's chest was still moving as he struggled for breath. Lee knelt over him, removed the boy's cap, and under all the hair and a scraggly beard, he saw clearly who it was.

"Joey!" he groaned. "My God!" He took hold of the boy's hand and squeezed it tightly. "I'll get you some help!"

"No," the boy pleaded, panting. "D-don't leave me."

Lee's eyes teared, and he moved to sit down beside the boy, picking his head up and cradling him in his arm. A Federal soldier ran up the hill.

"Sir! You all right?"

"Go away!" Lee ordered. "I'm all right, but get a doctor up here for this boy!"

The soldier frowned in curiosity at the way the words were spoken, as though Colonel Jeffreys were ready to cry over shooting a rebel! "Yes, sir," he answered, turning and running off.

Joey grasped the front of Lee's uniform and smiled. "Lee. What a . . . hell of a way . . . t-to meet again, huh?"

"Joey." Lee felt sick and empty. "I didn't know it was you!"

Joey kept smiling. "D-doesn't matter. I was so . . . bent on k-killing you, too, I d-didn't know . . . it was you, either." He winced and breathed deeply, began to tremble. "Here I was . . . so sure I'd make it through this without . . . a scratch," he said, his voice growing weaker.

"Dammit, Joey, don't you die on me! I'm getting you some help, and I'll make sure they don't send you to that prison camp, you hear? I'll give special orders that you get sent home once you're well. You've got to live, Joey, for Audra. She'll need you when this is over."

Tears began to form in Joey's eyes. ". . . won't . . . make it," he muttered. "You . . . have to t-take care . . . of Audra for me. P-promise me, Lee."

"You don't understand — "

"She'll still love you . . . even after all this. You'll see. Even . . . if she d-doesn't . . . promise me you'll f-find her . . . make sure she's all right. Please, Lee."

Lee studied the eyes that had always been so trusting. This stinking war had even cut down innocent, loving boys like Joey, who had no business being mixed up in killing and being killed. When Audra got word of this, she would never recover.

"I promise, Joey, but I won't have to. You're going to be all right." He hugged him closer, breaking into tears.

"It's all right, Lee. You . . . didn't know. I f-forgive you."

"Don't do this to me, Joey. Don't make me have to live with this, and don't make Audra have to go on without you. You're her only hope for happiness. I saw her, Joey. I saw her in Baton Rouge, and she was pretty as ever. All she talked about was you coming home, that somehow you'd find a way to save Brennan Manor. You have to live for that, Joey. I'll make sure you get the best care. I'm a colonel. I can pull strings. You'll be all right."

He knew that even before he finished talking, the boy was dead in his arms. He broke into bitter sobbing, not caring that several of his men had gathered around him to stare in dismay.

"We'd better tell the general," one of them said.

"No, just leave him be. He must have known this one. Just leave him here. He'll come down when he's ready."

They turned and left, muttering among themselves at the strange sight of a colonel in the Federal Army weeping over a dead rebel, holding him as if he had just lost a brother. It was several hours later and already dark when Lee came down to camp, his eyes red, deep circles under them. His uniform was covered with bloodstains. He went inside his own tent and came out with a whiskey bottle, then picked up a shovel and a lantern. Speaking to no one, he walked back up the hill. Some of his men watched curiously as he returned to where the dead body lay, and by the light of the distant lantern they could see Colonel Lee Jeffreys digging a grave, a duty usually assigned to the lowest ranks.

They all watched until they were too sleepy to care any longer. When morning came, their colonel still had not returned. "Better tell his commander," one of the privates spoke up.

Another nodded and left, and minutes later Major General West rode up the hill to find Lee passed out over the grave, an empty whiskey bottle in his hand.

JANUARY 1865

    Audra picked some old, dried flowers off the rosebush she had planted at the head of her father's grave. She hoped it would live, wouldn't know for sure until it bloomed in spring. She had dug it up from near the house and planted it here five months ago, and it had bloomed a while longer, so she held hope it would come to life again in two or three more months.

    Time seemed to have little meaning anymore. A day-by-day existence had made keeping track of dates pointless. She had only today realized that nearly five months had passed since her father had died. Her heart was filled with grief and guilt for having turned her back on him those first several months after finding out about Lena. Now a day did not go by that she did not wish he was with her, so that she could tell him again how much she loved him and needed his strength, his knowledge and wisdom ... and his love.

She had never doubted that love. It was the way he chose to show it that had brought her such unhappiness. For Joey it had been the same, but she knew her father's intentions had been good, and she was glad that she had forgiven him though forgiveness brought scant relief to her sore heart. Why did it take a person's death to make those left behind realize the depth of their own love? It seemed that everything in life was backward, that no one seemed to know what was really important. Right now she just wanted peace, and to know where her next meal was coming from. She glanced down the hill at Toosie, who was loosening the dirt from last year's garden with a hoe, keeping it prepared for planting again in a couple of months. Although it was January, it had been very warm, in the upper sixties, and the day was pleasant.

Lena sat in a chair on the porch, wearing a shawl, even weaker now since Joseph's death. She had wept pitifully those first few days and had not been able to eat. What a shame it was that Lena had lived her life loving a man she could never truly have, but Audra could no longer hate or blame her. Now she simply understood. She had secretly vowed always to care for Lena and Toosie, and though she knew deep inside how much she cared for them, she had never really been able to tell them.

Part of her still could not forget they were Negroes, and that she was not supposed to care for them as she did; but more and more, these people were the only ones she could depend on—not just Lena and Toosie, but Henrietta and the few remaining slaves who had stayed on at Brennan Manor. Even Jonathan Horne had finally left, the last white person on the plantation besides herself.

The Negroes were doing what they could to help grow food and to take care of at least the house and grounds. The house was in bad need of painting, but there was no money for it. The thousands of acres beyond the home were overgrown, as was the land belonging to Cypress Hollow. Audra was not sure what she would do if Joey did not show up soon. There was pitifully little money left.

She knew she might be forced to leave, but she did not want to go until she knew what had happened to her brother. This was where he would come when the war was over . . . home. She should be here. She did not like the thought of possibly having to sell some of her property, but it might be necessary just to survive. She looked at her father's grave once more, the old ache returning.

A horse came galloping into the back lawn, ridden bareback by a Negro man who charged up to Toosie and Henrietta and began shouting excitedly. Audra quickly left the gravesite and hurried toward the rider, alarmed when she thought she could hear more horses, a thundering sound, as though many riders were coming. Toosie threw down her hoe and yelled for her to hurry. When Audra reached her, Toosie grasped her arm and began pulling at her as she hurried toward the house.

"Get in the wood box in the kitchen!" she told Audra as they hurried up the back steps. "Henrietta, tell Mama to pretend she can't talk! No matter what happens, she should keep still!"

"Toosie, what's going on?" Audra demanded.

The Negro man who had ridden in galloped off to hide his horse, and Henrietta hurried her hefty frame past them and outside to talk to Lena.

"Union men!" Toosie told Audra as they hurried inside the kitchen. "The bad kind we've heard about—more like outlaws than soldiers! They've already been to Cypress Hollow and burned everything down. March Fredericks has turned traitor to his own kind and joined the Union outlaws. That was Freddie Washington that rode in. He said he got away and came straight here to tell us they're coming this way. March Fredericks is looking for you!" She opened the wood box. "You hide in here, and I'll cover you with more wood so they can't see you."

Audra turned to her before climbing into the box. "What about *you*?"

Toosie grasped her arms. "It's not me Fredericks is after. If he finds you here, he'll rape you and kill you, sure as I'm standing here! I'll go sit on the porch with Mama and try to convince him you aren't here anymore—that you've gone to New Orleans to live with Eleanor and her husband because your father is dead and there's nothing left here now. If March thinks you're gone, he might not do so much damage."

"Toosie, you're putting yourself in too much danger!"

The girl's eyes hardened. "I'm just a nigger, remember? They're not interested in niggers, just white women."

"Don't pretend with me, Toosie! You know good and well how beautiful you are to white men, you and Lean both! If they can't get hold of me, they'll take it out on you!"

"It's a chance we have to take. If we *all* hide, they'll know for sure something isn't right, and they'll tear this place apart looking for all of us. When they find us, it will just be worse for everybody! This is our only chance of getting rid of them without too much trouble! Now get in the box, Audra! Hurry! I can already hear them coming!"

Their eyes met, and Audra reached out and embraced her. "God be with you, Toosie." She wished there was more time to think, but the sound of oncoming riders told her there was not. She climbed into the wood box, at an end where a good deal of wood had been removed. Toosie began quickly taking logs from the other end and placing them over her. Audra covered her head with her hands, and she bent over from the weight of the wood, finding it hard to breathe and wondering how many spiders shared the woodbox with her. This was no time to be worried about dirt and bugs. This was a matter of life and death. Toosie grabbed up some nearby kindling from a basket then and threw it on top of the wood that covered her. "I can't see you at all," Audra heard her say. "Just stay there, no matter what happens."

Everything went dark when Toosie closed the lid to the box. "I'm going out onto the porch now to sit with Henrietta and Mama like we're just enjoying the day."

Audra heard nothing more, until she could literally feel the approaching horses. She could hear men shouting then, heard guns being fired, heard a scream. Who was it? The thought of March Fredericks turning on his own people sickened and infuriated her. She did not doubt that this was his way of getting back at the big plantation owners, men who had for years told him what to do, ordered him around. Richard and her father had both fired the man at different times, and she had never forgotten the sinister way he used to look at her. She knew Toosie was right about what he would do to her if he found her. She waited with a pounding heart, the weight of the wood becoming more and more oppressive. Something crawled over her hand, but she dared not move to shake it off.

Someone ran through the kitchen then, the footsteps heavy. A shot rang out, and a woman screamed again, followed by a hard thud. Someone heavy had been shot! Henrietta? No, not Henrietta! She heard more footsteps, several people, surely March and his men. There was a great deal of laughter, shouting and swearing, crashing sounds.

"I don't believe you, you nigger bitch!" It was March's voice. Audra knew it well.

"I told you she's not here," Toosie said, a pleading sound to her voice. An ache moved through Audra's heart. Toosie was risking her life to keep her from harm. They sounded as though they were only a few feet from the wood box. "Search the house if you want. She's gone to New Orleans to live with Eleanor. Look around! There's nothing left for her now. Joey is gone, and Master Joseph died five months ago. The place is in ruins. Mama and I only stayed because we've got no place else to go!"

"Yeah, and because your mama loved Joseph Brennan. He fucked her good for a lot of years. You think people didn't know that?"

Audra cringed, wanting to cover her ears.

"Now *you're* the young pretty one," March growled at Toosie. "I'm gonna find out what it was about your mama Joseph thought was so damn excitin'! I came here for a piece of ass, and if Audra Potter ain't here to give it to me, then you'll have to do!"

Audra heard a slap and the sound of someone falling. There came more shouting and the sound of heavy boots again. "Ain't no pretty white girl in this whole place, Fredericks," someone complained. "You lied to us, dammit, March! She wasn't at the other place either!"

"We're headin' out to the next farm," said another.

"Ain't nothin' left here worth lootin' except a few chickens and a couple of horses."

"What about this little gal here?" someone else spoke up.

"This one's mine," March told them all sternly.

"Ain't no other decent women left. The one out on the porch is pretty, but she's a damn cripple, and there ain't *no* man gonna have at that fat ole thing over there."

"Hell, she's dead, anyway. Let's go! Abel says he's sure there's a couple of young girls at the farm west of here. He used to work there."

The Benson girls! Audra thought. Herbert Benson owned a much smaller farm west of them, and he had two daughters, only sixteen and twelve. A man named Abel Runyon used to work for them. *Another traitor!* she groaned inwardly. Their own people were turning on them, using the war and the vulnerability of people who had lost everything as an excuse to come through and take what was left. How could men so easily turn into savages!

"Go ahead," March was saying. "They ain't the prettiest, but they're young."

"And they've got white skin. I'm sick of niggers. You can have this one."

Men trampled out. Audra almost gasped aloud when one stopped and opened the wood box, then slammed the lid down again. "Shit!" he cussed. "If the bitch is hidin' around here, I don't know where it could be. Hell, a place this big, there's a hundred places for her to hide."

"I told you, she's not here," Toosie spoke up. Audra thought she sounded as though she was in pain.

"Maybe I can get it out of the crippled woman," one of the others spoke up.

"No!" Toosie cried out. "My mama can't talk. She had a stroke back in sixty-two and can't speak."

"Well, then, if she's a cripple and can't speak besides, she's a pretty useless nigger, ain't she?" the man answered. "You know what happens to useless niggers."

The man walked out. "No! Wait!" Toosie screamed.

Audra heard a gunshot, and she felt like vomiting. Lena!

"No! No! Mama!" Toosie screamed.

There came a mixture of sounds then, men shouting outside, horses running again, combined with Toosie's screams in the kitchen, and the sound of a struggle. Something crashed, bodies fell. She could hear blows, and Toosie was begging March to leave with the others.

"I'm gettin' my piece, white or nigger," he growled.

Audra could hear him ripping and tearing at Toosie's clothes, and she could not let the horror go on any longer. Toosie was literally sacrificing herself for her, and she did not doubt that March Fredericks would kill her when he was finished with her. She strained upward against the heavy logs, pushing until the wood box opened and a few of the logs fell out. She wished there had been time to get her father's rifle that she kept in the parlor, but there had not, and it probably would not have done much good against so many men; but there was only one man now, and he was so engrossed in trying to rape Toosie that he was not even aware of Audra's presense.

March had Toosie down on the floor, and she lay as though in a daze, her nose and mouth bleeding. The skirt of her dress as well as her bloomers were torn away, and the man was positioning himself between her slender legs. Audra climbed out of the box, and finally March turned to see her standing over him with an upraised log. She brought it down hard against his head before he could stop her, and he fell away from Toosie, the front of his pants open. Audra brought the log down again, aiming for his privates, knowing that if she could hurt him there she could disable him long enough to find a way to kill him, but the man got to his feet too quickly. Her second blow glanced off his leg, and instantly he grabbed her around her throat with a powerful hand.

Only then she saw that in his right hand he held a knife. His head bleeding, the man pushed her to the floor, pressing the knife against her cheek, the tip of it near her eye. "So," he sneered through yellow teeth, his breath reeking of whiskey. "You *are* here, you haughty little bitch! When I'm through with you, you'll wish you had let me have at Toosie and stayed hidden, sweet little Miss Audra."

He kept the knife near her eye and raised up enough to reach under her skirt and rip at her bloomers, then ripped into the skirt of her dress and cut it away. Audra struggled to breathe, trying to think straight. All she could see was that big knife, but she wondered if it might be better to feel it cutting into her than to feel March Fredericks shoving himself inside of her. Either way, he was going to kill her. She would rather fight him and die in the struggle than allow him his pleasure first.

He came down closer then, rubbing himself against her thigh, holding the knife close to her face again. "I'm glad the rest of them left," he said with a hideous grin. "Now you're all mine! Not so high and mighty anymore, are you, Miss Audra? You ain't no better than me, and you never was!"

Audra stared at the knife, lying still for a moment to let him think she was going to submit. Suddenly she grabbed his right wrist with both hands and pushed it away, at the same time quickly ramming her head upward into his nose. March grunted and rolled slightly to his right. Audra used the moment to scramble out from under him and grab hold of a small black skillet that had fallen to the floor when the house was raided.

Instantly March was on her before she could get up. She swung the skillet, clobbering him in the head, but rather than hurt him, she only made him angrier. She wiggled to get away, hit at him with the pan again, but he grabbed her arm and slammed it hard against the floor. Audra screamed with a terrible pain in her right wrist.

"Bitch! Bitch!" he kept growling as a hard fist landed into her face twice. "I'll *kill* you!"

Then Audra felt the tip of his knife jab into her throat. From then on everything that happened seemed as though it was a dream, as if she were standing there just watching the struggle. She was startled to realize she felt no pain, even though she knew that March Fredericks had cut her throat. Straddling her, he leered at her, holding the bloody knife in front of her eyes. She thought he was telling her he would cut her eyes out when he was done raping her, but his voice sounded far, far away.

For one brief moment, she thought she could hear Lee's voice. *I love you, Audra.* She felt an amazing calm, and she stared at March Fredericks, while behind him Toosie stood looking down at them, Joseph Brennan's rifle in her hands. Still, all sound seemed muffled, and when Toosie pulled the trigger on the rifle and fired, Audra heard only a faint, faraway echo. March Fredericks's head caved in, and his body lurched to the side, pieces of flesh and skull landing on Audra's dress.

Audra lay helplessly, watching Toosie, who stood frozen for a moment, still aiming the rifle at March's body. She walked around Audra. "Your men killed my mama," she said coldly. She fired the rifle again, this time into the man's chest. Finally, as though coming out of a trance, she looked at Audra and threw down the rifle, ripping a piece of cotton slip from what was left of her clothes hanging on her body. She pushed the cloth against Audra's throat.

"Audra! Don't die on me, please!"

Audra tried to answer, but she could not make her voice work.

"Oh, my God," Toosie wailed. "Hold still!" She pressed the cotton tighter, pushed Audra's hair back to study her neck. "He didn't get the big veins. Hold this to your throat!"

Audra obeyed, still feeling no pain, wondering if she was already dying.

"I'll go get some of the Negroes at the camp houses, if they aren't all dead, too!" She leaned closer. "I'll have them take you into one of their cabins. If those men come back, they'll never think to look for a white woman in the Negro camps. I'll find somebody to help me hide March Fredericks's body. If those men come back and find out I killed him, they'll rape me and hang me for sure! I've got to find a way to get rid of the body!"

Toosie's face was bloody and swollen, and Audra could see her beginning to panic. She could hear a crackling sound, and she smelled smoke. Instinctively she knew that her precious home was burning. One of the Yankee raiders must have set a fire in another part of the house before he left.

She kept the cloth pressed tight against her throat. The

pain was beginning to set in now, and she kept swallowing something, soon realizing it was her own blood, but she told herself to stay calm. Somehow she had to help Toosie. She grasped the woman's wrist with her free hand, leaning up to her, trying to talk. "What is it? What is it?" Toosie asked. "I've got to get help, Audra!"

Audra squeezed her wrist, trying to tell her she had to stay calm. "Old . . . well," she managed to say in a rough whisper. It was as loud as she could speak. "Throw . . . him . . . in the . . . old well . . . put . . . the cover . . . on it."

Toosie was shaking. She nodded. "I'll get you help!"

Toosie picked up the rifle and ran out of the house, and Audra collapsed to the floor beside March Fredericks, wondering if she would bleed to death or be consumed by the fire before Toosie made it back.

Lee set the whiskey bottle down, staring at the sheet of paper in front of him. How many times had he tried to write this letter and been unable to do it? God only knew what had happened to Audra by now, and Joey's death would all but destroy her.

How could he keep his promise to Joey and see her again? There was a time when that was what he wanted more than anything on earth, even after she had screamed at him that day in Baton Rouge never to come back. He wanted nothing more than to find her and help her however he could, if she needed it; but how could he face her, knowing it was his own rifle that had killed her brother?

Over and over he relived the shooting in his sleep. He had continued the march with Sherman, doing his duty in numb obedience. He didn't care about anything anymore, nothing but to get this war over with, and for that, he needed his whiskey. So far his drinking had not interfered with his performance on the battlefield, if the raiding and burning of southern cities could be called "battles." By the time they reached most of these places, the Confederate defenses were long gone.

He took another swallow of fire and picked up a pen, dipping it into a bottle of ink and leaning over the desk in the back office of the church he had occupied in Savannah. From here his troops would be moving north into the Carolinas, continuing their march, encircling the Confederates and heading back into Virginia for the final kill. Sherman thought the war would be finished by summer, which meant he had to decide what to do about Audra.

Dear Audra, he wrote. He stopped, wadded up the paper, and took another sheet from his supplies. He couldn't write "Dear Audra," as though he knew her. This letter was going to be from a stranger, a Confederate who had known Joey. The stranger would tell her that her brother had been shot as he was bravely trying to escape from Union soldiers who meant to take him to prison. The stranger would tell her of all the heroic things Joey had done in the war. He would make up some wonderful stories to make her proud . . . her and her damn father. It was Joseph Brennan's fault Joey had even joined the rebels. If not for that man, Joey would have been home where he belonged, and if Joseph Brennan had not destroyed Lee's letters to Audra, Lee himself might still be with her.

It was all water over the damn now. The fact remained that Joey was dead, and he'd killed him. He had promised Joey he would find Audra and make sure she was taken care of, and he would keep that promise. But he didn't know how soon that would be, and he couldn't wait until then to tell her about her brother. Besides that, he wasn't sure he could ever tell her he was the one who had killed the boy.

Dear Mrs. Potter, he wrote the second time. *I regret to inform you that your brother, Corporal Joseph Brennan, has been killed . . .* Joey, a corporal. He smiled, thinking how proud the kid must have been of that. The smile turned to tears, just as it always did. He wiped at them with the sleeve of his uniform, wondering how and when he was ever going to get over this. If it weren't for the whiskey, and for his promise to Joey, he'd shoot himself.

He leaned back in the chair and took the letter from his pocket, a letter he had found on Joey. The boy had written to Audra, but the letter never got sent. Lee believed she should see it. Maybe it would help comfort her. He would

send it—with the letter from the stranger who would write
to tell her that Joey was dead.

He opened the letter again, picturing Joey writing it by
the light of a camp fire. *Dear Audra,* it read,

> *I am in Georgia now, and they say this war
> will end before much longer and I can come home.
> I guess you know by now that I won't come home
> victorious, but a least so far I am alive and unhurt.
> From what I have seen, I am lucky. I hardly know
> anymore what this war is about, and it hurts so
> much to see what is happening to the South. I
> worry all the time about you and Father, and I
> pray you are all in good health and that nothing
> has happened to Brennan Manor, for all I dream
> about now is coming home to the place I love, to
> my beloved sister, and even to Father. He will be so
> proud of my corporal stripes. When I get home, I
> will help however I can. We'll save Brennan
> Manor, Audra, and we'll be happy there. Maybe
> when the war is over, Lee will come back and you
> can forget all of this and be together like you
> should always have been. That would make me
> happier than anything I can think of. I know he's
> a Yankee, but he's one of the best people I know,
> and . . .*

The letter ended there. Joey never got the chance to
finish it, and Lee was sickened to read those last words
about himself. *. . . you can forget all of this and be together
like you should always have been . . . he's one of the best
people I know . . .*

"And he shot you, Joey," Lee muttered. "Lee Jeffreys
blew you away." He picked up the bottle of ink and threw
it against a wall. The blue liquid splattered against a
wooden cross, dripped down the wall. In Lee's eyes it represented blood. "Blue blood," he sneered. He stared at the
cross, thinking how he deserved to burn in hell for what he
had done. If only he and Joey had recognized each other
one second sooner. If only he had not joined the damn army

at all. He had been so sure he was right, so fired up to preserve the Union.

Well, now the Union was saved, for what that was worth. He had lost his own identity, his own reason for living; had even lost the only woman since Mary Ellen that he wanted to share his life with, all to save the Union. He had killed an innocent boy who had practically worshiped him. Just like Joey, he didn't even know what this war was about anymore.

He picked up the pen again, opened another bottle of ink on the desk, and kept writing. *Joey died bravely,* he continued, *and he did not suffer. He fought a Union soldier who was taking him to prison, and in the struggle the soldier's rifle fired, killing Joey instantly.* What was the sense of telling her the boy lived a few minutes? It would be agony enough knowing he was dead. Every time he thought about Audra getting the letter, and the unfinished letter Joey had been writing to her, pain seared his gut like fire, at times making him literally double over. He wasn't even sure himself how he was going to finish this war. If the pain in his stomach didn't finish him, the whiskey probably would, or maybe a bullet from his own gun. He was either going to have to learn to live with what he'd done and find a way to forgive himself, or end it all; but as long as Audra was alive and might need his help, he had no choice but to go on. She was all there was left to live for.

He kept writing. The letter had to be finished. It had to be sent, and that was that. Audra had a right to know her brother was dead. Why let the hope go on any longer? Why let her wonder or let her pray for something she could never have?

He swallowed more whiskey, then turned up the lamp and kept writing, while ink dripped from the corss, and in the distance yet another southern city burned.

28

Audra watched Toosie standing at the stove of the primitive little cabin in which they now lived. The beautiful Brennan home was gone, consumed by fire. Toosie and some of the other Negroes had managed to salvage a few dishes, pots, and pans from the kitchen, which was left standing. Only eight blackened pillars, and several fire-places with brick chimneys, also stood amid the rubble of the mansion.

It was a chilly January in Louisiana, but two days before, Audra had insisted on seeing what was left. She had managed to walk out to the rickety little porch of the cabin, and through a clearing left by winter-bare trees and fields that had been trampled by March and his men, she had seen the remnants of her beloved home. She could still feel the heat of the fire that raged around her that awful day, could still smell the smoke. Toosie and some Negro men had gotten her out of the house before the fire spread to where she lay, and they had carried her to one of the empty cabins in the Negro camp.

The rest of that day and the several days and nights afterward were a blank in Audra's mind. Toosie had been nursing her for two weeks now. For the last several days she had finally felt stronger, but the horror of what March Fredericks and his men had done would never leave her.

Poor, precious Henrietta was dead! So was Lena! It was all still so unreal, and at the same time all *too* real. Toosie had ordered some of the Negro men to bury them, and March Frederick's body had been dumped in the old, abandoned well, as Audra had advised Toosie to do. The man's horse had been run off, and everyone prayed fervently that the men March rode with would not come back looking for him. They never had—a small consolation for the horrors that had been visited upon them, but at least Toosie and the others seemed to be safe now from a hanging.

Audra was not sure how the hideous event had affected Toosie, who had herself been badly battered. March deserved what he got, and thank God Toosie had had the courage and fortitude to do the man in before he could rape them both; but killing a man was still something that weighed on a person's conscience. Toosie had remained amazingly calm and quiet, showing a strength Audra never realized the woman had.

She looked around the only room of the little cabin, staring at a fire in the little stone fireplace and thinking how ironic her situation had become. All her life she had looked down on Negroes as a lower class. All her life they had waited on her, and she had ordered them around without a thought. Yet in the end some of them had risked their lives for her—some had *lost* their lives for her. Now these people were her only friends, those who protected her, housed her, nursed her. She lay in a cabin that belonged to her father's Negro camps, in a homemade bed with ropes for springs and flannel stuffed with feathers for a mattress. Even the nightgown she wore had belonged to a Negro woman.

There were only six families left on the plantation. Besides Toosie there were six other women, two of them widowed. Among them were twenty-two young children. Eight men still called the Negro camps of Brennan Manor home, four of them husbands, the other four single. Audra had still not gotten straight which children belonged to which women, but through those children she had found some little bit of hope. In spite of what they had been through, and now living in near-starving conditions, the children remained happy and smiling, their bright, dark eyes full of mischief, finding wonder and excitement in the smallest thing: discovering a bird's nest or beating on an old tub with a stick or biting into a piece of fresh bread.

Audra thought how Toosie and the others had an amazing resiliency and an ability to overcome hardship. They seemed to have tremendous faith, and they found pleasure in the smallest of blessings. They prayed often, sang when they worked, could carry on in the face of tragedy. She knew Toosie was suffering over her mother's senseless and brutal death, but she had tried to accept it with a feeling of hope. *Mama's with Joseph now,* she had told Audra. *She's out of her physical pain and the misery of having lost your father. She hated walking with that cane, and she was lonely without Joseph.*

Audra had insisted on visiting Lena's and Henrietta's graves the day before, and an older Negro man helped support her when she was too weak to stand alone. He had gently kept hold of her as though she were his own daughter. Several of the Negroes had gone with them, and there had been praying and singing over the graves unlike anything Audra had ever seen or heard. She had never gone into the fields and listened to them sing, or ventured into the Negro camps at night. This place had always seemed so frightening and forbidding. She realized now that although she had lived with Negroes nearly her all her life, she knew hardly anything about them. There was nothing frightening and forbidding here.

Out in front of the cabin, little boys helped the Negro men with hoeing a field not far away, keeping the ground worked up so it would be ready for another planting of potatoes and vegetables as soon as the weather turned a little warmer. Thank goodness there was a long growing season in Louisiana. Some things they could plant and harvest twice They were determined to fend for themselves, feed themselves, learn to live without someone else providing for them. There was no money to buy anything, and none of them knew where they should go, what to do with themselves—so they would make do right here until and unless a better opportunity came along. They were free now, and some had talked about heading west to Kansas, where it was said even Negroes could homestead.

Their faces lit up at the prospect of living on land that was all their own, but there was no money to procure the necessary wagons and supplies for such a trip. Even so, they could dream, and Audra began to see that these people had the same hopes and desires and willingness to succeed as any white man. They loved, had families, laughed, cried, enjoyed being together, supported each other. The only thing they lacked was education, but if Toosie could learn to read and write, why not all of them? She felt almost ashamed that most of her life she had believed these people did not have enough intelligence for such things. Toosie had taken time to teach letters to some of the little ones, and they were learning quickly.

Audra put a hand to the bandages at her throat while she watched Toosie knead some bread dough. The woman had taken charge since Audra's injury, and all the Negroes had come together to help both Toosie and Audra. At first Audra had just wanted to let life slip away, for it seemed she had lost everything, even her voice. In all likelihood she would probably never sing again, and perhaps not even talk. Her beautiful home was gone, and there had been no word from Joey.

Everything that she had ever loved was gone. Lee would never come back, and even if he did, nothing could ever be the same. She knew he was a good man, but he was still a Yankee, and the hatred of the South for the North would prevail for a long, long time. Her only consolation was knowing she was among others who had also suffered tremendous losses, and the faith and courage of the Negroes helping her now renewed her own faith. They were as good to her as if she were one of their own. Some had even wept over the fact that she had lost her voice.

Our beautiful Audra used to sing prettier than any bird God ever made, one of the women said once when she was bathing her. *You will sing again, Miss Audra. God won't take away that voice forever.*

Audra had her doubts, and to bear the loss, she reminded herself that she was at least alive. She could not easily mourn the loss of her voice when the more immediate concern was to overcome the shock of March's hideous attack, Lena and Henrietta's tragic deaths, the sight of the black, skeletal remains of Brennan Manor. It was enough to bear the realization that her life would never be the same again, that her precious father was gone, that Joey still had not come home.

"I have some soup for you," Toosie was saying, interrupting her thoughts. She was carrying a tray over to the bed. "You have to try to eat again, Audra. You're much too thin."

Audra had no appetite, and when she did try to eat, swallowing was misery, and food did not always go down the right pipe. Sometimes she ended up coughing violently because something would get into her windpipe instead. The coughing would bring her unbearable pain and sometimes start the bleeding again, but every day Toosie made her try again, just to keep her from starving to death. March Fredericks had done a fine job of destroying her voice and had damaged her ability to swallow properly. Audra had not seen her own injury yet, and she wondered if it would leave an ugly scar. At least the knife had not found her jugular veins, and Toosie and the others had managed to keep her from bleeding to death; but Audra was still not sure that what was left of her life was worth living. Her only hope now was Joey. How wonderful it would be when he came walking through that door, her Joey. Together they could find a way to survive, maybe even find a way to rebuild Brennan Manor.

"Try this," Toosie was saying. "It's potato soup. I've got time to feed you while the bread is rising."

Audra shook her head and took the tray from her. "I'll ... do it myself," she whispered.

"Well, you just be careful. I'll sit right here. It's not too hot, so it won't burn."

Audra took a spoonful, realizing that for the first time in two weeks she had a bit of an appetite. The soup smelled wonderful. She put a spoonful in her mouth and thought how good it tasted. Now, if she could only get it to go down right, perhaps she could enjoy food for the first time since the horror of March's attack.

She swallowed, and to her surprise there was very little pain. She took another spoonful, another. She smiled, and Toosie smiled back at her, tears in her eyes. Audra felt like crying herself, finding it amazing, after the life of pampered wealth she had led for nearly twenty-three years, that she could sit in a Negro's bed, in a Negro's cabin, sharing this little victory with her Negro sister, and take such pleasure in merely being able to eat a bowl of soup.

She took several more spoonfuls before stopping to meet Toosie's eyes again. She reached out and took the woman's hand. "You risked ... your life for me," she whispered, still finding it painful to try talking.

Toosie squeezed her hand in return. "And you for me."

Their eyes held, and Audra could not hold back her tears. "I love you, Toosie." The words had come out so easily, and they felt so right. It was not something that she ever dreamed she would say to any Negro, certainly not a mulatto who was the product of her father's loving a slave.

Toosie was smiling, but her eyes were also brimming with tears. "And I have always loved you, way before you knew who I really was. We all love you, Audra. You will always have a home with us if you want it. We don't have much, and I don't know for sure where we'll go, but we'll share what we have with you for as long as you need it."

Audra set her tray aside and turned to sit on the edge of the bed, taking hold of both of Toosie's hands. "I'm so sorry ... about Lena ... and that you had to shoot March Fredericks. If anyone ... should ever come ... for him; if they find him ... I'll tell them *I* shot him. I have ... the scar on my throat ... to prove he attacked me ... and I'm white. It would go easier on me."

Toosie nodded, and suddenly they were embracing and crying. Out of tragedy had come something sweet and binding, a revelation for Audra, who realized that her best and most loyal friend had always been Toosie. She was still loved, still had someone who cared about her, still had family, even if that family was now Negro.

Someone knocked at the door then, and Toosie stiffened and pulled away. Audra felt her own heart pounding, as neither of them had gotten over the fear that March's men would come back looking for him.

"Who is it?" Toosie called out, wiping at her eyes and hurrying over to where she kept Joseph Brennan's rifle propped beside the door.

"Just open up and find out," a man's voice answered.

Toosie glanced at Audra with a frown, thinking the voice sounded familiar. She kept the rifle ready as she carefully lifted the wooden latch. When she saw who was standing there, she gasped and set the rifle aside. Audra could not see who it was, but she heard Toosie cry his name. "Elijah!"

The man came inside, swinging Toosie around in his arms, and Audra saw that it was Elijah Jakes, the man Toosie had once loved, the man her father had sold to keep them apart. It warmed her heart to see the joy in Toosie's eyes, and she thought again for a moment about Lee. There was a time when she would have wanted to greet him like that, to feel him holding her again, to know he had come for her. But there was no use in thinking about that now. Toosie wept with boundless joy, and Audra cried right along with her, but her tears were not just for Toosie's long-lost love. They were for a love she herself had lost ... and would never find again.

APRIL 1865

Audra smiled as Toosie and Elijah danced around the bonfire to celebrate the fact that Toosie was with child. Elijah was a free man now, and in eight years he had not forgotten Toosie or married anyone else. In spite of the fact that she missed her dead father, Audra could see even more clearly how wrong the man had been to sell Elijah, and she was happy for both of them. Out of all the tragedy of the past months had come a little bit of joy.

All six Negro families celebrated, as well as four more families who had joined them from the Cypress Hollow plantation, bringing with them three more single men and two old women. Although it was still the middle of the day, they had got the fire started so they could feed it and build it as darkness fell. They clapped, danced, sang to the music of one old man who played a fiddle. Elijah was a handsome, well-built Negro with a warm smile. He was thirty-one now, Toosie thirty. Not long after he came back, they had searched out a country preacher and gotten married. Audra had gone to live with one of the widowed Negro women so that the newlyweds could be alone, and now a baby was coming.

Audra's voice had grown a little stronger, but it still hurt to talk, and what came out was a low, rough, raspy sound that bore no resemblance to her once lilting voice. She was determined to keep using it and to do the special exercises she remembered Mrs. Jeffreys teaching her to strengthen her voice. Maybe what once made her lovely voice even more beautiful could be used to bring back a voice that was hardly there at all.

She helped care for the widowed woman's children, who ranged in ages from four to ten, and in spite of her voice being only a step above a gruff whisper, and the pain it caused her to talk, she was managing to teach the children their letters and numbers, delighted to discover that they learned willingly and readily. Their mother, known only as Wilena, could not get over the fact that her children would know how to read and write, or that it was Audra Brennan Potter who was teaching them.

The Lord surely sent us to live here when we was slaves, she would say, carrying on about Audra being so generous when she could leave them and find refuge and a more comfortable life among her own kind. Audra didn't feel she had any of her "own kind" left. She'd heard through news the Negro men brought from town that Uncle John was back, but he had not come to see if she was alive or dead, or to offer her help and shelter. Nor had she ever again heard from Eleanor. That was just fine with her. These people were her family now, her shelter, her comfort.

The only person she still cared about was Joey . . . and sometimes thoughts of Lee still plagued her. She could not deny that a little part of her still longed to be a woman again, longed to be held the way Elijah held Toosie, longed to lie in a man's arms again and make love not just out of physical need, but because she loved that man with every bone in her body. But it was partly because of men like Lee that she sat poor and destitute in this Negro camp, and that Brennan Manor lay in black ruins, weeds beginning to creep over and grow into what was left of the house. Things were the same at Cypress Hollow, and most of the valuables had been stolen, the livestock rustled away by thieves and other farmers, the rest having just wandered away. Because of men like Lee, outlaws could run wild through the South now, murdering innocent people like Henrietta and Lena, cutting Audra's throat so that she could never sing again.

That man is going to come for you, and you'll have to put the past behind you, Toosie had told her more than once. The woman wanted so much for Audra to find love again, and she was convinced Lee would come back for her. Audra had told her it would do him no good. It could never be the same, but Toosie insisted that it could. *Nobody will ever again love you as much as Lee Jeffreys loved you,* she was always reminding her. *Yankee or not, he's a man caught up in this war same as you were, and he's no more responsible for what has happened to us than your own father or the rest of our southern men who chose to fight for what they believed in. When this war is over, he'll just be Lee Jeffreys, and you have to put it all aside and let yourself love again, Audra. Don't throw that man away.*

Audra was convinced he would *not* come back, but as the war seemed to be drawing finally to an end, the realization that he might try was beginning to be an almost daily thought, and the things Toosie had told her weighed heavily on her mind and heart. Now, seeing Toosie and Elijah dance around the fire, knowing Toosie would be having a baby, made her ache for all of those things. No matter how confused her feelings were about Lee, the fact remained that when she thought about being a woman again, being a wife, having babies, she could not picture giving herself that way to any other man.

For now, she had to decide what she was going to do for the more immediate future. There was a total of sixty-three Negroes living here now, and since his return, all Elijah talked about was heading for Kansas soon to start their own settlement as a free people. Their only problem was money to buy the things they needed to get them there and help them get started in a new life. Audra had to decide whether she would go to Baton Rouge or New Orleans, or whether she should go to Kansas with them. She felt a strong desire to help Toosie and the others, as they had befriended and helped her. They had already said they would wait for her, knowing she would not leave until Joey came home. If Joey would come soon, he could help her decide what to do. Whatever they did, they could always be together.

There was really not much reason to stay in either Baton Rouge or New Orleans. The whole South was a shambles, people broke and starving. Some of the Negroes had managed to get to Baton Rouge a time or two and bring back a newspaper, which enterprising citizens still managed to print. In it she'd read about how people feared what would happen once the war was over. With everyone penniless, wealthy Northerners were sure to come down and buy up peoples' mortgages. For those like herself who owned their land outright but who were without money, Northerners could take over the banks, the county governments, maybe force some kind of heavy land tax on those with property. What could she do until Joey returned?

Elijah picked Toosie up in his strong arms and told her she must stop dancing or she would "lose that baby before it even grows its fingers and toes." Everyone laughed, and one woman announced that they all could eat now. In spite of the shortage of food and just about everything else humans needed to sustain themselves, the women had managed to prepare a little banquet table. They had cooked potatoes and squash in several different ways, and two dairy cows and a goat had provided enough milk for them to keep making butter, at least for as long as the salt supply in the root cellar lasted. The fire had not damaged the cellar, nor its supply of last year's harvest of potatoes, carrots, corn, squash, and jars of canned foods. A couple of the men had managed to catch a wild turkey, and it sat nicely roasted now, a royal feast for a people hungry to find something to celebrate.

Audra joined the line to fill her plate, a piece of expensive china that had once sat in a cupboard in the kitchen of her palatial mansion. Now it was used by the Negroes. All these little things kept bringing back stabbing, painful memories that would hit her at the oddest times, making her want to cry. She forced back the tears and put a small piece of turkey on her plate, not wanting to take too much, as the poor bird had to be shared by sixty-three people. Even if it was only a bite or two, real meat tasted wonderful. How strange that such things were a luxury now!

Joseph Adams rode in then on the one-and-only horse left to the plantation. Joseph was one of the single men, who Audra knew was romantically interested in Wilena. He had been visiting the woman often, playing with her five children. Because he was a strong man who had been used and sold frequently by slave owners who liked him because of his strength, he had never married, mainly because his owners would not allow it. According to Wilena, they had used Joseph like a stud horse, forcing him to mate with many Negro women to produce strong babies for future use in the fields. In one respect it would seem a man would not mind such a duty, but Audra could understand that Joseph had looked at it as horribly degrading. Wilena said he suffered from terrible guilt for having to force himself on some of the women because he'd been ordered to do it or be whipped. Joseph felt humiliated and guilty, and he was looking for a woman to love, a woman he could be with *because* of that love, a woman who wanted him just because she in turn loved Joseph and wanted him in her bed.

Audra had seen some ugly aftereffects of slavery, both physical and emotional, especially among the slaves who had come from Cypress Hollow. One man had the most hideous scars on his back and chest she had ever seen. They were from whippings, some at the hand of Richard Potter, and she felt less and less guilty over not mourning the man's death.

Joseph walked up to her with another newspaper. "You'd best read the headlines, Miss Audra," he told her, still addressing her in the old way all of them were used to calling her.

Audra turned and set down her plate, opening the newspaper while others quieted and watched her, most of them still unable to read. Toosie walked up next to her and gasped when she read the headline herself. It was dusk, but still light enough to read without a lamp. She turned to the others, knowing how difficult it was for Audra to speak up loudly enough for others to hear. "President Lincoln is dead! He was shot by an assassin!"

"Dear Lord!" one woman exclaimed, and others joined her in lamenting his death. Audra just stared at the headline, her emotions mixed. In her mind Abraham Lincoln had been responsible for the ruination of the entire South. She could not find it in herself to grieve for him, but she knew that to most Negroes he was a savior. In spite of their state of poverty and having no one to care for them now, they were free, and the man who carried the ugly scars turned away and wept.

"What's this country comin' to?" another man asked.

"Maybe he was shot by some southern man who's fixin' to start the war up all over again," another put in. "Maybe they gonna try to git things back the way they was, put us in chains agin."

Audra turned to look at them. "That will never happen," she assured them, straining to be heard. "There is no money nor means left . . . for any of us to go back to the way life once was. President Lincoln . . . already declared all of you free . . . before he died." She put a hand to her throat, her voice already weakening from just that small effort at talking louder. "A new President will simply . . . take over and carry on . . . where Lincoln left off."

Wilena approached her, touching her arm. "We is sorry life is bad for you now, child, but we can't help bein' happy for our freedom. We can't help mournin' Mr. Lincoln's death. You got to admit that no matter what has happened, Mr. Lincoln had a great dream in mind—a dream of stayin' united, a dream of freedom for *all* the people of the United States, not jus' the white folks. Slavery was wrong, Miss Audra. Surely you know that."

Audra moved her eyes to gaze at all of them again. She rubbed at her throat as she spoke. "I knew it was wrong . . . long before the war. Men like my father . . . *wanted* to end slavery . . . but they wanted to do it . . . in a way that would keep something like this from happening . . . all this bloodshed . . . all the burning and dying. Now . . . all of us have suffered for it."

"So has Mr. Lincoln," Wilena reminded her.

Audra's eyes teared as she once more contemplated the ironies of this hideous, needless war. "Yes," she said softly. "Everyone has . . . on both sides."

Wilena leaned close and hugged her, and when she moved away, Joseph held out a letter. "Miss Audra, this was waitin' for you at the newspaper office," Joseph told her. "They been holdin' it for many weeks, waitin' for you or one of us to come to town for another paper. Ah don' know how long it's been sittin'." He handed her the envelope, and Audra laid the paper aside, taking the letter with a shaking hand. She looked at Toosie.

"It could be . . . from Joey!" she said, her voice already reduced to a whisper again. "Or maybe it's *about* Joey!" She handed it to Toosie. "I can't open it, Toosie. You . . . do it."

Toosie took the letter, seeing the return address was a Private Larry Jones, Savannah, Georgia. No army regiment was given, no street address, nothing. "Do you know a Larry Jones?" she asked.

Audra shook her head, her throat aching, her heart pounding so hard that her chest hurt. Who was Larry Jones? Why wasn't the letter from Joey? A horrid dread began to fill her, but she clung to hope while Toosie opened the letter. Several of the Negroes gathered around her, many of them having known and loved Joey, all of them just as concerned for him as Audra and Toosie.

Something fell out of the envelope, and Toosie bent down and picked it up to see that it was stripes that had been cut off a uniform, as well as another letter. She opened it to see it was addressed to Audra. It took only a moment to realize what this must be. With tear-filled eyes she handed the cloth stripes to Audra, who took them with a shaking hand, her eyes wide with horror.

Toosie scanned the letter that had fallen, seeing it was from Joey. She folded it and pressed it into Audra's hand. "It's an ... an unfinished letter ... from Joey."

"Dear Lord!" one of the women groaned. "This day of celebration has turned to sorrow."

Audra just stared at Toosie, holding Joey's letter tightly, his corporal's stripes in her other hand. "Read the letter," she whispered.

Toosie took a deep breath for courage. Of all the hell she had been through, even fighting off March Fredericks and having to shoot him, nothing had been as difficult as this.

"Dear Mrs. Potter," she read. "I ... regret to inform you that your brother ..." Toosie fought back her own tears. "Corporal Joseph Brennan, has been ... killed ... fighting for the proud Confederacy."

It would be several days before Audra could bear to hear the rest of the letter. A darkness enveloped her, and she wilted into Joseph's arms, a blessed unconsciousness temporarily keeping away the pain of the most grievous loss she had ever known.

29

MAY 1865

Eleanor opened the door of her small but neat home, her eyes widening with a mixture of surprise and indignation, and finally a look of sweet satisfaction. There stood Audra, wearing a flower-printed cotton dress so cheap looking that one might expect to see in on a Negro woman. She wore a pink scarf around her neck, which did not go with the dress at all, and since it was such a warm spring day, she wondered why her cousin wore the scarf at all. She glanced past Audra to see a buckboard sitting out in front of the house, pulled by two sorry-looking horses. Two Negro men sat in the seat of the wagon, and an older Negro woman and Toosie both sat in the bed of the wagon.

"Well, my, my," Eleanor drawled, looking Audra over scathingly. "What terrible luck have you had, cousin dear?

And what are you doing clear down here in New Orleans? I do hope you haven't come begging." She smiled on the first words, but the smile turned to a sneer of hatred. "We don't give to traitors, certainly not a woman who would sleep with a Yankee while her aunt burns alive in a fire *set* by Yankees! It's a good thing Father isn't here right now. He would throw you right off the porch!"

"Uncle John is all right, then?" Audra asked.

"Yes. He came home four months ago, but he's not the same man. The war affected his mind, all the horror and all, then coming home to find Mama dead, the bank and our home destroyed. Poor Father is in a terrible state of depression."

"Eleanor, who is it?" the woman's husband asked, coming from another room to stand behind her.

Eleanor sniffed. "It's Audra. *You* know my cousin, remember? The one who whored with that Yankee soldier friend of hers while my mother was dying in that awful fire!"

She suddenly broke into tears that Audra suspected were fake. She turned to glance back at Wilena and Toosie, who sat waiting hopefully in the back of the buckboard. Joseph Adams, who had married Wilena, and Elijah also waited, hoping Audra would be able to do what she had come here to do. It had been a long, hard trip, and all along the way they had all seen the devastation left behind by the Yankees. There were few people left with any money or valuable possessions. Her only hope now was Eleanor's husband, Albert Mahoney.

She turned back to look up into Albert Mahoney's eyes. Eleanor's husband was a tall, gangly, rather homely man who was already balding, and Audra wondered if he had married Eleanor only because no attractive women would have him. Even so, he did not deserve a wife like Eleanor. He was a kind man who doted on his wife and was gracious to everyone. He also seemed very intelligent and enterprising, for somehow he had managed to salvage a lovely home out of this hideous war. He and Eleanor were well dressed. Apparently Albert was still doing all right, in spite of the poverty most of the South was in now. She hoped he was kind enough, and that he still had enough cash left, that he would be able to give her what she had come here for, or this arduous trip would have been for nothing. She had vowed once never to go to Eleanor for help, but she had no choice now. She told herself it would not be Eleanor she begged from, but rather Albert. "I would like to speak with you, Albert. May I come in?"

Eleanor suddenly stopped her crying and stared at Audra, surprised at her low, raspy voice. Albert, too, was stunned. He studied her gaunt look. Audra Potter had lost a considerable amount of weight. She looked as though she would blow away in a strong wind, and there were dark circles under her eyes. "What in God's name has happened to you, Audra?" the man asked, looking truly concerned.

"I will explain, if you will let me inside."

"Never!" Eleanor fumed.

"For God's sake, Eleanor, she's your cousin!" Albert argued.

Audra was grateful for the man's compassion. She looked boldly at Eleanor, refusing to crumble under the woman's venomous glare. "I was caught in the fighting that night in Baton Rouge," she told Eleanor. "I was attacked by Union soldiers, and I had been injured. Lee took me in only because I had no place else to go. If you will remember, your mother tried to shoot me that night. I *tried* to come home, but she would not let me, and I certainly didn't know someone would set fire to the house that night."

Eleanor pouted, folding her arms haughtily. "Maybe so, but—"

"Eleanor, can't you see something terrible has happened to Audra? She fared no better than anyone else, maybe worse. At least I managed to save my hotel and my savings and this home. If Audra was a traitor, she certainly hasn't received any special treatment for it. *Look* at her!"

The remark embarrassed Audra, but she held her cousin's eyes, showing no shame.

Satisfaction shone in Eleanor's eyes when she looked down her nose at her cousin. "What do you want? And what happened to your voice?"

"It's a long story. May I *please* come inside?"

Eleanor looked her over again, apparently relishing the little victory of presently being the one who was better off than Audra. "I don't know."

Audra took a deep breath. It was so hard to utter the words. "Eleanor, Joey is dead." Immediately the look on Eleanor's face changed to true sorrow and concern. "He was shot trying to escape Union soldiers who had captured him," Audra explained. Her voice broke on the last words, and Eleanor stepped aside.

"Come in," she said.

Audra looked ready to pass out. Albert took hold of her arm and led her into the parlor, ordering a maid, who Audra noticed was white, to bring some hot tea. He led Audra to a satin-covered settee and helped her sit down.

"I'm sorry, Audra, I really am," Eleanor told her, sitting down beside her. "I liked Joey. Everybody liked Joey."

Audra took a handkerchief from her handbag, wondering if she would ever get over losing her brother. No one's death, not even her mother's and father's, had affected her this way, for Joey was truly all she had left. "My knowing Lee . . . as you can see . . . did not keep me from suffering. I was not a traitor, Eleanor, and right now . . . if I could find a way . . . I would kill every Yankee who ever walked."

Albert took a chair nearby and pulled it close to the settee. He reached out and touched Audra's shoulder with a bony hand. "Tell us all of it, Audra. Why are you dressed this way, and who are those Negroes out there? Why did you come here in that shabby buckboard?"

Audra wiped at her eyes and spilled out her story. She had never even told Eleanor that Joseph Brennan had died. She told them about March Fredericks's attack, but she added that she had managed to get away and get hold of Joseph's rifle herself and had shot him. She never wanted anyone to know that it was Toosie who had killed the man. She told them about Lena's and Henrietta's deaths, how she lost her voice, and Eleanor gasped with horror.

"Both the mansions at Cypress Hollow and Brennan Manor are gone," Audra explained, "burned by the Yankee outlaws." She was still unable to comprehend fully all that she had lost. Joey's death had numbed her to the rest.

Nothing mattered now, not even Brennan Manor. Without Joey, she did not care anymore about trying to hang on to the only home she had ever known. "There is nothing left but the land, just the land. Even the guest house and the chapel are gone. All that's left are a few outbuildings and the Negro cabins. That's where I live now, in the Negro camp." She met Eleanor's eyes as she took a moment to sip some tea. She saw the shock and horror there, followed by disgust.

"Audra! You should move here with us. You *can't* be living with those nigger people! It just isn't proper, nor is it fitting for my own cousin!"

"They are just people, Eleanor, and they have become my only friends. They have sustained me, even saved my life after I was injured." She pulled away the scarf she had tied at her neck, showing them the scar March's knife had left. It was white and puffy, and it ran from just under her chin down the right side of her trachea, almost to the end of her collar bone.

Albert frowned sorrowfully, and Eleanor literally cried out with shock and turned away. Audra replaced the scarf and kept her attention on Albert. "I nearly died, but Toosie and the others nursed me and kept me alive. They have been very good to me, fed me, gave me shelter. They could just as easily have let me die, either by bleeding to death or burning up in the fire. They had no reason to save me, except that they are good people who for the most part hold no hatred for those who once owned them. I owe them, and that is part of the reason I am here."

Albert ran a hand through what was left of his hair. "What can we do, Audra?" the man asked.

"Wait!" Eleanor interrupted, looking at both of them. "I am sorry, very, very sorry for what happened to you, Audra. It was a terrible thing, and it must be awful for you to have lost your beautiful voice, let alone losing Joey. But the nigger issue is another thing. I won't do anything for those niggers, and it's wrong for you to try to educate them. They wanted their freedom. Let them find out the hard way that it is not all so grand and glorious as they thought, having to fend for themselves, learning to—"

"Be quiet, Eleanor!" Albert demanded, surprising Audra. The man had always seemed so timid. "Audra has been through hell, and those people out there helped her more than her own family has! Now if there is any way we *can* help, we'll *do* it! I am your husband, and I'll make the decisions. Let's hear her out."

Eleanor stiffened, her face reddening slightly. "As you wish," she said. Audra could almost hear the thunder, but she did not care what problems her request might cause between Eleanor and Albert. She cared only about helping Toosie and the others, and she had to get away from Brennan Manor and all the ugly memories or go crazy. If she could have at least buried Joey there, it would be a reason to stay; but her poor brother was buried someplace in Georgia, far from home. She would never even get to kneel beside his grave. All she had was that precious last unfinished letter.

She looked pleadingly into Albert's dark eyes. "Toosie and the others want to go to Kansas," she told the man. "They have heard even Negroes can settle there, claim land under the Homestead Act. It's their chance to start new, to have something of their very own. I am going with them."

"Audra!"

Audra kept her eyes on Albert, paying no heed to Eleanor's shock. "They're good people," she said. "I can help them get started, help teach the children. I have no place left to go, anyway. Brennan Manor is gone, and I have no means to rebuild it or to farm it. I was waiting for Joey to come home. I thought maybe he and I could save it, but without Joey, I don't even care anymore, Albert." She twisted her handkerchief in her hands. "I was hoping . . . hoping you might be able to give me some cash so that the Negroes can buy the necessary supplies to go west. I'd be willing to sign over the deeds to both Brennan Manor and Cypress Hollow. The buildings are gone, but there is always the land, Albert, and land is always valuable and can't be destroyed. An enterprising businessman like yourself can surely find a way to make money off that land again."

Albert sat back in his chair, rubbing his chin in thought. Eleanor rose, walking to look out a window at the

Negroes in the wagon. She looked back at Audra. "You
would *sell* Brennan Manor *and* Cypress Hollow, just to help
niggers?"

Audra rose. "They are my friends, Eleanor, and I wish
you would stop calling them niggers. They are Negro, but
more then that, they are just people, like you and me. They
are going to survive this. They just need a little bit of help."
She looked back at Albert. "And money to get started. Can
you buy the plantations, Albert? The deeds burned up with
the houses, but I will go with you to see an attorney and
draw up whatever documents you need to prove I have sold
the land to you."

Albert also rose then, towering over her. "I managed to
hang on to my hotel, Audra, and my savings; but with things
the way they are, and the possibility I would have to pay
some kind of taxes on that land to keep it, I have to be very
careful. I know we're talking about several thousand acres,
but I couldn't give you more than a thousand dollars; and I
would hardly feel right giving you such a paltry sum for so
much land."

Audra felt sick inside. The man was right. It *was* a paltry sum for thousands of acres of rich farmland. There was
a time when her father would pay more than a thousand
dollars for just one good Negro farmhand. Now she was expected to take a thousand dollars for all of Brennan Manor
and Cypress Hollow.

She watched Albert's eyes, knew he was an honest man
and probably telling her the truth. She really had no choice.
They could not continue to survive where they were, even
if she deeded the land over to the Negroes. As long as they
stayed here in Louisiana, they were going to have a hard
time of it. They would get no help, and already groups of
whites were banding together to harass and murder Negroes, blaming them for the problems that had now befallen
the South. They had to get out, many of them simply because there were too many bad memories on the old plantations.

"I'll take the thousand, but it has to be United States
money, not Confederate. We both know the value of Confederate money by now."

"I have a safe in my hotel with Federal money in it. I can get it today and we can go to my lawyer's office and have something signed."

"Fine." Audra put out her hand. "It's a deal then."

Albert shook her hand, but he did not look as happy as a man should look when he had just stolen a fortune in property. "I'm sorry, Audra. Are you sure you want this? I feel like I have robbed you."

"This is what I want. I just need to go away, Albert. I don't know if I'll always stay with Toosie and the others. Right now I just take things a day at a time. I can't think about tomorrow."

The man sighed and leaned down to kiss her cheek. "I am sorry about Joey. I never even knew him, but from talk of him, I can imagine what a fine boy he was."

Audra turned away. "Thank you."

"Just give me a moment to change and get the keys to the safe." The man left Audra and Eleanor standing in the parlor. Eleanor came closer, again a victorious look in her eyes.

"Now I will own Cypress Hollow, after all," she said, her chin raised high. "Richard would be happy to know that."

Audra ignored the remark. "I sincerely hope Albert can rebuild, Eleanor. I would be very happy to see homes at Cypress Hollow and Brennan Manor again. I would like nothing more than for that land to be a beautiful plantation once more, as elegant and peaceful as it once was, even if it means that you will get to be the one who owns it." She touched her throat, which still got sore whenever she had to talk much. "I don't care anymore, Eleanor, and I am tired . . . just terribly tired. You can hate me, feel victorious, whatever you want to feel. As for myself, I am tired of fighting and hatred of all kinds. I just want to leave and start over someplace new. I might never see you again, so let's just part friends."

Eleanor seemed to soften a little. She sighed, and her eyes actually filled with tears. "I truly loved Richard," she said.

"Yes, I believe you did," Audra answered. "And I truly loved Lee Jeffreys."

Eleanor nodded, swallowing and wiping at a tear. "Do you still?"

Audra shook her head. "I honestly don't know anymore. It isn't likely I'll ever see him again, so it really doesn't matter. I told him never to come back here when the war was over. Too much has happened for us to be able to pick up the pieces. Now, if he *does* come back, I won't be here. That part of my life is over, Eleanor. I have to go on to new things."

Eleanor nodded. "I suppose, but you shouldn't go off with those Negroes, Audra. Albert would give you whatever you need to go someplace else."

"Where would I go? I certainly can't go North and live among Yankees. Most major cities in the South are gone, burned. Right now there is no opportunity here for a single woman. There are no jobs, and there won't be for a long time to come. I can't farm the plantations all by myself, and I don't have the money to rebuild. I have friends among those Negroes, and they need my help. Besides, I need to keep busy however I can."

Albert came back into the room, coming up to take Audra's arm. "Would you rather rest here awhile first?"

"No. I'm all right."

"You are terribly thin, Audra," Eleanor told her.

"I wasn't able to eat much because of my throat. Actually I have gained back a little weight, but ever since hearing about Joey, I've lost my appetite again. I eat only because I have no choice if I want to live."

"It will get better," Eleanor assured her. "Time heals." She walked closer and embraced Audra, but Audra sensed her awkwardness, as though part of her wanted to care and love, and another part would never stop hating.

Audra put her arms around her cousin's hefty body and embraced her in return. "Be good to Albert," she told her. "He is a kind man."

Eleanor pulled away, tears in her eyes. "God be with you, Audra. You shouldn't be going off like this. You could stay right here."

Audra shook her head. "No. I have to do this. Good-bye, Eleanor." She took Albert's arm and the two of them left.

Eleanor sighed. "Good-bye, Audra." She began to smile a little, and she picked up the skirt of her dress and whirled about the room, imagining she was dancing with Richard at Cypress Hollow. Now she would own it! She, Eleanor McAllister Mahoney, mistress of Cypress Hollow *and* Brennan Manor! At last she would hold the position she once thought would always be Audra's. Poor Audra, so thin, penniless, her voice gone. Part of her truly did feel sorry for her cousin, but another part of her could not help celebrating.

She stopped dancing and hurried to a desk to take out paper and ink. She must make a list of what they would do first to begin rebuilding. The house must come first, for she intended to live on the plantations part of the time. Yes, Albert would rebuild. He always did anything she asked. Once a house was finished, she could vacation there, remind Albert how much she loved the country. It would be a way to get away from Albert, maybe take lovers there. It would be absolutely delightful, except for one thing. Richard would not be there. If only she could have spent those last few months with him, but Audra had stolen that from her, and that was the one thing she could never forgive.

"Go on to Kansas with your niggers," she muttered as she dipped the pen into an inkwell. "I'm sorry for what happened to you Audra, but you're getting what you deserve for keeping me and Richard apart."

Ballroom, she wrote. Yes, they must have a ballroom. No proper rich southern woman had a home without a ballroom, where she could hold grand parties, and there *would* be grand parties again, wouldn't there? Somehow life would return to the way it used to be. It just had to.

AUGUST 1865

Bennett James looked up from his desk, and he immediately sent three other men out of his room when he saw who was standing in the doorway. "Lee!" he exclaimed, coming around from behind his desk to shake his hand. "My God, man, I can't believe you're really back! It's been four years!"

Lee shook the man's hand firmly, and in the next moment they embraced. "How have things been, Bennett?"

"Fine, just fine! Oh, there are a few businesses that will have to make some adjustments now that the war is over, but that only means more business for us. Come and sit down!"

Bennett walked over to pour some whiskey for them both, noticing out of the corner of his eye that Lee had a slight limp. "I'm sorry about your father and brother, Lee. And that you'd been wounded." He turned, taking a good look at the tall, handsome young man who had left the firm to go off to fight for the Union. He had definitely aged some, and now was thirty-five. He was a little thinner, and there was a haunted look to those blue eyes. He had seen other men come back from the war with that same look, and from the horrors he had read about, he could not blame any of them for being deeply affected. It was reported that some had returned mentally unstable, alcoholics, some with wounds and diseases that were sure to plague them the rest of their lives.

"So," he said, taking Lee a glass of whiskey, "are you through with the army, Colonel Jeffreys?" he asked, putting on a smile and trying to bring a little cheer to the moment. Lee took the glass, and Bennett noticed he gulped the whiskey like water.

"Major General," Lee answered. "General Sherman gave me another promotion two months before the war ended. I spent the last three months since then in Washington, helping muster out other volunteers, making sure they got the proper pay and such, kind of a fizzle after all the cannon and shooting and fires of the last four years. It seems strange to know the damn war is over. I'm glad, but I don't really see what the hell was accomplished by all those men losing their lives." He handed out the glass. "Pour me another."

Bennett frowned, taking the glass and filling it again.

"Yes, well, it's a sad thing. War never does make much sense. Just a bunch of men battling it out to prove they're right about something. Have you been to see your brother Carl?"

"I have." Lee took a chair, then reached over Bennett's desk and took a cigar from a silver box the man always kept there full of fresh smokes. He lit it and puffed on it for a moment. Bennett handed him the second glass of whiskey.

"Cy Jordan died, you know. Our firm now represents Jeffreys Enterprises. Carl will be glad to work with his brother."

Lee swallowed more liquor, thinking sadly how just about everyone he ever knew before the war was dead now . . . even Joey. If he could just stop having nightmares about that day, maybe he could get back to living again, but the memory would not stop plaguing him, and he knew the only way he would be able to forgive himself was to be forgiven first by Audra. He had to find her.

"He won't *be* working with me. I've already talked to him, and he understands and has promised to keep you on anyway."

Bennett frowned, going to sit down at his desk. "What do you mean? You're all the family Carl has left, Lee. Surely you're going to stay here in New York now and come back into the firm."

Lee studied his cigar. "You're a good man, Bennett. You'll do fine on your own. You can take my name off the firm's title and figure up what you feel my share of the profits should be. I don't want much, considering the fact that you've been doing all the work for four years now. Consider yourself the owner of the firm. I'll sign whatever papers you want me to sign."

Bennett sighed, leaning back in his chair. "Lee, you can't let the war ruin your future. I have a damn good idea how bad it was because I've read it all and I've seen some of the aftereffects and a lot of the wounded myself, men without arms and legs, men returned from southern prison camps who are nothing more than walking skeletons. I also hear the South is in a hell of a mess, major cities burned—"

"It isn't just that," Lee interrupted. "Something happened that I have to try to set straight, if possible. I made a promise to a dying man, a boy, actually. I'm the one who killed him, and I intend to keep the promise I made him."

"A rebel?"

Lee could see Joey's face as vividly as if it had all happened yesterday, those trusting, forgiving eyes as he lay dying from Lee's own bullet. He felt himself breaking out into a cold sweat again, and he finished the second glass of whiskey. "Yeah. A rebel. It's a long story, and I'm not ready to talk about it." He sighed deeply. "I am also not ready to come back here, and I can't keep dangling as an absent partner forever. I'm sorry."

Bennett studied the tragedy in Lee's eyes, and his heart went out to the man. "I hope you can get this matter settled, Lee. How about that leg? Will it ever get any better? I noticed you limping. Do you still have pain?"

"Some. The doctors say I probably always will. I took shrapnel in my left thigh. They think maybe whoever took it out didn't get it all. I'll probably have to have it cut open again sometime, but I can't quite bring myself to think about that right now, after all the blood and stink I've seen in the makeshift army hospitals in the field. I just might decide to live with it the way it is."

Bennett rubbed at the back of his neck, thinking about all the good young men who had suffered so in this senseless war. Even Abraham Lincoln had ended up giving his life. "Well, you're a damn good lawyer, the best. You should get back to work, keep yourself busy."

"I will eventually. I just can't yet. I've talked to Carl, withdrew most of what had built up in my trust fund. I signed a paper taking myself out of any interest in Jeffreys Enterprises. He'll probably be contacting you about it. The only thing I wanted was Maple Shadows. I told Carl to keep withdrawing from future deposits to my trust fund until he has taken the amount we agreed I should pay for the place." Sweet memories swept through him then, of a summer long ago, a lovely young woman with a song for a voice, her hair glinting red in the sun. "I'd like to go back there some day,

when I can maybe be myself again, if I even know who that
is."

Bennett leaned forward, resting his elbows on his desk.
"What about that woman down in Louisiana you found out
had married someone else? I heard Baton Rouge was practically burned to the ground, and a lot of plantation owners
are penniless now. I don't suppose you're going to try to
find out if she's all right?"

Lee smiled sadly. "That's another long story. I was
among those who invaded Baton Rouge. Audra was there,
staying with an aunt because things had gotten too dangerous at the plantation. Her husband had just died about
a month before that—stabbed by a Negro with a pitchfork."

Bennett made a face. "Good God, what a way to
die."

Lee nodded, puffing on the cigar again. "At any rate,
we saw each other again, and we almost . . ." He rose, walking to a window. "Like I said, that's another long story. In
her mind now I'm just a stinking Yankee who is responsible
for whatever bad things have happened to her. Trouble is,
she doesn't know just *how* responsible." It was storming
outside, and Lee watched drops of rain splash against a
windowpane. He remembered another rainy night, down
in Louisiana at Brennan Manor . . . when a woman came
to him for comfort while the rain fell and thunder rolled.

"You're confusing me, Lee. What happened with
Audra?"

Lee faced him, and Bennett was startled by the terrible
agony in his eyes. "I can't talk about it now. After I've gone
to do what I have to do, I'll explain it all to you, either in
a letter or in person. It's still too hard to talk about. I just
thought I'd come by and explain why I can't come back into
business right now. I might even start over again someplace
else. It all depends on what happens while I'm gone."

"You're going to find her?"

Lee walked over and poured his own third glass of
whiskey, and Bennett felt a deep concern for whatever was
torturing the man enough to make him down so many shots
of liquor so quickly.

"Yes," Lee answered. "I'm going to fine her. God only knows what will happen then." He wondered what Audra would think if she knew he still carried that song. The paper was worn and thin, nearly ready to tear at the places where it had been folded and unfolded so many times. He still had not been able to throw it away.

30

"I got orders, missy. No niggers gets on this boat."

Audra glared at the captain of the steamboat that was heading upriver from Baton Rouge to St. Louis. "I will give you fifty dollars extra—yours to pocket."

The short, pudgy man grinned through tobacco-stained teeth, wondering at the low, raspy voice that came out of the mouth of such a frail-looking woman. "You don't understand, lady. They's a lot of white folks and former slave owners who don't think it's right for niggers to be tryin' to settle on they own. Some niggers tryin' to git out of Loosiana finds themselves arrested." His eyes moved over Audra, and he put a hand to her waist. "Now I don't have to tell you what would happen to a white woman if she was arrested for *helpin'* niggers git off on they own. Everybody knows what a white woman who travels with niggers is." His hand moved toward her breast. "You like them nigger men, do you?"

Audra pushed his hand away and pulled a revolver from her handbag, which she carried by its string over her left arm. She pressed the gun against the captain's stomach. "I'd rather hang for shooting you than pay for my passage the way you're suggesting." With her free hand she pulled down the high, laced-trimmed collar of the dress Wilena had made for her from deep-green cotton sateen. She raised her chin and let the man see her scar. "Mister, I've been through hell already, and there isn't one thing you can tell me that will frighten me off." She pushed the collar back up, glaring at him boldly. "I offered you fifty dollars. You can either take it, or I'll go to the steamboat docked beside you and try *that* captain. If you want *him* to make the extra fifty dollars, that's fine with me; but if you touch me again, your insides will be spilling over your belt, and fifty dollars will be of no use to you."

The man watched her eyes, green fire, they were. The woman meant what she said. He glanced past her at the group of at least fifty or sixty Negroes, including several children, who waited on the docks with wagons and supplies. He looked back at Audra. "They've got too much stuff. I can't git all that on this boat."

"You carry passengers and freight, Captain, and you're empty right now. I already checked with the clerk who handles your fares. You have plenty of room below for the wagons and most of the Negroes."

The man rubbed at his mouth. "You got livestock?"

"Only a few chickens in cages. We will buy livestock when we get to Kansas."

He looked her over scathingly again. "Where'd a bunch of niggers get that kind of money? They been raidin' and stealin' from poor, burned-out white folks?"

"It's *my* money. Now, will you take us on?"

She still held the pistol to his stomach. "All right," he grumbled, "but you tell them to stay below and out of sight as much as possible. I don't want people throwin' stones or shootin' at my boat."

"Fine. They will do whatever you want. Just get us to

St. Louis. If you will take us on from there along the Missouri to Independence, I will give you yet another fifty dollars in addition to the regular fare."

The man glanced around as though worried about who
might see him. "All right, but tell them to wait till dark, then
get on board fast as they can. They's men that watches the
docks. They don't like losin' their cheap labor, and they'll do
anything to keep the niggers from leavin', let alone bein' angry that them people thinkin' they can just go off and own
land and all. It ain't right."

Audra shoved her pistol back into her handbag. "There
are a lot of things that aren't right, Captain," she said, holding his eyes boldly. "I used to be one of the wealthiest
woman in Louisiana, and now I am reduced to this. If you
don't want to do this for the Negroes, then do it for people
like me and the rest of the South, *white* people who need
your help."

The man seemed to soften a little. "Show me the fifty
dollars so I know you ain't lyin'."

Audra's eyes displayed disgust. She reached into her
handbag and pulled out the bills. "Federal greenbacks, not
Confederate money. You'll get it when we reach St. Louis,
not before."

The captain adjusted his hat nervously. "All right. Come
back tonight at midnight, but not here. I'll move my boat
upriver to the docks of the burned-out warehouses and pick
you up there. They don't watch that area as much. Right
now just git the hell out of here. Make like I turned you
down, or I won't have a boat to take you in."

Audra had no choice but to trust the man. "Fine. We'll
meet you at midnight." She turned and left, telling Joseph
and Elijah and the others that the captain had turned them
down and perhaps they should make camp for the night.
"We'll hole up at the abandoned warehouses tonight where
we won't be in anyone's way. We'll try again tomorrow." She
would tell them the truth later. This was her family now.
Besides the thousand dollars Albert had paid her, she had
managed to make even more money by selling a few items
from the two plantations, buggies, a few of the livestock that
had not run off, even some valuable jewelry she had sal-

vaged. It was enough to pay their passage, which would make the trip to Kansas quicker and easier.

She wished they were not leaving so late. Here it was September already. Sometimes, she'd heard, winters could be harsh in Kansas, but she was determined not to wait out another winter here. It was becoming too dangerous. Bands of whites had been forming, men who rode out at night and harassed and brutalized Negroes, especially those who were trying to get out of the state. Some were arrested, their valuables and money confiscated. Poverty-stricken terrorists, fearing the loss of cheap labor, were forming mobs to discourage Negroes from fleeing. Some of the threats and whippings and murders were carried out by men who were angry that the Negroes seemed to be the reason for all the devastation in the South.

Everything Audra had feared and predicted would happen if the Negroes were freed was coming true, only it was all much worse than she had imagined. Her "family" of Negroes lived in terror of being the next target, and she was anxious to get them out of the state and to a free state that was so far welcoming homesteaders, even Negroes. She could only pray that the bands of white marauders and "nigger-haters" would not follow and cause trouble even in Kansas. Poor Toosie was not having an easy time with her pregnancy, and she should not be traveling, especially to a place where the winter could be much colder than anything she was used to; but they had no choice. To winter it out back at the plantation was to invite more trouble, and they had had their share of trouble with March Fredericks's attack, let alone hearing stories of what had happened to Negroes at other locations.

Getting everything sold that she could to raise money, then buying enough supplies for their journey, had taken more time than she had supposed. The biggest problem had been *finding* the supplies, as there was not much of anything left anywhere. She had been forced to travel to several different cities to get everything, and even then she had to convince sellers that the supplies were for her "white" family, not Negroes.

Wearily she walked beside the wagons as they made

their way along the docks toward the shell-like buildings that used to be warehouses. What was left of the supplies in those buildings had long ago been looted, by both Federals and citizens of Baton Rouge who had lost everything. She had no idea what kept her going, except the knowledge that she had to get Toosie and the others away from here. Until they reached their destination and decided where to homestead, these people needed someone who knew how to deal with white people. Long years of bondage had put the fear in them, leaving them all, even the strongest of the men, too timid to deal with men like the captain of the steamship. Audra had vowed not to leave them until they were safe in Kansas, but even then she was not sure what she would do, if she would ever leave. In some ways she had grown just as dependent on Toosie and Wilena and the others as they were on her. They all needed each other.

"The captain will pick us up tonight at midnight by the abandoned warehouses," she told Elijah quietly. "Don't tell the others until later. I want them to look dejected and discouraged. The captain thinks the wrong kind of men are watching. He wants them to think he turned us down."

Elijah nodded. "You don' have to do this, Miss Audra," he told her for probably the hundredth time. "It's too dangerous for a white woman."

"We'll be all right, Elijah. God took everything else away from me. He won't take this. We're going to make it to Kansas. I feel it." She put a hand on his arm. "You will all have your own homes and farms. With what money I have left when we get there, we'll buy some livestock. We'll build our own little town, and I'll open a school."

Elijah grinned. "Maybe we call our new town Brennan. Brennan, Kansas. How about that?"

Audra smiled in return, and Elijah thought what a rare sight it was. There was a time when he never would have dreamed that the young, spoiled Audra Brennan he had known before he was sold off by her father would be selling Joseph Brennan's plantation to raise money to help Negroes start a new life, let alone risk her own life and honor by going along with them and teaching their children. The war had certainly changed people, some for the worse, but some for the better. He watched her eyes begin to tear.

"That would be wonderful, Elijah! Brennan, Kansas." She squeezed his arm. "We can do it! I know we can do it! I haven't had this much hope in a long time."

Elijah's smile faded. "Hope is somethin' we knows all about, Miss Audra. For a long, long time it was all we had, hope that some day we'd be free, no matter what the cost. It feels good, Miss Audra, and God will bless you for helpin' us. If Joey was here, he'd be doin' the same thing."

The pain of Joey's death stabbed at her heart again, and Audra turned to keep walking. "Yes. He would."

Brennan, Kansas, she thought. She liked the sound of it. Joey would like that, too.

Lee halted his horse in front of the makeshift courthouse in Baton Rouge. There was at least some new construction going on, but so far the devastation he had seen was overwhelming. What haunted him the most was what he had found at Brennan Manor, a gutted mansion, a couple of graves that did not look very old, and a few families of trashy-looking white people squatting in what was once the slave quarters. None of them knew what had happened to Audra or Joseph Brennan, and none of the Negroes who had belonged to the plantation were anywhere to be found.

Who was in those graves? If one of them was Audra, he had nothing left to live for. He had been sorely tempted to dig them up, but he wouldn't have been able to bear looking at his once-beautiful Audra rotting away, and the bodies were probably decayed too badly, anyway, to tell who they were. The whites there said they had no idea where anyone had gone, but because of a horrible stench that came from an old well they had uncovered, they found the decaying body of a man.

What man? Someone had thrown his body into that well to hide it. What in God's name had happened at Brennan Manor, and where was Audra? His only hope was that someone at the courthouse would have some kind of records. Maybe Joseph Brennan had sold the place and moved on. Or was it Joseph's body in the well? Maybe the Negroes had murdered him and Audra both, then fled the law, if there *was* any kind of law right now in Louisiana.

He dismounted, tied his horse, and behind it a pack horse. Ugly memories plagued him being here. It was like coming back into the war, for the town remained burned out. He had stopped to ask a group of young white boys where he might find some records of land sales, and they had directed him to this church, one of the few buildings left untouched the night Baton Rouge burned. Those boys still followed him, and he felt uneasy. He was taking a chance coming down here so soon after the war, although other northerners had already started filtering in, men with money, ready to buy up the South and gather in the victor's spoils. It irritated him that on top of all the horror these southerners had already experienced, they would now have to put up with the humiliation of being raped by swindlers and the greedy wealthy from the North who would come down here and take advantage of people who had been stripped of everything they owned. The young men who followed him now probably thought he was one of those who had come to buy up land.

What's it to you, Yankee? one of them had sneered when he asked about a land office. He had explained he was just looking for someone he had known once and wondered if they had sold their property, but right now he was wishing he had tried to fake a southern accent, except he probably would not have done a very good job of it. A New Yorker couldn't stick out more obviously than in a place like Louisiana, and he had a feeling that if the boys following him knew he had been a Major General in the Union Army and had been here when Baton Rouge was burned, they would have pounced on him in a second.

Because he knew he was in dangerous territory, he wore a handgun strapped to his side under his fringed deerskin jacket, a jacket he found was most comfortable and practical for constant traveling in the out-of-doors. He wore brown wool pants and knee-high leather boots. It was cool even in Louisiana. It had been a very cold October in New

York when he left, and most leaves had already turned bright colors and were falling from the trees.

He walked up the steps of the church and went inside, approaching a gray-haired man wearing spectacles who sat behind one of several desks. Pews had been pushed to the sides of the interior, and several other people were there, one man arguing that someone had better find his deed because he needed to prove he owned a certain piece of land.

"I'm sorry, Mr. Jennings, but everything burned up in the fires. We're doing everything we can, mostly by people who know other people and can testify as to what they owned. Now give me a rough description of the boundaries of your property."

What an ungodly mess, Lee thought, feeling partially responsible. He felt guilty for a lot of things lately, but the one thing he would never get over was killing Joey. It ate at him until sometimes he would drink himself into oblivion and then be sick for the next two days. It was a vicious cycle he had fallen into, and he was struggling to get out of it, only because he needed to keep his senses straight until he found Audra. Once he knew she was all right, and once he had told her the truth, he could drink until the whiskey killed him. Death sounded pretty damn good sometimes. Maybe then he could find some peace.

"Excuse me," he spoke up. "I'm trying to find someone who knows something about Brennan Manor and Cypress Hollow, two big plantations that have been deserted."

The gray-haired man looked up at him, eyeing him suspiciously. "If you're another one of those Yankee bastards come here to steal what's left," he drawled, "you're too late. Mr. Brennan's property has already been sold, Mr. Potter's, too, for the paltry sum of one thousand dollars."

Lee felt a whirlwind of emotion, elated at finding someone who knew Joseph Brennan, appalled and concerned to discover Brennan Manor and Cypress Hollow had been sold for a mere thousand dollars. Why? "A thousand dollars for *both* plantations?" he asked in astonishment.

"Yes, sir. Reason I know without looking up the records is because I knew Joseph Brennan and Richard Potter both. I worked in the records office of our courthouse for years

. . . until it was burned down," he finished with a sneer, looking Lee over scathingly. He leaned back in his chair. "Just a few days ago the buyer was here, a Mr. Albert Mahoney."

"Mahoney?" The name sounded familiar, but Lee could not quite place it.

"He is the husband of Joseph Brennan's niece, Eleanor. They live in New Orleans."

Lee took a chair. "Of course! I remember now. Audra told me about Albert. He—" He leaned closer. "Thank God I found you, mister. Look, I'm not here to buy anybody's land. All I care about is finding out what happened to Audra Brennan Potter. Do you know anything about her? Is she still alive?"

The man eyed him closely. "Why?"

Lee sighed, removing his hat. "I'm Lee Jeffreys. My mother was Anna Jeffreys, and she gave Audra voice lessons in Connecticut back in fifty-nine. I kept in touch with Audra all through the war, then lost track of her. My mother was very fond of her, and I feel obligated to find out what happened to her and make sure she's all right."

The man studied him a moment longer, trying to decide if this Yankee was on the level. "Well, I expect she's still alive, seeing as how she's the one who signed her land over to Mr. Mahoney. Her father died, you know, and Mahoney told me her brother was killed in the war. Yankee raiders burned the place down, so Mahoney says. She needed money bad, and a thousand dollars was all Mahoney could pay her for the land. Crazy as it sounds, Mrs. Potter needed the money to help a bunch of Negroes get out of Louisiana. They headed for Kansas to homestead."

"Kansas!" Lee could hardly believe his ears. Audra? Selling her precious Brennan Manor to help *Negroes*? Audra? Leaving Louisiana for a rugged western state like Kansas?

"Lots of Negroes have been heading to Kansas and Nebraska and other places out west now," the clerk told him. "They can settle there under the Homestead Act. They all have big dreams of having their own land, but I'll wager a lot of them won't make it. They don't know how to take care of themselves. Why Mrs. Potter, of all people, would go with them instead of go to live with her cousin in New Orleans, I'll never understand. The woman had to be pretty destitute to sell that property for so little money, but Mr. Mahoney says she practically insisted on it. The man got a hell of a deal. He felt guilty about it, but that was all he could pay. A man has to watch his money these days, you know."

Lee hardly heard the man. What an ironic twist of fate! He remembered that first summer, how Audra had looked down on Negroes and had ordered him not to be too friendly with Toosie. She had been almost humiliated to discover Toosie was her half sister. Why would she go off to Kansas with Negroes when she apparently could have lived comfortably with her cousin Eleanor? But then Eleanor probably hated her for the night her own home burned and her mother died . . . while Audra lay in the arms of a Yankee man.

The memory hit him so hard that he drew in his breath and stood up. It would be wonderful to find her and be able to hold her again, marry her, keep her in his bed forever and live happily ever after. But there would be no happily ever after for either of them. He might as well quit fantasizing. "Do you have any idea how long ago this happened? When Mrs. Potter might have left for Kansas?"

The clerk removed his glasses and rubbed at his eyes. "Well, Mr. Mahoney was in here maybe two weeks ago to register for the land. The actual sale took place, oh, I think about August. I remember him saying something about her supposed to be leaving by the first of September."

"Damn! That means she's probably been gone a good six weeks already. I'll never catch up, and once she gets to Kansas, I'll have one hell of a time finding her."

"That's sure. Kansas is a big place. All those western states and territories are big, and with so many Negroes going out there, it won't be easy finding the particular ones she's traveling with."

"At least I know the name of one of them," Lee said, partly to himself. Toosie. How many people had a name like that? It was all he had to go on. "Thanks, mister." He left the building, wondering if he should go see Eleanor and her husband first in New Orleans. If he did that, it would cost him time, and time was important. They probably couldn't tell him much more than he already knew. The sooner he got to Kansas, the better. One man alone on a horse could travel a lot faster than a herd of families in wagons, which was probably how she was traveling with the Negroes.

Yankee raiders. What had they done to Audra? What a horror it must have been for her when they came and destroyed Brennan Manor. Had they also destroyed Audra? Hurt her, or maybe raped her? Perhaps that was why she was fleeing Louisiana, why she had given up on everything and left with the Negroes. Or maybe she had given up for another reason. Maybe it was the letter he had sent, telling her Joey had been killed. Yes, that would certainly make her give up. She had probably been trying to hang on to that land for Joey.

Again the memory made him take a flask of whiskey from his saddlebag. He took a swallow, wondering how in hell he was going to get through the rest of his life this way, waking up covered with sweat from the nightmare of his rifle going off, his bullet exploding into Joey's chest, the look of terror and surprise in those innocent eyes.

He put the flask back and started to mount his horse when something hit him in the back of the head. He fell against the horse, then slid to the ground, the initial blow leaving him unable to think straight or fight back. He was surrounded by leering faces of young men, and he recognized one as the boy he had talked to earlier, asking where to find a land office. Somewhere in the back of his mind he knew what was happening. The gang of young thugs in a now-lawless town had decided to "get themselves a Yankee," take out on one man their frustration from the war.

The attack was vicious and quick. He remembered there must have been at least ten of them. Even at that he might have put up a good struggle, since he was much bigger and more experienced than any of them—but for some reason he could hardly move. He could not even get to his pistol before fists and feet rained blows, brutal kicks to his head, back, and groin, and again to his head, until blackness swirled around him.

"Kill the son of a bitch!" someone shouted.

"You freed the niggers, you Yankee bastard!"

"You burned down my mother's house!"

"You killed my brother!"

Brother. Brother. The word stuck in Lee's head. Yes, he'd killed someone's brother. He'd killed Joey, and probably a *lot* of other people's brothers. But his own brother had also been killed. Was this his punishment for Joey? Memories passed through his mind as he lay motionless while the boys kept kicking him. Memories . . . Audra . . . the war . . . Joey . . . Voices became echoes, and there was no longer any sun . . . only darkness.

"Get the hell out of here!" a man yelled. Lee did not hear. He was not aware that the young men had finally run off. A stranger knelt over him. "My God, look at him! Somebody help me get this man to a doctor! They've practically beat him to death!"

"He deserves it. He's a Yankee," someone else spoke up.

"And we're all still human beings!" the stranger answered. He rose to look around at the crowd that had gathered around the northerner. They looked back at the minister, who preached in the very church that was now being used as a temporary courthouse. "Is this what the war has done to us?" the pastor yelled at the crowd. "Made us animals? Made us forget how to forgive, how to be *human*? The war is *over*! Some of you men gather round here and take this man to Doc Wilson's place. I'll tend to his horses and supplies."

A few men grudgingly picked up Lee's limp body and carried it away. The preacher looked up at the sky, then closed his eyes and prayed . . . prayed that somehow there could be true peace again, prayed that the South could find a way to forget and forgive what had been done to them. He opened his eyes to look around at a few people who had not left, some of them looking guilty and sheepish.

"I remind you of Jesus' teachings," he admonished them. "Matthew six fourteen: after Christ taught us the

Lord's Prayer! *For if ye forgive men their trespasses, your heavenly Father will also forgive you: but if ye forgive not men their trespasses, neither will your Father forgive your trespasses!* And First Kings," he continued, tired of all the hatred, wondering if there was any godliness left in mankind. "*And forgive thy people that have sinned against thee, and all their transgressions wherein they have transgressed against thee, and give them compassion.* The hatred must end, people! We will never rebuild and get our lives back together if we let the hatred continue to burn in our souls! Go now, and ask God to forgive you for not being willing to help this man here today!"

A few of them wandered off, and the preacher untied Lee's horse and led it, and the pack horse tied behind it, toward the doctor's office. He and the doctor would have to search through the Yankee's possessions and try to find out who he was, where his relatives might be. They should be notified if the man died. He shook his head at the realization that the war was not really over at all. For the South, it would not end for a long, long time to come.

SEPTEMBER 1866

Audra threw another potato into the sack she dragged along beside her. She stopped for a moment, sitting down wearily, smack in the dirt of the potato field. She took a moment to study her hands. The creases of her knuckles and her fingernails were caked with dirt from sorting through bunches of potatoes after she dug them from the ground with a fork, picking out those that had been stabbed. They would have to be eaten first, before they rotted. The best potatoes would be saved to sell.

She laughed lightly at how she must look, for it was better to laugh than to cry. The Negroes had taught her that. You looked at the bright side of things and took hope in that, for if a person dwelled too long on the dark side, he or she might wake up some morning and decide there was no reason even to get out of bed.

The bright side was that they had managed to claim some good ground in middle Kansas, that they had survived that first terribly cold winter, and that they had even been helped by Indians. At first they all thought the Indians had come to murder them, for they had heard only bad things about the Plains tribes; but the Cheyenne and Pawnee, although bitter enemies with each other, both seemed fascinated by the Negroes, who had managed to communicate with the Indians through trade—buffalo meat for cloth; hides for potatoes. That first winter the Cheyenne had come across their miserable little tent settlement, and they had shown Audra and the Negroes how to build much warmer shelter with skins. They had given them a good supply of buffalo meat, and Audra could not even imagine what her father would have thought to see her living in a tipi like some wild thing of the plains.

This past spring they had begun their first planting. One thing the Negroes knew how to do well was plow fields and plant seeds. Through the summer their land began to blossom into cornfields, potato fields, and vegetable gardens, thanks to a godsend of perfect rations of sun and rain. Audra decided she must have been right when she told Elijah that God meant for them to succeed, for they had made it here safely, and God sent those Cheyenne to keep them from starving or freezing to death over their first winter.

This spring some Pawnee had come along and traded them several horses for one pound of tobacco. They taught them they could make good fires with dried buffalo manure, which they learned later from white travelers were called buffalo chips. This summer they had managed to build a few homes, some from logs cut from cottonwood trees that grew along the Arkansas River not far away; most from sod dug from the earth in solid chunks that made for a cool dwelling in summer and, they hoped, a warmer place to stay this next winter. They had learned to build the sod houses from some settlers who had lived east of their little village and passed through as they moved on to Denver, deciding they might have an easier life in the new, growing mining town in Colorado.

Here and there, little by little, from Indians and whites alike, they were learning how to survive. Brennan, Kansas, had its own little school, where Audra taught whenever she was not needed to help in the fields. They had set up their own supply store, selling vegetables to travelers on their way to Denver. Soon they would also have corn and potatoes to sell. Out of sheer luck they had apparently picked an area frequented by people from many walks of life, all of whom usually were in need of food as they journeyed westward. Audra had helped the Negroes learn about money, how to count it, how to add and subtract and make change. They had also discovered that travelers in need were usually willing to pay ridiculous prices for food, especially those who were sure they were going to "get rich" once they reached Denver and the gold fields that lay in the Rockies.

Audra wiped at sweat on her forehead, realizing she had probably just smeared dirt from her hands onto her face, but what did it matter anymore how she looked? Her skin was a reddish-brown from a summer of working outside; she never seemed to be able to get her hands really clean; and she had not felt beautiful and elegant or worn a lovely gown in years. Perhaps she never would again.

She got to her feet and picked up the potato fork, plunging it into the stubborn soil again, straining to push down on the handle so that the prongs would come up through the ground and catch another bunch of potatoes. She grunted as she yanked them up, then shook them lightly to get most of the dirt off. She bent over then to pick through them, again throwing the good ones into one sack, the injured ones into another. To her surprise, she had discovered she found an inner peace and satisfaction working in the earth. She liked the smell of the dirt, enjoyed watching things grow that she had helped plant.

They had bought the corn seed and tiny planter potatoes in St. Louis, as well as seed for all kinds of vegetables; and as though God were performing some kind of miracle, she still had some money left. Now they would actually make a little money selling some of their food. If they handled things right, planted more every year, they could eventually make a very good living here. She did not doubt it, because she did not doubt the abilities and determination of the Negroes to make this work.

Toosie had had her baby, a healthy son she had named Joseph Brennan Jakes. What else would he be called but Joey? He was a happy baby because although he and his parents had little in the way of material things, they shared a wonderful love. Joseph and Wilena had also had a child, the sixth for Wilena. The little girl was certainly not Joseph's first child, but it was the first one he had been allowed to see and hold and love, the first child he had bred out of love for its mother.

This was a hard life, but she felt she had learned more these past few years with the Negroes than in all of her life before that. She taught them the basics of words and numbers, but they taught her the basics of survival. They taught her faith, strength, courage, and human values. She could laugh now, realizing that laughter was as much a healing factor as crying. She could laugh because there was no point to living if one could not see hope amid disaster. She could laugh because Joey would want her to laugh. In some ways Joey had been a lot like these people, able to take joy from simple things . . . like gathering seashells.

She stopped her work again, rubbing gently at a potato, smelling its earthy scent. Simple things. There was a time when Lee also knew how to find joy in simple things, when they picnicked together, when he taught Joey how to find snails. Her throat tightened and her eyes teared at the memory, which had struck her unexpectedly, surprising her with its vividness. How long had it been since she thought about Lee Jeffreys? When was it she had given up secretly hoping he *would* come looking for her, no matter how much she told others she didn't care anymore?

It was 1859, wasn't it . . . that summer she spent in Connecticut? Seven years ago! She could sing then, and people would sit and listen in near rapture to her voice. She touched the scar on her throat, tears brimming in her eyes, remembering Lee sitting in the audience watching her that first night, remembering how he had stood up for her when

Cy Jordan insulted her, remembering that first warm, wonderful kiss. He was the only man who had ever made her feel like a real woman, who knew how to bring out the brazen passion that now lay sleeping in her soul. No other man could awaken it. No one but Lee, and so it lay sleeping. She had not seen him or heard from him in over four years.

Should she even be giving Lee fond thoughts? Wasn't it men like Lee who were responsible for her being here in this potato field, her skin burned brown, her hands so dirty she might never get them clean again? Wasn't it men like Lee who were responsible for what had happened to Brennan Manor, for her attack and the loss of her voice . . . for Joey's death?

It's every man's fault, Elijah had told her. *South same as the North. Every man who thought he was right and wanted to fight for it. We are all to blame, the South for refusin' to give up slavery and for startin' the whole thing; the North for thinkin' they had to teach the South a lesson; and even us Negroes, for lettin' ourselves be stuck in slavery for so long. We was ignorant and afraid. Now, the more we learn and work hard to be on our own, the more we know we gonna make it okay, and life will be better for the little ones like Joey.*

She stopped digging then when several wagons of Negroes drove past the potato field and into their little village, where a wooden sign that read Brennan, Kansas, Population 72, hung between two posts on the dirt road that led into town. Audra watched Wilena and Joseph walk up to talk to some of those who stopped near the field, and then Joseph turned and signaled her and others to come out of the potato field. Audra dropped her fork and what potatoes she had collected and hurried toward the newcomers, stepping over other rows of potatoes. When she reached the procession of wagons, she noticed some of the Negro women crying. A few others just stared at her in surprise at seeing a white woman with red hair among them.

"We got trouble," Joseph told Audra. "These people are from a settlement east of here. They gathered their belongin's and run off on account of a band of white men that's been goin' around raidin' Negro camps, killin' and rapin' and destroyin' homes and crops. They ride in, usually at night, wearin' white hoods, settin' fires."

Audra felt her stomach turn. "Do they think they'll come here?"

"They say these men been goin' around findin' all the Negro settlements they can. This man here says they're a bunch of outlaws from the South, all mad about Negroes bein' able to come out here and settle on their own. They're just out to make trouble for Negroes anyplace they can. I expect they'll find us soon enough."

"But . . . we can defend ourselves if we stick together," Wilena put in. "There must be forty people here. If they want to stay in Brennan, we'll be over a hundred strong."

"That's includin' *children,*" Joseph reminded her. "You're talkin' maybe about seventy adults, and a lot of them is women. On top of that, we need guns, and we can't afford them."

Southern boys, Audra thought. Now that they were through with trouble from the Yankees, it was their own kind who would make life miserable for them. Yes, Elijah *was* right. *Everybody* was to blame for this war, and for some the war was still not over. "We have *some* guns," she spoke up.

"Yeah, and mos' of these men don't know how to use them very good. It's one thing shootin' at a rabbit or a deer standin' still in the woods. It's another to shoot at a man chargin' at you on a horse, especially when he's shootin' *back!*"

Audra looked out at the horizon, which in Kansas seemed endless. "They aren't going to chase us out, Joseph. We won't let them. We'll pray and we'll fight. God has been with us so far. He won't desert us now." She looked up at the man. "Have some of the others help these people settle in. We have to get the potatoes dug so we can have them to sell to travelers. And we still have corn to pick, you know. First things first. We have crops to get in if we want to get through another winter."

Joseph nodded. "Yes, ma'am."

"We'll hold a meeting tonight to decide how we can defend ourselves if these hoodlums come to Brennan."

Audra turned and walked back to her potato row, and Joseph watched her for a moment, then grinned at Wilena. "She still has a way of bossin' us around, don't she?"

Wilena just laughed. "It's in her blood, Joseph, but that's good. She's helped us a lot, takin' charge like she has."

"Who *is* that woman?" one of the newcomers asked.

"She's Audra Brennan," Wilena answered. "There was a time when she was one of the richest ladies in Louisiana, and a proud, bossy little thing she was, too." She looked at the Negro man who had brought them the news about the raiders. "Welcome to Brennan. You take your folks on into town, and people there will help you. God is on our side, mister. He'll help us through this."

The man tipped his hat and turned to guide the oxen that pulled his wagon. Wilena looked up at her husband. "We best get the potatoes dug like Miss Audra says. We can meet tonight and decide what to do about them outlaws. Seems this war ain't really over yet, don't it? Some folks seem bent on keepin' it goin', one way or another."

"Seems so." He looked out at Audra. "One thing is sure. If them men come, we got to hide her. They see a white woman livin' among us, it'll be worse for her than us."

"I agree," Wilena answered. "Why can't they jus' leave us alone and let us live in peace? We ain't doin' nothin' to nobody."

"We're free niggers doin' good on our own. *That's* what they don't like."

Joseph left her and returned to his work. Wilena watched Audra for a moment longer, then looked up at the clouds. "Please, Lord, don't let them men find us. Keep us safe, and especially keep Miss Audra safe. She's a good woman. Jus' let this war be over for all of us, for once and for all."

Wilena returned to her own work, but they all kept stopping to gaze at the eastern horizon, expecting at any moment to see a gang of men wearing white hoods riding down on their little town.

• • •

Lee opened his eyes to watch a woman fussing with a drapery she could not get open. She looked familiar, but he could not quite place her. Somewhere in the distance he heard someone playing a piano. It was lovely music, and it seemed to drift on a gentle breeze that came in a side window. The smell in that air was familiar, the smell of dry autumn, Indian summer. There was another smell mixed with it . . . the sea. He heard the cry of a sea gull.

How long had it been since he heard the sea gulls? He looked around the familiar room, his old room at Maple Shadows! Why, this was the very room where he'd made love to Audra for the first time, wasn't it? This was the room where he'd come searching for something that had belonged to her and had found the song. How in God's name had he gotten from Baton Rouge, Louisiana, to his old family summer home in Connecticut? And who was playing the piano? Had he died and was he with his mother now? And who was the woman fixing the draperies?

"Audra?" he spoke.

The woman turned as though startled. "Lee! My God, you spoke!" She stepped down from a chair and hurried over to his bed. "Lee, do you know who I am?"

He studied her a moment. Why was it so difficult to place her? Yes, she did look familiar . . . David's wife? No. Carl's.

"Beverly?"

She smiled. "Yes! Oh, Lee!" She touched his hair. "We wondered if you would ever come out of this! Lie still. I'm so glad Carl happens to be here! He came up for a week."

She left the room, and Lee looked around, totally confused. He was apparently alive, but how did he get here? What did she mean by wondering if he would ever come out of this? He looked out the window again, saw the deep colors of the trees outside. It was apparently one of those rare autumn days when it was warm as summer outside. He could hear the waves on the beach below. However he had gotten here, apparently not too much time had passed since he'd been to Baton Rouge. He could still find Audra by spring at least.

Audra! She seemed to fill this room. Oh, how happy

they had been here that summer! He and Audra and ...
Joey. Oh, yes, Joey. He'd killed him, hadn't he? When was
that? It was so hard to remember little things, like dates.
When had he gone to Baton Rouge? September, wasn't it?
September of sixty-five. It must still be roughly that time
from the look of the trees outside. He scrambled to remember how he might have landed here in bed. He could
vaguely see a man with glasses, telling him Audra had gone
to Kansas. He was going to go after her when something
had hit him in the head. That was all he remembered.

However he had gotten here, it felt good. He liked to
imagine it was his mother playing the piano downstairs.
How nice it would be if somehow he had gone back in
time, and both his mother and Audra would come into the
room, smiles on their beautiful faces—but that couldn't be,
could it? No, his mother was dead. Even his father ... oh,
how it hurt to think of it. So much had been left unsaid. So
much. Now the man lay buried out there beside his mother.
He had never even had the chance to visit his grave. When
he first came back from the war, he had gone only to visit
Carl, then Bennett James.

The war ... it had changed so many people's lives.
How had it changed Audra's? Where was she now? *How*
was she? Someone came into the room and leaned over
him. "Carl?" Why were there tears in his brother's eyes?

"Lee! My God! How do you feel? Can you move?"

Move? Why in hell shouldn't he be able to move? He
flexed his hands, raised his arms. Weak, he was so weak. He
looked at his arms, noticed they were terribly thin! "Carl,
what's happened? How did I get here?" He realized it was
even an effort to talk.

Carl pulled up a chair, and his wife Beverly stood behind him. "Do you remember anything about what happened?"

Lee looked around the room again. "Just ... I went to
Baton Rouge to find Audra. She's gone to Kansas. I ... have
to find her."

Carl put a hand on his arm. "Not for a while, Lee. It's
going to take you a long time to regain your strength. The
doctor said that if you ever came around, you'd probably

have to learn to walk all over again, after being immobile for so long. We've exercised your limbs as much as we could, just to work your muscles every day."

"I don't . . . understand. A couple of weeks shouldn't . . . make much difference."

Carl sighed, grave concern in his eyes. "Lee, some young rebels beat you senseless down in Baton Rouge. You were pretty broken up, but your bones have mended by now. When it first happened and they found your identification, the doctor down there managed to find me and told me to come get you and your belongings because you were unconscious, and he didn't know how long you'd be that way. By the time I reached you to bring you home, you were awake enough to eat and drink, but you just stared most of the time, didn't move, didn't know who we were, never spoke. We were beginning to think you'd be like that for years, alive but not alive." He squeezed his arm. "You have no idea how good it is to hear you talking, to know you remember us. We've managed to get soup and water down your throat, but that's it. You've lost a lot of weight, and it's going to take you a long time to get back to normal."

Lee tried to put his hand to his head, but he couldn't get it that far. Alarm began to move through him when he realized he couldn't possibly be this weak and thin after only a couple of weeks. "How long have I been this way?"

Carl closed his eyes for a moment, keeping a grip on his arm. "Lee, it's been a year. It's October, eighteen sixty-six."

Something close to horror swept through Lee's blood. A year! That couldn't be possible! Audra! My God, a whole year! What about his promise to Joey? What had happened to Audra by now? "That can't be," he said, feeling his voice growing weaker already. "I have to . . . go find Audra. I have to go to Kansas!" He tried to rise, but he had absolutely no strength, not even enough to raise his head. "My God!" Tears welled in his eyes. "A year!"

"Lee, just be glad you came around without loss of memory and without being paralyzed. The doctor wasn't sure just what would happen if you ever fully regained consciousness. The biggest damage was a blow to the head from a brick. There isn't much doctors know about injuries like that. All a person can do is wait and see. Just thank God you're alert. You were beginning to fail fast from poor nourishment. We weren't sure how much longer you'd live. I had you brought here to Maple Shadows because I knew how much you loved it here. I thought maybe it would help you recover to be someplace familiar, someplace Mother loved. Beverly moved up here with the kids to take care of you."

Lee closed his eyes against tears, feeling weak and vulnerable and horribly depressed. How ironic that his gravest injury had come *after* the war. "I have to get my strength back. I have to go to Kansas," he repeated.

"That's going to take time, Lee," Beverly told him. "The doctor said that if and when you came around, you would have to start eating solid foods very gradually. Your whole system has been shut down. Your stomach will hardly know what to do with solid food at first. And you're going to need help in learning to walk again. It will take months."

"No." Lee jerked in a sob, hating this ridiculous need to cry but unable to stop it. "I don't . . . *have* months. I have to . . . go to Kansas."

Carl bent over him, grasping his bony shoulders. "You *will* go, Lee. But not right away. I'm going to send for the doctor, and I'll bring in the best specialists from New York to work with you and help you get back your strength. A lot of people are going to be damn happy just to know you're conscious and haven't lost your memory. You remember Bennett James, don't you?"

Lee sniffed back more tears and breathed deeply for self-control. Carl took a clean handkerchief from his suit jacket and wiped his tears with it.

"Yeah, sure I remember Bennett."

"Well, he contacts Beverly weekly by wire, wanting to know if you're awake yet. I expect he'll be coming up here to see you real soon. Jeannie's been staying here off and on, too. Do you remember who Jeannie is?"

"David's wife."

"She's met another man. She's getting married soon, but she's been staying here a couple weeks at a time to relieve Beverly. It's been quite a project taking care of you, but we all love you."

"My God," Lee groaned. "I've . . . put all of you out . . . haven't I?"

Carl smiled through tears. "No. You gave us reason to come up here and have some time together. I was becoming just like Father, putting too much of myself into the business and not paying enough attention to my family. Your being here has made us spend more time here ourselves. It's actually been good for us. Maybe this is Mother's way of getting us back together. We're all that's left of the family, and I'm not going to let Maple Shadows sit empty anymore, Lee. I know it belongs to you now, but when you can't be here, I'll make sure it's opened every summer. Mom would want that. Hell, the house had been lived in all year. We had a hell of a winter, snowed in part of the time, but the kids loved it."

Lee took hold of the handkerchief and finally managed to get it to his nose. "Who's playing the piano?"

"That's our daughter Nichole," Beverly answered. "She's sixteen now. She's been taking lessons for years. I think she's inherited some of her grandmother's talent, don't you?"

Lee listened to the beautiful playing. He could see his mother so vividly, and he could see Audra standing by that piano, singing in that beautiful voice no one could match. "Yes," he answered. "That's good. Mother would like that."

"She even looks like our mother," Carl told him. He touched Lee's hair. "Hey, little brother, you're going to make it. Cooperate with the doctor and the specialists, and you'll be back to full strength sooner than you think. You can go find that southern belle that you've been after for so many years, and maybe you can finally be together. I just want you to know that we'll welcome her this time. It's time for the war and the hatred to be over, and it's time for you to be married and settled and happy."

Lee thought how he wasn't sure that would happen, once he told Audra the truth about Joey. So much had happened that would cause Audra to hate him that they might never again be able to find that sweet love and exotic passion they had once shared. She could even have remarried by now, maybe left the Negroes and gone on to Denver or some other new place to start over. Audra! Every day counted, and he couldn't do more than raise his hand to his face.

"Get those . . . specialists . . . soon as you can," he told Carl. He looked up at Beverly. "Thank you. How can I . . . ever repay you . . . for what you've done?"

She smiled. "Just seeing you awake and alert is repayment enough. The day you're able to walk out of here and get on a horse and go to Kansas will just be the icing on the cake."

He closed his eyes. Kansas. He hoped Audra was still there. If she wasn't, he might never find her. A whole year! It was incredible. "I . . . had a song I . . . carried in my pocket," he told Carl. "Audra . . . wrote it . . . for me. Did you find it? Do you . . . still have it?"

"We found it," his brother answered. "It's with your things."

"Get it, will you? Take it . . . to Nichole. Have her try to play it. Once she gets used to the tune . . . maybe she can sing it for me. I've never heard it sung."

"Anything you want, little brother." Carl rose, and Lee noticed how he had aged, graying heavily at the temples. Eighteen sixty-six—Carl would be forty now. He was thirty-six himself. How old would Audra be? She was seventeen that summer she spent here. That made her twenty-four, still young enough to have children, maybe his children. But then that was probably too much to hope for. "You just rest," Carl told him. "Beverly will take the song down to Nichole, and I'm going to send for the doctor."

They both left the room, and Lee lay staring at the ceiling, still finding it difficult to comprehend that a whole year could have gone by. A myriad of thoughts whirled through his mind, and tears wanted to come again. God, he hated being so weak! He had to get out of this bed.

He tried again to rise, but it was impossible. He lay back, listening then as Nichole began playing a different tune on the piano. She played it hesitantly at first, and he figured that by now the notes on Audra's sheet music were probably so faded that Nichole was having a hard time reading them. She played the tune a few more times until it flowed beautifully. It was a lovely tune.

Lee, my love, she began singing,
Just as the sun shines
And the ocean wind blows wet and wild,
I love you as a woman loves,
But you see me as a child.

Lee, my love,
When I am with you
I never want the days to end.
I love you more than life itself,
Yet to you I'm just a friend.

Lee, my love,
You stand before me
Tall and strong, your eyes so blue,
I long to feel your arms around me,
To hear the words, I love you.

Lee, my love,
We walk together,
We feel the sand and smell the sea,
I know we live in different worlds.
A life together can never be.

Was that true? After all these years, it certainly seemed so. Seven years it had been since that summer here. Seven years. By the time he was able to get out of this bed and find her, it would probably be closer to eight, but he'd made a promise to Joey, and he was, by God, going to keep it.

AUGUST 1867

Audra heard the riders first, then saw them, a long line
of men on horses, looking ghostly as the Kansas heat made
their images waver and ripple on the horizon. She dropped
her basket of corn and began running, catching up with
Toosie and telling her to scream at the top of her lungs for
everyone to take shelter. She could not raise her own raspy
voice high enough to warn them.

Intuition told her that the dreaded moment had come,
and she and the others did not have to wait until these riders came closer to know that the same gang of rebel outlaws
who had raided other Negro settlements was now paying a
visit to Brennan, Kansas. Because it had been a whole year
since the first Negro refugees had come to them, and there
had been no trouble, Audra had hoped they were going to

be spared. Other victims of raids had joined them, so that their little settlement had grown into a town of roughly 220 people, about 50 of them white. They now had a school where both Toosie and Audra taught in winter; a little church, where a white minister who had come to live among them preached sermons every Sunday; a livery; a blacksmith shop; a small rooming house; a clothing shop, where Wilena and some of the other women, both Negro and white, made men's and women's apparel; a general store, run by Joseph and Elijah; and several frame houses. Many of the people still lived out of wagons or tepees or sod houses, but the town's goal was that eventually everyone would have a real house, with windows and wood floors.

"Please help us!" Audra prayed as she ran, scooping up Wilena's youngest girl, Yolanda. Toosie carried little Joey in her arms, hollering for people to lock their doors and close their shutters. Many others had apparently already seen the riders, as Toosie was not the only one yelling out warnings. There were other shouts, men leaving barns and businesses to arm themselves with guns and clubs, women grabbing their children and running.

How can God do this to us? Audra fretted inwardly. They were a Christian community, made up of good people who were working together, sharing all they had so that no one went without, families helping families with chores and building homes and barns. They had accomplished so much here. Trade with travelers had been excellent, and they had even begun selling food to Fort Riley, and to the booming new cattle town of Abilene, both places many miles to the north but worth the trip by wagon for the profits they made.

Right now she wished the fort were closer. They could use the help of soldiers, and Audra had asked more than once for a patrol to be sent to guard their little town; but the commander at the fort had told her there had not been much trouble this year with outlaws. His biggest problem was with Indians who were growing more restless and resentful since more and more people had begun coming west to claim their lands. Audra suspected part of the reason they could get no protection was because the town was made up mostly of Negroes. Whites in general, even those from the

North who had been willing to fight to free the slaves, still were not ready to help Negroes survive the new world into which they had been tossed.

Audra's only hope had been that their little town had grown large enough that perhaps the outlaws had decided they were a little too much to take on, but from the thundering sound of horses approaching, it was apparent that the outlaws' numbers had also grown.

She found Joseph and handed little Yolanda to him. She saw the terror in the man's eyes, and she knew that in spite of the fact that a few of the Negro men had purchased guns and had practiced shooting them, facing the real thing was another matter. She had learned to understand their thinking. Most of these men were strong and healthy, and ones like Joseph could probably break any man's neck in a moment; but most of these Negroes had grown up learning to fear white men with guns and whips. Since the day they were born, they had been taught to submit, were torn from loved ones, many of them whipped mercilessly when they disobeyed or tried to run away. There was a deep terror in their blood that would make if difficult to fight these white men, even though they were themselves free now and had a perfect right to defend their town and their women and children.

"Don't be afraid, Joseph," she told the man sternly. "Stay calm, and don't shoot at anyone unless he's close enough that you're sure you'll hit him. When he is, don't you be afraid to pull the trigger. This is our town, and they aren't going to destroy it or chase us out!"

"Yes, ma'am," he answered, nodding and running off to his own home with Yolanda. Audra headed for the two-story frame house she shared with Toosie and Elijah and little Joey. Toosie was expecting another child, and Audra prayed nothing would happen today to make her lose her baby. She reached over and took Joey from her, worried about the woman having to run. All over town people were scurrying for shelter, closing the doors to their little shops, scampering for their homes, those unable to get that far hiding under boardwalks, taking shelter anywhere they could find it. The outlaws were already on the outskirts of town when

Audra and Toosie reached the house, relieved to see that Elijah was already there loading his rifle.

"Get under a bed with Joey!" he commanded Toosie. "You find a place to hide, too, Miss Audra."

"Like hell I will! This is *my* town!" she protested, going to an old china cabinet she had bought from a traveler and taking her father's rifle down from the top of it. "I can use this thing, and I *will* use it!" She took a position at a window, and Elijah knew there was no arguing with her. His own heart pounded with fear. He had never shot at white men before, and he could almost feel a rope around his neck.

"Some of them are riding through the cornfields," Audra said as she watched out the window, her voice amazingly calm. "Thank God we had an early season and a lot of it is already in."

"At least they can't hurt the potatoes," Elijah answered. "They ain't even dug yet." Both of them just watched, helpless to stop the pack of at least thirty men as they tied ropes to support posts of some of the buildings and ripped them away, howling and carrying on like wild Indians. One man threw a torch into the livery. A few headed toward Audra's house, and Audra wondered why the townspeople were not shooting at them. Was it that old fear? She looked over at Elijah, saw the sweat on his forehead. Why *shouldn't* these poor Negro men be afraid? They had never in their lives been allowed to fight back. She realized then that no one was going to fire a gun unless forced into it.

"Start shooting, Elijah Jakes!" she commanded, as though he were one of her hands. She fired her own gun, and to her surprise, one of the outlaws went down. Elijah let out a whoop and fired his own rifle, but missed. Audra shot at another man, hitting his horse. The animal went down, and the man cried out when it landed on his leg. Finally some of the others began shooting, and a few more outlaws fell from their horses. Many went on through town, and Audra knew they would most likely steal several head of their precious cattle. They had been working at breeding and building a herd, now that the railroad had come to Abilene. There was a lot of money in the cattle business, and the few they had were precious and valuable.

"Damn them!" she muttered, firing at another outlaw. The man's horse came to a sudden halt, and the wounded rider flew forward and landed smack on Audra's front porch with a thump and a cry of pain. He rolled away from her window, and for a moment Audra could not see him. Suddenly someone yanked Elijah's rifle right out of his hands. Elijah had been kneeling at the other front window with the rifle barrel sticking out. He gave out a yelp and ducked when the man on the porch turned the gun and stuck it back through the window and fired. Elijah ran into the kitchen, and before Audra could react, the front door was kicked open. The raider, whose fall had apparently done little to inhibit his mobility, charged into the house.

Audra turned to shoot at him, but her gun jammed, and in an instant the man ripped it from her hands and threw it aside. "Well, well," he said with a grin. "Look what we have here! A pretty white whore livin' with a nigger man!"

Audra reached for a vase and threw it at him, but he ducked just in time, then rammed the butt of Elijah's rifle into her middle, knocking the wind out of her. She fell backward, and the man was on her in an instant, jerking her to her feet with one hand, still holding Elijah's rifle in the other.

"Let's go, lady! Me and my friends know what to do with women like you." He dragged her toward the door, but Audra fought and struggled, managing to kick the door shut before the man could get her outside. He flung her sideways then like a rag doll, slamming her against a table. A terrible pain ripped through Audra's rib cage. The man forced her to bend backward over the table then, and he laid the rifle across her throat. "Where'd you get that scar, honey? Some jealous nigger man give it to you?"

"Get out!" she answered through gritted teeth.

"Word is you folks do a lot of sellin' to the army and folks at Abilene and such. You got money layin' around here? Hand it over, and I won't strip you naked and have at you!"

Suddenly Elijah sprang out of seemingly nowhere. He

knocked the man away from her, and the rifle went flying. The two men got into a vicious fight, crashing into furniture, knocking over plants and breaking vases and dishes. Toosie stood at the bedroom door clinging to little Joey, her eyes filled with terror for Elijah and her son.

Audra managed to find her own rifle, the pain in her side so fierce, she struggled just to breathe. She felt a wicked hatred welling up inside her soul. How dare these men come here and attack innocent people who had worked so hard to survive! Elijah landed a hard punch to the outlaw's jaw, and the man staggered backward. Audra tried again to shoot the man, but the rifle still would not fire. The man groaned and started to rise, and Audra saw her chance. She turned the rifle and whacked him in the head with the butt end.

All the horrors of the past crashed in on her then, and she took it out on the outlaw, beating him over and over with the rifle. This blow was for burning Brennan Manor. This one was for cutting her throat. Another for the loss of her voice. This one was for Richard's hideous abuse, that one for all the troubles between North and South keeping her from the only man she had ever really loved. This blow was for Lena and Henrietta, that one for burning Baton Rouge. Another for losing her home, her hope for happiness. Another for Joey . . . Joey . . . Joey, even though these men were southerners themselves. They were animals who had decided to take advantage of the victims of the war.

Elijah finally grabbed her and forced her to stop, and it was only then she realized the man's face was horribly battered and unrecognizable. The rifle was broken, the butt splintered and bloody. Her own dress was spattered with blood, and reality returned, bringing with it an awareness of the awful pain of her own injury. She grasped her ribs and bent over, gasping for breath.

"Take her to the bed," Elijah was telling someone. "I'll hide the body till we're sure they've rode off. Then we'll bury it with the others they leave behind. Them men's got our cattle. They ain't gonna come back right away. They'll herd the cattle off first."

"What if they do come back!" Toosie lamented.

"They're going to get their revenge, Elijah, because we fought back."

"Damn them all!" Elijah swore. "Get Audra to her bed and put Joey in that playpen I made for him so's he can't run off. I got to get my rifle and reload."

Audra could hear Joey crying. She wanted to go back and help with the fighting, but she wasn't even sure where her next breath would come from. She managed to crawl onto her bed, then rolled onto her back, gasping for breath, finally blacking out from the pain.

Lee halted his horse and took a moment to look at the little town before him. Brennan, Kansas, the commander at Fort Riley had told him it was called. The man had also told him a very pretty white woman named Audra Potter more or less owned the town and had dealt several times with him, talking him into buying corn and potatoes for the fort. Lee found it incredible that it could all be true, that the woman the commander told him about dressed like any rugged pioneer woman, had work-worn hands from helping dig potatoes and pick corn. Rumor had it the woman had founded a little school in Brennan, taught Negro children to read and write.

Audra—teaching Negroes, helping them build a town, getting her hands dirty. That didn't sound like the Audra he had known, but then, if anybody had the spunk and determination to do such a thing, Audra did. It was just that he never imagined she would go this far, helping Negroes build a town. Who else could the woman be but his own Audra? What other white woman would name a town Brennan? After two months of searching since he had arrived in Kansas, to think that she could be minutes away made his heart beat faster, and he took a deep breath for courage. Was it necessary, after all this time, to tell her he was the one who had killed Joey? Three years had passed, yet when he relived the event in his dreams, it seemed like yesterday.

He pushed back his Stetson and opened the top few buttons of his denim shirt. It was going to be another hot August day, and out here on the prairie there were no trees for shade. This land was certainly a far cry from Connecticut and even from Louisiana. He had never seen such endless horizons, and how anyone managed to break through the tough sod of this country and turn it into a farm was beyond his imagination; yet out there in the distance were cornfields.

He decided that in spite of its desolate, uncivilized state, he liked this country. He wanted to see more of it, maybe go to the Rockies. He'd been told there was a new city west of here called Denver, right at the foot of the mountains, a town growing explosively because of the discovery of gold. A railroad was being built, figured to connect clear across the continent within two years. With all the misery back east and in the South, the West was sure to grow fast now. A man who got in on the ground floor could make his own fortune, start new.

That was what he needed to do. Start all over someplace new. Everything back east brought back too many painful memories, and he supposed it was probably that way for Audra when she thought about Louisiana and Brennan Manor. There came a time when a person just had to stop looking back, and maybe once he told her about Joey, *he* could stop looking back, too. If he couldn't obtain Audra's forgiveness, he could never go forward and make something decent of the rest of his years.

He was done with the whiskey. A year of lying unconscious and going without had cured him of that. Months of rehabilitation had taught him the value of life and health, and he had discovered he had a great desire to live again, to be whole and enjoy life . . . and find Audra. Maybe, by some miracle, whatever future he formed for himself, he could share with her. Maybe she could find a way to forgive him, and they could both put the past behind them and go on from here, perhaps to Denver, where he could start a new law firm. There must be a need for lawyers out here where most places were just beginning to grow, where people were just beginning to enjoy the things taken for granted in more civilized places. He kind of liked the fact that a man could set his own laws out here. There were no constraints on how a man lived or even how he dressed. He wore denim shirts and pants instead of suits, leather boots instead of polished shoes. No one cared if a man got a little dusty or sweaty. They didn't even care what a man's name was, where he was from, what his background was. In most of the little towns he had visited in Kansas, people were just glad to see someone, especially those homesteading miles from any kind of town. Everyone was welcomed and fed.

He had found a new peace out here, and riding in the open air for weeks had strengthened him. His skin was browned from the sun, and a lot of riding and walking had firmed his muscles even more. Nearly everyplace he stopped to ask about Audra, the woman of the house cooked him a meal fit for six men, ham or beef, whipped potatoes, pies. When he left, they insisted he take some extra biscuits and dried meat, ears of corn and raw potatoes, so that he ate well even when he wasn't spending the night on someone's farm. He had gained weight but was still several pounds away from the weight he'd been before he spent a year wasting away in bed.

During the first several months of his recuperation, he had had to learn to walk all over again. It had taken nearly a year to get back his normal abilities and strength, but he had worked hard at it, anxious to leave for Kansas. He missed Maple Shadows . . . would *always* miss it. But right now the important thing was to tie up the loose ends of his past so that he could decide what to do about his future. That meant finding Audra. Maybe some day they could both go back to Maple Shadows, spend a summer there, rediscover the sweet love they had found.

He rode a little closer, squinting at what looked like a burned-out building. Now he could see that part of the cornfields looked trampled. He kept his horse at a gentle trot, saw a sod house flattened here, another there. At one of them a Negro man was restacking the chunks of sod, preparing to rebuild his house. The man looked at him warily, eyeing him with distrust. Lee halted his horse. "Good afternoon."

The Negro man just nodded.

"I'm Lee Jeffreys. I've come here looking for a Mrs. Audra Potter. Does she live here in Brennan?"

The Negro leaned on a pitchfork. "Why you want to know?"

"She's an old friend." Lee looked around. "What happened here?"

The Negro kept studying him, his dark eyes gauging and wary. "Outlaws. White men who don't like niggers settlin' in and havin' something of their own. They attacked us yesterday, tried to run us off, but Miss Audra, she told us to fight, so we fought. They left, but they said they'd be comin' back." He nodded to a distant hill. "Over yonder, we buried what's left of them white men we killed. Buried some of our own people that got killed, too. The rest of them outlaws, they're angry that nigger men killed their own. They're comin' back for us, all right." He looked back at Lee. "Maybe you're one of them, come to spy and see how many guns we got. We ain't got many, but we do okay, and we ain't leavin'. Miss Audra, she pretty near got herself killed helpin' us, so we're gonna stay and fight, for Miss Audra."

Alarm rushed through Lee at the words. "She's hurt?"

The Negro nodded. "One of them got into her house and attacked her, but she beat him, Elijah says. She beat him good with a rifle, smashed the man's head right in. Elijah, he helped her, got her away from him. That man, he hurt her good, broke some ribs. She's in a lot of pain, and she did it for us, so we stay, for Miss Audra."

Lee didn't know whether to laugh or go into a rage. He tried to picture Audra risking her life to help these people. *His* Audra? And she had beat the hell out of one of the outlaws! He would have liked to have seen that! My God, he hadn't even seen her again, and he already knew he still loved her.

"Where is Audra now?" he asked.

The man looked him over again suspiciously, then watched the horizon to make sure there weren't more men behind him. He pointed then to a frame house a little bit north of the main settlement. "She's there. She lives with Toosie and Elijah Jakes in that there house. Toosie, she's takin' care of Miss Audra."

"Toosie got married?"

The Negro seemed to relax more then, realizing Lee really did know Audra, and even Toosie. "Yes, sir. She got herself a little boy, calls him Joey. She's gonna have another baby 'fore too long."

Lee felt the old stabbing pain. So Toosie had had a baby boy and had named him Joey. Telling Audra the truth was going to be the hardest thing he'd ever done in his life, if he could find the courage to do it at all. "Thanks," he told the Negro. He rode off, leading his pack horse and heading toward the frame house. He looked up at the sign over the road leading into the little town.

Brennan, Kansas, Population 262, it read. The population number had been crossed off and painted over several times. A couple of buildings were burned down, but it was obvious this was a thriving town, and from the way people were moving about, picking up debris, hammers already pounding, men sawing new wood, the citizens of Brennan were determined it would continue to thrive, in spite of the outlaws who were trying to run them out.

Was all of this because of Audra? She seemed to be an absolute inspiration to these people. He approached the little frame house, noticing one window was broken and the door partially splintered. A well-built, handsome Negro man was removing the door to replace it. When he noticed Lee, he set the door against a porch post and moved to the steps of the porch, looking ready to fight.

"Are you Elijah?" Lee asked, deciding he had better set the man at ease right away. "Toosie's husband?"

The man frowned. "How do you know Toosie?"

Lee dismounted, tying his horse and leaving his weapons on the animal. "I'm Lee Jeffreys. Did Audra or Toosie ever tell you about me?"

Elijah's eyes widened in surprise. He looked Lee over, then grinned and put out his hand. "Mr. Jeffreys! Is it really you? Toosie!" he yelled louder then, before Lee could even answer. "Get out here! Come see who's here!" He shook Lee's hand vigorously, and a lovely Negro woman came to the open doorway. She stopped and stared, then broke into a smile.

"Mister Jeffreys!. God be praised!" She ran out to him,

and to Lee's surprise she threw her arms around his neck and hugged him. "You came! You really came! I told Audra you would find her again, but she wouldn't believe it."

Lee took hold of her arms and held her away from him, meeting her eyes. "Don't be praising God and all that, Toosie. You don't know the whole story."

"I know you're here! That's all that matters. Audra, she still loves you, you know. She denies it all the time, says it's men like you at fault for all that happened to her, but she's just trying to make herself believe that so she can forget you. But she never has. I can tell. Oh, and she needs something like this right now. She's been so lonely, worked so hard helping all of us, and now she's hurt and—"

"Slow down, Toosie!" Lee laughed lightly at the way she was carrying on. "I hear you have a baby!"

"Yes!" She turned and took hold of Elijah's arm. "This is my husband, Elijah Jakes. I knew him many years ago. Mr. Brennan sold him, and I didn't see him for a long time. After he got freed, he came looking for me, and we got married. We have a little boy named . . ." Her smile faded. "Named Joey. Joey was killed in the war, Mr. Jeffreys. Maybe you didn't know that."

When would he stop getting this burning pain in his gut every time Joey's name was mentioned? "I heard," he answered. *I killed him.* He removed his hat and ran a hand through his dark hair. "Toosie, can we go someplace and talk before I see Audra? I'd like to know more about all that's happened first, what's going on here with these outlaw attacks, how all of you ended up clear out here in Kansas in the first place. It might help me to know what to say to Audra when I see her again." He put his hat back on. "It's been five years, you know, since Baton Rouge."

Toosie grasped his hands. "Yes, sir. And you *should* know all that's happened. It's been bad for Audra. I'll never forget the day we got the letter saying Joey was killed. She had already suffered so much by then."

Lee stiffened, his eyes tearing. "Yeah. We've *all* suffered, Toosie."

Toosie looked him over, realized he was much thinner than she remembered him. And his eyes, those beautiful blue eyes, had a terribly haunted look to them. "It's been bad for you, too, hasn't it, Mr. Jeffreys? The southerners and the Negroes, we all think we're the only ones who have suffered; but it was bad for both sides, especially for the men who fought in that war."

Lee looked around. "Looks to me like the war isn't over yet."

"For some folks it might never be over. But the time comes when we have to forgive and forget and just start over, don't we?"

Their eyes held. "In some cases that might not be possible."

"Anything is possible, Mr. Jeffreys, with the Lord's help. Come over here by the shed. There's an old log we can sit on that's shaded by the building this time of day. I'll tell you all about what happened to Audra and the rest of us, and you can tell me why you're just now finding us when it's been two years since the war." She looked over at Elijah. "Don't you say a word to Audra till we come back."

"I won't say nothin'." Elijah turned and walked onto the porch to grab up a little boy who had toddled through the door. He brought the bright-eyed, grinning child close to Lee. "This is little Joey."

The little boy reached out, and Toosie made a remark about how readily Joey took to people, afraid of no one. Lee hardly heard her. He took the boy in his arms and hugged him, remembering another Joey, also with bright, dark eyes. But that Joey had white skin and red hair, and he had once told Lee he was the best friend he'd ever had.

It's okay, Lee. He could still hear the words so clearly, words from a dying Joey who forgave the man who shot him. Again he fought an urge to find some whiskey and just drink the memory away, but he'd tried that once, and it had solved nothing. There was only one way to get over this hell and go on from here.

He kissed the baby and handed him back to Elijah. "You have a fine son." He turned to Toosie then, remembering that first day he met her, struck by her beauty and suspecting she had an intelligence to match. It was good to see her free and married and happy. "I see you've got another one coming," he said, glancing at her swollen belly.

"Just a couple more months." She took his hand. "Let's go talk."

Lee walked with her to a shed at the rear corner of the house. They sat down on the log, and slowly the bright afternoon turned to dusk. While Elijah worked on the door, he looked their way several times, and once it looked as if Lee Jeffreys had his hands over his face and was crying. Was he crying over what had happened to Miss Audra? The loss of her voice? All the other things she had suffered? Or had that white man suffered something himself that nobody knew about? He was a good man. Elijah could see it in his eyes. He'd long ago learned to read white men's eyes, knew when they were sincere. Lee Jeffreys was sincere.

It seemed the Yankee and Toosie sat talking far longer than it should take to tell each other everything. Something was wrong. The white man still had his head in his hands, and Toosie was rubbing his shoulders, as though the man were suffering some terrible grief of his own. What was it all about? He heard Audra call out for Toosie, and he went inside the house to tell her Toosie had gone to help some others who needed it, that she'd be back soon.

"I thought I heard you both . . . talking to someone," Audra said, every breath painful.

"Jus' Joseph and Wilena," Elijah lied. "You jus' lie easy. Toosie'll be back real soon now. It's almost dark."

"What if . . . they come . . . after dark?" Audra fretted.

Elijah knew she was referring to the outlaws. He thought about Lee again. He'd been told Lee was a colonel or something like that in the Union Army. Now that the man was here, maybe he could help. One thing he ought to know about was fighting. "We'll be okay, Miss Audra. Somethin' tells me God has answered our prayers."

Audra glanced up at him in puzzlement. "What do you mean?"

"You'll see, soon enough." He grinned and left the room, and Audra tried to imagine what the man could be talking about. She wished she could get around better, but every movement brought a gripping pain. She would be no use now if the outlaws came back, and she knew what would happen to her if they found her, broken ribs or not. She was afraid, but she didn't want Elijah and the others to know it.

She heard voices then. Someone called to little Joey, told him what a big boy he was. The voice sounded very familiar. He didn't talk like most Negroes talked, and he didn't have the accent of a southern white man, either. Where had she heard that voice? Her first thought was Lee, but that was impossible.

"Toosie? Who's out there?"

Lee was close enough to the bedroom door to hear her, and he felt as though someone had knifed him in the heart when he heard her raspy voice. Audra! He could still hear her singing that first day he came to Maple Shadows, a voice so full and sweet, it gave a man the chills. She would never sing like that again, and he wished he had been the one to know the pleasure of killing March Fredericks.

"Someone very special is here," Toosie was saying. She went into the bedroom and leaned over the bed. "We're going to be okay, Audra. Somebody is here who can help us."

"A soldier? Did the commander at Fort Riley send us some help?"

"Not exactly, but he *is* a soldier, or at least he used to be." Toosie looked out at Lee and motioned for him to come into the room. At first Lee could not get his feet to move. Five years! He finally managed to make it to the doorway. Toosie stepped out of the room, and Lee moved closer to the bed.

For a moment they just stared at each other. "Hello, Audra," he finally managed to say.

Her eyes filled with tears. "Lee," she whispered.

In spite of all the mixed emotions Lee Jeffreys drew from her soul, Audra could not quell a quick smile of joy and relief at seeing him again. It seemed both impossible and miraculous, and although she no longer understood just how she felt about him personally, the sight of an old friend from a past that was once full of love and beauty was welcome. Still, she had spent years telling herself that she hated him, never wanted to see him again.

Oh, but for him to be standing here in front of her, this man who had known her as intimately as any man could know a woman, was another story. He was so many things to her, an old friend, yet just a stranger now. Was he still a friend? An enemy?

"How did you find me here?" she asked, looking him over. So thin. He looked older, and there were small scars on his face, as though he'd been beaten. Such tragedy in those blue eyes she had once loved beyond all measure. So he had suffered, too. "And why? Why now?"

Lee thought she looked like an angel from his dreams, lying there with her auburn hair spread out on the pillow, wearing a simple flannel nightgown, her face thin, actually burned from the sun and beginning to show just a hint of lines about her eyes. He struggled not to show his shock at her voice and the scar on her throat. It did little to mar her natural beauty, which to him was now a deeper beauty, one that came from the inside. This woman had matured into a strong, generous, courageous person, one with a determination to survive and make do with what she had. She was a far cry from the haughty seventeen-year-old he had met that lovely day in Connecticut, when she stood beside his mother's piano and sang . . . sang, with a voice she would never carry again. His own guilt for the wrongs of the past grew even heavier. He should have been there for her. She never should have suffered, but then, if her father had not burned his letters . . .

"The 'how' was easy," he answered. "I had gone to Baton Rouge, saw Brennan Manor." He saw the hurt in her eyes. "There were some whites squatting there. They told me they thought you'd sold the place but weren't sure who the owner was, so I went into town to find someone who might know. A clerk at the land office told me you'd sold the place to your cousin's husband and had left for Kansas with your Negroes." He turned and picked up a wooden chair, setting it beside the bed, then sat down near her. "Audra, you sold *everything* for a thousand dollars?"

Her eyes teared. "I had no choice. It was too dangerous to stay there . . . and I wanted to help . . . Toosie and the others. They had saved my life. They wanted to come to Kansas . . . but had no money to buy the things they needed, so I sold Brennan Manor."

Her words came slowly as she struggled to breathe against the pain of her broken ribs. She knew by Lee's eyes what he was thinking. Helping Negroes was the last thing she would have done a few years ago. She put a hand to her hair, thinking how different she must look from the elegant, perfectly coifed and dressed debutante he had first met in

Connecticut. She moved her hand to her throat in an effort to cover the scar there. Lee took hold of her hand and pulled it away.

"It's all right, Audra." He squeezed her hand lightly. "Toosie told me everything." He closed his eyes and rested his head against the back of her hand as he held it. "I'm so damn sorry. If things had been different ... if I had been with you, none of it would have happened. And if I could have found you sooner, you wouldn't have had to sell Brennan Manor. I would have given you the money to do whatever you wanted. You wouldn't have had to let the place go."

She studied the thick, dark hair, the handsome lines of his face, the broad shoulders beneath the denim shirt he wore. How old was he now? Thirty-five? Thirty-six? Where had the last seven years gone since they first met and she wrote that song for him? "I suppose no one person or group of persons can be blamed for any of it," she answered. "As far as Brennan Manor ... once I found out Joey was never coming back, it didn't matter ... anymore. It was all for Joey ... always for Joey."

God, there was the gut-wrenching pain again. For some reason he had found it easy to tell Toosie about Joey, and she had understood. She was a remarkably insightful, gentle woman, and she had forgiven him as easily as breathing, had understood the deep grief behind his tears. Toosie had told him that he must tell Audra and get it off his chest, and he knew she was right. There was no way around it. But he couldn't. Not just yet. He would let her heal first, see what he could do for these Negroes and their problem with the outlaws.

"I'm sorry about Joey," he answered. "More sorry than you'll ever know."

"I told myself ... I should hate you because of it, but now I know you shouldn't ... feel responsible for what some other Yankee soldier did. It was war, Lee. War makes men do terrible things. I know that firsthand."

You shouldn't feel responsible for what some other Yankee soldier did. He had to change the subject or go crazy. "Audra, I looked for you right away, right after I got mus-

tered out of the army, which was just a couple of months after Lee surrendered. When I was leaving the land office at
Baton Rouge, a gang of young rebel thugs attacked me,
clobbered me in the back of the head with a brick and beat
me almost to death."

"Lee!" He still held her hand, and although she hated
to admit it, the feel of his strength was comforting. In only
minutes this stranger was becoming just Lee again, her
friend above all else. She knew he'd meant it about giving
her whatever money she would have needed and helping
her keep Brennan Manor. After the way she had treated him
that terrible morning in Baton Rouge, she was surprised
he had bothered to find her at all. She had never forgotten
the helpless look in those blue eyes when she told him she
never wanted to see him again, yet here he was, and he had
apparently gone through hell to find her. "How bad was it?
That was two *years* ago."

"The doctor in Baton Rouge found out who I was, and
he contacted my brother Carl. Carl came for me, took me
by train up to Maple Shadows. I was only partially conscious, stayed that way for almost a year. My eyes would
open, and I could eat and drink, but only by someone else's
hand. They tell me I didn't speak or move all that time. By
the time I came around to full consciousness, I was practically a skeleton, pretty near death from not being able to get
enough nourishment. Carl and his wife and David's widow
nursed me back to health."

"David's widow? Your brother was killed?"

He rubbed at the back of her hand with his thumb.
"Yeah. I don't think there are many people left who didn't
lose someone they loved in that war."

"I'm sorry, Lee."

He sighed, finally letting go of her hand. "Well, at least
she met another man who is very good to her. She's
remarried now." He leaned back in the chair. "Mind if I
smoke?"

"No." She watched him take a thin cigar from his shirt
pocket. He took the chimney from a lamp near the bed and
leaned over to light the smoke, then replaced the chimney.
Although he was thinner, it was a lean, muscular kind of

thin, a man who was stronger again. There were harder lines about his face now, a face that told of a man who had seen horror and experienced it himself. He puffed on the cigar a moment before continuing.

"It took me months to learn to walk again, get my strength back to where I could leave for Kansas." He leaned forward, resting his elbows on his knees. "That's all that kept me going, Audra, knowing I had to come here and find you. Once I reached Kansas, it was just a matter of asking questions. I went to Fort Riley, and the commander there knew you." He grinned. "Once he told me the name of this settlement, I knew no one else but my Audra could be the white woman who helped build it."

My Audra. He had said it so naturally, as though the last time they had seen each other was only yesterday. Was that how he still thought of her, as belonging to him? Maybe she did. Maybe she had never stopped belonging to him all these seven years since she first met him. "I'm so sorry, Lee, for what you've suffered. It's been terrible . . . for both of us, and it's all different now . . . isn't it? Nothing can ever be . . . the same for us. You probably should not have bothered to come here."

He watched her eyes, and he didn't believe her. He was betting Toosie knew her better than anyone, and Toosie believed this woman still loved him. A trace of that old southern pride was rearing its ugly head again. She wasn't going to admit right away to any feelings for him other than an old friendship, and, after all, they were practically strangers now, weren't they? Where did he get off thinking they could be anything more after all these years? And what was the sense of even trying? Once he told her the truth about Joey, that would be the end of any feelings she might still have for him. He wanted to tell her he still loved her, but it seemed foolish at this point.

"I *had* to come. I couldn't leave things the way they were in Baton Rouge, Audra. I couldn't end this war in my own heart and mind without finding you, seeing you again, making sure you were all right. I had to do that much. I have to know we're at least still friends, that you don't still think of me as the enemy. I was *never* your enemy, Audra.

I never wanted you to suffer, but when a man has certain convictions, he has to act on them. I was helpless to stop what happened at Baton Rouge, or any of the rest of it. If I could have found a way to single-handedly end that war, I would have done it. And if I could have stayed in Baton Rouge and helped you, I would have done that, too, even though you didn't want me there; but I got my orders to leave, and I had to go."

"I know. I understand." She put a hand to her ribs. "A person suffers just so much . . . and then he or she realizes . . . there is no one to blame. Things happen that are out of our control, and we are left . . . to go on, to survive as best we can. I never thought I could find the strength or courage to face what I have faced . . . or that I could love the Negroes as I love these people who have been so good to me. After all the years I thought of them as beneath me . . . they saved my life and . . . took me into their homes and hearts. In some respects the war taught me a lot, Lee, about what is really important. Friends and faith . . . that is what is important." She reached out and he took her hand again. "I have told myself all these years that I should hate you, but seeing you again, knowing what you have suffered yourself . . . and realizing no one is to blame for any of this, the war itself is to blame . . . I must tell you I don't find fault with you, Lee. What you went through to find me tells me you are still my good friend, if nothing more. I am glad you came. I think you are right. The war . . . would have been unfinished if we had not seen each other again."

He studied her hand, astounded by how dark and rough it was, the creases of her fingers and the cuticles around her nails stained from months of working in the soil. These were not Audra Brennan's hands, but they were even more beautiful because of the generous sacrifices she had made, giving of herself to help others. If there was some way they could find love again, he would marry her and take her away from here, restore for her the life she'd been born to, find a specialist who might help her rebuild her voice. She should be wearing jewels, her skin soft and white, her hair done up in lovely curls. She should be dancing at balls and going to the theater. She should be Mrs.

Lee Jeffreys, wife of a prominent attorney. It was a nice dream.

He took another puff on the cigar, then looked around for an ashtray. Audra smiled. "This is . . . my room. Toosie and Elijah sleep upstairs. I have not yet . . . taken to smoking a pipe . . . or cigars."

Lee grinned then himself, surprised at the hint of a sense of humor in the midst of her pain. This was indeed a changed Audra, more courageous than he had imagined she could be.

"Use that tin drinking cup on the little table there," she told him, indicating the same small table that held the lamp.

Lee reached over and set the cigar in the tin cup, then leaned closer to her. "Tell me about these outlaws. How bad are you hurt?"

She moved slightly, wincing with the pain. "It's my ribs. The one who attacked me . . . slammed me against a table. Every movement . . . every breath hurts."

How he loved the sound of that familiar drawl, but the voice was no longer the lilting, musical voice of the once-wealthy and pampered Audra Brennan. "Toosie says you beat the hell out of him."

She closed her eyes. "I'm not proud of it . . . but I had no choice at the time. My rifle had jammed on me. I hardly remember myself how it happened. Elijah managed to wrestle the man off me, and I picked up my father's rifle and . . . started hitting him with it. Everything is kind of blank after that. I think my rage took over so that I was not even myself. I don't even remember . . . his face." Her eyes teared. "All I could think about was all the other things . . . March Fredericks, Brennan Manor, losing my voice and nearly dying, Aunt Janine, Baton Rouge, all of it . . . especially Joey. I thought about Joey, and I needed to kill someone. I just pretended he was the man who had shot him . . . and I couldn't stop hitting him."

Lee suddenly felt almost sick. *I'm the one you should have beat on,* he thought. He drew in his breath and got up, unable even to look at her for a moment. He took up the cigar again and walked to a window, looking out at some Negroes recovering what they could of one trampled cornfield. "Toosie and the others think the outlaws will come back."

"They will. We're sure of it. They'll be hopping mad because some of our Negroes . . . fought back and killed a few of them. I don't think any of them even owns land around here. They're just no-goods from the South . . . full of hate over the war . . . blaming the Negroes for all of it. They're the kind that will *always* hate Negroes and don't want to see them succeed at anything. The next time it will be worse. This time . . . they just damaged our crops and stole our cattle, burned a couple of buildings. There are other Negro refugees here, from other towns these men have attacked . . . and they tell of rapes and brutal whippings and murders. It will . . . get worse."

Lee turned to her, the cigar still between his teeth. "Not if I have anything to do with it."

"Lee, you're just one man—"

"I left the army a brigadier general. I've trained troops for years, and I can train those Negroes out there." He took the cigar from his mouth and moved closer again. "I'll teach them how to shoot, how to outsmart their enemy. This is no different from the war, Audra, and I'm not leaving here until I know Brennan, Kansas, is safe. It's the least I can do."

Her eyes teared at the thought that maybe something *could* be done. They had all prayed fervently for a miracle. Was Lee Jeffreys their miracle? Who better to train the Negro men how to fight than a brigadier general, even if he was from the Union Army?

"One thing I have plenty of is money," he was saying. "I'm going to Abilene and see about buying additional rifles, good repeaters, not the old muzzle-loaders Elijah tells me half these men are using. I can equip them right, Audra. And I'm also going to buy some cattle in Abilene. I'll take some of these men with me, and we'll herd some cattle back here so they can start rebuilding the herd they've lost. Toosie told me how important those cattle were, what with the railroad running all the way to Abilene now. Getting into the cattle business was a good idea." He leaned closer and grasped the wooden headrail of the bed. "We aren't going to let the outlaws win this one. The next time they come back, we'll be ready for them."

So close. Leaning over her as he was, her lying in a bed, brought back memories Audra thought she had managed to bury a long time ago. How strange to know that this near stranger had made love to her so intimately, and with such passion. He still wanted her that way. She could see it in his eyes, and it stirred something in her she had not felt in years. That was wrong now, wasn't it? All of that was behind them, and it was senseless to dredge it up again. "What will you do when it's all over . . . and you leave here?" she asked, trying to hint that that was what he should do. She could see the questions in his eyes, knew instinctively he was thinking it might be nice to take her with him when he left.

"I don't know," he answered, straightening again. "Maybe go to Denver. They must need good lawyers there." *I might never leave here,* he thought. *Once you know the truth about Joey, I might be buried here. If you shot me, Audra, I'd never blame you for it. I'd gladly stand and let you do it.*

"What about New York? Maple Shadows? Don't you want to go back home?"

He put the chair back in place. "It's all different now. Too many painful memories. I need to go on to something new, kind of like why you came to Kansas."

He turned to look at her, and she could see the truth in his eyes. The painful memories involved her, and that summer they shared at Maple Shadows. She missed the place herself, had dared to dream sometimes about being there again, pretending the past had never happened. But that was impossible. "I don't know what to say, Lee, how to thank you . . . for wanting to help . . . for even coming here to find me in the first place. After what I said in Baton Rouge, I thought you had decided never to bother. I even thought . . . maybe you had married by now."

He studied the green eyes that had haunted him for seven years. Was there a reason she had asked that question? "After what happened to me, there certainly was no time or occasion to be thinking about other women." *Be-*

sides, how could I ever give thought to loving anyone but you? He thought she surely had read his thoughts, for she suddenly looked away, her cheeks flushing slightly. "Toosie told me the white preacher who's come here to live is interested in you," he added. A fierce jealousy had surprised him when Toosie told him that. He hadn't even seen Audra yet, but after all these years, the thought of her ever being with some other man grated at his very bones.

"It's nothing," she answered. "He has shown an interest . . . that's all." She still did not meet his eyes. "There has been no official courting or anything . . . like that." She finally met his eyes again. *How could I ever love again, Lee, after loving you? How could I ever again find that passion with another man?* "Reverend Bishop is a nice man . . . a widower from the war." She touched her scar again, her throat starting to get sore from talking. "He's from Kentucky. I really don't think of him as anything but a friend . . . someone the community needs. He helped us build a little church." She finally looked up at him again. "Faith is just about all that has kept us going . . . and it's been nice having a real preacher to give sermons and help us pray, and no one minds when I pray with my rosary beads. They know I am Catholic, but religion doesn't seem to matter out here. We all pray . . . to the same God, and we all have the same prayer . . . just to be left alone to live in peace and be safe. It's been a long time since we have had those things. We're all tired, Lee . . . just tired."

He crushed out his cigar in the tin cup and leaned closer, giving her a look or reassurance. "Well, things are going to get better, I promise. You *will* find peace and be left alone. I'm going to make sure of it, just as I made sure Richard Potter quit abusing you." Their eyes held on the remark, and he knew she was remembering just as he was, that sweet, gentle night he had made love to her at Brennan Manor. "Seems like all I've ever been able to do is come in after the fact and protect you," he told her. "You always had to suffer first, because I wasn't there when I should have been. I don't know if I can ever forgive myself for that, Audra, but this time I'm going to make damn sure nothing bad ever happens to you again. I'm not leaving here until the situation with the outlaws is settled, and I'm going to talk to that commander at Fort Riley and make him keep a better watch on Brennan. I'll stay as long as necessary to make sure you're safe."

She smiled. Oh, how wonderful it would be to rest in his arms again, to give it all over to someone else, to let someone else be strong instead of having to do it all herself. But she didn't dare let this man hold her, for it might reawaken all the things better left asleep. She was almost grateful that right now she was in too much pain for him even to think about pulling her into his arms.

"Lee, I don't blame you for the times you weren't there. I told you that . . . it's both our faults. I was stubborn and determined . . . and proud. I'm as much to blame. Please don't say you can't forgive yourself. *I* forgive you, and . . . I need you to forgive *me* . . . for being just as responsible for some of the pain you suffered. So many times you offered to love me and keep me by your side . . . but I refused."

You don't know what you really need to forgive, he thought. If only it was this simple. He leaned down and kissed her forehead, wanting to taste her lips again. God, how tempting it was! But this was all new for them, and everything had changed. He'd killed her brother. "You get some rest," he told her. "Elijah said I could camp in the shed out back, so I'll be nearby if those men come back sooner than we think. Tomorrow I'm calling a meeting of all the men and we're going to get organized, go to Abilene and get the guns and cattle and get back here as fast as we can. Then I'm going to shape these men up into regular soldiers, as good or better than any army regiment."

Her eyes teared with gratefulness, and she thought how ironic it was that he would be fighting rebels again, only she and the Negroes would be helping him. "Thank you, Lee. Please be careful . . . I would hate to see something happen to you now after all you have been through . . . and getting through that whole war without being hurt. It's too bad you were nearly killed by civilians . . . after getting through all those battles unscathed. Everything about this war has been ironic, hasn't it? So many twists . . .

friends becoming enemies . . . enemies becoming friends. In the end I don't think anyone even knew why they were fighting anymore. That's the . . . saddest part of all." She rubbed at her throat. "I need some water."

Lee quickly poured her a glass from a pitcher on the nearby table. He leaned over and helped her raise her head, putting the glass to her lips. She swallowed some and he set the glass aside, noticing her rub at her throat again, as she had done several times. "Does it hurt to talk?"

"Yes. For a long time I couldn't talk at all . . . but I remembered some of the things your mother taught me about strengthening my voice . . . and it helped."

He noticed her voice getting weaker and raspier. Now she was forcing the words. "Audra, when we get this problem with the outlaws straightened out, I'm going to Denver or wherever I need to go to find a doctor who might be able to help you. I'll wire all the way back to New York, if necessary, pay whatever it costs to get a specialist out here if I can't find a good one close enough."

"You don't need to—"

"Yes, I do. I couldn't help you when you were attacked, but maybe I can help you another way. You're going to get your voice back, at least to the point where you can talk without it hurting. You might never sing again, but—" God, he hadn't meant to say that. He saw the grief in her eyes. "I'm sorry."

"It's all right. I know I'll never sing again."

"I said *might* never, not never," he reminded her. He reached into his back pants pocket and took out some folded papers. Whatever it was, it looked old, the edges frayed, the paper soft and worn. He took her hand and placed the papers into it. "Your song. I've carried it all these years," he told her, pressing her hand between both of his.

"Lee! You still have it?"

"It's all that kept me going sometimes. I have a niece who plays piano and sings beautifully. While I was at Maple Shadows, she played the song for me, sang it. You never got the chance to sing it for me, and I wanted to hear it. It's beautiful, Audra. Now that I've found you and the war is over, I can give it back to you. Promise me you'll always keep it, and that you'll do all you can to sing again. I think there's a reason God made me keep this all these years. He means for *you* to sing it, even if the words don't hold the same meaning for you now as they did when you wrote it."

Lee, my love ... She remembered some of the words, and she was not so sure they didn't still mean as much to her. She didn't know *what* to think now, how to feel. He had kept her song! He had searched for her, was going to help her. Lee was here again, rescuing her again, and she could tell by those blue eyes that the love was still there, just waiting to be rekindled. It was up to her.

A single tear fell from her eye. "I ... don't know ... how I feel about anything anymore."

"That's all right. I have more to tell you, Audra, but not now. You have some mending to do, and I apparently have my work cut out for me for the next few weeks. We'll just take a day at a time and get this place in order first, take care of those raiders." He gave her a reassuring grin, squeezing her hand once more. "You rest. I'll take care of everything."

He left the room, and Audra reveled in the peace and relief of having someone strong who could take some of the weight off her shoulders. *I'll take care of everything.* What blessed words. She was so tired of carrying the load.

Moments later Toosie came in to see Audra clinging to the papers. Lee had shown the song to Toosie, so she knew what Audra was holding in her hands. Audra was crying. "You still love that man, don't you?"

Audra's body jerked in a sob, pain gripping her ribs when she did so. "I ... don't know, Toosie." She pressed the song close to her heart. "I honestly don't know."

34

Audra sat at a kitchen table figuring up the profits from this year's corn and potato crop, which was planted, harvested, and sold as a communal project, the profits shared by all. Everyone had worked hard at retrieving and saving as much of the trampled corn as possible, and the potato harvest had been good. Fort Riley had purchased a good share of the vegetables, as well as carrots and turnips. More had been sold in Abilene, but, as always, a certain portion was kept for the community's use through the winter. Individual families made extra money at their own projects, Wilena with her dress shop, Silas Jones with his livery, Elijah, who had gotten into horse, oxen, and mule trading with travelers, and many other projects begun by other families, both Negro and white alike.

In spite of the outlaw raid, it had been a good year, and they were getting back on their feet faster than expected.

All had come together to rebuild the livery and the dress shop and three log homes that had been burned. Thanks to Lee's purchase of a fine herd of beef in Abilene, they again had cattle to breed, with two strong, healthy bulls to father the calves that should come in the spring. The cattle grazed north of town, constantly guarded.

Lee had also purchased rifles and ammunition, and practically every man in the community now owned a good repeating rifle and knew how to use it. Lee had drilled them regularly, set up schedules so that every man had time at least every other day for target practice. Many women had also been provided with rifles and pistols and had also learned to shoot, and Lee had helped the men build a fort-like barrier around the entire community, made up of a combination of sod, logs, hay bales, wagons, anything that would help stall a raid and would at the same time give men something to crouch behind to shoot at their attackers before they could even get into town.

Wilena called Lee their "savior." *Sent from God, he was*, she had said often. Audra had to smile at the thought of how everyone in their little town looked to the man as their hero. He had gained weight since arriving, for every woman in the village was anxious to stuff him with their best cooking, in gratitude for what he had done. Since he had arrived, Lee had not gone without a meal or a place to hang his hat—except for at Toosie's house. He always had an excuse for not being able to stay with them, and she knew why. They both knew why. It would be too hard to sleep in the same house without one of them wanting to go to the other's bed, to find out if the passion was still there. It was wrong, or at least she had managed to convince herself so far that it was; but more and more old needs and memories of the ecstasy of being in Lee Jeffreys's bed had been haunting her, keeping her awake at night.

Thanks to Toosie's gossiping, just about everyone in Brennan was apparently aware that she had once been in love with the man, and several had asked when they were going to be married. She set her pen aside, pondering their remarks. They all meant well. Most wanted "poor Miss Audra" to be happy again, to have a man of her own. They all thought Lee should be that man. What people were saying to Lee, she wasn't sure, but he had made no advances. It had been enough these past three months just to get to know each other again, to talk out the horror of the war, to learn all the little things that had happened to each other over the five years since he saw her at Baton Rouge. It was understood that the love was still there, buried somewhere under all the hurt, but neither of them had been able to bring up the subject. She suspected it was a fear on both their parts that maybe the other didn't feel the same way anymore. Neither of them wanted to hurt that way again.

She got up from her chair and opened the back door, letting the cool November air clear her mind. She couldn't help feeling that on Lee's part, there was another reason he was holding back, something deep inside that made him think loving him again was impossible. When they talked about the war, especially about Joey, he would suddenly freeze up, usually changed the subject. There was a look in his eyes that haunted her, as though he actually blamed himself for Joey's death. She had assured him several times that he shouldn't, but sometimes it seemed he felt as responsible as if he himself had pulled the trigger on Joey. The terrible grief in his eyes made her ache for him, and she wished he would tell her whatever it was that he was still holding back. He had seen or experienced some tragedy from the war that he still had not told her about, and she could only surmise that the killing he had had to do had deeply affected him.

She was sure that if they could find love again, it would probably be stronger than ever before, for they had both learned the hard way just how important love was. Seeing him again, watching how he worked with the others, how he really cared, made her remember the man beneath the uniform, the Lee Jeffreys she had known in Connecticut, who had been so good with Joey, who had loved her so deeply . . . the Lee Jeffreys for whom she had written the song she kept in a little chest now on her bureau.

That was what had touched her most. He had kept that song, and she loved him for it. He had struggled against death, forced himself to walk again, just so he could find her. He was spending his own money to help them rebuild, giving his own time to teach them how to defend themselves, had even helped with some of the harvesting.

Her thoughts were interrupted when someone outside let out a war whoop. "He's comin'!" someone shouted.

Audra frowned, turning and going through the sitting room to the front door. Elijah stood outside. "Look there!" he called to her.

Audra looked out across the vast horizon to see a rider coming. Lee had trained all the men in scouting and had set up a schedule for three men a day, three more every night, to ride the outskirts of the town watching for suspicious intruders. Today Lee himself was scouting, and even from this distance she could tell it was he who was riding hard toward Brennan. She recognized his buckskin horse, and the fringed deerskin jacket he wore. She liked that jacket on him. He'd grown more tanned, more rugged looking . . . and she desired him more than ever. She had been fighting that desire for weeks now.

Toosie hurried to the front porch from Joey's upstairs bedroom. She stood beside Audra to watch Lee approaching.

"The raiders must be comin'!" Elijah said, turning and rushing past both of them into the house to get his rifle.

"We'd best stay here with our guns in case they get through," Toosie said. "I'll put Joey in his playpen." She lumbered away, and Audra was worried about her. Toosie was due to deliver anytime. It was vital that this time they keep the raiders at bay, for if they got through, women and children would suffer even worse than before. She watched as Lee rode at a breakneck pace, his horse charging through the posts that held the sign of Brennan, Kansas. He shouted something to some men who stood nearby, and they ran to a wagon and began dragging and pushing it to the entrance to block it.

"Get your rifles! Get the women and children inside!" she heard Lee shout then.

A few families lived beyond the barriers, in little sod houses in the middle of their own farm fields. There was nothing that could be done about them, and she prayed the outlaws wouldn't bother with those families beyond the town. Their target was most likely Brennan itself, but this time they would get a surprise. She ran for her own rifle, checked to be sure it was loaded, then grabbed some extra ammunition. "I'm going to fight them at the barriers with the men!" she called to Toosie.

"No, Audra! You're supposed to stay here," Toosie objected. "Lee said for women and children to barricade themselves in the houses." She placed Joey in the playpen made of slender tree branches.

"I'm going to make sure they don't *get* to the houses this time!" Audra called back, running out before Toosie could stop her. She hurried through the street, noticing the town had come alive. Everywhere women and children scampered for shelter. Doors were bolted shut, shutters closed over windows. Men emerged from houses, businesses, barns, and corrals, to take their positions around the town behind their makeshift barriers. Lee was riding the entire perimeter, shouting orders like an army general, telling most of the men to line up on the south side, the direction from which the raiders were coming.

Audra headed for the south gate, and it was several minutes before Lee charged back to that area. He saw her kneeling behind several bales of hay, her rifle barrel resting on top of one bale for support.

"Dammit, what are you doing here?" he asked, dismounting.

"I'm going to shoot some outlaws," she answered, looking up at him, "same as you."

"It's too dangerous here. You should be back at the house in case they get through."

"They aren't *going* to get through this time!" She rose and faced him. "Let me stay, Lee. I want to be out here with you and the others. It's important to me."

Their eyes held, and Lee could not resist the sudden compulsion to lean down and kiss her. It was a soft, quick kiss, but it said everything, and in spite of the impending danger, for a moment Audra felt fire move through her loins and heart, a wonderful feeling she had not experienced for so long.

"You keep you head down," he told her, noticing tears in her eyes.

"I will," she promised.

He turned away and re-mounted, the taste of her mouth lingering on his own. They had had plenty of occasion to talk, to get closer again, to find and renew the friendship that had brought them together in the first place, except now it was better than ever, because there was nothing left to argue about. They thought more alike now, had an appreciation for what was important in life. She was healed, and he was stronger, feeling the old urges more keenly than ever since seeing her again. Something had to be decided soon. He ached for her, and he had to know if there was any hope in that. The problem was, he still had not told her the truth about Joey. He knew the time was coming when he'd have no choice. It had to be done, and once she knew, she would probably never want him to share her bed again.

There was no time now to think about that. The southern horizon was alive with men. From what he had managed to discern earlier when he first spotted them, he figured there were at least forty of them. They had apparently built their numbers again after losing some men in the first raid. This was going to be a real test of the training he had given these citizens of Brennan, but there were at least a hundred men lined up along these barriers. If they all picked their targets carefully and did not fire aimlessly with the repeaters he had bought them, there was no reason why the oncoming raiders should even get past the barriers.

The biggest test would be the ability of the Negro men to fire without fear. Audra had helped him understand what held many of them back the first time, besides their outdated weapons. These were men who had been brought up believing that to show any resistance or to fight a white man in any way meant death, or at the least a brutal whipping. Lee had lectured them, explaining that they were free now, free to defend themselves and their women and children. He had explained that he was himself a lawyer and that if any problems arose out of this, he would make sure no one suffered any unfair punishment. They were being attacked, which gave them every right to shoot back.

"Draw a good bead now," he called out to them, guiding his horse back and forth behind them. "Pick your target well and don't be afraid to pull the trigger. They aren't going to chase you out of your town or anyplace else! Wait till I give the signal before you begin firing."

Audra took careful aim herself. She had practiced shooting often once her ribs had healed, and Lee had taught her how to balance her heavy weapon, how to keep it steadier by squeezing the trigger with just her finger and not allowing her whole hand and body to move. A few times he had stood behind her and put his arms around her to show her how to hold the gun properly, and she had shivered with a desire to turn around and let him fully embrace her. She had liked the feel of his strong hands and arms, the security of his firm body pressed at her back.

The raiders were close now. They began firing, but everyone remained crouched behind the barrier, making difficult targets for the raiders. A bullet spit past Audra, tearing a path across the top of a hay bale. She heard Lee's horse whinny, but she dared not look back. She kept her aim steady and finally Lee gave the order to fire. Audra could tell by the faces of some of the raiders that they were surprised at finding behind the barrier a literal army of men, and a few women, with rifles ready. The minute Lee shouted the order to shoot, the air exploded with gunfire from a hundred Winchester .44 carbines. Men cried out, horses stumbled. Audra guessed that at least twenty men went down. The rest drew their horses to such a sudden halt that it drove hooves into the ground, and a few more fell. Those still mounted began to flee, while others scrambled to get back on their horses, cursing horrendously. The defenders of Brennan, Kansas, kept firing, downing more of them. A few of the wounded who tried to get up were also shot down, but some of them finally got away.

It was over so incredibly fast that Audra and the others watched in pure shock as the fifteen or twenty men who were left in one piece hightailed it away from Brennan as fast as they could ride. They had been vastly outnumbered and outsmarted, and they had not even come close to getting across the barrier. A few more of the wounded managed to re-mount their horses, and Lee ordered everyone to stop firing.

"They'll think twice before they come back," he told them. "Some of you go round up the dead men's horses. They're ours now. And we'll need a burial detail. You've won your first battle, men, in only ten minutes. How does it feel?"

The citizens of Brennan held up their rifles and began shouting and celebrating, giving out war cries and rebel yells. They began hugging each other, and Audra felt like crying from sheer happiness and relief. She looked up at Lee, and her smile faded when she saw blood pouring from his right cheek.

"Lee!" She threw down her rifle and rushed to his side, ripping off a piece of slip for him to hold to the wound.

"I'm all right," he told her, but he looked pale. "A little more to my left and I would have tasted the damn thing."

Audra shivered at the realization of how close he had come to taking a bullet in the head. He could have died in the short battle, and he would have given his life in defense of her little town. "Hang on to the pommel of your saddle, and I'll lead your horse back to the house," she told him, picking up her rifle.

The rest of the men continued celebrating. Brennan, Kansas, was a full-fledged town, filled with well-armed citizens ready to defend it. They could take care of their own now, and they were no longer afraid. Some of the men gathered up the raiders' horses, others collected bodies . . . fourteen dead, seven wounded. More wounded had managed to ride away, which meant only about fifteen raiders had been left unscathed. Those who had been left behind would be helped by the people of Brennan but kept under guard and taken to Fort Riley to be put under arrest.

Into the night many of the men kept up their vigil at the barricade, waiting for another onslaught. It never came.

•   •   •

Audra carried a tray of tea and biscuits into her bedroom, where Lee stood at a mirror that hung over her bureau and applied more whiskey to the wound on his cheek. "This ought to leave one hell of a scar," he grumbled. "As if I don't have enough already from those thugs in Baton Rouge. After everything I went through in the war, I get most of my battle scars from the aftermath. Isn't that something?"

A few scars certainly won't take away from that handsome face, Audra thought, setting the tray on a little table near the bed. "It's about time you got yourself back to this house to stay. You lost a lot of blood. You shouldn't have gone back out there."

"I wanted to make sure everybody stuck to the instructions and that the wounded outlaws were well guarded. We'll take them to Fort Riley tomorrow morning."

"We? You should stay here and rest."

He looked at her, just then realizing they were alone. Elijah planned to spend the night standing guard at the barriers. Toosie had taken Joey to Wilena's house, insisting that Lee stay the night at their house because of his wound. He could have her and Elijah's bed. Besides, she had told them, since she was so close to delivery, she wanted to be near Wilena, an experienced midwife who had delivered plenty of her own children. Lee was beginning to wonder if this was just Toosie's flimsy excuse to find a way to leave him and Audra alone together.

Maybe he should tell Audra the truth now and get it over with. He should tell her before something happened that would make her hate him even more if he waited. Still, he could see by her eyes she was thinking the same thing he was. They were alone . . . and would be all night.

"It's only a flesh wound," he spoke up. "I'm not dying, Audra." He grinned. "You did a hell of a job out there yourself."

She sat down on the bed. "Don't think I wasn't scared. A bullet whizzed right past me." She looked him over, stirred by his open shirt, the way his denim pants fit his hips, the drying wound on his cheek that showed his courage and his devotion to helping her and the citizens of

Brennan. Yes, she still loved her Yankee man. "I got a taste of what it must have been like for you, being constantly shot at, guns and cannons exploding all around you. Does your leg still hurt you?"

He picked up the bottle of whiskey and took a swallow. "Sometimes." He stared at the bottle for a moment. "I, uh, I got hooked on this stuff pretty bad for a long time," he added, "after Baton Rouge. Something else happened, Audra, something that—"

"Lee," she interrupted, unable to resist any longer the fire that was fast consuming old hatreds and resentments, leaving only the embers of love. "I might as well say it. After realizing today that you could have been killed, taken from me again in one swift second, I knew that I still loved you."

He just stared at her a moment, wrestling with his conscience. God, he wanted her again. If the only way to have her one more time was to wait and not tell her about Joey ... yet ... How could he turn away from that look in those exotic green eyes? He had never been able to resist her, but this time was different. He had killed her brother. She should know. "Audra—"

"Do you still love me, Lee?" Audra was surprised to see his eyes actually tear. He came closer.

"You know that I do. I didn't come here out of just friendship. I came here because I never once *stopped* loving you or thinking about you. All those years of not knowing what happened to you, if you were alive or dead, hurt, in need, just about drove me crazy."

Her heart ached with the wonderful freedom of letting go of her feelings and admitting to them. "It was the same for me," she answered, rising to face him. "I kept saying I hated you and never wanted to see you again, but deep inside ..." He own eyes teared. "Lee, the war is over. I want it to be over between us, too. We can start new. We can erase all the hurt and the ugliness. We belong together."

He watched her eyes, the house silent now, except for the ticking of a mantel clock in the main room just beyond the bedroom door. This was Audra, his sweet, sweet Audra, changed, matured, her magnificent voice gone; but she was more beautiful than ever, beautiful in spirit as well as in face and form. How many nights had he dreamed about finding her, holding her once more, tasting her sweetness again? How could he tell her? He argued with himself that it didn't matter anymore. She never needed to know. Maybe he could find a way to live with the guilt. He would do anything to have her back in his arms. "Audra—" Again the words would not come.

She touched his shirt, moved her hand to unbutton the rest of it. She opened it, resting her face against his chest. "I want to go back, Lee," she said softly. "I want to remember, to find what we had once before. I could never love anyone else as I loved you, still love you."

He trembled, a battle raging inside him. His love for her won out, and he grasped her hair, which tonight hung loose and full the way he liked it. She raised her mouth, and he leaned down and met her lips in a savage kiss that told both of them what had to be. Above all else, no matter what happened after he told her, he had to have her one more time; and he convinced himself she would want it this way, too. He groaned with ecstasy, running his tongue deep. He had not had a woman since his injury and long rehabilitation, and his body was on fire for her.

Once they realized what they both needed and wanted, there was no going back. He picked her up and laid her on the bed, moving on top of her, not even bothering to take down the covers and remove his boots. Right now neither of them even wanted to brother with the preliminaries. This was his Audra, his precious, precious Audra, whom he had loved for eight years. For the last five he had been denied this, had only been able to dream about it. She needed this as badly as he did, for it had been the same for her, five years of neglecting womanly needs. He had to be inside of her, and she needed to *feel* him inside of her. That was all that mattered now. Nothing else mattered. Nothing!

In moments he had pulled her bloomers off and entered her. They shared a wild, hot, grasping coupling, both of them still clothed. She drove him crazy when she moved her tongue into his mouth, her nails digging into his shoulders, arching her hips up to him in desperate desire. He rammed himself deep, felt his life spill into her, kept right on kissing her while almost instantly he swelled inside of her again. He literally tore at her dress then, and she helped him get it open so that he could draw a taut nipple into his mouth, taste of her sweet fruits again, while he felt himself growing hard and hot once more. He buried himself deep, needing, wanting, glorying in the way she cried out his name in her own spastic orgasm. They were both on fire, and the only way to consume the flames was to do this over and over until they were both weak and breathless.

Again his life surged into her. He took a moment to gather his breath, moved off her just long enough to close the bedroom door and undress. She watched him quietly, saying nothing. It was all in those green eyes. She wanted him as badly as he wanted her, and what he needed to tell her would have to wait, no matter how much she was going to hate him for it.

Audra drank in all that was man about him. She wanted him so badly she thought she might pass out from the utter ecstasy of being a woman again after so long. Who else could she have allowed to awaken old, buried needs but Lee Jeffreys?

He moved to the basin stand at the side of the room and poured fresh water into the pan. "Come here," he told her.

Audra obeyed, and he began removing her clothes until she, too, stood there naked. He handed her a clean rag from under the stand, and they each washed themselves, studying each other's nakedness, relishing the building desire that had still not been quenched. Audra shivered when his blue eyes raked over her, yet for one quick moment she again noticed that terrible, haunted look.

"Remember that I love you, Audra. Remember that above all else. I love you more than my own life."

She touched his face. "I know that."

He picked her up in his arms and carried her back to the bed, setting her on her feet to pull away the covers. He met her mouth in another delicious kiss, laid her back, both of them squirming farther onto the bed, naked skin touching. He fondled her breast, arousing her nipple with his thumb, and in the next moment he was inside her again. She arched up to him in glorious abandon, relishing the moment, because this time it didn't have to end. This time he wasn't going to leave her the next day. This time was forever. At last Lee Jeffreys was in her arms to stay. There was no war to tear them apart, no husband in the way, no drastically different way of life to interfere. They were free! Free of the past, free of the ugly memories, free of the awful mistakes they had made. God had brought him to her. He would surely never take him away from her again.

Audra stirred awake to see Lee standing at the bedroom window, quietly smoking a thin cigar. She watched the smoke float lazily upward on a shaft of morning sunlight. He wore his denim pants, but he was still shirtless. She studied him quietly for a moment, his provocative, masculine frame, the hard lines of this man who had been her first love, her only love. No man could make her feel the way Lee Jeffreys could. No other man could bring out the almost painful passion she had felt last night. She ached, and she was tired, but it was a pleasant kind of tired, and it felt so good to love again, to be a woman again.

"Lee Jeffreys," she spoke up, "I was planning on waking up in your arms and being able to lie there for once without one of us having to run off." She smiled and stretched. "Come back to bed." A little voice told her not to be too happy too soon when he looked at her with that terrible sadness in his eyes again. Why did he look that way? He should be a very happy man this morning.

"Toosie and Elijah could come back anytime," he said quietly.

"Do you really think they don't know what happened last night?" she joked, trying to get him to smile. She snuggled deeper into the covers. "And how can you stand there without a shirt? It's cold this morning. Come back to bed and I'll warm you up." There it was again—that terrible grief in his eyes. Alarm began to move through her blood. For once they had been able to make love with the knowledge that there was no reason for either of them to run away the next day. For once they had found true happiness . . . hadn't they? "What's wrong, Lee?" She sat up.

He kept the cigar in his mouth and pulled on his shirt. "I'm not sure *what* Toosie thinks we're doing. Maybe she thinks you've killed me and she's afraid to come home and find out."

Audra laughed nervously. "What on earth are you talking about?"

Lee buttoned his shirt. "I told her something when I first came here, something I've never had the courage to tell you." He pushed open the window and threw the cigar outside, then pulled the window shut again and latched it. "She might have told you herself if I had let her, but we both knew it was up to me. I should have done it last night, before we made love." He unbuttoned his pants and tucked in the shirt. "But I have a weakness when I get close to you. Every time I get near you, I do stupid things, things that I know damn well are going to hurt you, but I do them anyway." He buttoned his pants and walked closer to the bed.

Audra noticed he also already had his boots on. "You're confusing me. Are you telling me again that we can't be together after all? Is there another woman?"

He laughed bitterly. "I wish it *was* only that."

Her heart began to pound with dread. "Lee, don't do this. We've just found each other again. This time is for good. This time was supposed to be forever. There is nothing left to come between us."

He closed his eyes and sat down on the edge of the

bed. "Not on *my* part there isn't." He bent one leg and moved it up on the bed, facing her. "Audra, I meant everything I said last night. I love you more than my own life, and I'm telling you right now that if you'll have me, I want to get married and never be apart again. I want to move to Denver, start my own law practice there, find a specialist for you. I want you to be my wife, to give you a beautiful home and beautiful clothes and the kind of life you were born to. I want children, as many as we can have. I want to be the kind of father I never had, the kind *you* never really had. I want to share a family with you, and maybe after a while, when the transcontinental railroad is finished, we could take some time off to go back east and visit Maple Shadows, get back what we lost there. I want *everything* for us, for *you.* You have to believe how much I love you."

"Of course I believe you. Why are you talking this way? You know I want all the same things. I want to put the past behind us, Lee. This even helps me accept Joey's death, because he loved you so much. He would have wanted us to be together." There! There was that awful tragedy in his eyes again! "Lee, something has been eating at you ever since you first came here. I have always had the feeling you were holding back, that you didn't tell me everything about the war. Does it have to do with Joey? Did you see him, maybe in a Union prison?"

"My God," he groaned. He closed his eyes again, turning away and putting his head in his hands. "I'm such a goddamn fool. I should have told you last night. I *tried* to tell you, but you kept interrupting, and the next thing I knew we were kissing. . . ." He rubbed at his thick, dark hair. "All I could think of was being able to hold you and make love to you once more . . . just once more . . . before you told me to get out of your life forever."

"Why would I do that, Lee?" She noticed he seemed to be trembling, and she was surprised to realize the man was actually afraid to tell her whatever it was he had to tell her. "Lee, I love you. I have forgiven the past. Please tell me what's wrong."

He kept his head in his hands, sitting there quietly a few seconds before finally speaking. "You got a letter, Audra, from a private named Larry Jones, telling you about Joey's death."

The dread deep in her soul grew deeper. "Yes. How did you know? I never told you his name."

Lee kept rubbing nervously at his hair. "Maybe I thought using a name with my initials would somehow get through to you. *I* wrote that letter, Audra."

Her mind whirled with confusion. "You?" She tried to put it together, but it didn't make sense. "How? Why? If you knew something about Joey's death, why didn't you admit who you were when you wrote the letter?"

The room hung silent for several long seconds. "*I* killed him, Audra. I killed your brother. It was really . . . more an accident than anything else."

She just stared at him in shock. "What?"

"I was riding with Sherman then. We had just taken Atlanta. I was sitting on my horse on a rise, watching the city burn, thinking what a ridiculous waste it was, what a waste the whole war was. Below me some Union soldiers were herding along several Confederate prisoners. Some of them broke loose." He swallowed before continuing, still holding his head in his hands, but his hands were shaking. "Two of the prisoners headed my way. One had stolen a rifle from a Union soldier. He intended to shoot me with it, so I shot first. He went down, but by then the second one was there, grabbing for my rifle."

Audra listened in horror as he told the rest of it through broken sobs. "He just kept . . . pulling at the gun, not even looking up at my face. My hand was still on the trigger, and I had already . . . cocked it a second time. It went off. I'll never forget his eyes then. In that one . . . quick moment . . . we recognized each other. He spoke my name before he fell. . . ." He rose from the bed, wiping at his eyes with his shirtsleeve. "His hair was shoulder length . . . and he'd grown a beard and he was ragged and dirty. I didn't realize . . . who he was until it was . . . too late. If I had known . . . I could have had him freed . . . sent him home where he belonged! I had the authority . . . if I had just . . . known he was among those prisoners . . . if I had just recognized him sooner . . ."

He took a deep breath, walking back over to the window. "Do you want to know what he said? He said, 'What a hell of a way to meet again.'" He breathed deeply to stay in control of his emotions. "What a *hell* of a way to meet again! Yes, *wasn't* it!" He turned to face Audra. "He was typical Joey even to the end. He told me to take care of you for him. He made me promise. He said you'd still love me, even after you knew. He wanted us to be together, Audra, more than anything in the world. He wanted you to be happy. And do you want to know his very last words?" God, how he hated the look on her face, so much sorrow. He had awakened a painful grief, but it was done now. "He said, 'I forgive you.' I *forgive* you! He said it wasn't my fault."

He walked closer, clenching his fists, tears on his face. "And it *wasn't*, Audra! I didn't know it was him! But I knew I'd killed a lot of *other* Joeys in that war! I also knew that some day I'd have to find you and tell you, because I couldn't live with it. I started drinking to forget, and I drank and drank and drank until half the time I hardly knew where I was. I went on and finished my army duty because I had to be the good soldier! I even got promoted, and all the while I was going *crazy* inside!"

He took a deep, shuddering breath, watching her just sit staring at her lap. Why didn't she say something? Scream at him? Beat on him? "I . . . held him in my arms," he told her, his voice a little calmer. "I begged him to hang on . . . but being shot at such close range, I knew in my gut he wasn't going to live. It might sound strange coming from the man who killed him . . . but at least he died in the arms of someone . . . he loved . . . someone who cared. And you know damn well how much I loved that boy, Audra! You know I never would have let it happen if I had known. I wish I would have let him have the goddamn rifle and let him shoot *me* with it! And don't think I didn't consider doing that myself! For weeks after that I came close to putting a gun to my own head!"

She finally looked up at him, but he could not quite read those tear-filled green eyes. She turned away again, still speechless.

"I dug his grave myself," he told her. "I prayed over

him, put a cross at his grave. I stayed there with him all night, drank all night until I finally passed out beside the grave. I never stopped drinking after that. If not for being injured and in a coma for so long, I would have drunk myself into my *own* grave by now. Once I recovered, I knew I had to stay off the whiskey so that I could stay strong and clear-headed when I came to find you. I learned that whiskey only dulls the pain, Audra. It doesn't make it go away. And I guarantee you the pain I have suffered ever since then has been worse that any I could have suffered from a physical wound. The war ... wounds people in more ways than just physically."

She closed her eyes, and tears began spilling down her cheeks. "How well I know," she groaned.

Lee ran a hand through his hair, walking over to pick up his deerskin jacket. He pulled it on. "I found that letter on him ... the one he'd started to you and never finished. I decided it would be important to you to have that last letter ... so I sent it along. He was very proud that he was a corporal and a sharpshooter. For what it's worth, in spite of the horrors of the war and whatever he might have been through by then, I think he died happier than he had ever been. He had found something he could do himself and be proud of. He even died bravely ... forgave me because he knew I'd need to hear it. His last thoughts and biggest concern, though, were for you." He turned and picked up his hat from the back of a chair. "There is someone else's forgiveness I need more than Joey's, and you know whose it is."

She looked up at him, more tears coming. "You ... should have told me ... before."

He wiped tears from his own face, then put his hat on. "There are a *lot* of things I *should* have done over the years, Audra. It was the same for you. I can only tell you that nothing is changed for me as far as how I feel about you. I don't know why God sent that boy up the hill and caused me to be the one to kill him. There were thousands of Confederate soldiers out there all over the South. The odds against me ever running into Joey were tremendous. Maybe it was God's way of ... of letting him die quickly instead of

slowly in one of those stinking prisons. You don't know ...
Audra. You don't know what the prisons were like. It would
have been horrible for him. I've gone around with it in my
mind, in my nightmares, thousands of times. I hear that rifle
going off ... and I see his eyes ... hear him call my name
all at the same time. It haunts me ... eats at my gut. I
never even intended to shoot him, even *before* I realized
who he was, because he was unarmed. I wasn't that kind of
soldier, Audra. I never intentionally killed innocent people.
My God, you must understand *that* much about me!"

Her shoulders shook, and she covered her face with
her hands. "Joey," she sobbed.

Lee knelt in front of her. "Yes, you weep for Joey, because you have every right. But if you love me, Audra, you'll
weep for me, too. It's the ones left behind, who have to live
with all of it, that suffer the most. And when you're done
weeping, you think about the things I've told you and how
much I love you. It's either going to have to be over between us, Audra, or we'll be together the rest of our lives
and find the happiness we both deserve. I'll be back in five
or six days and we'll either leave for Denver together, or I'll
leave alone. If I do, that truly will be the end of it."

She looked up at him. "Where are you going?" she
asked sobbing.

"To Fort Riley. I'm going to help take those prisoners
in, and I want to talk to the commander there about patrol-
ling this area better. I'm better off leaving for a while. You
need time to think about all of this."

Part of her wanted to get up and embrace him, tell him
it was all right. She knew what a horror it had to have been
for him, knew how he had felt about Joey. Yet the fact remained that this Yankee soldier had killed her brother. What
a cruel twist of fate! She watched his eyes, understood now
the strange agony she had seen there so often, yet for the
moment she saw him again as the enemy, the epitome of all
she had hated for so long ... hated and loved with the same
passion. She just closed her eyes and looked away, and in
the next moment she heard the door close. Should she run
after him? Would he really even bother to come back?

She turned and crawled back into bed, her body racked

with sobs, Joey's loss reawakened now with the vivid picture of how it had all really happened. Each time she drew in her breath, she caught the scent of Lee Jeffreys still on the pillow next to her. She had shared a bed with her brother's killer, yet strangely, it was what Joey would have wanted. She knew deep inside that Lee's killing the boy was just as awful for him as if she herself had accidentally killed him. She drew the pillow to her, and she realized her tears were not just for Joey. They were for *all* the Joeys, and all the Lees, and all the women like herself who had been left behind.

Toosie walked out onto the porch, carrying the four-day-old little baby girl she'd named Lena. She had given birth the very day Lee left for Fort Riley, and she had not been outside the house since. It felt good to breathe some fresh air, even though that air was cold. She draped the baby's blanket over her tiny face and walked close to Audra, who was sitting in a chair watching the horizon. The frayed pieces of paper on which she had written her love song to Lee eight years ago lay on her lap. "Would you like to hold little Lena for a while?" Toosie asked.

Audra seemed startled, as though she didn't even realize Toosie was standing near her. She quickly grabbed the papers and shoved them into a pocket of the wool jacket she wore. "Yes, I'd like that," she answered, putting on a smile.

Toosie leaned down and placed the tiny baby girl in Audra's arms. Audra cuddled the child close, lifting the blanket and kissing her dark little cheek. Toosie pulled her shawl tighter around her shoulders. "He's going to be back pretty quick," she reminded Audra. "Maybe even today. Are you going to Denver with him?" she asked cautiously.

Audra sighed deeply. "I still don't know what to do, how to feel."

"Yes, you do, Audra Brennan Potter," Toosie answered firmly. "You know that you love that man, and that he loves you with every bone in his body. You'll never find another like him. He's suffered enough over what happened. Don't punish him more by sending him away alone. You've *both* been alone too long already. You know good and well being together is what Joey would want. There is no greater gift you could give to your brother's memory than to marry Lee Jeffreys."

Audra looked up at her. "I know that." Her eyes teared. "I'm afraid, Toosie. It seems like every time we find each other again, something happens to destroy our happiness. I'm afraid to let go and care again."

Toosie drew up a chair beside her, sitting down wearily. Taking care of little Joey and breast-feeding a new baby following a difficult birth had left her worn out, though she was feeling stronger today. "Audra, the war is *over*. Nothing more like that is going to happen. Once Lee comes back, if you'll just let go of the past, you could be so happy. Don't turn him away. Don't let that pride get in the way one last time, because this time it *will* be the last. The hurt will be too deep. If Lee Jeffreys leaves here without you, he'll never come back. Can you live with that?"

A tear trickled down Audra's cheek, and she wondered where it came from. She had shed so many that she was sure there were none left. "God help me, I don't think I can."

"Of course you can't. And God *is* helping you. He means for you and Lee to be together, or He wouldn't keep bringing that man back into your life. Look at that little baby there. Wouldn't you like one of your own? You need children, Audra, a family. So does Lee. Forgive the man and let yourself be happy. If you won't do it for yourself, then do it for Joey."

Audra pulled the baby closer, pressing her cheek against little Lena's cheek. "What about you and Elijah? Wilena and the others? I can't leave you."

"Before long there's going to be a railroad all the way through Kansas into Colorado, you'll see. In a few years we can visit as much as we want." Toosie touched her shoulder. "We're all going to be fine here, now that we've shown ourselves against the raiders. They won't be giving us any more trouble, and if they do, we know how to handle it. And you've taught us so much, Audra, about how to manage things. We can run Brennan all on our won. You've given up so much to help us. Do something for *yourself* now. Go to Denver and be the wife of attorney Lee Jeffreys. Live in that fine home he wants to build for you. You were born to that life, Audra, and nothing would make all of us happier than to see you living in grand style again, happy and in love, a string of little ones at your feet. Why, I can just picture you coming here to visit, dressed all fine and fancy, showing off sons and daughters all handsome and beautiful. Maybe you'll have a daughter who can sing like you once sang, or who can play the piano. You could even have your own grand piano like that one Mrs. Jeffreys had. Lee can give you a good life, and you deserve it. All of us here, we'll be doing just fine on our own. We're happy, too. This is a better life than any of us dreamed we could have a few years ago. Don't you be worrying about us, Audra."

Audra looked at her, thinking about all the wasted years when she had treated Toosie so callously. "I'm sorry, Toosie, about the past."

"There, you see? It's the same for Lee. Now you know how he feels, wishing he could change the past but knowing it's impossible."

Audra smiled through tears. "You've always been so good to me, Toosie. All of you have. I would miss you so much."

Toosie grinned. "But you'd rather miss all of us than miss just one man, wouldn't you?"

Audra turned to watch the horizon again. "Yes. Part of me says I should want him to hurt, but I can't do it, Toosie. I can't let him go this time, and I know Joey would be so unhappy if I did. God help me, but I love him. It isn't wrong to love him, is it, knowing what I know?"

Toosie grasped her hand and pressed it lightly. "You know it's not wrong. There isn't a soul I know of who would think that it was."

Audra held little Lena close to her breast, thinking how wonderful it would be to have babies of her own. Joey would want her to go on with life, to put all the hatred behind her. She wondered sometimes if her brother had ever even known the feeling of hatred. He'd seemed incapable of it, and she was tired herself of hating. She wanted to love and be loved, and only one man could do that for her.

"We'd best go inside. I don't want the baby to breathe this cool air too long," Toosie spoke up.

Audra kissed the baby again and handed her over. "You go ahead. I'll sit out here a while longer."

Toosie followed Audra's gaze. "Seems like you've been waiting for that man half your life. Stop waiting and denying yourself, Audra. It's time to start really living again."

She went inside, and Audra shivered, pulling her woolen jacket closer around herself. Cold. It seemed she had been cold for years, even in the worst Louisiana heat. It was a cold that came from the inside, an ugly kind of cold that was much worse than the winter air. Winter, it seemed, was the season she had lived with since the summer she had left Maple Shadows. There had been no more summers, except for the few brief times Lee had warmed her in his arms.

Two more days passed, and Lee and the rest of the men still had not returned. Audra began to worry that something had happened. The trip to Fort Riley could usually be made in six days, but eight days had gone by. All kinds of possibilities flashed through her mind. They could have been attacked by Indians, or maybe the outlaws' had pounced on them in the night to retrieve their wounded and had murdered Lee and Elijah and the others.

She had to stay busy and not think about the possibilities. They had to be all right. She bent down to trim dead, dried roses from one of several rosebushes Elijah had purchased in Abilene earlier in the spring. She and Toosie had planted them around the house, trying to bring a little more life and color to the flat, treeless land. Audra wanted to plant some trees, but so far no one in Abilene sold such things.

She trimmed up another bush, and she was behind the house when she heard a horse ride up, heard Elijah call out happily to Toosie. Her own heart beat faster. Was Lee finally back, too? After all the time she had spent watching the horizon, they had come when she was busy behind the house and couldn't see them coming.

She stood up, walked to the back door that led to the kitchen. Elijah was hugging and kissing Toosie, and she looked away, the longing in her strong for a man to be with every night like that, without it being forbidden and wrong.

"We got caught in the worst storm you ever did see," Elijah told her. "Held us up at the fort almost two days. Didn't it rain here?"

"No," Toosie answered. "We were so worried, Elijah. We thought Indians or the rest of those outlaws had attacked you."

Elijah just laughed. "Just rain. We would still have left, but it was a black, drivin' rain that no man would dare go out in. We jus' had to wait till it was done with. We were all worried about *you*, thinkin' it was doin' the same thing here."

"We're fine. You didn't see other outlaws?"

Audra did not hear Elijah's answer. She had noticed someone ride up to the shed at the back of the house. It was Lee. He dismounted and took his horse inside, not even noticing her at first. Audra could hardly believe her own reaction, but she found herself running off the back porch and across the yard to the shed. He was all right! He'd come back as he'd promised! Part of her had been afraid that because she had been silent when he told her about Joey, he would decide never to come back. She hurried inside the shed, then stopped short when he exited a horse stall and saw her standing there out of breath.

They just watched each other for a moment, and Audra could see the mixture of hope and despair in his eyes. She studied him, so rugged and handsome, standing there in that fringed deerskin jacket and leather hat, a long white scar on his cheek from a bullet that could have taken him from her in an instant. The scar would fade with the years, years they would spend together. *You stand before me, tall and strong, your eyes so blue* . . . Some of the words to the song she had written suddenly came to her, along with all the love and passion she had felt for him at seventeen. Suddenly she was young again, and they were standing on a beach in Connecticut.

Lee waited for Audra to speak first. She was out of breath, as though she had run here. Should he take hope in that? She was beautiful, her cheeks rosy from the cold air, her auburn hair pulled up in a clumsy pile on top of her head. How could he leave her this time? He had never prayed harder in his life than he had been praying the last few days that she would not turn him away again.

"I'd like to stay here one more winter," she spoke up. "It's already November, and it would be dangerous to travel anymore before next spring. Besides that, I want to be sure Toosie and the others get through another winter all right, and the baby is still so little—"

"Are you saying you'll go to Denver with me?" Lee interrupted.

She blinked back tears. "Yes, if you still want me to. I would just like to wait until spring. I hope you'll ... stay here with me. We have a real preacher. He could marry us. Maybe when we get to Denver, we can have a second wedding, by a Catholic priest, if you'd be willing."

Lee's eyes misted. "You sure, Audra?"

A tear slipped down her cheek. "You didn't kill Joey, Lee. *All* of us killed him by creating that war in the first place. You were right when you said a lot of Joeys died in the war, and we're all responsible. I'm tired of all the hating and fighting, and the pride that has kept us apart for so many years. I want to love, and *be* loved. I want—"

Before she could finish, she was in his arms. There was the warmth, the wonderful warmth only Lee could bring her. "I love you, Audra," he groaned. "I never want to be apart again."

He held her tight against him, her feet completely off the ground. She hugged him around the neck, kissed his cheek. "I love you, too. I have loved you for the longest time, Lee Jeffreys, just like in my song ... *Just as the sun shines and the wind blows wet and wild ...*" She tasted his tears when she kissed his cheek again.

"I need to hear something else, Audra," he said then, his words broken. He set her on her feet, touching her cheek with the back of his hand, watching her green eyes. "Joey ... forgave me. Can you?"

She reached up and wiped at his tears. "There is nothing to forgive, Lee, but if you need to hear it, then I forgive you. I wouldn't have decided to spend the rest of my life with you if I could not forgive you."

He pulled her back into his arms. "Then the war . . . is finally over."

The cold November wind picked up, rushing through the open door of the shed; but Audra did not feel it. She was in a place where she was warm and protected. She was in Lee's arms, where it was always summer. She was never again going to let go of him.

FROM THE AUTHOR...

Many famous Civil War battlefields have been preserved and can be visited today, a still-vivid reminder of a hideous time in our nation's history that left wounds which to this day continue to fester. There are times when one has to wonder if the war ever really ended, or if it has simply taken a different form. As long as prejudice, hatred, and intolerance of other human beings exist, a more silent civil war continues in America. My hope is that one day it truly will end.

ABOUT THE AUTHOR

An award-winning romance writer, ROSANNE BITTNER has been acclaimed for both her thrilling love stories and the true-to-the-past authenticity of her novels. Specializing in the history of the American Indians and the early settlers, her books span the West from Canada to Mexico, Missouri to California, and are based on Rosanne's visits to almost every setting chosen for her novels, extensive research, and membership in the Western Outlaw-Lawman History Association, the Oregon-California Trails Association, the Council on America's Military Past, and the Nebraska State Historical Society.

She has won awards for best Indian novel and Best Western Series from *Romantic Times* and is a Silver Pen, Golden Certificate, and Golden Pen Award winner from *Affaire de Coeur*. She has also won several Reader's Choice awards and is a member of Romance Writers of America.

Rosanne and her husband have two grown sons and live on twenty-nine wooded acres in a small town in southwest Michigan. She welcomes comments from her readers, who may write to her at 6013 North Coloma Road, Coloma, MI 49038-9309. If you send her a stamped, self-addressed #10 (legal size) envelope, she will send you her latest newsletter and tell you of her other novels and her forthcoming books.

Don't miss these fabulous Bantam women's fiction titles on sale in October

• OUTLAW

by Susan Johnson, author of SINFUL & FORBIDDEN

From the supremely talented mistress of erotic historical romance comes a sizzling love story of a fierce Scottish border lord who abducts his sworn enemy, a beautiful English woman — only to find himself a captive of her love.

____29955-7 $5.50/6.50 in Canada

• MOONLIGHT, MADNESS, AND MAGIC

by Suzanne Forster, Charlotte Hughes, and Olivia Rupprecht

Three romantic supernatural novellas set in 1785, 1872, and 1992. "Incredibly ingenious." — Romantic Times
"Something for everyone." — Gothic Journal
"An engaging read." — Publishers Weekly
"Exemplary." — Rendezvous   ____56052-2 *$5.50/6.50 in Canada*

• SATIN AND STEELE

by Fayrene Preston, co-author of THE DELANEY CHRISTMAS CAROL

Fayrene Preston's classic tale of a woman who thought she could never love again, and a man who thought love had passed him by.   ____56457-9 *$4.50/5.50 in Canada*

Ask for these books at your local bookstore or use this page to order.

❑ Please send me the books I have checked above. I am enclosing $ _____ (add $2.50 to cover postage and handling). Send check or money order, no cash or C. O. D.'s please.

Name _____

Address _____

City/ State/ Zip _____

Send order to: Bantam Books, Dept. FN118, 2451 S. Wolf Rd., Des Plaines, IL 60018
Allow four to six weeks for delivery.

Prices and availability subject to change without notice.   FN118 10/93

THE VERY BEST IN HISTORICAL WOMEN'S FICTION

Iris Johansen